*The*
# CAFÉ
# BETWEEN
# PUMPKIN *and* PIE

# Books by Stacy Finz

The Nugget series
*Going Home*
*Finding Hope*
*Second Chances*
*Starting Over*
*Getting Lucky*
*Borrowing Trouble*
*Heating Up*
*Riding High*
*Falling Hard*
*Hope for Christmas*
*Tempting Fate*

*Choosing You*
*Holding On*

The Garner Brothers series
*Need You*
*Want You*
*Love You*

The Dry Creek Ranch series
*Cowboy Up*
*Cowboy Tough*
*Cowboy Strong*

# Books by Kate Angell

The Barefoot William series
*No Tan Lines*
*No Strings Attached*
*No Sunshine When She's Gone*
*No One Like You*

*No Breaking My Heart*
*No Time to Explain*
*No Kissing Under the Boardwalk*

# Books by Marina Adair

The When in Rome series
*RomeAntically Challenged*
*Hopeless Romantic*

The Sweet Plains, Texas, series
*Tucker's Crossing*
*Blame It on the Mistletoe*

The Nashville Heights series
*Promise Me You*

The Sequoia Lake series
*It Started with a Kiss*
*Every Little Kiss*

The Eastons series
*Chasing I Do*

The Heroes of St. Helena series
*Need You for Keeps*
*Need You for Always*
*Need You for Mine*

The St. Helena Vineyard series
*Kissing Under the Mistletoe*
*Summer in Napa*
*Autumn in the Vineyard*
*Be Mine Forever*
*From the Moment We Met*

The Sugar, Georgia, series
*Sugar's Twice as Sweet*
*Sugar on Top*
*A Taste of Sugar*

# *The* CAFÉ BETWEEN PUMPKIN *and* PIE

Kate Angell
Stacy Finz
Marina Adair

KENSINGTON
PUBLISHING CORP.

www.kensingtonbooks.com

KENSINGTON BOOKS are published by

Kensington Publishing Corp.
119 West 40th Street
New York, NY 10018

All Kensington titles, imprints, and distributed lines are available at special quantity discounts for bulk purchases for sales promotion, premiums, fund-raising, educational, or institutional use.

Special book excerpts or customized printings can also be created to fit specific needs. For details, write or phone the office of the Kensington Sales Manager: Kensington Publishing Corp., 119 West 40th Street, New York, NY 10018. Attn. Sales Department. Phone: 1-800-221-2647.

The K logo is a trademark of Kensington Publishing Corp.

ISBN-13: 978-1-4967-3321-4 (ebook)
ISBN-10: 1-4967-3321-5 (ebook)

ISBN-13: 978-1-4967-3320-7
ISBN-10: 1-4967-3320-7
First Kensington Trade Paperback Printing: September 2021

10 9 8 7 6 5 4 3 2 1

Printed in the United States of America

# Contents

# Love Over Easy

## KATE ANGELL

*For Alicia Condon, editorial director, thank you for including me in another visit to Moonbright, Maine. Such an incredible fictitious town. That always seems to come alive before my eyes.*

*For Donna Kauffman, I miss you. You were always such an amazing author and good friend. Inspiring and joyful. We will always have* The Bakeshop at Pumpkin and Spice *together.*

*And for Debbie Roome, my closest and dearest friend.*

# Chapter 1

"Bo Peep, you're losing your sheep," a man standing on the curb called to Hannah Allan. His voice was deep with a hint of humor.

*Her sheep?* Hannah heard him but didn't look his way. She stood in the middle of Pumpkin Lane, awaiting the start of Moonbright's annual Halloween parade. Fifteen minutes and counting. She was dressed as Little Bo Peep. She'd pinned her hair beneath a pink bonnet with white eyelet trim, then tied it under her chin. Her pink satin dress featured puffy sleeves, a faux lace-up bodice, and polka dot trim. A stiff crinoline flared the skirt. Adult sheer white thigh-high stockings decorated with flirty blue bows brought sexiness to the childhood nursery rhyme. She'd debated the pink ruffled panties and decided to stick with the costume. No plain white cotton. Black patent leather Mary Janes completed her outfit. She carried a bright blue plastic shepherd's crook.

She grew weary. This was not her costume of choice. She wore it on her older sister's behalf. She was doing Lauren a big favor. She had come down with a cold and could not participate in the holiday festivities. Her husband was a police officer, on duty, and so, equally unable to carry out the family tradition. She'd begged Hannah to take her place. To take her four-year-old triplets to the parade, then trick-or-treating. Which was actually asking a lot. Hannah was single. She had no experience with children of her own.

Hal, Howie, and Harry were a handful. The nearly identical boys were costumed as sheep. Their one-piece fluffy white Sherpa jumpsuits, hoods with ears, and shoe covers made it difficult to tell them apart. A tiny gold bell was sewed at the neck of each costume. Their heads bobbed, and there was a lot of jingling going on.

One such jingle had wandering feet. She turned to her young flock and discovered Howie's focus was on the numerous live animals lining up behind them. He liked all things Disney and wanted to pet the Saint Bernard wearing Mickey Mouse ears.

Hannah motioned to him. "Come back to me, Howie."

He ignored her. "Right now," she said firmly. "All small hands on the shepherd's hook. We walk together, remember?"

The guy at the curb chuckled. "Need help with your flock?" he asked.

The wide brim of her bonnet framed her face. She refused to look his way. "I've got things under control." Or did she?

"You've lost a second sheep," he pointed out.

So she had. Hal's interest was centered on the Moonbright High School band. Costumed as skeletons, they tuned up their instruments in preparation for marching down the street. Hal had joined their drumline.

Worry took over. She was two sheep down, and the third, Harry, took interest in the man curbside. One quick look in his direction and familiarity struck home. She shivered. Not from the cold, but in response to the man himself. *Jake Kaylor in the flesh.* A Halloween shocker.

He thumbed down his mirrored-lens aviators and stared at

her over the rim. His eyes were a green so deep they were almost black. No more than ten feet separated them. He defined edgy. All hard faced, daring, and hazardous to her heart. He held her attention with a shadowed gaze and sexy cool smile. Then reset his shades.

Her knees nearly buckled. She'd had a crush on him for more years than she could count. Unrequited and from a distance. She was so lost in the moment of looking at him that she nearly forgot who and where she was. Including her responsibility of the triplets. She blinked, adjusted to his presence. Then raised her voice to be heard over the trombone section. "Hal, Howie, right here, right now."

The boys glanced her way for all of a second, only to ignore her request. Bribery became her best friend. Hannah knew their weakness. "Whoopie pies at the Corner Café if you behave."

The enticement worked. They stopped short and returned to her as fast as their small feet could carry them. Hal ran. Howie hopped. They loved the chocolate cake circles filled with a creamy vanilla frosting. Their favorite treat. She extended the shepherd's crook and each grabbed hold. They stood appropriately still. For the moment. Harry, however, took his sweet time.

Jake now held his full attention. Harry wasn't the only one fixated on the man. Anyone standing within twenty feet of Jake openly stared. He made an immediate impression, biker tough. The men admired him. A sexual rush made women blush. He was a turn-on. There was a wildness to Jake that unsettled the ladies. A roughness that dared them to domesticate him.

Other guys were equally tall, broad shouldered, and muscled. It was Jake's face that set him apart. Angular and strong boned. Alpha and masculine. His sharp gaze undressed and penetrated a woman's deepest thoughts. His cheekbones slashed to a single dimple, unshaved jaw. Wicked grin. His mouth promised midnight arousal and morning satisfaction.

Hannah recalled that her sister had dated Jake a number of summers ago. It had been short-lived. Lauren was oftentimes vain and liked being seen with him. However, he hadn't shown her the consideration she felt she deserved. He was a man of strong convictions. Blunt and truthful. There was no small print written into his character. Lauren's nagging, criticism, and ultimatums hadn't set well. He didn't change for anyone. They'd parted ways. He on friendly terms, she silently fuming.

Jake rallied by playing the field. The single women of Moonbright missed him terribly when he left town.

Lauren rebounded with policeman Grant Atwood before the growl of Jake's motorcycle had cleared the city limits. Grant was madly in love with her and went out of his way to please her. They'd married and had three adorable boys. All curious, a bit unmanageable, and growing like weeds. Hannah needed eyes in the back of her head to keep track of them.

At that very moment a preoccupied young Harry was checking out Jake. Hannah studied the man too. A black bandanna wrapped his long hair. He wore a faded gray T-shirt scripted with *Ride Hard* beneath his black leather jacket, the collar turned up. He packed a pair of frayed jeans like no other man. He emitted an intimidating strength and purpose that left her breathless but didn't faze Harry in the least.

Undeterred, Harry scrutinized Jake's scuffed black boots. *Boots with attitude*, thought Hannah. The boy stooped low and touched the steel toe, the side zipper, and the double snap flap. His gaze widened in awe. Hero worship. "Snow boots?" he asked Jake.

"Motorcycle boots," Jake informed him. "I ride a '70 Ducati Monza."

The brand of bike was lost on Harry. But he liked Jake's clothes. "Nice costume."

"Thanks." Jake didn't correct Harry. He let the mistake slide. His outfit wasn't a disguise—it was his everyday attire.

Jake held out his hand to the boy. "I'm Jake. The parade looks fun. Mind if I walk with you?"

"I'm Harry." The child straightened so fast, he nearly tipped over. The excitement of holding Jake's hand along the six-block route would make his day. Nonetheless, he hesitated. *Smart boy*, Hannah realized. His parents had taught him well. Jake was a stranger and Harry sought Hannah's permission before taking the man's hand. She nodded, and Harry grabbed on to Jake, jumping in place, his sheep bell jingling.

"Hal and Howie," she introduced the other two boys.

"Dudes," Jake acknowledged.

"Dudes" drew their laughter. Silly belly laughs.

Hannah observed them from beneath the rim of her bonnet. The triplets had taken to Jake. She was taken by him too. She'd recognized him, standing nonchalantly on the curb, but she didn't know him well. Nobody did. Rumors and reputation preceded him. He never corrected misconceptions. He knew who he was and didn't care what people thought of him.

She'd grown up in the small Maine town of Moonbright, a shy, oftentimes clumsy girl. Her family owned the Corner Café. Established in 1946, the restaurant had a generational soul that went deep in Moonbright history.

Jake had no such ancestral roots, wasn't even a full-time resident of the community. The majority of his family lived in Bangor. Jake and his father restored classic cars and, over the years, had established platinum status for their business. Jake had further branched out to collector motorcycles. Repairing, rebuilding, and reselling the bikes. His only link to Moonbright came through his grandfather, military veteran Major George Kaylor. Jake visited the older man on occasion. More often now since his grandmother's passing. He apparently deemed Halloween a homecoming event, Hannah thought.

"You sure about the parade?" she hesitantly asked him. He had volunteered, but she didn't want to disrupt his day.

Jake nodded. "I've two hours to kill. Afterward I'll locate my granddad and let him know I'm in town. On our last phone call, he indicated he would be at the café late in the afternoon, seated on a counter stool, enjoying a cup of coffee and piece of pie."

Hannah had served the older man over the years. He was a regular. "Black coffee and pumpkin pie."

"He lives for that pie."

Baking was near and dear to her grandmother's heart. Nan's pies were celebrated throughout the county. She made them from scratch. "I crack one egg at a time," she often said. She baked daily. The pies were in the oven long before dawn. She made one specialty pie each day along with the standard favorites. The kitchen always smelled fruity, cinnamon-y, and delicious.

The coordinator of the parade soon drew everyone's attention. The woman had climbed an aluminum ladder near a corner stop sign. Her voice was amplified by a megaphone. "Your attention, please." Those on the street quieted. Only a beagle and a pug exchanged barks. "Welcome to *Boo to You!*" The theme of the parade. "Get in position. It's almost one PM. The Halloween Queen goes first in the vintage Cadillac, followed by the mayor and city officials in separate vehicles. Third, the high school band. Play loud; play lively. Fourth, anyone in costume. From babies to adults. Pets fifth. Hold tight to those leashes. No runaways. The hayride and floats sixth. An enormous new pumpkin-faced helium balloon will wrap up the parade. Handlers guide the balloon straight down the street just above the rooftops. No higher. Looks like a windy day. The route ends at the city park. Disperse with care. Once the street fully clears, the stores and cafés will open for trick-or-treating. Have fun, everyone!"

She blew a whistle, loud and piercing, and the parade was

underway. Exhilaration marked the day. Moonbright laid claim to the largest pumpkin patch in the state of Maine. Located on the outskirts of the village, the acreage produced hundreds of pumpkins, from palm size to four hundred pounds. Locals and tourists alike bought pumpkins to carve, then display. Both grinning and grumpy jack-o'-lanterns now lined the parade route. It was a sight to behold.

The parade was inclusive. Anyone who wanted to participate could participate. No one got left out. It was a tight fit on the narrow streets of Moonbright, but the outcome made every person happy.

The weather was overcast and cool with no snow in the immediate forecast. The sun poked holes in the clouds and lit up patches of blue sky. The pale sunshine cast a false warmth.

"The band is on the move," said Jake. He motioned them forward. "It's our turn, guys."

Little Bo Peep, her sheep, and the motorcycle man fell in behind parents pushing baby carriages and those with toddlers. They got their fair share of stares. Hannah didn't like being the center of attention. Shyness overtook her and she withdrew inside herself. Jake was comfortable in his own skin with nothing to hide, nothing to prove. Numerous locals recognized him. Most seemed surprised that he walked in the parade. Quite tame for him. He received short nods and curious grins. The triplets seemed to believe the parade was in their honor. They marched with pride and waved like crazy.

A peevish northern wind joined the parade. It tipped Hannah's bonnet over one eye. Sketched goose bumps on her arms. Then blew up her skirt. The hoop-style petticoat swung above her knees. She flashed sheer white thigh-high stockings right up to the pretty blue bows. She swatted down her errant skirt. And nearly dropped the shepherd's crook. The triplets hadn't noticed the mishap, but Jake definitely had.

She felt his gaze from behind his mirrored aviators. He cocked his head and grinned. A teasing grin, so sexy and unsettling that she nearly tripped over her own feet.

He edged close, lowered his voice, and said, "Naughty wind peeked up your skirt."

"So did you."

"Nice legs, Peep."

Her blush was immediate. Worse still, the wind had a mind of its own. It continued playing with her hem, unrepentant and determined to lift the layered polka dots once again. She didn't want to draw further attention to herself. However, the gusts were relentless.

The crowd had thickened, and she couldn't let go of the staff or her two sheep would wander off. Hal and Howie were still hands-on as long as she guided them. Panic set in. She feared the next stiff breeze would flaunt her pink ruffled panties. Despite the fact they were part of the costume.

Overly modest? Perhaps. Even so, she preferred that no one see her undies. She flattened the front of the skirt over her legs with one hand only to have the wind riffle the back. A stiff draft slid between her thighs. Tickled her bottom. She sidestepped into Jake.

He sensed her predicament and saved her. He grasped her by the elbow and eased both her and the sheep toward the curb. The parade swerved around them. Continued on. Not missing a beat. No one paid any attention to their momentary break. Even her nephews behaved.

Once curbside, he shucked his leather jacket and handed it to her. "The wind's really kicked up. Put it on; zip it up," he told her. "My jacket will fall below your hips. At least it will pin your skirt down. No panty flash."

How had he known her worst fear? There was something about the man that both relieved and bothered her. She was

glad to have his jacket, yet flustered by how easily he'd read her mind.

Jake kept track of the triplets while she slipped on his jacket. It was large, roomy, and scented with his maleness. All earthy and musk. The bottom leather edge fell mid-thigh and, once zipped, held down her polka dots. His body warmth embraced her, chasing away the chill and further indignity. Grateful, she smiled and mouthed, *Thank you*.

He spoke low. "We've denied the wind the big reveal."

*We*, as in he and she. Together.

A lusty gust pressed his gray cotton T-shirt to his chest. Etching his firm pecs and six-pack. The man was built. "You won't get cold?" she asked.

"I've plenty of heat, Peep."

That he did. She was feeling overheated herself. Not only from the jacket but from his nearness. "The parade," she managed. They needed to join the folks in costume before the animals caught up to them. The dogs, cats, and a Shetland pony required their own space. And would prove distracting to the boys.

Jake found the perfect moment for them to reenter the procession. They ducked between a Flintstone family and a row of Caped Crusaders. They'd walked four blocks with two to go when Hal's shoulders drooped, his one hand dropped off the staff, and he began to drag his feet.

"Tired, Hal?" Hannah was quick to ask the boy. The triplets had been hyped at the beginning of the parade and expended a lot of energy. They were winding down. She gently suggested, "Let's step aside and watch the remaining pets and floats from the sidewalk."

"Keep going." Hal pushed forward on a sigh and a yawn. His sluggish steps slowed the parade behind them. A few people shouldered past. The dogs pressed close. A black Labrador sniffed Hal's costume.

Jake still held Harry's hand, yet his concern for Hal was evident. He stepped behind Hannah and hunkered down beside the boy. He patted his shoulder, encouraged, "Piggyback." Hal climbed on. Jake carried him easily, and they continued down the street.

Jake's thoughtfulness wasn't lost on her. She glanced at the tall man holding one small boy's hand while piggybacking another. They were quite the sight. She saw a photographer on the sidewalk snapping pictures for the small-town newspaper the *Moonbright Sun.* The young woman focused on Jake. Clicked several frames. He'd make a great feature photo.

Hannah looked at Howie, still holding on to the shepherd's crook. "You doing okay, little man?" she questioned. Hoping he was.

"I'm fine," he assured her. He was all smiles as he marched along to the band's rendition of "Monster Mash." "Whoopie pie," he reminded her of the promised treat.

Hannah had not forgotten. It was fresh on her mind. They progressed down the street, streaming past the redbrick storefronts. Seasons came and seasons went. The autumn russet awnings would soon be retracted and winter frost would curtain the storm windows.

They'd nearly reached the end of the route. The courthouse marked the southwest corner of the final block. Constructed in gray brick, the 1889 town landmark had aged gracefully. The two-story structure had weathered countless harsh northern blizzards. The clock tower created a sense of time and place. The wide cement steps provided seating for those watching the parade. A vendor costumed as a skeleton sold popcorn and caramel apples from a rattling-bones portable food cart.

The town park spread out just ahead at the end of Pumpkin Lane. October painted a sparse cropping of trees in faded russet and sienna hues. Few leaves survived on the branches; the bark on the white oak had turned patchy. The grass browned by fall.

Two police officers directed traffic as everyone dispersed along Pie Street. She debated inviting Jake to join them at the café. He'd gone above and beyond helping her with the triplets. The least she could do was offer him a homemade sweet before she took the boys trick-or-treating. Their father would pick them up at the conclusion of his shift.

She looked at Jake now. A big man encircled by little boys. He still held Harry's hand. Hal's arms were still wrapped about his neck. The little boy had fallen asleep over the last two blocks, his cheek pressed against Jake's shoulder. A much-needed short nap. He stirred now. Jake twisted about and Hal slid off his back, stood, and stretched. Wide awake and fully revived.

Howie tugged on Hannah's hand. "Whoopie pie!"

Her nephews weren't the least bit hesitant about inviting Jake to join them. "Come with us," they begged.

"He may have other plans," Hannah said, giving Jake an out.

"There's nothing more important than whoopie pie," he replied. "Once inside, I'll speak briefly with my granddad, then join you for a snack."

"I appreciate your help today," she told him.

"I like a grateful woman." His suggestive tone stroked her.

"I never expected you to—"

"Join the parade?"

"You don't seem the type."

"There's a first time for everything. I was at the right place at the right time. You had your hands full. Harry did like my costume," he reminded her.

His clothes fit him, a physically hard man. Yet she'd also seen his softer side. He liked kids.

As did she. "I love children," she admitted. "Sadly, I don't discipline; I bribe."

"They aren't your kids," he reminded her. "They'd listen to their parents, but you're the aunt and an easy mark. There's nothing wrong with a little bribery."

She accepted his take on the day.

He removed his mirrored sunglasses and hooked them in the collar of his T-shirt. Humor crinkled the corners of his midnight green eyes. "It was a fun afternoon. There was a lot going on, and the boys survived all the stimulation and distractions. They were actually quite good."

She crooked her finger. "Cooperation comes with whoopie pie."

An appealing treat, Jake thought. He willingly followed her the short distance to the Corner Café, one of his favorite places in town. The triplets had gotten their second wind and were all bounce and boundless energy. They jerked the front door wide and entered ahead of Hannah. Jake held the door for her, and she passed beneath his arm. The wind had pinkened her cheeks and the tip of her nose. Her shoulder brushed his chest and her feminine scent enveloped him. Fresh, crisp, and clean. Innocent. Awareness jolted him. Sudden and unexpected. A sexual surprise.

*What the hell?* Hannah was pretty and sweet but not his usual type. Maybe it was her costume, he mused. Sexy role play in the bedroom wasn't new to him. Sinful nurses and naughty nuns turned him on. Little Bo Peep was mild by comparison. Nursery rhymes were meant for children. Be that as it may, her thigh-high stockings were damn sexy and very adult. She had shapely legs.

His wayward thoughts were lost to his memories of the café. The casual atmosphere included a pressed-tin ceiling, wood-paneled walls, green vinyl counter seats, and wooden booths with coat hooks. The old-fashioned tile work had survived the wear of spring sandals and winter boots.

Each time he had visited his grandparents they'd brought him to the café for a meal or two. A wide chalkboard on the far wall displayed the daily specials. A wooden sign off to the right was carved with the café slogan: *Your Favorite Food Comes in a Pie—Lobster, Chicken, or Fruit.* Jake's favorite was lobster pot pie.

Mounted photographs of the Allan family along with time-honored customers framed one wall. All from different decades, showing folks at various stages of eating their meals. The locals felt a sense of celebrity to be pictured among diners of another era. Jake planned to look more closely at the photos as time allowed. He hoped to spot Hannah as a young girl.

All around him local residents hung out on the counter stools or settled into booths. Tables didn't turn over quickly. More often than not, new arrivals would pull up chairs where people were already seated for extended conversations. The home-style atmosphere offered generous food portions at a fair price.

The waitresses were older, in their fifties and sixties. Most had aged with the café. Their customers were predictable. The servers could write up an order when someone entered the door. That's how well the waitstaff knew what the regulars ate. To this day, Hannah's grandmother Nan left bite-size sugar cookies in an antique cookie jar next to the archaic cash register. Everyone left with a smile on their face and a sweet in their pocket.

A few people drifted toward the door, which Jake presently blocked. He moved aside. He'd lost Hannah and the boys during his reflections. They were halfway across the café, headed for a corner booth. She corralled the triplets in the booth while he searched out his grandfather.

His gramps was easy to spot. He sat shoulder to shoulder on a counter stool beside retired electrician and longtime friend Will Moody. The men were known as Moody and the major. Both were widowers and had reached their eighty-fifth birthdays within the same month. A need for companionship drew them to the café twice a day. Like clockwork. A routine never broken. Their morning breakfast and afternoon coffee and pie gave their day purpose. They showed up for each other.

Jake felt a flicker of regret that he hadn't visited his grandpa more often. Regrettably, work got in the way. Which was his own fault. Days turned into weeks, into months. He'd recently restored a 1956 Harley-Davidson KHK motorcycle. A hell-raiser bike. An intense and time-consuming overhaul. The owner had been pleased. The Californian had added a large bonus to the bill. Jake had subsequently decided to take some time off. He planned to stay in Moonbright until the major sent him back to Bangor.

Jake crossed the café and came to stand behind his granddad. He curved his hand over the older man's shoulder and squeezed. Both his gramps and Moody swiveled on their stools. They faced him, equally gray haired, bespectacled, in their flannel Pendleton shirts and dark trousers. No belts, Jake noticed. Apparently, they were too restricting for pie a la mode.

The major grinned at Jake, and years faded away. "You're here," he greeted Jake. He pushed off the stool and the two exchanged man hugs and thumps on the back.

Jake next shook Moody's hand. "You've been gone too long, boy," the older man declared.

"So I have," Jake agreed. He had no one to blame but himself and his busy schedule. "I'm here now and hope to stay awhile."

His grandfather raised an eyebrow, asked, "What's a while?" There was hope in his voice that Jake would stay longer than a day.

"Until you tire of me."

"That would never happen. You are my grandson."

Jake's schedule was presently open-ended. He didn't have a set agenda. He scratched his jaw and his gaze strayed to Hannah and the triplets. He hadn't realized the major and Moody also followed his stare. An open, revealing look, apparently, given their grins. He wished he hadn't taken off his aviators. No one could trace his gaze when he wore them. Too late now.

"Cute kids," his gramps said. "Hannah's nephews, I believe."

"They're costumed for the parade," added Moody.

"We walked together," slipped out. Jake set his jaw. He didn't feel the need to explain himself.

"Old news. We've already heard." There was humor in Moody's voice. Moonbright was a small town. Word spread fast. Gossip had run ahead of Jake into the café. His name was now linked to Hannah's.

"Little Bo Peep never looked so pretty," his grandfather admired.

*Gentle and shy too*, Jake thought. He mainly knew Hannah through the café. She worked for her grandmother. Waitressing. Hannah occasionally mixed up orders, but no regulars seemed to mind. The customer who received country fried steak and eggs instead of flapjacks switched plates with the other person. Food was eaten. Everyone left the café full and happy. Hannah always received big tips.

"The kids are enjoying whoopie pies," noted the major. "There's an extra treat and glass of milk on the table untouched, as if they're waiting for somebody."

"That someone would be me," Jake admitted.

"You'd better go and get it," said Moody. "The little boy on the end has finished his treat and is eyeing yours. He's got shifty hands."

Jake cracked his knuckles. "Guess I'll head that way then."

His grandfather cleared his throat, hinted, "You're looking open-road scruffy. You might consider a haircut someday soon. A shave even."

Jake couldn't help but smile. His gramps had lived his life with a military buzz cut. His hair was close-cropped even in retirement. His jaw was cleanly shaved. Jake, on the other hand, wore his own hair longer. A bandanna worked for him or, on occasion, a short ponytail. His facial scruff protected his jawline from windburn when he rode his motorcycle.

"I'll think about it," was as far as he'd commit.

Moody spoke up. "You'd need an appointment at Theodore's Barbershop. With the recent cooler weather it's become as busy as the café."

Jake understood. The drop in temperature drove everyone inside. The old-fashioned barbershop drew the male population. It specialized in classic, hot-lather shaves, conservative haircuts, and shoeshines. The shop had three vintage barber chairs and a striped pole out front. Extra slat-back chairs bordered the walls of the shop to accommodate those individuals hanging out, just being sociable. Friendships made time pass quickly. Companionship came with a cut and a shave. Theodore had been in business as long as the café. Both were local institutions.

Jake finished by telling the major, "I may go trick-or-treating with Peep and her sheep. Where can I find you early in the evening?"

"Upstairs in my apartment," he was told. "Moody and I will be playing gin." The men enjoyed card games. The bets were nickel-and-dime.

Jake's granddad's studio apartment was one of four built above the café. Both he and Moody rented from the Allans. The rooms were small and cozy, perfect for the men and their modest possessions. They'd downsized following the loss of their wives.

Jake wondered who else leased from Nan. His gramps filled him in. "One apartment presently stands empty. I asked Nan if you could stay there for a single night or several weeks, however long you were in town. She was fine with it."

"Thanks, Gramps." Good news for Jake.

He'd called around before arriving in Moonbright, checking vacancies at Amelia Rose's Rose Cottage bed-and-breakfast along with a few smaller hotels. Even those on the outskirts of town. He'd been too last-minute. Halloween weekend drew an enormous crowd to the village renowned for its celebrations. Every place was booked with out-of-towners, oftentimes a year in advance. That hadn't discouraged his visit. He'd have bought a cot or a sleeping bag at the hardware store and slept on his granddad's living room floor as a last resort. No need for such purchases now. He had his own space. He was grateful.

The major's brow creased. "What about your motorcycle?"

"Parked in a side bay at Morrison's Garage during my visit." A few blocks south. "I figured this might be my last round-trip bike ride before it snowed. I drive my Hummer in winter."

A waitress skirted the counter, topping off coffee cups. She held up the pot. "Welcome home, Jake. Coffee?" she asked.

*Home* sent an unexpected warmth through his chest. This was his grandfather's town. Jake had few ties. Still, it was nice to be accepted. "I'll pass for now," he told her. "I've milk and whoopie pie waiting for me at Hannah's table."

"There's soon to be a three-way split of your snack if you don't hurry over there," the waitress warned him. "The sheep are restless."

Definitely hyped, Jake noticed. It was hard to tell the boys apart. At that moment all three bounced and rocked in the booth. They were already wired on whoopie pie, with trick-or-treating yet ahead. He watched as Hannah caught their attention. She raised her hands, then lowered them, a silent request that they settle down. The triplets scrunched their faces but obeyed. For how long was debatable.

"Get going. Join them," his gramps encouraged.

"Thanks for understanding." He turned to leave.

"I understand your interest in Bo Peep," the major said slyly. That stopped Jake. His jaw worked. He lowered his voice, said, "Don't assume, Gramps. I'm merely lending a helping hand with the boys. That's it."

The major nodded. "If you say so."

"I've said so."

"For now." Moody got in the last word.

Jake shook his head. Matchmakers, both. His status as a confirmed bachelor served him well. Marriage didn't fit his lifestyle or future. Still, the older men hinted and nudged him toward Hannah. He sensed without really knowing her that she was caring, kind, and family oriented. He was hard-core. A ride or die kind of guy. He dated, but at thirty-five he was more involved in his work than with any special lady. He operated free and easy. He came and went as he pleased.

Locals nodded and greeted him as he walked from the counter to the corner booth. "Jake!" the boys whooped his welcome with the enthusiasm of a days-long absence when it had been only minutes. Hannah gave him a small smile. He slid in beside Harry. He'd walked beside the boy in the parade and noticed his blue eyes were a tint darker than his brothers'. But not by much.

The sheep had flipped back their hoods. Static electricity stood their hair on end. They'd eaten their treats with gusto. White milk mustaches framed their upper lips and chocolate cake flaked their chins. He passed them napkins from the metal tabletop dispenser.

Harry pointed to Hannah. "She needs a napkin too."

Yes, she did, Jake noted. As with the triplets, cake flecked her cheek and the corner of her mouth. He couldn't help but smile. He instinctively made a man's move on a messy woman and gently brushed away the crumbs. Her cheek was smooth and soft to his touch. Her pink lips gently parted with the press of his callused thumb. She exhaled and the moist warmth was as startling as if she'd sucked on the tip.

A turn-on for him.

Embarrassment for her. Her eyes were wide.

She blushed and looked away.

He was struck by her reserve. He lowered his hand and leaned back against the booth. Bo Peep was naïve, he realized. Inexperienced. He'd unintentionally made her self-conscious. He should've passed her a napkin as he'd done for the boys. And not touched her. He hoped he hadn't drawn attention to them.

A side-eye at those seated nearby proved people were deep in discussion and minding their own business, not his. He was relieved. Not necessarily for his sake, but for Hannah's. His harmless gesture could be construed as affection. Gossip was contagious and spread rapidly in a small town. She lived in Moonbright. He was passing through. He didn't want to leave her as a topic of conversation. Not linked to him, anyway.

Harry bumped him from the side, gaining Jake's attention. "You going to eat your whoopie pie?" he asked.

"I'd planned to eat part of it."

"What part?"

"At least half."

The boy smacked his lips. "The other half?"

"I could divide it into thirds."

Harry scrunched his nose. He understood half, but thirds confused him.

"Three pieces," Hannah helped out.

"Milk too?" asked Harry. His fingers inched toward Jake's glass. His was empty.

"Let Jake have his own glass," Hannah was quick to say. She slid out of the booth, unzipped and slipped off his leather jacket, then hung it on a coat hook. "I'll get refills for you guys."

Her skirt once again swung wide and the hoop bumped into the backs of chairs and the edges of tables as she headed toward the beverage station. There she filled three small glasses with milk and placed them on a serving tray. Her gaze was downcast and she didn't look all that steady on her return. Her hip caught the corner of a tabletop and milk sloshed in the glasses but didn't fully spill over. She arrived and set down the tray. Her breath rushed out in relief. The boys snatched the glasses and had chugged half the milk by the time she resettled in the booth.

Jake eased his plated whoopie pie across the table along with a table knife. "You do the honors, Peep," he requested.

Her nephews leaned forward, their elbows on the table, eyeing her slicing, wanting their fair shares. Hannah had a good eye. She evenly halved the pie and gave Jake his piece. She held the blade over the boys' half, debating the remaining thirds, when Harry pressed her for the largest piece. "Little more to the left."

"No, to the right," insisted the boy Jake believed to be Howie.

Hannah did her best. She sliced the treat into clear-cut thirds. Although Howie insisted that Harry got more than he did.

"Eat slowly and it will last longer," Hannah told them.

Their chewing was measured and unhurried. A game in which no one wanted to finish first. Silliness prevailed. They drew out their enjoyment of the snack.

Howie, his teeth chocolate, looked at Hannah. "Tell us a Halloween joke," he pleaded. "Make us laugh."

She hesitated. "My jokes aren't that funny."

The boys ganged up on her, chanting, "Joke, joke, joke."

Jake had finished his whoopie pie and glass of milk. He wiped his mouth with a napkin, said, "Humor us."

They hadn't given her a choice. She gave in, saying, "This one's for you, Howie. What does a child monster call his parents?"

He came back with, "Monster Mom and Dad?"

"Good guess," Hannah praised him. "The answer is *Mummy and Deady.*"

The boys all grinned, hooted. "My turn," said Harry.

"Where does a ghost go on Saturday night?" she asked him.

Harry rocked on the booth, deep in thought. He finally shook his head. "Don't know?"

"Anywhere he can *boo*-gie."

Smiles all around. Hal sat on the edge of his seat. He pounded his palm on the tabletop, said, "Me next."

"Why is a ghost such a messy eater?"

Hal didn't bother to guess. "Tell me."

"The ghost is much like you guys," said Hannah. " 'Cause the ghost is always *goblin.*"

The boys' amusement drew attention to their booth. Customers turned their heads, smiled, even without knowing what had caused their laughter.

Jake eyed Hannah while the boys finished their milk. They were having a slurping contest. Loud with bubbles at the corners of their mouths. He snuck in, "Do you have a joke for me too?"

She reacted with, "What is a skeleton's favorite song?"

He had no idea.

" 'Bad to the Bone,' " she dared.

He grinned. "Good one." He knuckled his jaw and asked, "Is that how you see me?"

His question took her aback. She folded her hands in her lap, answered, "It was only a Halloween joke. No assumptions, Jake. I don't know you well enough."

"We'll have to rectify that."

"Rectify what?"

"Us." He tested her willingness to spend time with him. Her reaction disappointed him. She bit down on her bottom lip. Her expression was skeptical. Her lack of interest wasn't impolite, merely telling. She wasn't into him. A minor blow to his ego.

What had he expected? A hint of interest, perhaps. However small. Just not a silent shutdown. Jake immediately debated the wisdom of his suggestion. There were dos and don'ts of dating in a small town. Especially when the guy was an outsider. Hannah had caught his eye over the years, but he'd never pursued her. They'd barely exchanged a dozen words. He had, however, dated her sister, Lauren, which might put Hannah off dating him now.

Resolve prevailed. He wasn't ready to give up on her, not yet anyway. He felt comfortable around her. Hannah was attractive and her innocence appealed to him. Fate had placed him on the sidewalk at the start of the parade. That's where he'd first spotted Little Bo Peep. He'd been amused by her costume as well as her inability to keep track of her sheep. Her nephews were wide-eyed and wandering. Moving in three different directions. He'd offered assistance and she'd reluctantly accepted. He'd never walked in a parade but found it fun.

Their paths would continue to cross while he was in town. The café was where everyone met to enjoy a good meal. His grandfather and pal Moody wiled away hours seated at the counter. They rehashed the good old days and discussed the weather. It was only logical that Jake would join the two on occasion.

Be that as it may, his conscience waved a red flag. A reminder that Hannah's grandmother and mother were very protective of her. So were the regular customers. She was undeniably special. A friendship with her would be fine. Intimacy, off-limits. Difficult for him. He liked sex. A lot. Nothing felt better than the hard vibration of a bike between his thighs unless it was the smooth, naked slide into a soft, wet woman.

There were those ladies who could handle an affair and those who sought stability. Permanence made his palms itch. His feet were programed for an about-face. His boots were made for walking.

Realistically, he couldn't just make love to Hannah, then roll out of bed, dress, and depart. She was too damn sweet. There was too much at stake. His grandfather would disown him if he hurt her. Logic ruled. He decided to move slowly and see how things shook out.

Hannah's grandmother soon walked through the swinging doors that separated the kitchen from the dining room. Jake recognized Nan Allan immediately. The Allan women all held a strong family resemblance. Fine features and slim figures. The older woman had pinned her gray hair in a bun at the nape of her neck. An orange apron designed with a scarecrow covered her kitchen whites. She stopped briefly at the counter and spoke to the major and Moody before approaching their corner booth.

"Gran-gran Nan!" the boys greeted their great-grandmother.

"My handsome sheep," Nan returned. She came armed with plastic pumpkin-shaped buckets. She set one before each boy. Then affectionately ruffled their static hair.

Harry pointed to her face. "There's flour on your nose."

Nan swiped it away with the back of her hand. "All gone?" she asked. Harry nodded, and she explained, "I'm elbows deep in dough. Baking bread."

"*Elbows deep.*" The boys found that funny.

"Are you having a good time?" Nan asked them.

"We marched in the parade," said Harry. "Jake too."

Nan nodded to Jake. "I heard about your visit from the major. It's good to see you. Stay a spell."

Jake wasn't certain how long "a spell" might be, but he planned to stay awhile. He leaned back in the booth, legs extended, relaxing in the moment. Enjoying the family exchange.

"We ate whoopie pies," Howie told her. "Jake shared his."

Nan approved. "How generous of him." She then singled

Jake out. "Stop by the kitchen anytime and I'll have a whole whoopie pie set aside with your name on it."

He appreciated her offer. "I'll do just that."

"Hannah told us jokes," Hal informed his great-gran.

Nan grinned, revealed, "Hannah told me one at breakfast. What does a mother ghost say to her kids in the car?"

The boys all shook their heads.

" 'Fasten your *sheet* belts.' "

Nan laughed along with the triplets.

Jake chuckled too.

Seconds later the boys drummed on the pumpkin buckets with their spoons. They'd grown impatient. There was no holding them back. They climbed across Hannah and hopped from the booth. "Trick-or-treat. We want candy," they collectively demanded.

Nan leaned toward them and gently laid down the law. "All candy that's collected goes in the pumpkin buckets. Hannah will make the rounds with you. You'll walk north on Pumpkin Lane to the bed-and-breakfast, then back to the courthouse. All businesses are handing out treats. No munching along the way. *Not one bite*," she emphasized. "Your dad will pick you up at the café on your return. He can decide how much candy you can eat before bed. Got it?"

Hal screwed up his face and was the first to whine. "Not even one piece? I'll get hungry walking."

Nan was determined to prevent a sugar high. "Not one tiny bite."

"What if it's a Tootsie Roll pop?" asked Howie. His favorite candy.

"Not even if it's a red one."

The boy blew raspberries.

Jake slid from the booth. "If you guys can't eat candy, then neither will I," he said, hoping to make them feel better. It seemed to work. Their frowns faded.

The triplets looked at Hannah. She also gave her word. "Nothing for me tonight either. However, should a store owner hand out Butterfingers, I expect you to share one or two with me that I can enjoy tomorrow."

Nan turned to Jake. "Would you mind herding the sheep to the door? I need to speak privately with Hannah. Two of my waitresses costumed as gypsies are handing out Dragon's Teeth candy corn on the sidewalk outside the café. One pack per sheep."

Jake snagged his leather jacket off the hook. He flipped it over his shoulder. "On our way out. Let's go, dudes."

The sheep pumped their arms and bounded across the dining room, dodging customers, full of energy and excitement, their bells jingling.

Jake had exceptional hearing. He hadn't meant to eavesdrop, but Nan's whisper carried to him. "Have you recited the Halloween chant?" she asked Hannah.

"Chant" caught his attention. Curiosity slowed his steps. Hannah's answer was barely audible, "No, Gram, not yet."

"Embrace the Halloween magic, my dear," Nan pressed. "Don't let the night pass you by. The women of Moonbright have faith in the legend. Over the years they've spoken the words with heart and soul and believed in the outcome. Their wishes came true. Yours can too."

*Moonbright legend?* Jake was baffled. He wondered if the folklore was known only to the women or if the men were aware of it as well? He would tap his grandfather for information. Surely he'd have a clue.

Further contemplation went out the door with the triplets. They were temporarily Jake's responsibility and he didn't want them on the sidewalk alone. He had to limit each boy to one pack of the strawberry-and-chocolate-flavored Dragon's Teeth.

Outside, the wind had died. Hannah no longer had to worry about it blowing up her skirt. Although he wouldn't mind a second peek at her sexy Bo Peep stockings. The late-afternoon sun split the clouds, bright enough for him to slip on his mirrored aviators.

That's when he caught Harry fumbling with a pack of candy corn pressed against his stomach. The wrap crinkled, split open, and quick as a blink the boy shoved several pieces into his mouth. Jake had never seen anyone chew so fast. He swallowed equally as quickly. He was lucky he hadn't choked.

Jake cleared his throat from behind the boy. Loudly enough that Harry jumped. He had a Halloween joke of his own to tell. "What do I say to a sheep who sneaks treats?"

Harry shrugged guiltily.

Jake bent close, his voice deep and low. " 'You are baaad,' " he bleated like a sheep.

Harry grinned for a single second before turning serious. He nervously dropped the partially opened package of candy corn into his bucket. "You going to tell Aunt Hannah?" he asked.

Jake debated. It was Halloween. Candy was a hot commodity and hard to resist. He cut Harry some slack. "How many Dragon's Teeth did you actually eat?"

"One."

"I thought I saw two pop into your mouth."

"I ate three."

"No more from here on out."

"No more *what*?" Hannah had joined them. The sweep of her hoopskirt grazed the backs of his knees.

He cut her a look over his shoulder. He wasn't a tattle tale. "No more walking ahead of me," was all that came to his mind. "The street is crowded and the sheep are eager. The candy is calling their names."

Hannah arched an eyebrow, not quite believing him. "I'm sure there are plenty of treats to go around," she assured them.

Harry took Jake's hand. "I'll walk with you," he said.

"Want me to hold the pumpkin bucket?" asked Jake.

Harry shook his head. "I can manage. I don't want to miss out on any treats."

"You already have a package of candy corn." Hannah squinted into the bucket. Noticing, "Is one corner of the package open?"

Harry fidgeted, not wanting to fib to his aunt.

Jake spoke for him. "Nope, still closed."

Harry heaved a huge sigh of relief for such a small boy. The broken seal was a dead giveaway.

Hannah saw through Jake's white lie. "If you say so, Pinocchio."

"Not my costume, Peep."

A crush of trick-or-treaters soon surrounded them.

Jake, Bo Peep, and her sheep moved up the street.

# Chapter 2

Trick-or-treaters packed the sidewalk. A physically tight fit. Fortunately, there wasn't any pushing or shoving. People progressed at a leisurely pace. Hannah walked behind Jake and the triplets. The boys were bouncy. Jake's stride was smooth and athletic. She discreetly admired his backside. Wide shoulders and narrow hips. A butt that could've modeled boxers or blue jeans.

Several people spoke to him. The conversations were short and friendly. Most everyone wanted to know why he was in town and for how long. Jake repeated the same answer over and over again. *He was visiting his grandfather with no set departure date.*

An hour went by, and the afternoon sky darkened. Dusk flipped a switch and the antique lampposts illuminated Pumpkin Lane. Brightly. Jake still wore his aviators. Each time he glanced over his shoulder, she couldn't tell if he was looking at her or at someone behind her. Hannah wished it were at her. However unlikely.

She rewound their conversation at the café. She'd told him

a Halloween joke and he had teased her back. Suggesting that they spend time together. His proposal had bounced off her. She hadn't believed him serious. She was plain and shy and not all that interesting. Her life was routine, varying little. She went to work, joined friends for an occasional movie, and turned in early.

She wished with all her heart she'd handled things differently. She should've kept the moment light. Perhaps a witty comeback, something sassy but not too snide. Letting him know that she was aware he was kidding her and that he didn't actually want to hang out. Sadly, all her words stuck in her throat. The silence had suffocated her. She'd come off as stand-offish. Uninterested. Rude. Which was so unlike her.

The Corner Café offered a fairly steady turnover of male customers. Many of the men were personable and hardworking. Even so, she'd never met any man like Jake Kaylor. He was handsome, hot, and in town for such a short time. She despaired. She might never meet anyone like him again. He wasn't the type of man to ask a woman twice. Still, she wished for a second chance with him. Moonbright had its fair share of single ladies. He wouldn't lack company.

She rubbed her forehead. Her grandmother's words were imprinted on her mind. A stark reminder of Moonbright Halloween lore. She must repeat the chant prior to the bewitching hour in order for it to come true. Then, if the legend was to be believed, she would glimpse her future husband in a reflective surface before midnight.

Pretty farfetched, but she'd give it a try. She searched the area. No mirrors or shiny glass in the vicinity. Skeptical and feeling foolish, she reluctantly honored her grandma's wishes. She dipped her head, partially closed her eyes, and whispered, *"Mirror, mirror on Halloween, will my future spouse be seen?"* She repeated it twice. Dubious of the outcome.

Preoccupied with the chant, she found herself on a collision course with Jake. He'd stopped short on the sidewalk and she walked smack into him. She and her hoopskirt bounced off his hard body. She lost her footing, fell back a step. Clumsy and humiliated. Wide-eyed and panicky. She made a grab for whatever or whoever could steady her.

That turned out to be Jake himself. Her outstretched fingers scraped down his side and sank inside his jeans. Her thumb hooked a belt loop. The force of her grip drew down the waistband by several inches. Her fingertips grazed the muscular curve of his hip. A commando-bare hip. His body heat stroked between her fingers, crept over her hand, and skittered up her arm. Her breasts tingled. She wished the sidewalk would open up and swallow her whole. Her wish was denied.

Jake turned with a slowness that further unnerved her. He flexed his butt cheek and his voice was deep-husky when he asked, "What's up, Peep? Are you scratching my back, picking my pocket, or getting in my pants?"

She swiftly withdrew her hand. Awkwardness made her apology a stammer. "F-forgive me. I tripped."

A man costumed as a Tyrannosaurus had witnessed her pitch forward. "She mumbled and stumbled," he verified. "There are cracks along the sidewalk. Sorry I couldn't catch her." His dinosaur costume was authentic, and the very small arms were pinned against its body. No way could he have saved anyone. He gave a dinosaur bellow and shuffled off.

Jake put the moment in perspective. "So it was either grab me or face plant?"

"More or less."

He single dimpled. "I'm fine with you grabbing me. Anytime."

Harry took that moment to pull on Jake's arm. "Hurry up."

Hannah saw that they were holding up the trick-or-treaters. The boys weren't happy. People were starting to pass them, cutting in line. "Onward," she said, keeping her hands to herself.

They continued on. Their next stop was Bellaluna's Bakeshop. Sofia, the baker and owner, handed out the best treats in town. Jumbo cupcakes made with chocolate cake, topped with orange icing and tiny marshmallow ghosts. All wrapped in clear cellophane. A tasty indulgence not to be missed.

"*Harry*," Hannah warned when her nephew poked his fingers through the wrap and into the thick, creamy frosting, then went on to lick them clean. "No sweets. You're cheating."

"You mad at me?" the boy asked.

"Not mad-mad," said Hannah.

Harry grinned. "Then it was worth it."

Jake took the cupcake from him and placed it safely in the pumpkin bucket. "For later," he stated.

They made it four additional blocks without mishap, finally reaching Rose Cottage at the northern end of their loop. Amelia Rose stood on the walkway of her front yard. The bed-and-breakfast was surrounded by a magical forest of enormous pumpkins and twinkling lights. Amelia sparkled as Glinda the Good Witch from *The Wizard of Oz* in a pale pink gown with puffy sleeves and an organdy skirt sprinkled with silver glitter stars. A bejeweled circlet crowned her soft gray hair. She welcomed everyone with a wave of her dazzling wand. Two costumed Munchkins circulated through the crowd, handing out Tootsie Roll pops.

The hard-candy pops were Howie's downfall. He pulled a face and was ready to argue with Hannah when Jake took away all temptation. He dropped the red lollipop into the boy's bucket before he could even touch the stick. Howie frowned but didn't fuss further. He was a trooper as they headed down the opposite side of the street to collect additional treats. Their containers were nearly filled to the brim by the time they reached the courthouse. The mayor and his staff passed out bite-size Snickers.

"Daddy!" her nephews shouted as they crossed the road to

the Corner Café. They ran to their father and hugged him. Officer Grant Atwood had just finished his shift. His formal police uniform fit in with the costumes. Others had paraded as law enforcement earlier in the day. Together, he and his boys quickly entered the café so the kids could show off their candy.

Inside, the café-style shutters were drawn. The lower halves of the windows were covered in Halloween artwork of ghosts, pumpkins, scarecrows, and black cats, all painted by glass muralist Mila Cramer, owner of First Impressions. Talented Mila produced seasonal paintings for the downtown storefronts and restaurants. Her Halloween creations would soon be transformed into Thanksgiving themes. Always innovative. Amazingly eye-catching. An asset to Moonbright's curb appeal.

Above the mural, the upper casement reflected the corner lamplight and intruding night. A Hunter's Blue Moon was on the rise. Rare and eerie. Few customers remained. The café had closed early so the staff could participate in the Halloween festivities. Private and public parties. Music and dancing in the streets. The boys retreated to a nearby booth. They poured out their buckets on the tabletop and began an immediate exchange of candy. Deciding which pieces they wished to keep and which they wanted to give away.

Howie nabbed the red Tootsie Roll pops.

Harry went for Starbursts.

Hal gathered the Hershey's Kisses. Adding Jolly Ranchers and Twix. Howie and Harry called him out when he grabbed all the mini-bags of M&M's. Hal glared but reluctantly shared.

Grant managed to shake Jake's hand and give Hannah a big hug while keeping an eye on his sons. "You saved the day," he told her. "I just called Lauren, and while she's feeling better, she's not at one hundred percent. My boys would've missed out on the parade and trick-or-treating if not for you."

"Jake helped out too," she said, giving credit where credit was due.

"Appreciated." Her brother-in-law next drew a breath and had to ask, "How were they?"

"It was a long day for everyone," she admitted. "They did well." She glanced toward their table and caught Hal jabbing Harry in the arm with a blue Rock Candy Swizzle on a wooden stick. Harry smacked him back with a red Twizzler. Howie fired Skittles at them both. She sighed and added, "They're on the verge of a candy war. Time to take them home, Grant."

He agreed. "We're gone." He crossed to scoop the candy off the table and to collect his sons. The boys were all smiles as they left. Each one passed Hannah a bite-size Butterfinger on their way out the door. Jake was rewarded with three packets of Dragon's Teeth. The candy corn spilled onto his palm from the pack Harry had originally opened. Jake ate them quickly.

"I saw that," Hannah accused.

He held up his hand. "Empty, Peep."

"You're as bad as the boys."

"Bad to the bone."

Her heart stuttered. Life had hit the reset button. Offering her an opportunity to explain herself. "I don't think that of you," she softly said.

"I wasn't so sure earlier."

"I made a joke and so did you."

He scratched his jaw. "I don't remember my joke."

They stood off to the side, in an aisle of empty tables. Several diners trickled out. Looks were cast, but no one outwardly stared. Their conversation was as private as it could be in a public place.

Shyness shortened her breath. She gave a small indifferent shrug in an attempt to lessen the significance of his earlier comment. "You mentioned rectifying something or other."

He puzzled, then remembered. "Rectifying us. Our getting to know each other better." He paused. "You found that funny?"

"I thought you were kidding me."

"I never joke about spending time with a woman."

"Why me?" slipped out.

He flattened his palm over his heart. "I have a soft spot for Little Bo Peep."

"You're into nursery rhymes?"

"Into you, if you have time for me."

She worked a lot of hours. "I'll find time."

A heartbeat of silence before her grandmother broke them apart. "Here you are, Hannah." She stood beside the front counter in her Red Hat Society costume. She'd changed from her kitchen whites into a frilly satin purple dress and feathered red hat. She dangled a ring of keys from her fingers. "I'm meeting Naomi and Margaret at the Thirsty Raven for our traditional Bloody Mummy. Would you mind locking up for me, sweetie?"

"Happy to. Anytime."

Her gram delivered the keys. She leaned close and whispered, "Did you chant?"

"I chanted."

"Excellent. So glad you listened to me."

Hannah waved her out the door. "Party hearty with the Red Hatters." Those women over fifty who regularly socialized and whose friendships stretched a lifetime. "I'll see you bright and early."

She secured the door, then turned back to Jake. "Your plans?" she asked. "Coming or going?"

"I'm headed upstairs to visit my granddad and Moody. How about you?"

"The cooks and dishwasher have set the kitchen in order. It's my job now to clean up the dining room."

"All by yourself?"

She scanned the room. "There's usually two or three of us to wrap up the supper shift. The other waitresses wanted the night off to celebrate Halloween. There's lots of activities going on in town. So I volunteered."

"You're more Cinderella than Little Bo Peep."

"Hardly. I've no evil stepsisters or stepmother."

"Don't you mind missing out on the fun?"

"The married ladies should be with their families, and the single girls have dates."

"What about your date?"

"I've a date with the side work."

"Side work?"

He apparently had never worked in a restaurant. She ticked off the tasks on her fingers. "Wiping down booths, tables and chairs, and menus, filling salt and pepper shakers and condiment baskets. Stocking the drink station with glasses and cups. Setting bus pans under the counter for dirty dishes. Rolling silverware in napkins. Then sweeping and mopping the floor. I'm organized and quick."

"All while wearing your costume?"

"Quick change. I have an apartment on the second floor."

That seemed to please him. "We're neighbors then."

Her eyebrows raised. "How's that?"

"I'm renting the empty studio while I'm in town."

"Oh . . . ," escaped her. No one had warned her. He would be right next door. Only a wall would separate them. They'd be sharing a bathroom. Undeniably close. She could no longer run around in her pajamas. She'd be forced to wear a robe or be fully dressed. How would she be able to sleep, wondering what he wore to bed? She imagined he slept nude. Naked would look good on him.

Her expression must have revealed her concern. He removed his sunglasses, guessed, "Problem, Peep?"

She couldn't deny him a roof over his head. She drew a breath, said, "I'm fine. You need a place to sleep."

"Trust me," he assured her. "I called around town. There

were no hotel rooms available." He grew serious. "If my presence makes you uncomfortable, I can always sleep beside my motorcycle on the cement floor at Morrison's Garage. Your call."

"My decision, huh?" She kept a straight face when she said, "The floor at the garage will be cold. I'll get you a pillow and a wool blanket."

A ticking of seconds before he laughed aloud. A deep, hearty laugh that stroked her hot. She blushed. "At least you'd allow me some comfort. Although I'd prefer a bed."

"There's a single in the studio apartment."

"Small, but not an issue."

He was a big guy. A king-size mattress would've served him far better. Him and a lover. The thought left her overly warm.

She cleared her throat, asked, "Have you been up to the second floor?"

He nodded. "From the outside staircase last time I visited my grandfather. I held on to the entrance key."

She touched her forefinger to her lips as if sharing a secret. "There's also a narrow set of steps located off the storage room. Known only to family and trusted boarders. Used only after hours. The outside key works inside too." She crooked her finger at him. "Follow me—I'll show you."

He followed her across the dining room. They entered the kitchen through the swinging door. Gray linoleum tiles had withstood years of spills, rolling carts, and hundreds of footsteps. The aromas of Yankee Pot Roast and cooked vegetables still lingered. Pot roast had been a dinner special and was one of Hannah's favorite meals. The meat would've been meltingly tender. The veggies seasoned and baked in the rich broth. She'd missed supper and wished there were leftovers. But her grandmother generously sent any remaining food home with the employees. Most being family. A café perk.

Hannah admired the shiny stainless-steel kitchen. Whereas

the dining room reflected the past, the kitchen functioned on modern upgrades. Her grandmother was practical. Business was brisk and profitable. Equipment breakdowns would close the doors. Repairs would eat profits. Quality commercial brands were used to cook and bake her recipes.

The only spot of color in the kitchen was a bright butter yellow Hobart mixer. A splurge by Hannah's gran. Arthritis gripped the older woman's hands. They often ached from all the stirring, mixing, and kneading. The large countertop mixer eased her pain.

Hannah *felt* Jake on her heels as she bypassed the food prep station and convection oven. His knees bumped the hem of her hoopskirt. Swinging it sideways. He helped her pat it down. His palm settled low on her back as they headed toward the storeroom. Her heart jarred at the hot rush of intimacy.

Unsteady, she thankfully made it to the storage area without mishap. There tiered metal shelving lined the walls. One separate rack was piled with bags of flour, sugar, and rice. Casters rolled it aside, revealing a narrow hidden door. Hannah ran her fingers along the upper frame and recovered a brass skeleton key. "An extra key should you forget yours," she said. She fit it in the lock. Then turned the knob and the door squeaked open.

"A secret passage?" Jake was intrigued.

She explained, "Secret to most. Decades ago when my grandparents first opened the café, housing in town was limited. They found residing upstairs a practical solution. Over time they tired of living and working under the same roof and eventually bought a house on Starry Night Court. Two blocks south, and still an easy commute for Gram. She continues to drive a 1970 Ford Pinto. It clinks, clanks, putt-putts. She refuses to trade it in for a newer model."

Jake grinned. "The major is much like your grandmother. He's hung on to his 1940 wood-paneled station wagon."

Hannah smiled back. "The Woody Wagon."

"The one and only. It's a classic. Countless collectors have offered to purchase the Packard. He's turned down every one. He continues to rent secured space at Morrison's Private Storage behind the main garage. I'll check out the wagon while I'm in town. He doesn't drive much anymore. Even so, I want to be sure it's winterized."

Very thoughtful of him. She liked how he took care of his gramps. She motioned to him, then said, "Time to climb. Be careful. The staircase is narrow with a sharp curve near the top." She clutched the wooden railing with one hand and her skirt with the other. Then headed up ahead of him.

Steep steps, and the sway of her skirt couldn't be contained. Instead of side to side, it flounced front to back, flashing Jake from behind. She cringed.

He chuckled, deep and admiring. "Sexy thigh-highs. Those blue bows along the seams do it for me."

His compliment sent heat up and between her legs. Her composure slipped. The hoopskirt would be the death of her. She would never wear one again. Sheer will pushed her up the remainder of the stairs. Once on the landing, she struggled to turn and face him. The light overhead flickered and dimmed, needing a bulb replaced. Jake's face was shadowy, but she could make out his expression, equally intense and indulgent.

She would have immediately taken to her room, but his gaze detained her. All dark heat and sinful appreciation. His face was hard cut. His mouth curved, wicked by design. Tension stretched between them. Nerves overcame her. She felt inept with this man.

She stepped back, only to have him step forward. Her skin prickled and goose bumps rose. She rubbed her arms. Heaved a breath. Her voice wavered when she asked, "Are you hitting on me?" The question sounded rather juvenile.

"Do you want me to make a move?"

"No. . . ."

"Then I'm not."

"That's what I thought."

"Did you really?"

"I just wanted to be sure."

"And now you know," he said easily. "Don't worry, Peep; this is as near as I get. Your crinoline's like a chastity belt."

"The hoop comes off shortly."

"Stripping down is good. Go get comfortable."

She was five minutes away from changing clothes. She pointed down the hallway. "Your room is the second door on the left. There's a private key above the doorframe."

He nodded. "Thanks. I want to spend an hour or so with Gramps and Moody; then I'll head to Morrison's Garage and retrieve my helmet and saddlebags from my motorcycle."

"You travel light."

"I don't need much. I never stay anywhere overly long."

Which meant he could leave Moonbright on a moment's notice. Or no notice at all. Her stomach sank. She felt a sense of loss, and he hadn't even left yet.

She finished with, "I need to get busy. The dining room tables won't wipe themselves down. The napkins won't fold around the silverware. The salt and pepper shakers won't refill each other."

He shifted his weight from one hip to the other and casually said, "I may come down to the kitchen before I turn in. I'd like an evening snack. Your grandmother promised me a whoopie pie."

"She always keeps her word," said Hannah. "I'm sure there's one in the refrigerator with your name on it."

"One I don't have to share with three hungry sheep."

The memory of her nephews eyeing, then devouring half of Jake's whoopie pie made her smile. "All yours and well deserved."

His booted footsteps took him across the durable Maine

Coast Rope Rug in black with green flecks. Constructed with recycled lobster float rope, the floor covering was locally produced and found in most homes. This particular rug had survived decades. Hannah's parents had lived a short time in one of the apartments after they'd first married. She'd crawled and taken her earliest baby steps on the rope rug.

A collection of photographs on one wall outside his grandfather's door caught Jake's attention. "Neat photos," he said. "The black-and-white of the coastline covered with fog has a supernatural vibe."

Hannah found it ghostly. Spooky.

He tapped a heavy wooden frame with his finger, noted, "There's strength and survival in the bull moose crossing the watery wetland."

She nodded her agreement.

"Which picture do you like best?" he asked her.

No hesitation on her part. "The colorful lobster buoys hanging from the faded blue fence."

"Wood, handmade, vintage. Durable." He met her gaze. "The lobster industry is as much a part of Maine as the Corner Café is of Moonbright. Generational and familiar. Stable."

His assessment pleased her. He understood her fondness for the photo. There was something about the buoys that represented longevity and legacy. Lobster was a mainstay at the café. Lunch hour lobster rolls and lobster pot pie sold as fast as breakfast hotcakes.

Jake proceeded to knock on his granddad's door. The major answered. The older man waved at Hannah. Jake looked back and winked at her. "Later, Peep." And he closed the door.

His wink unsettled her. He left her weak-kneed. She turned to enter her own apartment only to walk straight into the wall. Fortunately, her stiff crinoline protected her. She bounced back instead of running face first into the wood. She sighed heavily. She needed to be more careful. Less clumsy. Difficult to do with Jake Kaylor in her life. She needed to get a grip. To set thoughts of him aside and clean the dining room. Scrubbing tables would distract her.

"You missed a spot." Jake came up behind Hannah as she sponged a tabletop in the dining room. He leaned close, removed his aviators, and pointed to a smear of ketchup at one corner.

She startled, and her hip bumped the table leg. Soapy water splashed from a small plastic container, pooling on the Formica. She seized one of the clean rags tucked into the waistband of her jeans and quickly soaked up the excess water. She wrung it out over the container.

Lady was jumpy, he thought. He straightened, notched his shades at the neck of his T-shirt, and apologized, "Sorry. I didn't mean to scare you."

She didn't look up, only said, "I thought you'd be longer with the major and Moody."

In truth, so had he. "The time we spent together was good. All their games are played with two people, so I sat off to the side and watched. They are night rivals and crazy competitive. They compete in gin, backgammon, chess, checkers, and double solitaire. Gramps set up a dry eraser board with colored markers and they keep score. The loser at the end of the week buys the winner Saturday pie."

"On occasion, I've taken cookies and milk to them as an evening snack," said Hannah. "They thank me, but seldom look up. I've never taken offense and don't stay long."

Jake had spent an hour with the men. One of the longest of his life, however comfortably seated in an overstuffed armchair, pulled up to the card table. The two had been intent on their cards, and even though they'd included him in their conversation, his attention had been fixed on Hannah. Images of her looped like a mind reel.

He half listened to the men's questions, reacting with a nod or short comment. His gramps had asked about trick-or-treating, to which Jake answered, "Nice time."

"Big crowd?" from Moody.

Jake nodded. "Uh-huh."

"The town always turns out for Halloween," said the major.

"Yep."

His gramps switched to, "Have you settled in your apartment?"

"Soon."

"The place is minimally furnished," his granddad informed him. "If you need extra towels or bedding, I've got plenty."

"Okay, thanks."

His grandfather shuffled the deck, side-eyed him, and snuck in a personal question when he thought Jake wasn't fully paying attention. "You planning to date her?"

"Date who?" he shot back, wise to his gramps's probe. He never let anyone, not even his family, interrogate him about his private life. He narrowed his gaze on his granddad. A silencing glare.

The major grinned. "I've seen darker looks."

Moody snorted. "You don't intimidate us, boy. If we have questions, we'll ask them."

They could ask, but Jake had no plans to answer. He did have one question of his own, however. "You've lived here a long time. Tell me about the Moonbright legend."

Moody raised an eyebrow. "How'd you hear about it?"

"I overheard Nan mention it to Hannah."

"Eavesdropping, boy?" asked his gramps.

"Nan's whisper carried to me."

The major scratched his jaw, said, "Halloween magic. The single ladies have a specific chant—supposed to be spoken before midnight. It's believed they will then catch a glimpse of their future husband in a mirror or other reflective surface."

Jake rolled his eyes. "You've got to be kidding."

"Truth, boy," came from Moody. "It's happened too often not to be believed. Nan trusts in the lore. Along with numerous women in town. They saw likenesses of their husbands before the men arrived in their lives."

Jake couldn't wrap his head around it. "Still hard to believe."

"We know of what we speak," hinted Moody.

"Your wives envisioned you both?"

"Both saw us clear as day," from the major.

"Personal experience made us believers," Moody asserted.

"I'm still skeptical."

"Nan adores her granddaughter," his gramps informed him. "Hannah doesn't date much. Nan is hopeful she'll meet a nice man. Get married. Perhaps a reflection in a mirror will give her a sneak peek of her life partner."

That said, the older men went back to playing cards.

Jake sat still, unconvinced.

The apartment was small. He stayed until restlessness claimed him, then pushed to his feet. He repositioned the armchair in its original spot. On his way out the door he offered to buy the men breakfast in the morning. At an hour of their choice.

The major readily accepted. "Sounds good. Hannah will be working. She opens the café at six. Moody and I wander downstairs at eight to avoid the early rush."

"Eight works," said Jake. He set his own hours back home. He rose at six. Jogged three miles when the weather permitted. Then fixed a bowl of organic whole-grain cereal. The family business was housed in a renovated warehouse nearby. He was on the job by seven thirty. He lost himself in his work. Time spun the hands on the clock. He closed down the workshop at dark.

But that was Bangor and this was Moonbright. He was presently on vacation. He would adjust to the older men's schedule.

"Should you beat us downstairs, take a booth in Hannah's section," Moody requested. "She's our favorite waitress."

"Such a gentle soul," injected Jake's gramps.

"There's a possibility she'll mix up our orders when she gets busy," Moody cautioned. "Don't be an ass and give her a hard time."

"Food is food. I wouldn't complain."

"You'd grumble if she served you corned beef hash." His grandfather knew him well. It was Jake's least favorite dish.

"Not a problem," he reasoned. "I'd switch plates with Moody and eat whatever he had ordered."

"That would be corned beef hash."

Both men chuckled.

They enjoyed needling him. Jake let it pass. "We'll catch up at breakfast then."

He was halfway out the door when Moody called after him, "You better tip big, boy."

"Got it covered. I'll be generous."

"*Really generous,*" his gramps emphasized.

Moody added, "Don't make us look cheap or we'll take you to task."

"We would, if we had to," ended the major.

The men were brave with their words.

Jake cleared the door. A smile broke across his face in the hallway. The two were very protective of Hannah. That pleased him greatly. Her waitressing skills might not be the strongest, but he'd never purposely hurt her feelings. It wasn't his style. He was a tolerant guy. Little fazed him. He crossed his fingers against a corned beef hash breakfast. He would be forced to eat it so as not to offend her.

He decided to take the outside staircase, which landed him

in an alley between the café and Keepsake Antiques, which
fronted on Pie Street. Then continued to walk the two blocks
to Morrison's Garage, a one-pump gas station with a three-
bay auto shop. Mac Morrison was just locking up, and the men
conversed for a short time. Their exchange ended with Mac's
mention that his master mechanic had given notice and his last
day was Monday. Mac knew that Jake was visiting his gramps,
and although he didn't want to disrupt his vacation, Mac was
in a significant bind. He was backed up with minor tune-ups
and major repairs and, if Jake had extra time on his hands, Mac
could use a temporary mechanic until he was able to hire someone full-time.

Moonbright didn't have a new-car dealership. Used and vintage models populated the town. While Jake preferred to work
on motorcycles, he remained knowledgeable about cars and
trucks. Mac sweetened his proposition by allowing Jake to set
his own hours. No pressure. Mac would sweeten the deal with
a hefty commission on each invoice. Jake promised to consider
the offer and would get back to Mac shortly.

He'd gone on to grab his helmet and saddlebags and return
to the café, taking the outside stairs to his apartment. He'd
dropped everything on his bed, then found his way down the
secret inside steps to the kitchen. He'd entered the dining room
through the swinging doors. That's where he'd found Hannah,
hard at work cleaning tables. Humming to herself. He'd surprised her. She'd been slow to recover.

Her breathing remained shallow, erratic, even now as she
wiped away the ketchup he'd mentioned. She fully dried the table
before facing him. They stood close enough to breathe the same
air. He looked down as she gazed up. Her expression was questioning while she waited for him to say something, to do something. He had nothing.

Nothing, that was, until he glanced around and realized she

had a long way to go to put the dining room in order. "Let me help you," he offered. "Tell me what you need done and I've got it covered."

A corner of her lips twitched. "You could marry the ketchups."

That stumped him. "Vows and 'I dos'?"

She rolled her eyes, clarified, "Collect the ketchup bottles. Take them to the counter by the sink. Caps off, and wipe down the necks. Then you pour a half-full bottle of ketchup into another half-full bottle so you have one full bottle."

He nodded. *Easy enough.* "I can do that." He hoped without making too big a mess.

In spite of his good intentions, messes were made. He mentally kicked himself for staring at Hannah and not concentrating fully on the bottles. He liked watching her move. A lot. The swing of her high ponytail. The fit of her light blue café T-shirt with the steaming coffee cup logo. The easy way she leaned over the tables, along with the stretch of her spine and curve of her butt when she erased today's specials from the menu chalkboard, then wrote the new ones for tomorrow. He blew out a breath when she printed the breakfast specials: biscuits and gravy, lumberjack pancakes, and corned beef hash.

He planned to enunciate "lumberjack pancakes" very carefully when he ordered in the morning. He didn't want his food to get mixed up with Moody's or his granddad's should they go for corned beef hash. The older men would find humor in Hannah's accidentally serving him his least favorite breakfast.

Sidetracked and totally into her, he'd allowed the ketchup bottles to overflow. Big spills and splatters brought her to him. She didn't comment or criticize. Instead she grabbed a sponge and bus tub from under the counter and cleaned up after him. She took over his task and, in a matter of minutes, filled the remaining bottles and discarded the empties.

He felt like a fool. "Sorry," he said. He'd botched a basic job.

"It's minor," she assured him. "My spills are far worse. Besides, we all have our skill sets. Side work is quick and easy for me, but I could never rebuild a motorcycle engine."

"You don't know that unless you've tried," he refuted. "You might be great at assembling and restoring big bikes."

"That's your niche," she insisted. "Mine is the café."

"You've never wanted to do anything else?"

She shook her head, slowly, thoughtfully. "I love my life. I get to see my family and friends every single day. I eat the best meals in town." There was an innocence to her words. He admired her sense of self. She obviously felt safe, secure, and comfortable at the café. She knew who she was and where she belonged. Small-town living agreed with her.

He, however, preferred a bigger city. Bangor worked for him. He enjoyed sharing a shop with his dad. He'd never met anyone smarter in the field of mechanics than his old man. Jake had learned at his father's knee. Their camaraderie was invaluable to him.

Truth be told, he could work anywhere he chose. Even in Moonbright, which had never crossed his mind until that moment. He ran one hand down his face. There was something so natural, so familiar, and so relaxed about standing here with Hannah, despite the fact they didn't know each other well.

He cleared his throat, asked, "Any other condiments you want me to marry? Mustards? Maple syrups? Give me a chance. I can do better."

She shook her head. "Nothing more. I'm good to finish. Go to the kitchen, get your whoopie pie from the refrigerator, sit, and enjoy it. I'll clean up around you."

That wasn't going to happen. He refused to eat while she worked. It didn't seem fair. He briefly remained behind the counter while Hannah moved on. She had side work down to a science. There had to be something he could do. That's when he noticed that the salt and pepper shakers on the counter were low, as were additional shakers on the tables. It didn't take him long to locate the larger canisters of each spice. He opened the metal spouts, went around the café, and topped off the shakers. He found some of them sticky and wiped them down.

His task completed, he looked up and found Hannah seated on a counter stool nearby. His small contribution had had a big impact on her. Her eyes were bright, her expression soft. "Thank you," came with a small smile. "Nice job."

"Not a big deal."

"A big deal to me."

He liked that she felt that way. "What's next on your list?"

"I'm almost done. Quick sweep and mop."

That was easy enough. "You sweep and I'll mop."

"You don't have to do that."

"I want to."

She secured a broom and he filled twin wringer buckets, one side with lemon Lysol cleaner and the other with clean water. He grabbed the mop. They started near the front door and worked their way back to the counter area. Hannah swept ahead of him. She had a way with a broom. Her strokes were short and efficient, causing a graceful shift of her shoulders and sensual roll to her hips. Distracting as hell.

He followed her with the mop. More than once he kicked a bucket, splashing water over the side. He mopped over the spots twice. Luckily for him Hannah didn't seem to notice. She located a dustpan and swept up the dirt and dropped napkins.

They worked well together and their tasks were completed in record time. Although he would've liked to drag out her sweeping for a few more minutes.

She motioned him toward the kitchen. "Let's get our desserts. The tiles will be dry by the time we return."

He pushed the buckets through the swinging door and emptied them. Then came up behind her at the commercial refrigerator. She handed him his whoopie pie on a paper plate. He couldn't wait to dig in. Hannah took her sweet time peeking beneath the domes on several plastic cake and pie containers before making her selection.

She sighed. A gentle rise and fall of her chest. "It's hard to decide. A toss-up between Indian pudding, peach cobbler, and blueberry butter cake."

He nudged her toward the cake. "So I can have a bite."

She smiled at him, agreed, then cut and plated a large piece. "Forks are in the dining room," she told him.

The floors had dried. She retrieved silverware from a flatware tray under the counter. He followed her to the first two-seater booth. She set down her dessert, then scored glasses of milk. They sat across from each other. Companionship and sweet treats. Jake could think of no place he'd rather be.

He dug in then. He'd eaten almost all his whoopie pie before noticing Hannah lagged behind. She was all about small bites and savoring. He appreciated the sight of a woman enjoying her food. It was sexy as hell. Her eyes would close and he swore a soft moan escaped with each taste. He stared at her until she sensed his eyes on her.

She blushed, set down her fork, and wiped her mouth with a napkin. She nudged her cake plate toward him. "Feel free to take a bite," she offered.

"I'd rather watch you eat."

"I can't imagine why."

"Tell me, Hannah, which is more important to you, love or food?"

"I'd keep on eating."

He grinned. "I would too."

"My grandmother would disagree with us. She believes food sustains, but love makes life worthwhile."

"Have you ever been in love?" he asked her.

She took a sip of milk, grew thoughtful. "Not love exactly, but like. There was Gregory Manor in the fourth grade. I was once on the playground swing set, but couldn't kick my legs hard enough to gain height. He got off his swing and pushed me so high, I felt like I was flying."

"Flying on a swing is fun."

"We were close friends all through school. He took me to summer picnics in the park. He invited me to the senior prom when I didn't have a date. He was my first kiss."

"First kiss, huh?"

"A quick one that landed more on my cheek than my mouth."

"Sounds like he had a crush on you."

"Or he felt sorry for me."

He denied her theory. "I don't think that was the case. Whatever happened to buddy Greg?"

"He was smart, ambitious, and graduated with honors. He entered Yale. A major accomplishment for a small-town boy to gain admittance to an Ivy League university. He received his law degree and chose to practice in New Haven."

"You've kept track of him?" An unexpected curiosity.

"Moonbright has kept track, not just me. We're a connected town and care about what happens to our own. Gregory was a success story. We're all happy and proud of him. His parents still live here. He comes back to visit often."

"More often than I visit my gramps?"

"A passing comment only," she assured him. "I wasn't pointing my finger at you, Jake. Honest."

He didn't want her to think poorly of him. "I should've come around sooner," he hated to admit. "I'll do better in the future."

"You're here now," she eased his conscience. "The major is excited to see you."

"What about you, Hannah? Are you glad I'm here?" his ego asked.

"Here, to help me with my side work. I'm appreciative. You mop real good for a motorcycle man."

She'd skirted his question. He didn't mind. He'd gotten too personal for the small amount of time they'd spent together. He finished off his whoopie pie, then sampled her dessert. Moist cake, fresh blueberries, and melt-in-the mouth frosting. "Best ever." He understood her slow savoring and the licking of her lips.

"I could eat blueberry butter cake for breakfast, lunch, and dinner," she confessed. She tapped her fork on the plate, encouraging him. "There's plenty; have a second bite."

He shook his head; she was his indulgence. All happy, uninhibited, and turned on by cake. "I enjoy dessert now and again," he conceded. "But I'm more a meat-and-potato guy."

"There's steak and eggs on our breakfast menu," she said. "Gram makes amazing home fries. Sliced potatoes, chopped onions, and sweet bell peppers cooked in bacon fat. Don't get me started on her buttermilk biscuits."

He grinned at her. "I've invited my granddad and Moody to breakfast. We'll see you around eight."

She rolled her shoulders, yawned behind her hand. "You tired?" he asked. He hoped not; he liked talking to her.

"I'm winding down. I thought you might be weary," she returned. "You rode your motorcycle from Bangor, walked in a parade with the triplets, and took them trick-or-treating. Then helped with my side work. A pretty full day."

"I was cool with the boys." He tucked his shoulders deeper into the booth, stretched out his legs. His booted feet bracketed Hannah's tennis shoes. He crossed his arms over his chest and hooked his thumbs in his armpits. Laid-back and content. He revealed a part of himself that he seldom exposed. "Riding my bike brings order to my world. It's a way of life. Adrenaline charged. The open road calls my name and I answer. I live in the moment. An amazing freedom."

He watched her watch him. She'd rested her elbows on the table, cupped her chin in her palms. Her gaze brightened with interest. Flatteringly attentive.

He kept on. "Being at one with my bike is almost surreal. Total Zen. People ask me why I ride—it's because I can't not ride. I've taken dozens of road trips. I have more of a bond with my motorcycle than with most people."

She gave a small nod. "You can't buy happiness, but you can buy a Ducati."

He liked her insight. She got him. "What bakes your cake, Hannah?" he asked her.

"My cake?" She grinned, reflected. "All states have their beauty, but Maine is a place unto itself. The landscape is untouched, dramatic, and soul stirring. The air smells like brine and pine needles and moss and wood fires, depending on the season. Every incredible sunset deserves to be painted and framed."

"I appreciate a gorgeous sky." The deep blending of paint box colors, with nature the artist, drawing a thin line on the horizon. Masking the day in darkness while unveiling moonlight. "What else, babe?"

"I love Bean boots and fisherman sweaters. Picking apples and blueberries. Hiking state parks, visiting lighthouses, and hunting for sea glass on the coastline. I once spent two days on a windjammer on Penobscot Bay. Maine is the most beautiful place I've ever been."

"You've traveled a lot then. For comparison."

"Not exactly."

"What exactly?"

"I've taken trips throughout Maine. Always returning to Moonbright. It's kept a special hold on me. I've never wanted to live anywhere else."

"You're safe here."

"Safe and sane. I know myself and what's important to me. I

don't need to travel the world to be content. I could walk across the street and do the happy dance."

She was wholesome and disarming, Jake realized. He felt her peace. Her pleasure. The joy in her heart. Her commitment to the small town where her roots were deep and forever settled.

He accepted her life. She had no reason to change. For anyone or anything. No reason to go somewhere that left her longing for Moonbright. Home was home.

Hannah was so different from her older sister, Lauren. Lauren felt no such connections to the town, from what he'd witnessed five years prior. Lauren envied him and the open road and had hoped he would take her with him when he'd left, early one spring morning. The least encouragement and she would've climbed on the rear seat of his Ducati and waved good-bye to Moonbright. He had known from their first date that they weren't suited. Not the least bit compatible. They'd never been intimate. It was far better she'd stayed behind. She'd made a life with Grant the police officer and had three terrific boys.

Enough on Lauren. Hannah had finished off her cake. She went as far as to tap the tip of her forefinger over the crumbs. Then skim the rim of the plate for the last bit of frosting.

He stared at her now with an intensity that seemed to unsettle her. She accidentally frosted her chin. She grabbed a handful of napkins, dabbed at the smeared buttercream. "Look what you made me do," she accused him.

His tongue pressed against his teeth. He felt a craving to lick the frosting from her lips. To nibble on her chin. To fully taste her. An urge he tamped down. "How's missing your mouth my fault?" he asked, amused.

"You were staring at me."

"Did I make you nervous?"

"You looked . . . hungry."

"I'm quite full, actually." Hannah was inexperienced. She was unaware that his hunger hadn't been for the cake; it had been for her. He said honestly, "I enjoy looking at you. Get used to it."

She wasn't appeased. She looked him straight in the eye. "What if I stared at you?" Her expression was stern, all narrowed gaze, tight-lipped, and not terribly effective. She looked cute, not intimidating.

"Be my guest. I like your eyes on me."

# Chapter 3

Hannah blinked. Swallowed hard. He rendered her speechless. Jake liked her looking at him. Something she could've done for hours on end. He exuded rough-edged masculinity. All hot gaze and sexy smugness. An extreme sexual draw. Her face grew warm. Air caught in her lungs. Her tummy tingled. She hated to be the one to come undone. He left her on the edge of her seat. She fidgeted, shifting her hips, crossing her legs, flexing her foot.

She cut her gaze sideways and attempted nonchalance. A major fail when she came face-to-face with one of her childhood photographs hanging on the wall. She grinned as she pointed out the picture to Jake. She'd been sitting in a high chair on her second birthday with a piece of cake before her. "I was always a messy cake eater."

He studied the color photo. His smile brought out a single dimple. "How old were you?"

"Two."

"I can't see your face for all the cake," he teased her.

"Gram said I loved the texture. It was angel food with fairy pink frosting. I squished it between my fingers. Smeared it in my hair, got it in my nose, rubbed it over my lips, but ate very little."

"Looks like you had fun."

"I guess so. I don't remember much. The photo is the memory."

He drank his glass of milk in two long swallows, then stood. He wandered the aisle, checking out the collection of photographs. He chuckled, said, "Neat older pic of my granddad and Moody seated at the counter. They sit on those same stools today."

She had a soft spot in her heart for the two older men. They were a constant in her life. "Some things never change. Although Moody's slightly balder."

Jake paused before a photo of her grandmother. Nan was holding up her famed apple-plum pie in one hand and a blue ribbon in the other. She'd won first place in the pie-baking contest at the county fair in 1975. There'd been lots of ribbons since. "Nan was quite a looker in her day," he commented. His gaze swung back to her. "You resemble her."

Numerous people had likened Hannah to her grandma. She didn't see the similarities. Her gram was far prettier, blond and slender with expressive features. Nan's smile made everyone smile. She'd been praised for her baking from the moment she mixed the batter and baked her first cake. She'd written a cookbook on soups, chowders, and bisques: *Tastes Like Fall in a Bowl*. A New England best seller.

Jake tapped a red, white, and blue frame and said, "Your parents seated with the governor. There's a lot of people standing in the background."

"A campaign year from what I remember. Mom and Dad backed Dale Clark. They worked the local election headquarters. Small potatoes to some, but every vote counted. Clark won by a narrow margin. Afterward he traveled the state to thank his constituents. He stopped at the café and had lunch. It was a pretty big deal."

"How are your parents doing?"

"They're on a cruise, celebrating their thirty-fifth honeymoon."

"I heard that they renew their vows every fall."

"During the year Mom is wrapped up in the café—she does the bookkeeping and all the ordering. Dad was recently promoted to the Chief Financial Advisor at the courthouse. They work hard, love each other like newlyweds, and always set aside two weeks each year for themselves and no one else."

Jake nodded. "Cool. Good for them." He leaned toward a second photo of Clark and her grandma. "She's handing him—what? A tray of cookies?"

"A dozen of her cream cheese sugar cookies with yellow royal icing. Made especially for him and his staff to take back to the state capital."

"I'm sure the cookies were eaten long before they reached Augusta."

"The governor sent Gram a personal handwritten note. Thanking her for the café's hospitality and the cookies."

"Nice of the man." He took a long moment at the next photograph. "You and Lauren," he mused. "Although the shot captures more of your sister with that handful of menus than you carrying a tray of food."

"Lauren's the hostess most days. She likes fashion, not our khaki uniforms. She dresses to impress and likes to be the center of attention," said Hannah. "She greets the customers, seats them at their favorite tables, and hands out menus without breaking a nail. I, on the other hand, am a career waitress."

There were people who would put down her job, believing she lacked ambition. She shielded herself from his own snub.

He respected her choice. "You work at what you enjoy most."

"In my mind," she shared, "I serve the community in a small way. People come into the café hungry and leave full and content. If there's the occasional disgruntled customer, he's not usually upset with the food; he's just having a bad day. A breakfast cherry cheese Danish or dessert at lunch on the house can turn his day around."

"You're kind, Hannah."

She lowered her gaze.

"And humble."

She dipped her head.

"You don't take compliments well."

"I don't always feel deserving of them."

"I mean what I say."

He returned to the booth. She looked up. Regarded him. This man with the dangerous face and daredevil features. Wide shoulders and a wicked hard body. She wanted to know everything about him. Where to begin?

To her relief Jake took it upon himself to start. He slouched his shoulders, rested low on his spine. A big man, all casual and chill. He made the booth look so much smaller than it actually was. He stared at her. Steadfast. "I believe in eye contact. I tend to stop whatever I'm doing and look directly at someone before I talk to them."

"So I've noticed."

"It's a good way to judge honesty and character."

It was also unnerving. She attempted nonchalance but lacked his confidence.

He saved her from her uncool self. "Keep it simple. Random thoughts, secrets, or confessions," he stated. "Don't overthink our convo, Hannah.

"My man stats," he went on. "I'm thirty-five, born April twentieth, a Taurus. I read my horoscope on occasion. I'm six-three. Tip the scale at two-twenty."

She shared too. "I turned thirty-two on February twenty-fifth. Pisces." She was the gentle fish to his muscled bull. "Five feet five inches. One-ten."

"You're a lightweight."

"Fast metabolism. I'm on my feet all day. I eat plenty. I work at the café but can't cook or bake," she admitted. "I enjoy food preparation, the chopping and dicing of ingredients, but I burn the edges of pancakes on the grill and my omelets become scrambled eggs. I read a recipe one way, Gram another. Our bakes aren't even close."

He admitted, "Cereal, sandwiches, and takeout are mainstays for me. Your favorite restaurant other than the café?"

"Tito Rico's Mexicana on the outskirts of town serves a yummy taco salad."

"Yummy, huh?"

"You're making fun of me."

"Never. We'll have dinner there some evening. I like watching you eat."

"When the food reaches my mouth." Her observation was self-critical.

"We all spill on occasion."

"Which is daily for me."

"Should that be your worst trait, you're close to perfect, babe." Short pause. "Do you like to dress up for an evening on the town or keep it casual at home?

"Casual for me. Jeans and sweats. Lauren's the one who loves fancy clothes, perfect hair and makeup. I only wear lip gloss."

"You're a natural beauty."

"Flattery?"

"Truth."

She warmed with his kind words. "Your quirks or misbehaviors?" she asked him. Hoping he had at least one.

"I have several," he admitted.

She felt a sense of relief. The man had faults.

"A peculiarity of mine—I pat down my pocket to check for my wallet and keys right after I put them in."

Back to her. "I don't drive often. But when I do, I park, then repark my car until I'm in the middle of the lines."

"You're conscientious. You give those drivers around you plenty of space." He paused. "What else?"

"I'm constantly tucking my hair behind my ears." She did so now.

That made him smile. "Every time I sit near a candle, I try to put it out with my fingers. I've never been burned, but not successful either."

"I sidestepped cracks in the sidewalk in my early years. I once knocked down Lauren avoiding one."

"How'd Lauren take it?"

"She was clucking her tongue while walking, a clip-clop sound. Pretending to be a horse. I foolishly laughed at both her clomping and her fall. She punched me in the stomach."

"A solid hook?"

"She hit me so hard I gasped for breath. I ended up stepping on the crack I'd danced around." She scrunched her nose. "I tend to laugh inappropriately at times. Often hysterically. Over a current incident or even something funny from years ago. I try to make myself stop, especially when waitressing. But I only laugh more. Gram just shakes her head. Lauren gives me a dirty look. Customers smile along with me."

"Laughter's healthy." He took her side. "Nothing wrong with belly laughs."

"Every so often I cry when I'm happy. I get hiccups. Heaving hiccups," she said. "People frequently mistake my tears for sadness. Not so."

He next revealed, "I've a behavior trait that might shock you. I find clothes confining. I strip down immediately upon getting home. Door closes. Bam! Naked."

A hot flush heated her face, her breasts, and between her legs.

"Too personal?" he asked.

"No. . . ." Not really. He was all about freedom. Riding his Ducati, living his life, and stripping down. He'd look good in his skin.

His gaze was knowing. He was amused by her thoughts. "Bedtime, and I bet you tuck yourself under the covers like a mummy. And that you wear thick socks to keep your feet warm."

"Leave me with a little mystery." A contemplative pause. "I will share that I sleep with a night-light on. I often wake up at midnight for a snack."

"I wouldn't kick a woman out of bed for eating crackers. Or for eating cake with her fingers."

Good to know. "I can't whistle, but I like to hum."

"So I heard when you were cleaning tables. Any particular song?" he asked.

"Something popular or something I make up."

"Optimist or pessimist?" he quizzed.

"Optimist. You?"

"Realist."

No rose-colored glasses for the man.

"I play hard, Hannah. I'm a daredevil and a risk taker."

"I pack a safety net."

His dimple flashed. "I like learning about you."

"Same for you."

He lowered his voice conspiratorially. "Full disclosure, I've had moments of questionable behavior."

"How questionable?" *A crime, probation, jail time?*

"Nothing too terribly wrong," he assured her. "I should've done one thing but instead did another."

"Did you lie about it?"

"A slight twist of the truth," he reflected. "But for a good reason. I had a football scholarship to college. Wide receiver. My father nudged me toward Business Administration. Work hard. Work smart. While on campus I dated an English literature major. Charlene Wells belonged to a highbrow book club and dragged me to a discussion at her professor's home."

"She must've been hot," Hannah mused. Jake didn't look like the reading group type. Unless intellectual stimulation led to sex. That she could believe.

He conceded, "Char was smokin', but she quickly cooled toward me. I claimed to have read *Ulysses* by James Joyce, the entire book, but actually I just started it, got bored, and took a nap after forty pages. I went on to watch the 1967 movie instead. Needless to say, my comments and observations didn't resonate well with the other book club members. They dissected the themes while I barely scratched the surface. Charlene was embarrassed by me. I spent more time at the refreshment table than listening to the discussion. I split after several chicken salad finger sandwiches, three chocolate brownies, a handful of cream cheese mints, and a cup of tea." He gave her a crooked smile. "I ate a doily."

*No way.* "The lacy circle under the food?"

He nodded. "Those fancy thin papers are pure decoration and not to be eaten. I hadn't noticed the doily stuck to the bottom of my brownie. I didn't realize there was a little china dish on the table to discard them. I'd chewed and swallowed. Mine was in my stomach."

"Did anyone see you eat it?"

"Only the caterer. His eyes nearly popped out of his head. I lacked the sophistication of the other members."

"Oh . . . Jake." She felt both sympathy and amusement. Her laughter won out. *This very hot motorcycle man had eaten a delicate doily.* She crossed her arms over her stomach and laughed until her belly hurt. He chuckled too, at his own expense. "That's quite the confession," she finally managed. "Tell me, was there a second date with Charlene?"

"Not a chance. She considered herself an intellectual and me an illiterate biker."

"That was harsh."

"The situation taught me not to lie to get laid."

"And to look at the bottom of a brownie before you put it in your mouth."

"That too."

"We have a similar history," she confided. "We've both met *Ulysses*. You through a book club, me through Library Week. Moonbright promotes and celebrates literacy in April. A time when both young and old are encouraged to read. My gram suggested that Lauren and I take part in the accompanying lectures. We agreed, to please her. Those involved would give five-minute speeches on a particular genre chosen by the librarian.

"A big meeting was held in the conference room. I arrived late and sat in the back. Lauren was there too. I crossed my fingers, held my breath, and hoped to speak on women's fiction or mysteries. Regrettably, all categories had been assigned. My sister got children's books. Lucky her. Only modernist literature remained. The media specialist handed me *Ulysses* to review. Awkward for me. I hadn't a clue as to the avant-garde of the early twentieth century, but then neither did anyone around me. I received pity looks and sympathetic mumbles. Junior college hadn't prepared me for *Ulysses*. I initially wanted to bail on Library Week."

He sat up straighter and said, "I feel bad for you even now. The book is a tomb. Over seven hundred pages. It's not a pleasure read. Even scholars would've struggled."

"I managed."

"Damn, I'm impressed."

She shook her head. "Don't be. The dust jacket confused me.

The book itself was unreadable. For me, anyway. Not wanting to disappoint my grandma, I took a shortcut, much as you did with the book club."

His grin was immediate. "You're a lady after my own heart. I'm liking you more and more."

He gave her a high five then. Their palms touched and he gently squeezed her hand. Their fingers unexpectedly twined. They were now holding hands. His grasp was warm, callused, relaxed. Pleasant. She waited for him to release her. He did not. Instead he lowered their hands to the table. Their connection felt good. Natural. Genuine. Right.

"Tell me, Hannah, what was your alternative to reading the book?" he asked.

"I bought the CliffsNotes, which made my eyes cross. James Joyce may have been one of the most influential writers of his time, but I found him tiresome. Draining. I next turned to Wikipedia. I memorized several pertinent pages."

"The perfect five-minute abridged version."

"Pretty much so. I'm good at retaining information. I was the last to speak and incredibly nervous. I complimented my audience, noting they were smart and progressive and that *Ulysses* would provide a life-changing experience. That caught their attention. I mentioned that Joyce's modernist experiment was hailed as a revolutionary work of genius by T. S. Eliot and Ernest Hemingway. Many readers were familiar with Eliot and Hemingway."

"A good comparison."

"I somehow managed to push forward. Those in the media center were attentive. Although I doubt they fully grasped my speech. But then neither did I. There were both confused and awed expressions. All wide eyes and dropping jaws. Heads were scratched when I tossed out phrases like 'scandalously frank,' 'wittily erudite,' 'mercurially eloquent,' 'resourcefully comic,' and 'generously humane.' Tongue twisters. Sounding smart without really understanding what I was talking about.

"I finished and silence grabbed the room until Gram clapped. She was so proud of me. She called me gifted. High praise for a cribbed speech. The question and answer period followed. Fortunately, no hands were raised."

"You were brilliant," he commended. "Innovative in finding a way to give a speech on a tough topic."

"I did cheat."

"I see you as clever. You were resourceful, lady. You gave a solid review. Not many people could recite five minutes of Wiki, especially on such an academic level. I'd have given you a standing ovation." He paused, curious. "How did Lauren do with her children's books?"

"Lauren wore a fuzzy bear outfit that she'd rented from Charade, the local costume shop. She spoke well and read a few pages from one of the Berenstain Bear books. Her audience ranged from toddlers to ten-year-olds. The kids loved her. Children's books are heart-warming. Youngsters get attached to characters. Curious George, the Velveteen Rabbit, Winnie-the-Pooh, or even Fancy Nancy. There were lots of smiles."

"What did you wear?"

She blinked. "Do you honestly care?"

"Merely fantasizing, babe. I can picture you as a brainiac. Hair in a bun, small rectangular reading glasses, buttoned-up white collared blouse tucked into a plaid pleated skirt. Saddle shoes."

She corrected him. "Your imagination's more schoolgirl than scholarly. Substitute the plaid skirt for a black A-line with short heels and you've got me."

"Still hot."

"I was going for professional."

"I'm sure you succeeded." He rubbed his thumb along her wrist, warming the soft skin. "Lauren might have proved entertaining, but you were thought provoking."

"More like mind-numbing." She suddenly smiled over a

memory. "I've checked out a lot of library books over the years. I used to leave positive unsigned notes in the pages for future readers."

"Nice gesture. What are you reading now for fun?"

"A mystery set in the South."

"I just picked up the latest John Grisham."

A companionable silence joined them at the table. Their attraction was strong. Tangible. They looked at each other, really looked, and formed an invisible bond. Unintentional but evident. Scary yet reassuring. She'd never felt so in tune with another person. All in a very short time.

He grinned, a sexy uptick of his lips. "No matter what else happens in our lives, we'll always have *Ulysses* between us."

That they would. Be that as it may, his words gave her pause. He could leave tomorrow and return to Bangor. His visit would undoubtably be short-lived. In that moment she decided that while he was in town she would enjoy his company, his friendship. Maybe even a kiss, should he be so inclined?

"You work, you read, what else, Hannah?" he asked.

"At the end of my shift, I often head upstairs to quilt, but it's not something I do well. The last comforter I made didn't land on my bed, but found its way to my sofa. Irregular in size, it's more triangular than square."

"Nothing wrong with a triangle."

"True." She appreciated his positive spin on the asymmetrical shape. She liked to snuggle deep into the navy and gold pinwheel stars.

"The rest of your spare time?"

"I like art. I sketch landscapes."

"Stick figures here."

Which drew her grin. "I often go to the movies," she told him.

"Most recent show?"

"Double feature. *Jaws* and *Jurassic Park* at the Strand Cinema on Spice Street. The owner runs popular oldies. I love the buttered popcorn."

"Movies are nice, but I prefer streaming Netflix at home. *SEAL Team* and cop shows. Stretched out on the sofa. Beer in the fridge. Pizza delivery. A bowl of mixed nuts. When I've time to kill, I often choose movies with awful reviews to see how bad they really are. Flicks are subjective—not all of them deserved low ratings."

She wondered, "Favorite time of year?"

"Fall and winter. I like the outdoors. Hiking, camping, ice fishing. I've survival skills."

"Spring or summer for me. I enjoy daily walks as long as the weather permits. Your grandfather joins me on occasion."

"I jog. Maybe I'll join you sometime too."

"We stroll. You'd be jogging in place."

"What about Moody?" he asked.

"He prefers the café counter stool to exercise. He's a people person. Very social."

"Sports?" he posed.

"Baseball and gymnastics. Watched on TV. I'm not very athletic. You?"

"I always liked football. However, there were no professional draft prospects after college. Graduation, and I joined my dad's business. I presently have a younger brother who's just started working part-time. Janson was a late-in-life baby. He's conscientious and smart. A good mechanic."

"A family business then."

"Same as with you and the café."

They'd covered a lot of ground. She didn't know him well, but she knew him better than when they'd marched together in the parade. She liked every aspect of the man.

She snuck a peek at her watch. It wasn't terribly late. She

wasn't sure if she should call it a night or continue with Jake. He was a good time. She'd give anything to stay. However, Sunday morning would come too soon. The café would be swamped. She needed a solid night's sleep. There'd be no pushing the snooze button.

Her practical side had her rising from the booth. She stood, then stacked their plates and glasses. Jake took the hint and rose beside her, aviators in hand. He was tall. She looked him up and down, smiled, more to herself than at him. "When I was a kid, I was absolutely sure that everyone taller than me was on stilts. I'd eyeball their legs, checking them out."

"In elementary school I would enter a room with my left foot first. No idea why. It became a habit." A grin spread as he remembered. "I'd reinvent myself every day and go by a different name."

"How'd that work for you?"

"Not well. Kids would call out to me on the playground, but I didn't respond. I'd forgotten the names I'd created for myself. They thought I was a snob."

"I like your imagination. I once believed I was invisible in the kitchen. Until Gram accidentally stepped on my toe. She took me by the shoulders and gently suggested I was in the way and should go outside to play."

"So much for your superpowers."

"I also practiced magic, but my hands weren't quicker than the eye."

"I'm ambidextrous," he added. "I can write or work with either hand, which drove my kindergarten teacher crazy. She wanted me to print the alphabet only with my right hand. I'd switch."

"So much talent." *Such skilled hands.* She eased around him. "Thanks for today."

"So you're kissing me good night?"

"*Wishing* you a good night," she corrected. "I'm done for the day. You might not be." She cupped her hand behind her ear, listened, and then said, "I hear music in the street. People will party well into the night. You could join them."

"No need. If you're turning in, I'm turning in." She went wide-eyed and he made clear, "Not together, sweetheart."

"I wasn't assuming otherwise."

"I'm sure you weren't."

She turned off the dining room lights. The full face of the moon peeked through the window. The emergency lights cast a red glow.

Jake shadowed her to the kitchen, his steps heavy on her heels. She could feel his heat. She hurriedly washed off the plates and glasses and set them on a drying rack.

She turned around and found him inches away. She felt time slow down. Awareness nuzzled. Arousal stirred. Impressions surfaced. He seemed to wrap around her, shift into her, and embrace her without touching, in a mystifying oneness.

Feelings swelled, and untried sensations were exchanged between them. She'd never felt anything like it. His solidness and strength stroked her physically. She wanted to touch him, to press her palms to his chest, to feel his heart pulse beneath her fingers. She suppressed all emotion. Balling her fists, she held them at her sides.

He sensed her distancing and stepped out of her way. She slipped by him. Their hips brushed and electricity sparked. A simultaneous sizzle. She inhaled sharply. "That was odd."

"We generated heat."

She wouldn't have believed it had she not felt it. "I've never—" *What? Sparked off a man?*

"We have chemistry."

She groped for words. Nothing.

He took her by the hand. "We're headed the same way. I'll

walk you home." He led her through the kitchen and into the storage room, where they took the back staircase to the second floor.

She liked having him see her to her apartment. They soon stood before her door. She clasped her hands before her. His mirrored aviators dangled from his fingers.

She grasped for something to say. "I like your sunglasses."

He slipped them on for effect, grinned. "Wiley X is my brand. Nearly indestructible. I'm prone to setting them down and forgetting about them. I've lost many pairs over the years. I've gone to wearing them day or night. People have no idea where I'm looking."

"Where are you looking now?"

"At your mouth."

"Look away."

"Can't. You have very sexy lips."

She went red in the face. Self-conscious.

He was bold, blunt, and spoke his mind. She liked that about him. Emotion soared. Arousal slipped up on her. She wanted him in her life.

He apparently wanted her too. His desire came in a kiss. Light and gentle and lasting no more than a heartbeat. Modest and restrained. Sensitive, yet sensationally hot. Memorable.

Afterward he rested his forehead against her own. Their noses bumped. They both smiled. A seamless bond. A perfect connection.

She stared deeply at her reflection in his shades. She saw herself as he saw her and recognized the hope in her eyes, the optimism in her expression. Her expectations ran high. Time for bed—they would part ways shortly. She wished with all her heart that they might take up tomorrow where they left off tonight.

An unforeseen jolt stole that likelihood. An awakening zap. The moment took on a life of its own. The Halloween chant echoed in her head. Growing in volume. Jake's sunglasses gleamed like a polished mirror, then shimmered like a mirage, became muted and dull. Her own image vanished. A new face emerged. The cloudy profile of a man. Her future husband. All cleanly shaved with short hair. Not long-haired and rugged with a sexy dimple. The haze blurred his features. He was unidentifiable. The image faded as quickly as it had appeared.

Her stomach sank. Numbness overtook her. The stars had not aligned. She felt utterly foolish to have harbored the hope that Jake Kaylor might be her destiny.

Halloween was not her friend.

The legend had let her down.

Her knees buckled. She would've collapsed had Jake not grasped her about the waist. He held her for what could've been seconds or possibly minutes. His strength flowed into her, along with an undeniable sense of oneness.

They weren't one, she reminded herself. Never would be, if the legend was to be believed. Countless women in Moonbright swore by the Halloween reveal. It was now her turn. The sunglasses had introduced her to a new man. Someone who was chosen and meant for her. Despite the fact she'd wished for another.

Her heart hurt. Her feelings were crushed. She placed her hands on Jake's forearms and eased back a step. He was slow to release her. His thumbs pressed her abdomen and his long fingers stroked high on her hip. Loss flooded her once he'd fully let her go.

She felt alone and vulnerable.

Jake looked as confused as she now felt. The lenses on his aviators were once again mirrored. A solid reflection of her. He tipped them down his nose, his green gaze hard. "What happened, Hannah?" he asked. "We shared a friendly kiss and then you went MIA on me."

A friendly kiss? For him, maybe.

For her, an awakening to what might have been but would never be. The legend foretold that she and Jake would travel separate paths. Painful to say the least.

She needed to get away from him, for her sanity's sake. She forced a small smile from deep within. It didn't last long. The corners of her mouth drooped when she said, "Guess I'm wearier than I thought."

"My kiss made you even sleepier?"

"I'll sleep like the dead."

He frowned. "Not the effect I was going for."

"What were you after?"

"Appealing, maybe arousing. Soft kisses can be a turn-on. You're a sweetheart, Hannah. I didn't want to come on too strong. Guess I'll have to try harder next time. To keep you awake."

His next time wouldn't be with her. The man definitely had impact. He'd evoked emotions. An exciting sensitivity. A single day together and he'd left imprints on her heart. Compelling and significant. Lingering.

"Night." Her voice sank just slightly. She could barely lift her legs. The world had gone somber and sluggish around her. The air heavy. She turned to leave. She cast him one final look. He didn't look happy. He stood bold, inflexible. All squared shoulders and widened stance. His expression was troubled. His jaw worked. He looked about to comment further, to come after her, but she denied him. She removed the key from the back pocket of her jeans and unlocked her apartment door in record time. She entered, closed the door, and leaned back against it. Exhaled heavily.

This was a Halloween she'd remember and not in a good way.

She'd never look at Jake the same way. Neither would she gaze into his mirrored aviators ever again.

\* \* \*

Jake lay flat on his back, naked and restless. His left hand rested on his abdomen. His right at the crease of his thigh. He sported an erection. Morning sex was the best sex. It relieved all the pressures of the day ahead. But he was minus a partner. He faced a cold shower. Not his first choice, but his only option.

The bed was comfortable enough. A single, fitted with white cotton sheets. The scent of lavender detergent lingered. Soothing and sleep inspiring. Which hadn't worked on him. Night had allowed him to close his eyes, but thoughts of Hannah had invaded his peace and stolen his sleep. A first for him.

He rolled onto his hip, raised himself up on his elbow, and cut his gaze to the alarm clock on the nightstand. It was six thirty. Breakfast with his granddad and Moody wasn't until eight. He had time to kill. He shook his scrunched pillow, punched it twice, and then eased back down. Meditative. His thoughts drifted back to her disappearing act.

All had centered on that hint of a kiss. He'd gently tasted her. Her lips were sweet and soft. Slightly sugary from the cake. Afterward she'd stared at him. Not directly into his eyes, but into his shades to be exact. That was the start of the finish. In mere seconds her face turned pale and a stunned sadness clouded her eyes. He'd never seen a woman faint, but Hannah had come close to it. Her body just gave out. He'd tightened his hold about her waist to keep her upright. He would've pulled her close had she not pushed back. A tangible distancing. An emotional closure. Untimely and unfounded.

He'd stood in the upstairs hallway for ten minutes following her departure. Staring at her closed door. Taken aback and hesitant. He didn't handle uncertainty well. She'd shut him out. He had no idea why. He wanted an explanation, but she was long gone before he could request one. He'd find some time today to talk with her. To feel out the situation. To see if she was still willing to date him.

On the far side of midnight he'd hashed over Mac Morrison's offer of part-time work at the garage. He decided to give it a try. His granddad and Moody had their own daily routines. He figured he could have breakfast and lunch with them. Then the men would go about their day. Days often spent gathering at the barbershop, then playing bingo and selected games at the senior center. His gramps was the center's champion at the mentally stimulating Word Searches, discovering and circling all the hidden words in a grid of letters. Their lives were routine and reliable. Social and safe.

Jake hoped to take Hannah out to dinner. Maybe even a movie, if she was willing. Slow and steady seemed the way with her. He had every intention of seeing her again. Sharing a kiss that didn't make her sleepy.

He rolled out of bed, a man with a plan. He retrieved his black leather travel kit from his saddlebags. He assumed the bathroom was free, because Hannah worked the sunrise shift. Still, he knocked before entering. No response, so he cracked the door. There was no sign of her. Although the scent of her body wash lingered, fruity and floral. He breathed it in. *Nice.*

He grinned then and imagined her standing before him now, naked, her skin damp with dewy droplets. Temptation sinned with the flick of his tongue along her moist neck and the tip of her nipple. Foreplay came in toweling a woman dry. Gently patting down soft breasts, a rub over her belly, and a deep slide between her legs. Arousal teased him unmercifully. He sucked air. His sex thickened. Throbbed. An intractable ache.

He unzipped his kit, set out his toiletries on the counter beside the sink. He snugged his Black Amber bar of soap, shampoo, and shaving gear beside Hannah's toothbrush holder and deep moisturizing body lotion. He'd never shared a bathroom with a woman. The intimacy was undeniable.

He collected what he needed, shoved back the shower curtain, and placed the items on Hannah's corner shower caddy beneath her pear and lily body wash and purple mesh shower sponge. A tangible sense of togetherness stepped with him into the tiled stall. He turned on the water, rotated the handle to cold. Ice-cold. The spray hit his shoulders, chest, and groin. Shock and shiver. A total boner kill.

He tempered the water, warmer now, and soaped up. Shampooed his hair. Rinsed off. Toweled dry. He dressed and took off for Morrison's Garage, open six days a week and a half day on Sunday. Vehicles broke down whenever, wherever. A mechanic was as valued and well regarded as the mayor. Weekends often proved as busy as weekdays.

He entered the office. Mac was at the coffee machine. He greeted Jake with a grin over his shoulder and a Styrofoam cup of freshly brewed coffee in his hand. "Good to see you," he said.

Jake accepted the cup, then chuckled when Mac turned his way. The mechanic wore beat-up jeans and a logoed gray T-shirt: *I Couldn't Fix Your Brakes, So I Made the Horn Louder.*

"A great advertisement for your business."

"People are always worried when they bring in their vehicles. How much damage? The cost? A little humor takes the edge off. Most honk when they leave the garage."

Jake took a sip of his coffee, strong and black. He liked the way Mac did business. Customers hated a jacked-up bill. Mac was known to be fair. If he knew someone was in desperate straits, he took payments on the repairs.

Jake eyed Mac now. "I wanted to catch you first thing," he said. "Unless you've hired a part-time mechanic overnight, I'm interested."

Mac gave him a thumbs-up. "The job is yours."

Jake glanced through the side office window and into the three-bay garage. He noticed four vehicles in need of work. "Nice Range Rover," he complimented.

"Nothing major there. The owner will be in town for a couple of days. The job can wait until tomorrow. He's a stickler for maintenance. A routine tune-up and rotation of tires. Easy enough. I like those who take care of their vehicles and don't run them into the ground."

"I think I can handle an oil change."

Mac cracked up. "Dude, you're known for dismantling and reassembling engines."

"I prefer to work on motorcycles."

"I doubt you've lost your touch on cars and SUVs."

"I often work alongside my dad on difficult overhauls."

"No pressure, but when can you start?" asked Mac.

"I'm headed to the Corner Café for breakfast with Gramps and Moody," Jake told him. "I need to bring them up to speed on my part-time job. So how about Monday, around nine?"

"Sounds good. The Camry needs a new muffler; the Jeep, replacement brake pads. You know how to work the lift. Tools are on the magnetic storage panel and in the drawers of the rolling work chests. Should you need to order a part, I keep a clipboard with a running list by the phone. Jot it down."

Jake approved. He liked organization.

"You are your own man," added Mac. "Repairs are nonstop. Come and go as you please. Spend as much time as you can with the major."

And with Hannah. She'd quit on him the previous evening. Somewhat disturbing. A reason for her departure would be nice. He glanced at his watch. It was closing in on eight. Time to cut out. He finished off his coffee. Gave Mac a two-finger salute. "Tomorrow, then."

He left the garage and walked the short distance back to the café. The air was cool but not chill. The sun stole a look beneath the low-lying clouds. Retreated. Traffic streamed smooth and orderly. The clock tower at the courthouse chimed on the hour. Sounding eight o'clock and creating a sense of place and presence. Tradition and normalcy. All of which Jake valued. He was right on time to meet the older men.

He entered the Corner Café through the front door and breathed in the mingling scents. Homemade baked bread, cheesy potatoes, biscuits and sausage gravy. Wild blueberry muffins. His stomach growled, low and hungry.

The café was packed and he took his place at the end of the waiting line. Until he caught his granddad waving to him from a corner booth. He eased out of line, excused himself to those ahead of him, then crossed to the major and Moody. The men must have arrived early. Smart on their part considering the crowd. He would've been ahead of schedule had he not stopped at Morrison's Garage. He was here now and that's all that mattered.

He'd nearly reached their booth when he heard a whoop and his name shouted. He turned toward a table nearby. His smile widened. The triplet boys were enjoying breakfast and totally into their food. Napkins were tucked into their shirtfronts. Syrup drowned their plates of pancakes and gooey spills stained the tabletop. Orange juice rings circled beneath their glasses.

"Dudes." Jake gave each one a high five and drew away with a sticky palm. He scored a napkin from the holder and wiped off his hand. Then crushed and dropped it onto a growing pile of those already smeared with syrup.

The boys looked him over. All curious and intent. "You're still wearing your Halloween costume," came from Harry.

Jake realized the boy's mistake. "Different clothes, similar style," he informed them.

He routinely wore jeans, a T-shirt, and his leather jacket when fall arrived. Broken-in biker boots. He'd pulled back his hair beneath a black bandanna. His stubble was another day old, his jawline scruffy. His mirrored aviators hid his gaze.

Howie pointed to the middle of his chest. "What's on your shirt?" he asked.

Jake looked down on the sketch of an abstract motorcycle. He read the logo aloud, " 'Four Wheels Move the Body, Two Wheels Move the Soul.' "

Blank expressions from all three. "In other words," he explained, "I like cars, four tires, but prefer a motorcycle—"

"Two tires!" Howie shouted, quite proud of himself.

"You are so smart," Jake praised Howie. He remained at the table a moment longer, watching them shovel in their pancakes. "Chew," he commented. "Your stomach doesn't have teeth."

Which drew a round of laughter. A second's pause and Jake added, "You guys look nice." All three wore white button-down shirts and navy slacks.

"We took a shower," said Harry. His hair was still damp.

Howie fingered his shirtfront. "Mom made us wear buttons."

Hal stuck out both feet from under the table, kicking Howie in the process. "And shoes that pinch my toes." He wore brown Oxfords.

Harry scratched his armpit. "Church clothes make me itch."

"You'll survive Sunday school. It's only once a week," came a voice from behind Jake. Female and recognizable. Hannah's sister, Lauren.

Jake eyed her over his shoulder. Lauren was the hostess at the Corner Café. She seated customers and passed out menus. Copies, too, of the *Moonbright Sun*, the morning newspaper. While the waitresses hustled in their khaki uniforms, Lauren had chosen a red sweater dress, fitted soft on her curves. She liked to be noticed and was hard to miss.

He scanned the diners, hoping to catch sight of Hannah. No sign of her. She must be in the kitchen. "Busy morning," he offered, making small talk.

"We serve the best breakfast in town."

"Your kids are doing those pancakes justice."

"They're bottomless pits."

Jake was ready to move on but didn't want to appear rude. "I heard you weren't feeling well yesterday. Better today?" he asked.

"Improved enough to work," she returned. She angled to stand by his side. "Thank you for walking in the parade with my boys, then taking them trick-or-treating."

"Hannah and I had fun." He linked his name to her sister. It didn't set well with Lauren.

Her expression tightened, showing narrowed eyes and pinched lips. She shifted the menus in her arms, located a copy of the local newspaper from beneath the stack, and slapped it onto his palm. "An article on the parade and a photograph of your good time is on the front page." Her tone was sharp, unpleasant.

He folded the paper under his arm. He'd check it out once he'd joined his gramps and Moody. He turned back to the triplets. They were on the edge of fidgety. Squeezing maple syrup onto empty plates. Resulting in a syrup lake. Followed by sticking their tongues deep into their empty glasses of orange juice. Licking the sides for pulp. Boys would be boys, Jake mused.

Fortunately, Lauren's husband, Grant, arrived to pick up his sons. Off duty and out of his police uniform, he wore a dark gray suit. He nodded to Jake, then motioned the three toward the restroom. "Wipe your mouths and wash your hands. Let's get a move on."

"I need to move on too," said Jake. He looked directly at Grant, then briefly at Lauren. "Nice to see you both." He wove between the tables to reach the major and Moody.

Jake's gramps tapped his watch face. "Quarter past eight, boy."

"Sorry, I got waylaid." He slipped off his jacket, hung it on a hook. Then slid into the booth next to his granddad. He set his creased newspaper alongside his napkin-wrapped silverware. He told them about his stop at Morrison's Garage and his plans to work part-time. The men approved.

Moody mentioned his arrival. "We saw you talking to Hannah's nephews."

"And Lauren," added his gramps.

"It was all about the kids," Jake relayed.

"For someone who once swore her love to you, Lauren didn't look that happy to see you," noted Moody.

"I've come to terms with our short history and she apparently hasn't—"

"Fully gotten over you?" suggested Moody.

Jake shrugged. "She's married with triplets. Grant seems a good guy. He'll make her happy."

Moody lowered his voice. "Making her happy will never be easy. She's a flirt and fickle. I've overheard Nan tell her granddaughter to act like a married lady."

The major elbowed Jake. "What about your happiness, boy?"

His pleasure depended on the woman now picking up orders from the pass-through window that connected the kitchen and the dining room. The cooks shelved the meals there beneath heat lights to keep them warm. The waitresses then stacked the dishes on trays.

Hannah hoisted and shouldered such a tray. Piled with plates, it tipped slightly, but she managed to keep it upright. She turned slowly, safely, and delivered the breakfasts to a four-top near Jake's booth. The customers affectionately thanked her. One elderly woman patted her arm. Hunger ended their conversations. Their orders of biscuits and gravy went down easy.

Jake smiled to himself. The expression on his face must have reflected his interest in Hannah, as both Moody and the major cleared their throats and grinned.

"Hannah will get to us shortly," Jake's gramps informed him. "We went ahead and ordered coffee before you got here."

Her turnaround time for the carafe of coffee and three mugs wasn't as quick as they'd expected. "She's slammed," Moody whispered. "The café is busy and Hannah's running behind."

"She'll catch up," Gramps said, sounding quite certain. "It's always that way on Sunday. She runs like crazy before church, then again after the service as well. The crowd doubles in size following the closing 'Amen.' People are patient. The other waitresses help her when they have a free second."

Those free seconds were far and few between. The major eyed the creased newspaper. "We've already read the paper. You should take a look at the front page while we're waiting," he nudged. "There's a picture and article on the parade."

Jake shook out the paper and took a look. His gramps had not prepared him for the half-page photo spread. Hannah, he, and the triplets were front and center. Hard to miss.

The photographer had captured them in black-and-white. He and Hannah walked close together. He piggybacked Hal and held Harry's hand. She clutched Howie's. She wore Jake's leather jacket as protection against the gusty wind. The hem of her skirt possessively wrapped his left knee. Like a hug.

Despite the multitudes and crowding, their expressions were engaged. She was peering up at him from beneath the rim of her Little Bo Peep bonnet as he glanced down on her. They looked completely into each other. Her face had softened and his own was relaxed too, less harsh without his normal locked jaw. The photo revealed their compatibility. A notable attraction. There was a core oneness about the two of them that hinted at a possible relationship. It was that evident.

Jake didn't care what anyone thought of them.

The Halloween parade had brought them together.

He wasn't big on having his picture taken.

However, this one touched him.

They looked like a couple.

Somehow that didn't bother him in the least.

"So . . . what do you think of the front page?" Moody prodded.

Jake folded the paper, ducked a response, "I've yet to read the article."

"Don't worry; they spelled your name correctly."

"Good to know, Gramps."

"It's a sweetheart of a picture of Hannah," added the major. "Even the boys seem content. Not so squirrely."

"You look less hard-ass than usual."

Jake narrowed his gaze on Moody, his teeth set.

Moody grinned. "Yeah, that's the look."

Jake ran one hand down his face. Exhaled. The men would razz him on the photo the entire day if he let them. He held up his hand. "Let it go."

"For now." Moody would only let it drop for so long.

Jake's gramps nudged him with his elbow. "Behave. Hannah's headed our way."

She was coming toward them now. Jake started to smile, only to swallow it instead. Her steps were tentative. Longing flickered in her eyes, fading to wariness. He'd told her the previous evening that he'd be at breakfast. There was no warm greeting on her part. Only a new detachment. A quick look his way and she focused on Moody and the major. Jake became the invisible man.

She placed a mug before each of them, then poured their coffee from a thermal carafe. Steam rose. A dark-roasted brew. She placed the carafe in the center of the table, an easy reach for all three.

Pen and order pad in hand, she addressed the older men with genuine warmth. "What sounds good this morning?"

They rattled off their breakfast choices. Jake came next. He stared at her hard from behind his sunglasses, willing her to look at him. She did not. Instead she eyed his bandanna as she took down his order.

Afterward she read back their selections, starting with Moody and Jake's gramps. "Two corned beef hash topped with eggs, sunny side up."

Moody blinked. "We didn't order eggs."

"You need your protein."

Jake's granddad chuckled. "She's always looking out for us."

"Two glasses of orange juice." She stared down their raised eyebrows. "You need your vitamin C."

"You're like a granddaughter," Moody approved.

Jake was mildly amused. He liked the way Hannah watched over the older men. He hoped she'd take care of him too. Perhaps by adding something special to his own breakfast. He listened intently.

"One order of lumberjack pancakes," was all she gave him.

"And . . . ," he pressed, "don't forget my sides of scrambled eggs and bacon."

"And . . ."—the major winked at her—"his side of corned beef hash."

Jake removed his aviators, jammed them atop his head, and canceled, "Real funny, Gramps. Erase the hash, Hannah. I'll pass."

She had avoided looking at him while he was wearing his shades, but didn't hesitate to meet his gaze without them. *Strange.* She held up her order pad for him to see. "I never wrote it down."

His granddad grinned. "Gotcha, boy."

Her gaze flicked off his. "I'd planned to bring you a side too, Jake. One of Gram's vanilla-maple Danishes."

The best Danish on the planet. She'd thought enough of him to add an extra. He liked that. A lot. Things were improving. Somewhat. "Thanks," he said.

Jake stared at her with such intensity that she moved on, distancing herself from him. He hadn't missed the clouding in her eyes. A hint of sadness. The heaviness in her steps as she proceeded to clip their breakfast ticket on the order wheel at the service window. He took a sip of his coffee. Brooding and reflective.

She confused him. He didn't like uncertainty. He preferred clarity. Especially with women. What had appeared the start of a relationship the previous day had weakened overnight. For no apparent reason. Which made him crazy.

Crazier still with Moody's observation, "Hannah doesn't seem too fond of you this morning."

"She seemed more sad than mad," his granddad reflected.

Jake shrugged. "I've no idea. Maybe she got up on the wrong side of the bed."

"As long as it wasn't your bed." His gramps spoke low and direct.

"Nope, not mine. I slept alone," he assured him.

"She usually has more pep in her step," said Moody.

"Bigger smiles too," added Jake's gramps.

"Don't blame me." Although he already blamed himself for Hannah's changed attitude toward him. He felt like the fall guy in a relationship that never got off the ground.

"We're not pointing any fingers, son," the major said appeasingly. "I'm sure her mood will improve."

Her mood did, in fact, take a turn. Five minutes, give or take, and a tall man with short brown hair dressed in a brown sport coat and knife-creased khaki slacks entered the café. All clean-cut and polished. Preppie, Jake thought. The man stood just inside the door, sharply eyeing the crowd. He wasn't familiar to Jake. But that meant little. He didn't know everyone in town.

Moody noted the new arrival. "Gregory Manor, our local success story," he said with pride. "He's a fine lawyer."

Jake recognized the name from his conversation with Hannah. Greg and she had grown up together. They had a history. He'd been her first kiss. An off-target kiss, more cheek than mouth. Still, he'd gone in lips first.

"Bet Gregory came home to check on his father," the major assumed. "His dad had a bad fall off a ladder while cleaning the gutters at his home. Damn autumn leaves."

"Bet he planned to see Hannah too," added Moody.

Jake was curious to observe them together. He had little time to wait. Hannah came toward them now, clutching a tray piled with plates that looked like their order. All attentive and careful. She managed to avoid the crush of departing customers, as well as the brush of waitresses running circles around her. Including hostess Lauren, who cut her off at a corner table. Thankfully, there were no upsets. She focused on safely reaching their booth.

All the while the buzz around Greg increased. The excitement circled throughout the café as customers focused on the man. He was welcomed with handshakes, slaps on the back, and wide smiles. As popular as any politician.

Drawn toward the commotion, Hannah glanced his way. The man stood in profile to her. Jake watched her watch Greg. She started. Color drained from her face. Her grip on the tray turned her knuckles white.

Her body suddenly sagged and the tray swayed. Jake's gaze shifted to their meals. His Danish rolled off its plate and his order of bacon flipped onto a serving of corned beef hash. Orange juice splattered the rims of the glasses. An accident waiting to happen.

He reacted. He straightened from the booth before she dumped the dishes onto their table and the floor. His best efforts weren't good enough. Hannah came out of her trance too late. The tray teetered and the edge smacked him square in the chest. He took the brunt of the mess. A serving of corned beef hash cleared the rim and coated his T-shirt. The egg atop it smeared the logo on his chest, the yolk runny. A full glass of orange juice splashed his groin. Sticky. He smelled of hash.

Shaken, Hannah lowered the tray onto the table. "Oh no, Jake," she said brokenly. "I'm so sorry. It was all my fault." Her worry touched him.

He hated to call attention to himself, but everyone was now looking his way. Even Greg eyed him. "Not a big deal," he was quick to say. "I stood up too quickly and unsettled you."

She fidgeted. "That's not quite—"

"It was exactly how it happened."

There was a deeper stir throughout the café when Greg approached them. He squeezed Hannah's shoulder, greeted her warmly, "I came to have breakfast." He cut Jake a look. "I'd rather eat it than wear it." He scrunched his nose. "You could use a shower."

*A shower?* An obvious observation. Jake lived by his gut feelings. He took an instant dislike to the lawyer. He wondered how Greg would react to corned beef hash squished on his starched white shirt. Citrus splashed down his zipper. Undoubtedly not well.

Word of the mishap had already reached Nan in the kitchen. She shot through the swinging doors and came straight to them. She carried two dish towels, one damp and the other dry. She handed them to Jake. "Maybe these will help," she said. "Wipe yourself off."

He swiped at his T-shirt, but the stain only sank in and spread. His chest flexed. The hash smell was all over his skin. He passed the towels back to Nan. Said, "I need to clean up. Change clothes."

"What happened?" the older woman asked.

Jake looked at Hannah. Her expression was downcast, so he gave his own brief accounting of the incident. "Greg—" he began.

"Gregory," the attorney corrected.

"Greg," Jake continued, "came into the café and everyone was glad to see him. His arrival caught Hannah off guard. Surprise tipped her tray. She would've recovered had I not jumped up to help her. I jarred it further. My interference caused the plates to shift. This is the end result." He indicated his ruined shirt and damp jeans.

"Your helpful hands weren't so helpful after all," Greg said.

"I appreciated the rescue," said Hannah.

"Not really a rescue but more of a disaster," from Greg, his tone distasteful.

Jake had heard enough from the man. He threatened the attorney with a look that had him taking a step back. Behind Hannah. His shield. What a wimp.

"So everyone's okay, then?" Nan asked, making certain.

"We're cool," Jake assured her. "This is far from the worst thing ever to happen to me."

Nan eyed her granddaughter. "I'm fine," Hannah said.

She next took note of Greg. "Nice to see you." A warm and genuine welcome.

"You'll see quite a bit of me during my father's recovery," he announced. "I'll be in town for several days."

Greg was the good son with strong family ties. Jake had had enough of him. He snagged his jacket off the hook, tossed it over one shoulder. He dug a fifty-dollar bill out of his jean pocket and handed it to Hannah. "That should cover our breakfasts along with a tip."

Hannah gasped. "Way too much." She tried to pass the bill back to him.

He refused to take it. "You deserve it."

"Return and I'll fix you a special breakfast," Nan offered.

"Will do," he agreed.

He cut his gaze to his gramps and Moody. They'd observed the incident but remained silent. Unusual for Moody, who always had two cents to share. The major spoke now. "Mind if we start without you, son?"

"Chow down."

Hannah quickly served the remaining breakfasts. The men dug in. Forking down the leftover plate of corned beef hash along with Jake's lumberjack pancakes. He couldn't fault them. They were hungry.

So much for their family breakfast together.

Better luck tomorrow.

# Chapter 4

Hannah watched Jake leave the café. His shoulders were set. His stride long. Purposeful. She felt awful about the tipped tray and food slide. All dumped onto him. She needed to apologize further without everyone in the diner staring at them. Soon, she hoped.

She quickly checked on her remaining customers, clearing away plates and refilling the carafes with coffee. Most had headed out the door for church. Tray in hand, she headed to the kitchen and dropped off the dirty dishes with the dishwasher. She sought the comfort only her grandmother could provide. Always warm and nonjudgmental.

Hannah found her gram at the big yellow mixer. "Muffin batter," she was told. "Butter pecan."

Hannah's favorite. She became mesmerized by the circling mixing bowl. The snap of her grandma's fingers made her blink. "You don't seem yourself this morning," Nan noted.

"Just feeling a little . . . off."

"How so? You should be in high spirits after that great parade photo and article in the *Moonbright Sun*. You and Jake were quite the pair. I've heard lots of positive comments on the spread. Did you have a good time?"

"Pretty much so."

"What's gone wrong since?"

Hannah sighed heavily. She had no problem confiding in her gram. Nan had been her confidante over the years. Broadminded and wise. "It has to do with the legend."

"What about it?" Her grandmother slowed the speed of the mixer, asked, "You chanted. Did you catch an image of your future spouse?"

Hannah kept Jake's kiss to herself, held deep within her heart. She did, however, explain that she'd seen an unknown man's reflection in Jake's mirrored aviators.

"You must've been standing quite close."

Hannah blushed. "Close enough."

"You didn't recognize the man at all?"

"The profile was hard to determine. The vision looked a little like Gregory."

"A little or a lot?"

"Too hazy to honestly tell."

Nan eyed her thoughtfully. "You expected someone else?"

Hannah shrugged. "Merely hoped."

"Ah, perhaps somebody in a black leather jacket?"

More heat in her cheeks. A question she couldn't confirm or deny.

Nan stopped the mixer. She laid out several muffin tins with liners. Then used a measuring scoop to fill each one. "Gregory's home now," she said. "Are you glad to see him?"

"He's a good friend."

"He's a fine man. Accomplished and established. Keep an open mind, little one."

"Is the legend always right?" Hannah needed to know.

"Do you want it to be wrong?"

"I'd merely like some leeway."

Her grandmother read her well. "A chance to know Jake better?"

"I haven't been friendly with Jake since I saw the image," she confessed. "I pretty much blew him off afterward. He may have already lost interest."

"From what I know of Jake, he may be mildly put off but never discouraged. Should he decide to date you, he will." Her gram winked at her. "Even with some competition."

"Gregory?"

"He's always been devoted to you." Nan sprinkled a pinch of cinnamon sugar atop the muffin mix. "My best advice, sweet girl—it's not the worst thing in the world to be pursued by two men. Rather exciting, I'd imagine. Why not divide your free time between them? Enjoy them both. Gregory will be in town as long as his parents need him. Jake"—she shrugged—"who knows? He's a loner, on his own schedule."

"He could leave at any moment." Realistically speaking.

"But I doubt he will." Nan moved two trays of muffins to the convection oven. Already preheated. She set the timer. Paused. Adding, "Don't force life. Let it happen. Sooner or later the image you saw in Jake's sunglasses will become clear and you'll know who's meant for you. Have faith in the legend's choice."

Hannah's heart lightened. Possibilities emerged. Gained life. She would be patient.

Her grandmother went on to gently massage her hands, which were reddened with swollen knuckles. Hannah sympathized. "Your arthritis is acting up."

"My fingers are sore today," Nan admitted.

"What can I do to ease the pain?"

"Nothing at the moment, honey. But easier days ahead. You've met Sydney Byrne, I believe."

Hannah nodded. "Pretty lady. Medium height, brown hair worn in a bun. Her parents were killed in a car accident, from what I remember. She came to live with her grandmother in the large Victorian on Maple Street. She finished up her last two years of high school here."

"Exactly right," Nan confirmed. "Sydney moved away and only recently returned for her grandmother's funeral. She owns Bread and Cie in San Francisco. After her grandma's passing, she came back to Moonbright to settle the estate. She's fixing up the place and I hope she'll stay awhile. She bakes amazing homemade bread and I'm going to talk to her about making weekly deliveries. I hear she makes a wonderful honey wheat loaf. Sourdough and marble rye too."

"No more kneading and rolling out dough for you." Hannah cupped her grandma's hands in her own, holding them lightly. Relief settled deep. Nan worked so hard, even in pain. Hannah was grateful for Sydney and hoped she and Nan could come to an arrangement.

"Order up, Hannah," one of the line cooks called to her.

"Gregory's breakfast," she told her gram.

"Feed the man. Then I have a favor to ask of you."

"Anything."

"The dining room has quieted down for the moment. The other waitresses can cover your section. I'd appreciate your going upstairs and checking on Jake."

"Whatever for?"

"A courtesy call. He saved your tray from fully toppling over and took the brunt of the hash and juice. Bring him back downstairs and I'll fix you both breakfast."

"I don't have time to eat."

"Make time."

Hannah managed a smile. "Yes, ma'am."

She located Gregory at the front counter and served him a sizzling plate of country fried steak and eggs. He patted the empty stool next to him. "Join me?"

An offer she might have accepted, if not for Jake. Gregory

was good-looking and personable. He'd been a great playmate and friend when they were younger. He'd always shown interest in her. She liked him a lot. Their relationship was comfortable. Caring and easy. But he didn't make her heart race or her stomach go soft. Jake did both.

Be that as it may, the image she'd seen last night in the mirrored lenses persisted in her mind. Just out of focus. More blur than believable. While the vision wasn't Jake, she wasn't certain it was Gregory either.

She touched his arm but turned him down. "I have an errand to run for Gram." She left out who and where.

Gregory cut a bite of country fried steak. "Care to catch a movie later?"

"Thanks, but no. I've seen the double feature twice already."

"I'll think of something else for us to do then."

"I'm working until three."

"I'll give you a call. We'll touch base later."

Hannah topped off his coffee mug, then cut back through the kitchen. She took the storeroom steps to the second floor and crossed to Jake's apartment, where she stood outside the door. She breathed deeply, slowly raised her hand, and knocked. There was no immediate response. She fist-bumped the door a little harder. Still no answer. She wondered if she'd missed him. Perhaps he'd gone down the outside staircase as she'd come up from inside. A considerate move on his part. He wouldn't disrupt the busy kitchen staff.

She decided to quickly freshen up before heading back to the kitchen. She'd wash her face, comb her hair, and readjust her ponytail. Go as far as to change her khaki shirt, which showed several small stains. She'd splattered coffee earlier. The triplets had hugged her around the waist with sticky syrupy hands. They'd left small fingerprints.

She slipped her key from her pant pocket. Unlocked the

door. Entered. She unzipped her slacks, untucked her uniform top. Then gripped the hem and drew it up and over her head. She tossed the shirt into her wicker laundry basket.

The doorknob to the bathroom twisted easily. She stepped inside in her white sports bra and unzipped slacks and inhaled steam so thick and humid it felt like a sauna. She gasped for air.

It was apparent Jake had taken a hot shower. The air was scented with amber and musk. Enticingly male. She spotted him when he turned away from the sink and cut her a look, sharp with surprise. He was a heart-stopper. He stood nearly nude. A knotted towel hung low on his hip bones. The gap near his groin was shadowed. Neither managed a word. Silence held between them. Engulfing and immodest.

She dared to stare. His masculinity merged with the mist. Her gaze flicked over his damp hair, hard face, and thick-muscled chest. Alpha and carnal. All slickened sexiness and raw strength. His legs were long and strong. His feet big and bare.

A sigh escaped, low and throaty. She sagged against the doorframe. A dead giveaway that she liked what she saw—a little too much. She was so into him that she twitched when he said, "Are you flashing me, Hannah? Bra and pretty pink panties."

"Not on purpose." The split V of her zipper exposed her cotton undies. She hurriedly zipped up, grabbed a towel off a nearby rack, and covered her breasts. Her sister would've laughed at her modesty. Lauren considered sports bras public, unrestricted workout wear; Hannah felt exposed and vulnerable.

She was slow to explain. "Gram sent me to check on you. I knocked on your door, and when you didn't answer, I thought that you'd already left. I felt it safe to clean up."

"Instead you got hit with steam and me."

That's how it had gone down. She held up the flat of her

hand in an attempt not to look at him. "Sorry to have bothered you."

"You never bother me," he told her. "Put your hand down. You're peeking between your fingers."

Busted! She lowered it. Steadied herself.

He pushed back his hair. The ends touched his shoulders. The majority of the mist had dissipated. He was full-on staring at her. Intense and hard. A muscle ticked in his cheek. "I'm glad we're speaking again, Hannah. After last night and breakfast this morning, I wasn't sure we would. You went all cold shoulder and quiet on me, woman. Care to explain?"

"Maybe we should get dressed first."

"Naked conversations resolve issues quickly."

A bare Jake Kaylor would be far too distracting. She'd lose herself in his big buff body. Wanting only to touch him rather than talk. He dimpled, aware of her dilemma.

"I'll get dressed, you do whatever, and we'll meet on the landing," he suggested.

She nodded. "We'll go downstairs together. Gram wants to fix you breakfast."

"You'd rather go public than private with our conversation?" he asked.

"Eat first, talk second."

"Doable. I'm hungry. I can live with that."

They parted, did their own thing, then exited their apartments at the same moment. Both were cleaned up and recharged. Hannah was no longer sticky from syrupy fingerprints and Jake had escaped the smell of corned beef hash. From his black bandanna down to his biker boots, he was all male and disturbingly handsome. He gave her goose bumps.

"Outside stairs or cut through the kitchen?" he asked.

"Kitchen works fine. Gram is expecting you."

"You'll join me?"

"I'm on the clock."

"We'll stop time for thirty minutes."

"We'll see."

"If you decide to serve and not sit with me, be warned that I'll pull you onto my lap in the booth. Breakfast gossip."

Idle threat? Doubtful. Jake was a man of action. Whispers had circulated earlier over their photo in the newspaper. There'd been enormous curiosity and speculation. All unfounded. Should he draw her across his thighs, rumors would spread in seconds flat. Her face heated.

Jake gently stroked her cheek with his thumb. "You look pretty in pink. The same color as your panties."

He looked dark and dangerous in all black.

He reached for the sunglasses hooked to a belt loop, ready to put them on. She associated his aviators with the legend. She didn't want a repeat vision. "Would you mind not wearing them just now?" she softly requested.

He agreed. "Sure, no problem." He secured them atop his head. He followed her down the back staircase and into the storeroom. That's where they found Nan bent in an attempt to lift and empty a fifty-pound sack of flour into a portable bin. She struggled.

Jake was there for her. "I've got it." He upended the open bag in one fluid motion. Then stuffed the empty sack in a garbage can.

Nan released a breath. She touched him on the arm. "I think I'm strong, but my hands tell me differently. You saved me from spilling flour all over the floor."

"He saved me earlier too," Hannah reminded her grandmother. "Had he not steadied my tray, all those around us would've worn breakfast food. Not just Jake."

"We thank you," Nan said. "Now let me place your orders. Hannah likes blueberry pancakes. Is there anything you don't like, Jake?"

"Corned beef hash." He and Hannah spoke as one. They smiled at each other.

"Grab a booth," Nan indicated. "I'll have Dolores deliver your food."

Dolores was a second cousin on Hannah's mother's side. She'd worked at the Corner Café for as long as Hannah could remember. She'd mentored Hannah in the dining room. A plump woman who'd sampled every item on the menu and offered recommendations to indecisive customers.

"It's Sunday. Busiest day of the week. You're sure, Gram?"

Nan looked from Hannah to Jake. "Never been surer in my life." She reached for the flour bin, only to have Jake give it the needed shove into the kitchen. He placed it near the prep table where Nan had laid out pie tins for her daily special. "Pumpkin," she told them. "Requested by Moody and the major."

He and Hannah left the kitchen then, Jake walking so close beside her, their bodies brushed. She liked the feel of him. Solid and strong. Several locals followed their progress to the small corner booth. A two-seater wedged behind a larger six-top. A tight fit for Jake. He couldn't stretch out his long legs. His thighs splayed and he trapped her own tightly squeezed knees between his. His rough denim jeans rubbed against her cotton khakis. His heavy boots pressed her tennis shoes.

Hidden intimacy under the table. Bold and infrequent for her. He caught her eye across the table and winked. She gave him a small smile just as her sister approached, frowning, huffy, and confrontational.

Lauren hovered over their booth. "What's the deal?" she demanded. "You should be preparing for the next church rush, not sitting on your butt."

Jake calmly intervened. "Take your complaints to Nan. Your grandmother suggested we have breakfast together after the tray mishap."

"Then grab a quick bite and get back to work," Lauren hissed at Hannah. A very bossy hostess. "This booth is a favorite for couples."

"We are a couple." His response turned Lauren on her heel, and she stormed off.

Hannah nervously tucked her hair behind her ears. "A couple? Us?" Not possible. She was sure his comment was meant to tick off her sister, not hold any truth.

"We can be whatever we want to be," he said. "Being a couple seated in this booth works for us now."

Now . . . but for how long after their breakfast? How would he see them later in the day? Tomorrow?

Take it slow, her gram had advised. Be persistent but patient. Don't rush fate. The right man would surface. With love and good intentions.

Dolores soon brought mugs of coffee and glasses of orange juice to their table. She followed up with a tray laden with food and unloaded their dishes. "Blueberry pancakes for Hannah and the Mainers Platter for Jake. A sampler of nearly everything on the menu, minus the corned beef hash. Compliments of Nan." She left them to their breakfasts.

Jake stared at all the food. "Your grandmother was generous. There's enough here to feed three people. It all looks amazing."

"Far better than a doily?" Hannah couldn't believe she'd said that out loud. An untimely comment followed by inappropriate laughter. She couldn't help herself. The moment hit her as funny. She'd warned Jake the previous evening that if she recalled something humorous she would laugh hysterically. The doily anecdote had stuck with her. She doubled over in amusement now.

Jake chuckled right along with her. "I can laugh at myself," he told her. "But maybe not as long as you're laughing at me." He tapped his watch. "Minutes now, Hannah."

She barely gained control. Heaving a breath, she bit down on her bottom lip and said, "I really lost it."

"Nothing wrong with letting go," he assured her. "I liked watching you laugh. Seems I have entertainment value."

Hannah had laughed so hard she felt weak. Her stomach hurt. Breakfast awaited. She poured warm blueberry syrup on her wild blueberry pancakes. "Let's eat."

Jake went with maple syrup on his waffle.

Lauren appeared before they'd taken their first bites. "Keep it down over here," she ground out. "You're laughing like a hyena and disturbing the customers."

Hannah eyed those seated around them. No one appeared upset or uptight. Not one person knew what had sparked her outburst, yet several folks grinned and shared in her amusement. "We're not bothering anyone," she finally said.

Her sister stiffened. "I'm bothered."

Jake turned his gaze on Lauren. His tone was low and chill. "Hannah's laughter is contagious, unlike your scowl." He then forked a generous piece of waffle and popped it in his mouth. End of conversation.

Lauren's nostrils flared. She left in a huff. Hannah watched her go. Her sister met arriving customers at the door with a toss of her hair and a pinched-lip welcome.

"Eat, Hannah," Jake encouraged. "Don't worry about Lauren."

She complied. The pancakes were light and fluffy. Fresh wild blueberries teased her taste buds. She closed her eyes and chewed slowly. Swallowed and sighed.

"That good?" came from Jake.

"I'm savoring."

"I take pleasure in you."

No man had complimented her so. She warmed from the inside out. Her outlook bright. "I enjoy you too."

"How can we experience each other further today?"

She took two more bites, then went on to suggest, "It's nice outdoors. We could take an afternoon walk when I get off work. The park is pleasant."

"A quiet place for us to talk?"

"Benches provide privacy. The only noise might come from the playground, if kids are there for fun. It can get loud. No indoor voices used. The kids shriek and shout each word."

"It's good to play at the top of your lungs."

"I'll want to clean up after my shift," she told him.

"I won't break in on you while you shower."

"Both doors will be locked."

"I've picked a lock or two."

She believed him. "Front door, four o'clock, then?"

He nodded. "I'll be the guy in the black leather jacket."

"I'll be the girl in the navy Moonbright sweatshirt."

"I'd recognize you anywhere, babe."

It was the nicest thing any man had ever said to her. "Thank you," she softly replied.

One corner of his mouth tipped up. He understood her shyness and insecurity. "Welcome."

A comfortable silence saw them through the remainder of their meal. Afterward Hannah was so full she wanted nothing more than to take a nap. Instead she faced the lunch rush. Three hours of hustle.

Jake took a last sip of his coffee, then stretched his arms along the sides of the booth. He breathed deeply. "I can't believe I ate the entire Mainers Platter."

"You deserved every bite after our earlier fiasco."

"It's time to move before the food fully settles and I can't get up." He pushed from the booth, added, "I'm headed upstairs to visit with Gramps and Moody while you work. Maybe even work out before we hook up."

Hannah rose too. "Moonbright doesn't have a gym."

"I don't need exercise equipment for crunches, push-ups, and jogging."

Hannah had a mental flash of him getting physical. All sweaty muscles and heavy breathing. Her own breath hitched. She managed a, "See you later," as she cleared their table for the next customers.

His good-bye wasn't spoken, yet his touch meant more than words. He grazed his fingers down her arm, then squeezed her wrist. His slow grin left her expectant and excited about their walk in the park.

Jake spent an hour with the two older men, seated in the same chair as the previous evening, this time watching them play chess. Moody wore his bifocals. The play was intense. The conversation minimal. Words were only spoken between moves. Jake didn't mind. He felt a sense of family just being there. In between comments he flipped through two fishing magazines and checked the emails on his iPhone. One message from his father indicated business was booming and slightly backed up. Jake's brother was helping to pick up the slack. There'd been numerous inquiries as to when Jake would return to Bangor. He was in demand with an anxious clientele. Motorcycles didn't fix themselves. Classic bike owners were particular about the mechanic. He had earned favor among the largest collectors.

Despite the requests, Hannah came first. She was his priority. He'd put all bike repairs on hold for a week or two.

Moments later, the major called, "Checkmate." Moody's king was under threat of capture with no legal move to prevent it. The game was over.

"I should've taken out your bishop two moves ago," Moody complained.

"You went after my queen and missed your chance."

The two men shook hands. "We're celebrating my win with

a piece of pie in the café this afternoon," the major declared. "Strawberry-rhubarb with a scoop of French vanilla ice cream."

Moody grumbled, "Guess I'm buying."

"No guessing about it. I won. You lost. Grab your wallet, old man."

Moody snorted. "Old man?"

"You're older than me by ten days."

Moody included Jake. "Join us, boy."

"Thanks, but I already have plans."

"Plans alone or with someone we know?" asked his gramps.

"Time with Hannah."

"So we figured," Moody said.

The major nodded. "No surprise there."

Jake wasn't afraid to admit, "I like her."

"We know," said by both men.

"How could you?" Jake was just coming to the realization himself.

His granddad explained, "Your expression is telling. Others have noticed too."

*His face gave him away?* Perhaps only to those who knew him well. "Who, exactly? Name names."

His gramps answered, "Anyone who's seen your photo in the morning newspaper or observed you at breakfast with Hannah."

"You're both crazy."

"You're crazy for her," Moody said.

"I'm just getting to really know her," Jake reminded them. "I've been in town twenty-four hours. Cut me some slack."

Moody eyed Jake through the magnifier on his glasses. "Seems longer than that given the way you look at her."

The major agreed. "Love doesn't tell time."

Moody was philosophical. "One day or twenty years—the heart just knows."

"A man should recognize his feelings and act accordingly," Jake's grandfather advised. "Don't ignore the obvious."

Jake let their advice soak in. The men were looking out for his best interests. Hannah was his interest. Their support meant everything. Still, he knew his own mind and refused to be rushed. "Friendship first. Whatever follows I'll take in stride. Hannah's not a race to the finish line."

Moody snorted. "In stride, huh?"

"Keep a steady pace, son," Jake's granddad nudged. "Gregory Manor's in town, single and partial to her."

"That sounds like a warning," Jake said.

"Merely a cautionary comment."

Moody's grin was sly. "Ever compete for a woman, boy?"

"No, never."

"First time for everything."

Jake exhaled. Moody was needling him. He refused to take the bait. He'd been fortunate with the ladies. They willingly chose him. Dates and short-term relationships came easy, no strings attached. But Greg and Hannah had a history. Jake hoped the attorney wouldn't interfere with his own plans to date her. That was yet to be determined.

He pushed off the chair. Stretched. "I'm off. I want to exercise and take my bike for a ride. Cruise around town. Explore the outskirts."

"Moonbright hasn't changed much since your last visit," the major said.

Moody counted, "It hasn't changed in fifty years."

The men waved him off with, "Have a good afternoon."

Jake went to his apartment and exercised for sixty minutes. He took his third shower of the day. Then rode his Ducati for an hour. A part of him gravitated toward the familiar. Time had enhanced Moonbright's appeal. The town remained genuine and quaint. Generations of families had walked the sidewalks.

Grandchildren shopped the same stores as their grandparents. People waved as he passed by, smiling and friendly. One young boy raised his hands, curving them as if holding on to handlebars. Jake got the message and revved the engine for him. The boy pumped his arm.

In due course Jake took to the back roads. A winding landscape of barren trees and browning foliage. Winter would soon push autumn aside. Nature would go dormant in the whites and grays of the long winter season ahead. There would be snow. Lots and lots of snow.

He debated his future. Relocation crossed his mind. Where he might want to live and who might accompany him. That *who* could easily be Hannah. There was a lot to consider. So much that he lost track of time. Riding his Ducati twice as far as he'd planned before turning around and heading back toward town. He refused to race above the speed limit. He didn't need a ticket. He arrived in Moonbright twenty minutes late.

He locked up his bike at Morrison's Garage. Jogged to the café. He rounded the corner at Pie Street and Pumpkin Lane and immediately spotted Hannah. It wasn't cold out, but she stood huddled against the brick building, her head lowered, her hands deep in the pockets of her sweatshirt. She shuffled her feet.

"Hannah," he called out to catch her attention.

She looked up, her expression blank. She blinked several times, as if she saw him but didn't really see him.

"You okay?" he asked when he reached her.

"You're here." Her voice was weak, faint.

He gently touched her arm to reassure her that he was. "We agreed to take a walk in the park once you got off work. I took my motorcycle out to clear my head and got caught up in my thoughts. I'm sorry. I'm here now."

"I wasn't sure you'd show up."

"Why would you think that?"

"Lauren saw you ride by earlier," she explained. "She announced you'd grown bored with Moonbright and were likely leaving town. Here today, gone tomorrow. No good-byes."

His chest tightened. "You believed her?"

"You once left Lauren."

"You're not Lauren."

"Still, my sister was convincing," she confessed. "I don't know you well enough not to have considered the possibility."

"Trust me, babe. I have no immediate plans to leave town. I want to spend more time with my granddad and Moody. I've taken a part-time job at Morrison's Garage until Mac hires a new mechanic. I'd planned to share that with you during our walk."

He tipped up her chin with one finger. Her blond hair fell away from her face and over her shoulders. The shadows in her eyes vanished when he said, "I'm seriously hot for a woman in a navy sweatshirt. I plan to stick around and see how we shake out."

"I'm into a man wearing a black leather jacket," she said. "Who accidentally ate a doily." She covered her mouth and swallowed her laughter.

"The doily, again?" he muttered. "I tell you my secret and you still find it funny."

"Funny forever," she admitted. "Whenever I think of you."

"Think of me often then. Your laughter does it for me."

He took her by the hand. Small, soft, and finger laced with his own. Holding hands in public meant something in Moonbright. The gesture wasn't taken lightly. It went beyond a casual friendship and labeled them a couple. Hannah didn't resist, so he took that as a good sign. Passersby cast inquiring looks and a few nodded support. Several others narrowed their eyes, unconvinced of his sincerity. Gossip would debate their future together. Let people talk. He knew how he felt about Hannah. He was genuinely fond of her. That's all that mattered.

They crossed the street and entered the city park. The cement path was wide, for both walkers and bicycle riders. It was well maintained, Jake noticed. And fairly quiet. The bike racks stood empty. The gazebo looked lonely. A very pregnant woman sat on a bench while her two young daughters bounced on the horse spring rides and slid down the short sliding board. All giggles and wiggles as tag came into play. The lady waved to Hannah and she waved back.

"That's Mary Jane Dennison—she's expecting twin boys any day now," Hannah told him. "Her husband runs Keepsake Antiques. The girls are Rebecca, age six, and the itsy-bitsy is Betsy, age three."

"Cute girls," Jake said as he and Hannah settled on a bench nearby, their shoulders, hips, and thighs aligned. He liked the feel of her against him. Soft and feminine.

She lifted her face to the sun, sighed. "The park is so peaceful. Fresh air raises the spirits."

He squinted against the sunshine. "So do good company, bonding, and relaxation." He debated putting on his sunglasses, decided against them. They seemed to upset Hannah. She'd refused to look him in the eye at breakfast. So he left them off. For the time being.

"The park is an active part of the community," she told him. "The Events Coordinator at the courthouse, Lara Shaw, plans amazing seasonal events. The entire town gathers for the Halloween Pumpkin Carving. In December, it's Build the Snowmen. There's an Easter Egg Hunt in the spring and a huge picnic with games and sparklers on the Fourth of July."

Jake had always been more loner than joiner. Still, he admired the unity and kinship of Moonbright. People came together, formed tight-knit relationships. Lifelong friendships.

He nudged her with his elbow. "Let's talk," he requested. "It's quiet, apart from the girly giggles. I need to know why you split last night. I thought we were getting along well. What suddenly upset you?"

She shifted on the bench and was slow to answer. He sensed her hesitancy. "It has to do with the Halloween legend, which some call foolish and others hold great store by."

He squeezed her hand encouragingly. "My granddad mentioned the legend."

"The major's witnessed it at work firsthand."

"So he said. Moody too." Still seemed farfetched to Jake. "Do you believe in the myth? Did you chant?"

She blushed. "Yes to both. Gram insisted."

He'd been with her much of the day on Halloween. "When, exactly, did you recite it?" He thought back.

She scuffed her feet. Dust flecked the toes of her tennis shoes. "During trick-or-treating."

He guessed, "On the sidewalk when you bumped into me?"

"I closed my eyes," she admitted, "and didn't realize you'd stopped. I grabbed you for support."

"Here I thought you were trying to get into my jeans."

Her color deepened. "Total accident."

"The end result?" He was curious but dubious. "Did you catch a man's reflection in a looking glass?" He made the legend sound like a fairy tale.

She withdrew her hand from his, putting a tangible distance between them. This was a bigger deal to her than he'd imagined. She was a believer in tradition. Reluctance lowered her voice. "I saw a man, but it wasn't through a looking glass."

He gentled his tone. "Where, then?"

"It happened upstairs right after you kissed me," she whispered. "When I looked into your mirrored aviators."

He knew what was coming and it hit him hard. Frustrated him. "You saw another man in my reflective lenses?"

"A hazy silhouette. Unrecognizable."

"The legend failed you?"

"I was initially disheartened. I'd hoped for a clear reflection. Gram believes in happy endings. There hasn't been a Moonbright woman disappointed by the outcome of the legend. Right place, right time, right man. But my vision was just plain confusing. I'll await transparency."

He let her words soak in. "A mystical secret." He hated secrets. He liked things candid and decisive. No gray area.

He ran one hand down his face, rubbed the back of his neck. He found the muscles tight. His stomach hollow. He'd faced challenges and competitions throughout his life but had never gone up against small-town folklore. Dubious to him, yet familiar and credible to the locals.

He had questions for her. Important ones. He kept his calm. Spoke slowly, "I care for you, Hannah. What happens next? Can we still date? What if we become involved? How much power does the legend have over you?" Would she dump him for another guy?

She clasped her hands, looked out across the playground. Sunshine captured her expression; concentration furrowed her brow. She worried her bottom lip, seemingly lost within herself. For a considerable time.

His own hands flexed and his fingers itched. Vulnerability was not his friend. Such an emotion was new to him. Love was a progression. He wanted to move forward with Hannah. He needed to touch her, to pull her into him, to have her accept him as a friend, her man, and a possible lover—should midnight take them to his bed.

Instead he sucked it up, backed off. Gave her space. Hannah was smart, capable, and he trusted her judgment. One way or the other. Minutes had never moved so slowly. He sat stiffly. His back ached. He waited and waited and waited some more for her decision.

Significance scored her words when she finally said, "I'm

curious about the man profiled in your sunglasses. I'm also my own person. I like being with you, Jake. We move forward. Get to know each other better."

She was open-minded. He had a chance with her, despite the pressures of the legend. Jake exhaled the breath he hadn't realized he'd been holding. Relief settled bone deep. "Good plan." They'd made progress.

He had more to say, hoping to schedule time together. Dinner dates. Movies. A ride on his Ducati. Regrettably, they were interrupted by the littlest Dennison, toddling toward them. A chubby sweetheart in a purple sweater, matching leggings, and a gauzy red tutu sparkling with sequins. She held up her arms, entreated, "Help, Han-Han."

Hannah was up in a heartbeat. She lifted the girl against her chest, dropped a light kiss on her forehead. "What do you need, Betsy?"

Betsy pointed between the low wooden balance beam and the monkey bars. "Whirly," she squealed.

Jake stood up too. The whirl was an older child's ride. It featured a wide, round metal platform with multiple handgrips to provide support whether users sat or stood. One person would push the whirl, possibly break into a run, while the others spun wildly. It was a dangerous ride for such a tiny girl.

He came up beside Hannah. "You and Betsy climb aboard." They did so. He gave Hannah a boost from the back, his palm cupping her butt. She had a nice ass. "Sit near the middle," he instructed, "cross-legged, and secure Betsy on your lap. Hang on; here we go."

Betsy bounced on Hanna's thighs. "Fast." She giggled.

He waited until Hannah had a solid hold on the girl as well as a handgrip before he set the whirl in motion. There was fast and there was cautious. He started out slow, a mere shuffling of his feet, his boots kicking up dirt, before he widened his stride and took several giant steps.

Betsy shrieked at the increased speed. He slowed again. Then sped up. He circled countless times, watching the girl go from wide-eyed and breathless to silly giggles.

"Do me next," Rebecca called from the swing set. "Push me high."

Jake stopped the whirl and helped Hannah, holding Betsy, back on firm ground. His fingers curved over Hannah's upper arm at the same time his knuckles pressed the side of her breast. High and firm. He was slow to let her go. She cast him a look over her shoulder. He winked. She blushed. They all crossed to the swings.

Rebecca slid onto a canvas belt swing and began pumping her legs. Hannah settled Betsy in a bucket swing and fastened the seat belt, for safety's sake. Hannah and he circled behind the two and gently pushed them to a moderate height. Nothing too high. Although Rebecca called for "higher."

Jake glanced over at Hannah. She liked kids. For a split second he imagined her as a mother. She was patient and kind and was having as much fun as the girls. She threw back her head and laughed when Betsy let go of the metal chains and clapped excitedly, all the while snug in the high-back bucket.

The girls eventually tired of their swinging. They weren't allowed to walk on the low beam or climb the geometric dome. They wanted Jake to do both. He showed off for them. He pretended the low beam was a high wire. He tipped from side to side, his arms stretched out for balance. Applause resounded when he finished. He hadn't scaled a dome since he was twelve. He shot to the top like a mountain climber. The girls *ooh*ed and *ahh*ed.

Their mother struggled off the bench and joined them near the monkey bars. She glanced at her watch. "Time to go," she told her daughters. Who moaned and groaned. "There's pizza for supper," which had the two jumping like pogo sticks.

She smiled at Jake and Hannah. "I appreciate your entertaining my girls. I'm not much fun at the moment. Every movement's labored. I get winded easily."

The girls grabbed their mother's hands. "Car!" They led Mary Jane off, dancing alongside her.

The sun was shuttered behind a bank of clouds and a cool breeze swept the park. "What are your dinner plans?" Jake asked Hannah.

She looked down, seemingly reluctant to tell him. She spotted a heart-shaped rock, picked it up, and slipped it in her jean pocket. Her gaze lifted and she said, "Gregory called right before I met up with you. He invited me to Sunday supper. I'll be joining him and his parents for clam chowder and game night."

"Sounds nice," he managed, thinking it actually sucked. He should've asked her out sooner. Not last-minute. He hadn't known how the day would resolve itself. Their conversation had gone well. He would miss taking a meal with her. "What kind of games?" he asked with forced interest.

"Scrabble, Monopoly, charades."

"Good times."

She poked him in the chest to make her point, deliberate in her intent. "I've known his family all my life. They're kind and supportive. Gregory's father was hurt falling off a ladder, cleaning the gutters. He could use some cheering up."

"You're cheerful, all right."

She pulled a face. "Sarcasm, Jake?"

A bit cynical, perhaps. She was comfortable with Greg, with his family's homey atmosphere. Jake relented, "Let's get you back to your apartment so you can dress for dinner."

"I'm wearing what I've got on."

Casual then. He was mildly relieved she wouldn't be wearing her Sunday best. He took her hand and they returned down the path from which they'd come. The café had served breakfast and lunch but was now closed for supper. They took the outside staircase to the second floor. There they stood silent, facing each other. Neither one was ready to part company.

"See you later, Hannah," he finally said.

She released his hand. A slow slide of palm against palm. "It won't be a late night."

It would be, however, a night spent with Greg and not with him.

"What will you do while I'm gone?" she asked.

"Hang out with Moody and Gramps."

"They're good company."

They weren't Hannah.

# Chapter 5

It was ten o'clock by the time Hannah returned to her apartment. Dinner and game night had proved enjoyable but had dragged on. Her mind had wandered to Jake, so much so that Gregory had eyed her strangely when it was her turn at Scrabble and she sat staring at the tiles. Unable to form the simplest words.

The two had partnered in charades. Gregory had acted out her favorite movie, *The Princess Bride*, and she'd missed his clues. She'd guessed badly. He wasn't a good loser, even to his parents. His frown only deepened throughout the evening.

He'd borrowed his dad's Subaru to drive her home. He'd attempted a good-night kiss, but she'd turned her head. The kiss landed off-center, more chin than lips. A red flag from their childhood. He'd looked surprised but not discouraged. He'd gone in a second time, which she also evaded. She'd then quickly unfastened her seat belt, opened the SUV door, and hopped out. Finger-waved her good-bye.

She'd climbed the stairs, contemplative, and came to a decision. She couldn't kiss Gregory with a clear conscience. She liked him a lot, but only as a friend. Jake Kaylor presently held her interest. She nearly collided with him on the landing as he was leaving his grandpa's apartment.

At the very sight of Jake, her heart quickened. Crazy wild.

He stood in a casual stance and grinned down at her, sans sunglasses. His stare was fixed on the rapid pulse at her neck. "Turned on by Greg or hot for me?" he asked her.

Her entire body blushed. She shut her eyes for several heart-beats. Her lashes lifted and she found he'd closed in on her. Silently. So near they almost touched.

His gaze was steady on her. "Did Greg kiss you good night?"

"M-mm, sort of."

"He did or he didn't?"

"Does the chin count?"

"He missed his mark."

She'd avoided his kiss. "More or less."

"So no lips."

"No lips."

"Not very memorable. Your call or his?"

"None of your business."

"I'm making you my business."

Her stomach softened.

He grinned, got cocky. "I'm guessing good old Greg wanted to fool around. Instead you came home to me."

"I *live* here."

"So do I."

"For the time being."

"I'm not going anywhere, Hannah. I told you that this after-noon."

She feigned a yawn. "I'm tired. I've got an early-morning shift, and I open the café. Time to turn in."

He recalled, "You once said my kisses made you sleepy. Should we test your theory again tonight? One good-night kiss and you'd be out like a light."

Or she could just as easily lie awake, thinking of him. Silence, heavy and thick as foreplay, settled between them. She wet her lips, nervous yet expectant. She didn't resist when he eased her fully against him. She let the moment play out. There was a big difference between knowing someone casually and knowing someone intimately. Their embrace was private, personal, appealing.

Their bodies coupled. Her breasts pressed against his chest and their hip bones rubbed. He curved his arms about her shoulders. She settled her hands at his waist. The man was solid. His muscles taut. She shifted between his legs, flush with his groin. A groin that stirred. Arousal struck hard.

He bent to kiss her.

Just as she stretched up to him.

Time slowed with the exchange of breath.

The heat of his slightly parted lips blew across her mouth.

His unshaved jaw brushed the softer skin of her chin.

Seconds were magnified as each memorized the impact of the moment. It was startling. Unsettling. And unforgettable.

He moved on her without reservation. The pull between them was inescapable. He slanted his mouth over hers, flicked his tongue along her upper lip, and nipped the bottom one. Then sucked both hard. She nearly came out of her skin.

He penetrated her mouth with his tongue. A seductive pulse of slow, then fast. Raking the roof of her mouth, then thrusting deep. He was skilled in kissing. She lost herself in the mating rhythm. Her heartbeat sounded in her ears. Her nipples poked her sweatshirt. Her belly warmed. Her skin felt supersensitive. All from a kiss.

She clung to him, not nearly ready for him to release her. He stepped back. She felt frustrated. Uncertain. Far from satisfied.

She touched her lips with her fingers. Fingers that trembled. She drew a deep breath.

His eyes were dilated. A muscle ticked in his cheek.

Neither spoke. Neither looked away.

Calling it a night was a difficult choice. For both of them.

Jake lightly took her by the shoulder and turned her toward her apartment door. "Take the memory of my kiss to bed with you," he said.

His kiss would still be with her in the morning.

Hannah slept little. An hour here and an hour there. She'd tossed and turned and awakened physically stressed, tangled in her top sheet, her pillows on the floor. Her body hummed, physically charged and unfulfilled. Her emotions were stirred up.

She showered, dressed, and hurried downstairs to the café. The lights were on in the kitchen. Her grandmother stood at the prep table, measuring ingredients for the pancake batter into the commercial mixer. Once on the griddle, the pancakes would rise, thick and tasty.

"Morning, sweetie," Gram greeted Hannah. "I hope you slept well. Dolores is already in the dining room. She noticed a line forming at the door. Early birds in need of their caffeine."

Hannah glanced at the kitchen clock. She swung her arms at her sides. Fifteen minutes before service began. "I'm ready to go."

"Are you sure?" Gram eyed her closely. "You've dark circles under your eyes."

Thanks to Jake. She would not admit as much to her grandmother. "I went to bed on a full stomach," she hedged. "I ate too much clam chowder at Gregory's house."

"Chowder can be filling," Gram agreed. "Did you have a good time?"

She'd enjoyed seeing Jake on her return home. "I like Gregory's parents."

Her grandma stopped what she was doing. She'd measured a tablespoon of baking soda but momentarily held off adding it to the batter. "His parents, hon? What about Gregory?"

Hannah shrugged. "I don't think we can move beyond friends."

"Friendship provides a solid basis for a future together."

"I'm sure you're right."

"Although I could be wrong," Gram relented. She pursed her lips, thoughtful. "A long, long time ago the legend sent me a man who made my heart race." Her eyes misted. "Norman gave me goose bumps from across a room. I think of him even now and feel blessed we had fifty incredible years together. I miss him every single day." She swiped at a tear on her cheek. "I want that same love for you."

Hannah went to her, hugged her from the side. "I want a Norman too."

"You will find him, sweet girl. Keep the faith." She went back to work.

Dolores popped her head through the swinging door between the dining room and kitchen, called to Hannah, "Your section is filling up fast. I've served coffee to your regulars. There's a darkly handsome man at the counter requesting you take his order."

She hoped it was Jake. He'd planned a sunrise breakfast before heading to the garage. "On it." She followed Dolores back to the dining room, grabbed an order pad from beside the archaic cash register, and surveyed the diners.

"Darkly handsome" sat tall and broad shouldered on a stool at the far end of the counter. Sipping a cup of coffee. He was dressed all in black. His aviators atop his bandanna. His hair in a short ponytail.

She caught his eye and he stared back. A lingering look that hastened her heart and made her smile. She was glad to see him. She went to take his order. "What can I get for you?" she asked him.

He set down his cup, crooked his finger for her to lean close.

When she did, he whispered against her ear, "You, over easy." Bold and suggestive. Teasingly sexy.

"Not on the menu."

He kept his voice low. "Not even as a breakfast special?"

"Not even." She drew back slowly, so as not to draw attention their way. Too late. A few customers had noticed their exchange but not overheard his request. They were all ears now, curious, hoping he would speak up.

Hannah looked him in the eye, said, "How did you want your egg with the corned beef hash? Poached?"

Jake chuckled deep in his throat. "Good one, Hannah. You got me. I'd prefer three scrambled eggs, grilled ham, and home fries."

"That you will get."

She turned and placed his ticket on the order wheel. Then filled a carafe with freshly brewed coffee and topped off his cup. She wished she could stand and talk to him longer, but she had six tables of customers awaiting her attention. She hustled to take their orders.

Dolores passed her in the aisle with a brief, "Hope you don't mind, but Jake's order came up and I served him for you."

Hannah didn't mind in the least. Jake was a distraction. She couldn't neglect her regulars. The Miltons were her priority. Husband and wife were pushing ninety and lived on their Social Security checks. Often spread thin.

Hannah took extra time with them. She stood by their table and asked, "What would you like for breakfast?"

She was patient as they adjusted their bifocals and debated the menu. "We'd like to split a meal," Helen Milton finally said. "One cheese omelet, marble rye toast, two plates, please."

Hannah placed their order, after adding a few extras. Gram was the soul of generosity and encouraged her waitresses to keep an eye out for those less fortunate. No one left the café hungry. Hannah returned to the Miltons' table with two plated omelets, toast, along with bowls of plump blueberries. Both Miltons patted her arm, thankful.

"It's my birthday, Hannah," announced a middle-aged man, prematurely gray, after he motioned her to his table. He sat alone. Always alone. No friends or family. "I get a free meal, right?" he boasted.

Hal Hanson had ordered the Mariners Platter and eaten every bite. He'd also consumed an extra side of sausage. Nearly a full carafe of coffee. "Didn't we just celebrate your birthday last week?"

He shook his head. All innocence. "No, not mine."

"My mistake then." She pretended to believe him. "I'm going to circle the date on the kitchen calendar, so we remember your birthday next year."

"Circle the date, huh?"

"One birthday a year is enough for anyone," she said. "My grandmother applauds special occasions. Family or work related. I'm sure you'll find something else to celebrate in a month or two."

"That would mean another free meal?"

"Periodically, not frequently." She relented and picked up his breakfast ticket. "On the house, Hal. Have a good one."

The big man rose. "If I were twenty years younger, I'd court you, girl." He left her a quarter tip.

Jake finished his breakfast and came to stand behind her. She sensed his presence before he spoke. "Hanson was hitting on you. Should I consider him competition?"

"Hal's a good man. Despite his white lies for a free meal. He's lonesome and seeks attention. All the waitresses are wise to him." She half smiled. "Although four birthdays in a month is a bit much."

Jake gave her shoulder a light squeeze. "Breakfast tasted

good, but I'd have enjoyed it more if you'd been able to join me. We're both working. I'm headed to the garage. I'll be back to have lunch with Gramps and Moody."

"You know where to find me."

"Where can I find you after four?" he asked, planning ahead.

"At my apartment, reading."

"Read until I arrive. What about supper? Dine out or order in? Your restaurant of choice."

"The café. Gram will feed us."

"What about breakfast in bed?" spoken low.

Tomorrow was her day off. She could sleep in. Or sleep with Jake. "Still proposing over easy?"

"My favorite position."

He left her then. She stared after him, a man larger-than-life who wanted her. Sex would be phenomenal with him. The image of his big naked body in bed stole all thought and left her breathless. Until Dolores brushed by her and said, "Table four is done eating and ready for their check. Table six wants a second order of applejack hotcakes."

Hannah got her rear in gear. The morning hours passed quickly. Lauren arrived for the lunch rush. She glared at Hannah for no good reason. Hannah diligently prepared for the noon customers while her sister showed off her new green skirt suit and handed out menus.

Lauren purposely filled up Hannah's section. All six tables, and not one was open when the major and Moody came in to eat. Hannah sighed her disappointment when Jake showed up and her sister seated all three at Dolores's four-top near the front windows. She removed one chair.

Hannah felt his gaze on her throughout the lunch hour. She warmed, no longer shy or objecting to his outright stare. His dark green gaze was hot and intense. Possessive, if she chose to believe they were a forever couple. It was a nice thought.

The lunch crowd came and went. The tables and booths

turned over quickly. The major and Moody waved to her on their way out of the café. Jake came to her at the counter. He pulled her toward him. Not too close, but close enough to feel his heat. He dropped a kiss on her forehead. Such a kiss meant more to her than if he'd taken her mouth. It was both casual and familiar and perfect for the moment. He winked his good-bye.

Dolores walked past Hannah, put her hand over her heart, and said, "No man deserves to be that good-looking."

Hannah agreed. He had a raw-edge appeal. Women did a double take. He brought silly grins to their faces even when they didn't feel like smiling. Their hearts beat faster. Tummies tingled. Sighs rose from the breast. Tangible arousal. They fantasized intimacy.

She was deep in her private thoughts when Lauren cornered her by the soda and ice machines. The confrontation was unexpected and jarring. The space barely fit one but squeezed in two. Lauren clutched a stack of menus to her chest. Her color was high, her tone resentful, as she attacked Jake's integrity with swift and frenzied words. "He's not into you. He's all about himself. I'm warning you off a man who could break your heart."

Hannah was taken aback. She listened, maintaining a degree of skepticism. She'd faced off with her sister countless times over the smallest issues. Jake was a big deal to Hannah. A part of her recognized Lauren's jealousy, perversely misplaced and ongoing. Jake had once dumped her and bruised her pride. She'd been the center of gossip for months afterward. Lauren had never forgiven him. She now took her anger out on Hannah. It was inexcusable and groundless, but understandable.

Hannah kept her voice even. "Your reason for discrediting Jake?"

"He doesn't do long hauls."

"Maybe not a lifetime, but we're living in the present and enjoying each other's company right now."

"He could leave town any second."

"That's your opinion only."

"Don't think you can hold him here. You don't have what it takes."

"And you did?" She should've bitten her tongue.

Lauren fluttered the edges of the menus with her fingers. Halfheartedly said, "I let Jake go and got Grant."

Hannah seized the positive. "You're very fortunate. Grant is a fine man." Her praise of her sister's husband slowed Lauren's rant. "You have three adorable boys."

"A husband and sons," Lauren stated. "A family."

"Lucky you. You have it all."

"More than you."

"Maybe someday I'll have what you have."

"Not with Jake," she asserted. "Despite what you may think, he really isn't all that. I'm speaking from experience. Cut his long hair, take away his biker's jacket and Ducati, and he's any townie off the street."

"He's smart and strong and his own person."

"Whatever." Lauren and her menus turned to leave.

One step, and she faced their grandmother. Neither of them had heard her approach. There she stood, arms crossed over her kitchen whites, disapproval in her eyes.

Lauren turned pale. "How much did you hear?"

"You tell me."

Hannah and Lauren traded a look. In spite of their disagreements, they remained sisters. Hannah characteristically apologized first, even if it wasn't her fault.

Lauren surprised her this time and spoke first. "I was interfering in Hannah's love life."

Gram raised an eyebrow. "Hannah has a love life?"

"She might if I left her alone."

"Then leave her alone," said Gram.

"I was warning her off Jake," admitted Lauren.

"Whatever for?" Gram wanted to know.

"I knew Jake *when*," said Lauren.

"I know him *now*," Hannah inserted.

"I was trying to be a good sister," added Lauren. "He could leave her. Break her heart."

"Or not," said Gram. "History doesn't always repeat itself." An objective observation.

She narrowed her gaze on one sister, then the other. "You're too old to be bickering over boys."

*No boy in Jake*, Hannah reflected. He was all man.

"Are we done here?" Gram demanded. "I've biscuits in the oven."

"I'm good," said Lauren.

"Fine too," agreed Hannah.

"Finish your shifts in peace," the older woman concluded. "Mind your personal business. Live and let live." She headed back to the kitchen.

The sisters went their separate ways.

Hannah exhaled, suddenly tired. Dealing with her sister stole her energy. Lauren's good intentions were debatable. Hannah looked forward to seeing Jake later in the day. No chaos around the man. He had a calming presence.

The day sped by for Jake. He'd returned to the garage after lunch at the café with his granddad and Moody, mildly disappointed that Hannah hadn't been their waitress. Leave it to Lauren to seat them at a table not in her sister's section. A typical move by a woman who took jealousy to the extreme. Jake believed she loved her husband, Grant, but her pride at his rejection years ago still made her bitter. She didn't know when to let go. He hoped she'd come to realize the foolishness of her actions.

He was presently under the hood of the Range Rover when footsteps approached him. He expected Mac, only to glance over his shoulder and find Gregory Manor instead. The man was well dressed in a light blue button-down and navy slacks. Polished wingtips. He carried a trench coat over his arm. His attire was better suited to an office than a garage. Jake wondered what the hell he might want.

He straightened, set down his wrench, and wiped his hands on a work rag. Greg might well be a good customer, so he went with polite. "If you're looking for Mac, he's in the office," he directed the attorney.

"It's you I'm wanting to see."

"See me then."

"We need to talk," he confronted Jake.

*About what?* Jake wondered. He had no business with this man. "I'm working—can't it wait?"

"That's my Range Rover."

"I need to change the air filter and I'm done."

"Take a break. I'm in no hurry on the tune-up."

Jake leaned back against the door panel. Crossed his arms over his chest. He took a dim view of Greg. "Speak to me."

"It's about Hannah."

"I won't talk about my woman."

"Your woman." Greg was visibly set back. "Since when?"

"Since I arrived in town."

"You've been here a short time."

"Long enough."

"What are your intentions toward her?"

"What is your interest in my interest in her?"

"I'm fond of her."

The man had balls. Jake kept his feelings for Hannah to himself. He'd come to several realizations overnight. He needed to sort through them with her before anyone else. He kept quiet.

Greg didn't deal well with silence. "Hannah and I had a date last night. She's close to my family."

"Family is important." Jake gave him that much.

"Back off, Kaylor," was more a demand than a request. "You distract her. She loses focus on our future."

"On your life together?" It was the first he'd heard.

"I've serious intent."

Rather presumptuous. "Hannah feels the same?"

"She will when you're out of the picture."

Jake had heard enough. "I'm here to stay." And left it at that. He'd witnessed Hannah's return from dinner and game night. There wasn't much chance of a permanent relationship with Greg. She hadn't even let the man kiss her.

Jake directed their conversation back to the Range Rover. "Fifteen minutes and you can drive off." *Good riddance.*

Greg huffed, "Mind my words." He stormed off. Profanity echoed in the bay. No legalese. He might be used to winning cases in court, but he'd lost his argument in the garage.

Jake again focused on the SUV and finished the tune-up in ten. He lowered the hood and stepped away from the vehicle.

"Done for the day," he called to Mac Morrison on his way out. He'd returned his tools to their proper places and swept the bay. Time to fly.

He wasn't physically tired, but Greg had ridden his last nerve. He disliked a man who claimed a woman without her permission. Hannah was her own person. Greg believed their childhood closeness would automatically lead to marriage. Not in the adult world.

Jake stopped in the café before heading upstairs to Hannah's apartment. They'd agreed to dine in. Lauren had clocked out for the day, but Dolores was still waiting tables. He asked her to take his order. The chalkboard listed the early-bird special: a cup of seafood bisque, baked jumbo shrimp, wild rice, and a slice of lemon meringue pie. "Two specials," he decided. He remembered Hannah's affection for cake. "Lemon meringue for me and replace the other pie with a big piece of—"

Dolores winked at him. "Blueberry butter cake?" She recognized his dining partner.

"Thanks." There were a handful of customers in the café. No one he knew. So he walked to the wide front window and stared out at the street. There was a sameness about Moonbright, a day-to-day predictability and certain peace that appealed to him. Traffic flowed steadily, no evening rush hour. Those on the sidewalk waved pleasantly to one another at the end of the workday. All calming benefits of a small town.

Moonbright had opened his heart. Hannah had too. Time meant little to their relationship. They'd set the groundwork and would grow and love together. They had much to discuss.

Dolores came to him in a matter of minutes. She handed him a zipped carryout food warmer along with two plastic containers for the desserts. "No charge. Nan wishes you a good evening. I wish you a night to remember."

He gave Dolores a sizeable tip. She pressed her hand over her heart in thanks. He didn't want to impose on the kitchen staff, so he walked back outside, around the corner, and took the exterior staircase to the second floor. The fried-fish sandwich he'd had for lunch hadn't stuck with him. The aroma of the seafood made his mouth water and his stomach growl. He hastened his steps.

Hannah was waiting for him in the sitting room attached to the tiny kitchen in her apartment. She set her book aside and smiled her welcome from the roll-armed sofa upholstered in brown fabric. The enticement of food drew her up and to the round café-style table. She looked fresh and cute in a peach waffle pullover and laddered jeans. Wool socks. No shoes.

He shrugged off his leather jacket. Removed his aviators and set them on the tabletop out of the way. Together he and Hannah unloaded the carryout and plastic containers. Careful of the steaming bowls of bisque and the jumbo shrimp. The smell enticed them. They both breathed deeply.

Hannah opened a plastic container and bounced on her toes. "Cake." A happy sound from a hungry woman. "Thank you," heartfelt. She nodded toward the mini-fridge. "Iced tea okay?"

"Fine, but don't pour mine just yet," he said. "I smell like an oil change. Let me grab a quick shower."

"You expect me to hold off eating?"

"You'd start without me?"

"On dessert."

He grinned. "Be my guest."

She unwrapped a set of silverware, scored a fork, and dug in without him. A big bite of cake and a low moan followed him across the room. He stopped at the bathroom door, looked back, and declared, "There's something you need to know before I forget."

She paused mid-bite. Set down her fork. "You look serious."

"I had a visitor at work today." Jake figured someone in the area would've seen Greg at Morrison's Garage. It was obvious the man hated his guts. His resentment festered. Greg would bad-mouth Jake to anyone who would listen. He sought to relay their talk to Hannah before the gossip made the rounds.

Her gaze was questioning. "Who stopped by to see you?"

"Your buddy Greg."

"What did he want?"

"You."

"Oh." She was startled. "What did you tell him?"

"That you were my woman." He wasn't certain how she'd react.

Fortunately, her response was positive and in his favor. "I rather like that, if it's true."

He flattened his hand on his chest. "Heart-swear."

"I believe you." She cleared her throat. "Full disclosure, I have something to share with you too."

"Go for it. My shower can wait."

She scrunched her nose. "Lauren confronted me about your sincerity this afternoon. My sister warned me off you. She swore you'd leave me and never look back."

"How did that make you feel?"

"I felt sorrier for her than worried for me. She has a jealous streak. Gram intervened and indicated history didn't always repeat itself. I believe that to be true."

"Faith in me is good."

"I've something else as well." She rested her elbows on the tabletop, steepled her fingers. "I've come to a decision. A major one for me. For us. I no longer care about the outcome of the Halloween legend. My feelings for you are stronger than any Moonbright lore. I trust and believe in us, together."

He whistled low. This was huge. "I like your decision."

"I thought you might."

"You're absolutely sure?" He knew what the legend meant to the ladies of Moonbright. He didn't want Hannah to break from tradition, not even for him. "No regrets down the road, babe?"

"I'm positive, Jake," she said with conviction.

Fortune had been kind. She'd chosen him over tradition. And over her history with Greg. Relief sent him back to where she sat. He leaned down, kissed her full on the mouth. Parted lips and lots of tongue. He wished he could wrap his arms around her, pull her flush against him, but not before he'd cleaned up.

"Don't go anywhere," he requested.

She wouldn't. She had cake.

He stripped down in the bathroom. He'd need to locate a laundromat fairly soon. The longer he stayed in town, the more work clothes he would need. He'd noticed a Work Warehouse north of Morrison's Garage. Advertising construction clothing, automotive uniforms and gear. He'd make a few purchases soon.

A warm shower, fast scrub, and he toweled dry. He retrieved a fresh black T-shirt and jeans from his apartment, got dressed. Then stood at the sink and studied his reflection in the mirror. His granddad had called him scruffy, which he couldn't deny. He wasn't yet sure where his night with Hannah might take them. There would be kissing. Stubble abraded tender skin.

He decided to shave. There'd be no whisker burn on his woman. His jaw was soon smooth. The ends of his hair flicked against his neck. He hadn't cut it in years. He withdrew a short pair of scissors from his shaving kit and clicked them together. A lengthy debate.

He had no idea what possessed him to trim off an inch, then another, up to four. The strands fell into the sink. He hadn't worn his hair this short since high school. He wasn't a barber, but the mirror reflected a decent attempt. He'd set up an appointment at Theodore's Barbershop later in the week. To even the ends.

He wasn't sure how Hannah would receive him. She'd taken to him rough. He was still himself but looked different. More groomed and respectable. A look he could live with.

He cleaned up the sink. Then scored a couple condoms from his shaving kit. Prepared for the night ahead. He returned to the kitchen. There he waited for Hannah to look up from her last bite of cake.

She never met his gaze. She glanced to the side instead. He observed her closely. A sudden flash from the lenses on his aviators left him guarded. He wouldn't have believed it, had he not seen it. The distinctive glint gave him pause.

Hannah witnessed it too. She reacted as if in a trance. She

reached across the table, pinched the bridge on his shades, and held them at eye level. She stared and stared into the lenses. Seconds ticked by as her gaze shifted between the sunglasses and him. Disbelievingly.

Time stretched. Until she blinked, trembled, and her eyes misted. She set his aviators aside and a sob escaped on a hiccup. Tears fell on her cheeks.

Jake felt helpless. He crossed to the table, pulled up a chair beside her, and drew her close. He stroked her hair, massaged the back of her neck. Comforted her. She sniffled, dabbed at her face with a napkin. Her eyes were puffy, her nose red. Her smile was watery.

"You're not going to believe what just happened," she said.

"I could guess, but you tell me."

She did so. "Total transparency. The lenses gleamed and mirrored my husband."

She'd gotten clarification, he realized. "That man would be?"

"You, Jake. You are my future." She explained, "On Halloween you had long hair and stubble. The murky profile showed a clean-cut man. You've since cut your hair. Shaved. A big difference. The reflection was of you, as you are now. According to the legend, you are the man for me. That's why I lost it. Happy tears."

Legendary approval. He let her words sink in. Most important to him was that she'd chosen him before she'd seen that second vision. Which proved how much she loved him. She'd had no doubts. He might just become a believer after all.

He cupped her face in his hands. "You are amazing and so incredibly beautiful."

"You've always been hot." She admired him. "But your new haircut makes you a heartbreaker."

"I'd never break your heart."

"I'll hold you to that."

They both agreed that dinner could be reheated as a midnight snack. They craved each other now. Food was quickly stored in the refrigerator. He noticed a copy of the newspaper and a heart-shaped rock on the corner of the kitchen counter.

"What are these?" he asked, curious.

"I'm storing memories for my scrapbook," she softly said. "The article and photo on the parade, along with the rock from the park. We can now add your aviators to my collectibles. Important mementoes to me."

Significant to him too. Emotion felt hot and thick in his throat. He hugged her tight, said, "Love wasn't something I went out and looked for. The parade brought us together. We were destined." He grinned then. "We have the legend's blessing. Let's make a future. Marry me, Hannah Allan."

She nodded against his chest. Spoke into his shirt, "You and me. Together always."

Always started now. No words were needed as to where they would make love. Her bedroom was closer than his. Mere steps away.

Feminine and floral came to Jake's mind when he entered her room. Her space was decorated in soft peach and mauve tones. A corner armoire, overstuffed chair, and bedside table finished the room. They stood at the foot of her bed. Anticipation touched them both, a sensual pull and stirring promise. He made the sex all about Hannah. Wanting the very best for her.

He began by touching her with her clothes on. Then gently taking them off. He encouraged her to do the same for him. Until they were both naked.

His hands were steady.

Hers shook.

"I've only done this once before," she admitted.

"More than once for me."

"You've more experience."

"You're keeping up just fine, sweetheart."

He introduced her to him slowly. A hard man showing his

soft side. A slight shift of his shoulders and he grasped her hips. She was a small woman. Delicately boned. Their thighs brushed and his sex pressed her belly, as their bodies became acquainted.

She raised her hands between them. Skimming her fingers over the cut and contour of his muscles, then tracing the arrow of his chest hair down to his groin. He liked her hands on him. Tentative and appreciative. She squeezed his length. His throat constricted. He moaned.

The moment was seamless, timeless. He took great pleasure in foreplay. Kissing her gently. Then again with thrusting intent. Mating with her mouth and mimicking sex. Her lips were sugary from the cake, and the flavor of blueberries lingered on her tongue. They kissed for a very long time.

Until she embraced him fully. She wrapped her arms about his neck and pulled him close. She nuzzled his collarbone, kissed his throat, and then placed a kiss over his heart. His rough hands were tender on her smooth skin. He outlined her nipples and stroked the underside of her breasts with care. They explored each other with thoroughness.

His fingers wandered, worked their way across her stomach, hand-spanned her hips, and then traced the sensitive crease between her thighs and torso, stopping short of her sweet spot. She shivered, grew restless. Nearly ready for him.

Jake scored a condom from the pocket of his jeans. He ripped the foil with his teeth, was quick to cover himself, smoothing out the latex. He took her to bed and drew her down with him. He settled over her, set his knees, and eased her legs apart. She pushed up, offered herself to him. A calculated shift of his hips and he entered her. Careful not to crush her. He was twice her weight in muscle and doubly strong. They still fit as if made for each other.

She hugged him close. He buried his face in her hair. Her

neck. Breathed in her scent. Aroused woman and feminine musk.

They moved together.

Uninhibited and indulgent.

Power and pleasure.

He thrust, and she throbbed.

She arched against him.

He strained against her.

A sensation hit him that he hadn't expected.

A sense of oneness settled in his soul.

His rhythmic pace coaxed her, drove her higher.

They climbed fast and were suddenly there.

They came undone.

Both stiffening.

Both shattering.

Both boneless. Mindless. Replete.

He was drained. She was exhausted. However, they weren't too tired to eat. Their shrimp dinners called them to the kitchen. He rose, disposed of his condom. Then slid on his jeans. She donned a short cotton robe. They heated the meals and ate in intimate silence. He split his piece of lemon meringue pie with her.

They sat for a long time. Hannah was something to stare at with her tousled hair, kiss-swollen lips, and sexy serenity. Her robe slipped off one shoulder. Baring her collarbone and the top of her breasts. She did it for him. He'd never felt so relaxed in his life. Never more satisfied. Never more hot for a woman.

They held hands, kissed often, and discussed their future.

"Long or short engagement?" he initiated.

"Six months."

He groaned. Seemed like forever. "I'll need to get you a ring."

"It's not necessary. I have you."

"It's important to me, Hannah," he told her. "I actually have one in mind. How do you feel about vintage jewelry?"

"Classic and lovely," she returned. "I often browse Keepsake Antiques. There's a history behind each gem."

"I have such a ring if you're interested. A family heirloom."

She was attentive. Intrigued.

"We'd need to go to Bangor for you to see it," he said. "We can visit my parents and brother then too. Share our good news. My mother recently handed down my great-grandmother's engagement ring, in hopes I would marry someday. It's stored in a safety deposit box at the bank." He recalled the jeweler's description. "A two-carat round diamond with double-halo accents styled in a filigree setting. I want you to have it if you like the design."

She placed her hand over her heart. "How exquisite. I'd love to see it."

"The ring would look good on your finger." She had slender fingers. Short, clear-polished nails. "We'll pick out our wedding bands together."

She nodded her agreement.

"Our wedding?" he next asked.

Her smile was sweet. "Large. I grew up in Moonbright. I know everyone. I couldn't exclude a soul."

His gut clenched. He wasn't one for public displays. Crowds closed in on him. But he could live with the townsfolk for one day. He gave in, for her. "When and where?" came next.

"Spring. Outside when the air is crisp and cool, at the gazebo in the park. It gets a fresh coat of paint every April."

Lots of room at the park for the guests. "Where will we live?"

"We can start out above the café."

"A bit cramped, babe."

"I like being close to you."

"Close it is then."

"Your motorcycle business?"

"Clients will find me. I can work anywhere." He'd thought to rent a bay from Mac Morrison. At least at the outset.

"When do we share our news with Gram, the major, and Moody?"

He'd let her decide. "Whenever you're ready. Just not tonight. I want you all to myself."

They soon cleared away the dishes. Bed called to them again. They went willingly. They stripped down and spooned for hours. He tucked her so tightly against his body, she became an imprint on his skin. A sensual tattoo, invisible, yet memorable.

They dozed sporadically, woke, and made love. The more they had sex, the more they wanted each other. They were that good together. His condom supply dwindled. They kissed until their lips were numb. Until neither could draw a full breath. Until they wore themselves out and sleep drew them deep.

Seven thirty, and sunlight creased the window shade. A flickering of rays across Hannah's cheek and Jake's bare chest. He blinked awake. She peered at him through heavy lids. It was her day off. Jake was in no hurry to get to the garage. He could call Mac and skip work, if he so chose. He'd just gotten engaged. Mac would understand.

Life felt lazy, no worries, just the two of them holed up in bed. She lay fully across him, hugging him tightly, as if she'd never let him go. The feel of her calmed him. He'd never felt such peace. Such hope. Or so much love.

His stomach gave a growl. Food crossed his mind. So did fooling around. The latter won. Without question.

Hannah lifted her head, licked her lips. "Breakfast in bed?"

He deftly eased her onto her back. Then rolled atop her. She yielded beneath him. So soft. So warm. So willing. "Love over easy, babe."

"Double that order."

*Love Rising*


# STACY FINZ

*For my husband, Jaxon Van Derbeken*

# Chapter 1

*What . . . the . . . hell?*

The screeching noise was so incessant Sydney bolted straight up from her grandmother's bed. At first, she thought it was a bad dream. A buzz saw running rampant through the little town of Moonbright, Maine. She didn't need Freud to know that the buzz saw represented the current state of her life.

But now, wide awake, she realized the noise, which also included a pounding that reverberated through the walls, was no dream. Just your garden-variety construction nightmare. It was happening all over San Francisco, where new buildings were going up faster than jetliners over the bay.

But in Moonbright?

She threw her covers off and padded to the window. There was a red pickup truck parked in the driveway, and the carriage house doors were flung wide open. Syd grabbed the first things her hands touched in her suitcase, dressed, and flew downstairs, straight out the back door.

There was a man tearing out the walls of Gram's beloved crafts room.

"Excuse me," she shouted over the hammering and Mick Jagger wailing that he couldn't get any satisfaction. "Excuse me!"

The man whirled around, took a longer than necessary look at her, and grinned.

"I guess you don't remember me."

She remembered him all right. Right up to the moment when . . . well, she'd gotten the thankless jerk through his junior year of Algebra II. Except Nick Rossi was no longer a high school student. The once rangy teenager had turned into a full-fledged man. There were now a few crow's-feet dancing around those chocolaty brown eyes of his, and the broad shoulders she'd once ogled in math class had doubled in width.

Even in the brisk autumn air, he wore only a white, slightly damp T-shirt that clung to his chest like a second skin. He still had that thick head of wavy brown hair, though. Not like Gage, who by the time they'd broken up had started a regular regime of Rogaine.

"My dad retired," Nick said. "My brothers and I took over Rossi Construction about two years ago."

Okay. But that didn't explain why he was destroying the carriage house.

"What's going on here?" She pointed at the walls or, rather, lack of them.

The question seemed to surprise him, judging by the look on his face, which was a combination of mystification and *you're joshing me, right?* "I'm installing the kitchen Stella wanted."

Kitchen? The Victorian already had a kitchen. And Stella . . . was dead.

"I think we'd better start at the beginning because I have no idea what you're talking about. Why don't we go inside?" In her haste, she'd forgotten a jacket and was cold. October in California was still like summer. Not so much in Maine.

He nodded, rubbed the stubble on his chin, and followed her to the kitchen. "I know it's only a short time since the funeral. But the last time Stella and I talked . . . before she, uh, passed . . . she was in a rush to get it done."

*What done?*

"I guess that's where we need to start," Syd said. "Gram never said a word to me about turning the carriage house into a kitchen." Gram loved to cook, but a second kitchen seemed a little excessive for an elderly woman suffering from cancer. Not to mention that for years the spacious granny unit had been Gram's refuge, a place where she'd gone to sew and work on her many craft projects.

Nick shrugged. "I don't know what to tell you. But if you'd like to see the contract, I've got it in my truck."

"Yes, I'd like to see it." She crossed her arms over her chest.

He blinked at her in surprise, then became a little less congenial. "What? You think I made the whole thing up? That I get my jollies sneaking into people's homes and rebuilding them for shits and giggles?"

"I don't know; do you? What I do know is there is absolutely no reason my grandmother would've wanted to turn her carriage house into a kitchen." She'd had pancreatic cancer, not a brain tumor.

Nick snorted, turned on his heel, and returned a short time later with the contract. At the bottom of the paperwork was Gram's signature, clear as day. "You happy?"

No, she wasn't happy. Why would Gram have done this without consulting with Syd? They were as close as mother and daughter. Syd had traversed the country ten times in the last year to be with Stella in her final days and not once had she mentioned converting the carriage house. Hell, if she'd wanted a new kitchen, why not remodel this one? Syd glanced around the room, noting all the ways it could be updated.

Other than adding a few modern appliances, her grandparents had kept the kitchen the same as when they had purchased the Victorian more than fifty years ago.

She let out a deep breath. "I don't know what to say. This has caught me completely off guard. Obviously, a second kitchen is no longer necessary. And of course I'll pay you to put everything back the way it was."

Nick rubbed his jaw. "Yeah, that's a problem."

"Why's that?"

"Because your grandmother paid me in full and I've spent a good chunk of the money on lumber, cabinets, materials, and appliances."

"Can't that stuff be returned?"

He stared at her as if she'd lost her mind. "The things are custom for the job, so, no, I can't return them."

This was certainly a conundrum. One Syd didn't need, considering all the other complications in her life. Besides her losing the most important person in her world, her ex-boyfriend had just announced his engagement to Syd's former assistant. On top of that, Syd was knee-deep in starting a new business.

"Well then, just put them in here." Syd thought the idea inspired. It would kill two birds with one stone—restore the carriage house back to a granny flat and spruce up the Victorian's dated kitchen. "I'd like to get the house listed, and bringing the kitchen into the twenty-first century might help sell it."

"Oh," he said, taken aback. "I'd assumed you'd be staying."

She couldn't fathom what had given him that idea. Syd had hightailed it out of Moonbright right after graduation. Sure, she'd come back often to visit her grandmother, but small-town life wasn't for her. After culinary school, Syd had preferred the hustle and bustle of San Francisco, a foodie mecca and the perfect location for her bakery, Bread & Cie. She was already scouting sites for a second bakery and was hoping for a grand opening to coincide with the release of her first cookbook.

"No," she said. "I'm just here for a few weeks, enough time to deal with my grandmother's estate." She glanced up at the peeling plaster on the ceiling where there'd been a leak from the upstairs bathroom. "So it's settled. We'll just do the work in here and I'll reimburse you for whatever you've done so far on the carriage house."

Nick gazed at the furniture-style cabinets and the old farm sink. "What part of 'custom' didn't you understand? None of the stuff your grandmother ordered will fit in here. The ovens alone would take up a third of the space."

"Do you like being difficult?" He certainly had in high school.

He threw up his arms. "Who's being difficult here? Stella hired me to do a job, and I'm following through with my obligation." He rubbed his hand down the back of his head and searched the room until his eyes fell on the coffeemaker. "You mind if I make a pot? I think we could both use a cup of coffee to figure this out."

"I'll make it." She rifled through the cupboard, found a bag of ground beans, turned on the machine, and got down two mugs. Nick didn't strike her as a cream and sugar kind of guy, so she served him his coffee black. He motioned for her to take a seat at the small table.

"Isn't there any way you can just make it work?" she said. "Cut down the cabinets if you have to."

Nick frowned. "The stuff for the carriage house is sleek and all commercial grade. I don't think your grandmother would've wanted that for here. The house is original. We should keep it that way. Then there's the small issue that I was hired by your grandmother, not you. And she wanted the kitchen in the carriage house."

Syd bristled at his presumptuousness, but the truth was Stella Byrne had loved this house like her own child. And while the upkeep had become too much for her in the last decade, she had preserved the Victorian as one did a piece of treasured history. With respect and affection.

"Did she tell you why she wanted a commercial grade kitchen?" The whole thing baffled Syd.

"Only that she had big plans for Moonbright and that she was keeping things under wraps until she got further along in the process."

"When? When did she tell you that?"

"Two months ago."

That was crazy. Three months ago, she had received her diagnosis. Pancreatic adenocarcinoma.

"She wanted me to get going on it as soon as possible," Nick said. "I kind of got the impression that it was her . . . you know."

"Dying wish?"

He nodded, his expression solemn. "We were just waiting on permits. And now that I've got them, I'm gonna finish the job."

She wanted to say that he wasn't the boss here. She was. But it would only sound childish. Furthermore, she didn't want to go against her grandmother's wishes, even if she was flying blind to the reason for them. It just seemed so wasteful to build a commercial kitchen in a residential property. Unless Syd sold the house to a restaurateur—the chances being slim to none—it made more sense to leave the carriage house as a spare room. That way the family who bought the place could use the granny flat for anything they wanted.

She blew out a breath. "Do you have an inventory of the materials I can see?" Maybe it would give her a clue about her grandmother's intentions.

"It's back at the office. I can get it for you." He paused, then said, "Stella was explicit that there was a plan for all of it. I'm sure if you did a little poking around, you could find out what she had in mind."

Syd didn't need Nick Rossi's condescending advice. She was about to tell him that when she thought better of it. Why spare the energy? Of course she planned to *poke* around. The question was where? If Gram hadn't told Syd her plans, whom had she told? "In the meantime, get me that list?" She rifled through her purse and shoved a business card at him.

"Yes, ma'am." Nick dropped his own card on the counter.

"Great, then I'll let you clean up." She leaned her head in the direction of the carriage house in a not-so-subtle hint. "I'm sure you have other things to do today."

She walked him to the door, then poured herself another cup of coffee. The temperature had dipped into the forties and she turned up the thermostat, pondering what to do about breakfast. In San Francisco she had a plethora of options, including her own bakery, which served a mean scone. Here in Moonbright, the locals were most likely to eat at the Corner Café, a family-owned restaurant and Gram's favorite. The café's whoopie pie was off the charts. And everything else on the menu had that delicious hearty homespun quality that San Francisco's chichi restaurants and coffeehouses lacked.

But it was the morning before the town's big Halloween parade and the Corner Café would be a zoo. Syd wasn't up for seeing Gram's friends and neighbors so soon after the funeral. Though Gram had been sick for a long time and her passing hadn't been unexpected, Syd was still grieving.

She grabbed some eggs from the fridge and found a package of English muffins in the bread box. Comfort food for a chilly autumn morning. She'd just begun to whisk a little cream into her bowl of eggs when the racket started all over again.

"What the . . . ?"

She peered out the window. Nick was on the roof of the carriage house with a circular saw. She rushed out the back door.

"Hey," she called up to him, but he couldn't hear her over the noise. She scurried up the ladder. "Hey!"

That caught his attention and he turned off the saw. "What's up?"

"I thought we decided to wait on this until I saw the materials list."

"I thought I told you that Stella hired me to do a job and that I planned to see it through."

"Are you serious? You can't even give me a day to digest this cockamamie scheme or find out why Gram hired you in the first place?"

He pointed at his watch. "Time is money. So nope."

She would have ordered him off her property if it weren't for the fact that she didn't legally own it yet. Until Gram's estate was settled, everything had to go through Stella's lawyer. And Syd would be damned before she bothered the man over stupid Nick Rossi.

"Well, then, keep it down. I have work to do." She started to get down from the ladder when it swayed.

Nick steadied it before she toppled to the ground, and hauled her up onto the roof. "Sit. Otherwise you're liable to kill yourself." He grabbed the spot next to her. "You're still pissed at me, aren't you?"

"Over what?" She pretended not to know what he was talking about, because only a loser would hold a grudge that long over something so petty. So ridiculous. Besides, it was ages ago. She was a successful businesswoman now, not a lonely teenage girl.

He searched her face, trying to determine whether she was telling the truth. Apparently satisfied that she was, he said, "Syd, I'm just trying to do the right thing here. This was important to Stella. I don't know why she wanted a commercial kitchen in her carriage house, but she did. Enough so that she paid me in advance because she knew she wouldn't be around to see it finished. I won't renege on the deal she and I made. When it's done you can pull it all out if that's what you want to do. Sell everything on Craigslist. But I'm not walking away until I've fulfilled my promise."

She couldn't argue with his dedication, even though she wanted to.

"I just want my grandmother back." She squeezed her eyes shut, valiantly trying to stop a flow of tears.

"I'm sorry about Stella, Sydney. We all were. In fact, I don't remember a funeral that well attended in Moonbright in a long time. That's how special she was."

Had he been there? The day had passed in such a devastating haze that Syd could barely recall the service, let alone the attendees. She'd moved through the postfuneral reception, accepting condolences like a ghost.

"Thank you," she said, her voice near a whisper.

They sat there for a long time, neither of them speaking. Syd tried to collect herself, but being back in Moonbright only served as a reminder of all that she had lost. First her parents sixteen years ago. And now Stella.

The sooner she left this town the better.

Nick's phone beeped, breaking the silence. He studied what seemed to be a text and said, "Today's your lucky day. I've got to put out a fire at another job site. So you've got a reprieve until Monday."

He got up and readjusted the ladder. "I'll go first and hold it for you. Promise me you won't break your neck. Last thing I need is for my insurance premiums to go through the roof."

She gave him a dirty look, then followed him down the ladder. When she landed on the middle rung, he hooked her around the waist, lifted her into the air, and gently dropped her on solid ground. *Show-off*, Syd silently muttered to herself. But an unwanted tingle went up her spine just the same.

She stood to the side of the driveway as Nick packed up his stuff and locked up the carriage house.

"See you at the parade tomorrow," he called over his shoulder as he headed to his truck, his tool belt hugging a slim pair of denim-encased hips.

*The parade.*

She hadn't planned on going, which was sacrilege in Moonbright. Every year, the entire town gathered for the big event, a processional of costumed locals that included everyone from the high school marching band to fifth-generation families. The Macy's parade it was not. But it was Moonbright's thing the way the Bay to Breakers was San Francisco's. Gram—Gramps, too, when he was alive—had loved it, planning and sewing her costume months in advance.

Perhaps it would be good to get out, Sydney thought as she watched Nick drive away. An opportunity to ask around about Gram's kitchen. She'd avoid Nick Rossi like a colonoscopy.

Last she'd heard, he'd gotten engaged to Jennifer Gerard, his high school sweetheart. Back then, Jen had been voted the girl most likely to become a movie star. Tough to do from tiny Moonbright, Maine. Syd guessed Nick Rossi was Jen's consolation prize, such as it was.

Unfortunately, for the next few weeks he was going to be the bane of Syd's existence.

# Chapter 2

Nick passed the Corner Café and Bellaluna's Bakeshop on his way home that evening, pondering the wisdom of stopping for takeout. But parade prep, including blocking off the main route, was in full swing and finding a parking space would be a bitch. Quicker to pop leftovers in the microwave.

He bypassed the chaos, taking a side street to the east side of town where his small Cape Cod was nestled in a tidy, tree-lined neighborhood of modest homes. It was a far cry from the colonial he and Jen had shared on one of Moonbright's most prestigious streets. And to tell the truth, he hadn't done much to keep up the little house. The shutters were rotting, the paint on the siding chipping, and soon he'd need a new roof. What was the saying about the cobbler's kids having no shoes?

Rossi Construction was so busy he barely had time to eat and sleep, let alone do work on his own house. Things were supposed to let up in fall with the bad weather, but the jobs kept coming. Everyone wanted a kitchen redo or a bathroom makeover in time for the holidays. But hey, it was good for Nick's bank account, so he wasn't complaining.

He'd actually been looking forward to Stella's job. Not so much because the work interested him but because he'd always been fond of the old woman who'd defied age. Hell, the last time he'd seen Stella, she'd been dancing in her kitchen to a Guns N' Roses song. Only in the last few weeks of her life had she shown the ravages of cancer.

*She would've been a lot nicer to work with than her damn granddaughter, who still walked around with a stick up her ass and a severe superiority complex. Just like in high school. The only thing that had changed about her was her looks.*

Sydney freaking Byrne had surprised the hell out of him at the funeral. As a kid she'd been what you would call a late bloomer. Gangly and awkward. She'd come to live with her grandmother after the deaths of her parents. Her mother and father had slid off the road near Portland in a snowstorm and had wrapped their car around a tree. Syd's dad had grown up in Moonbright and the entire town mourned the couple's death. But Sydney never fit in.

She'd left right after high school, and except for the times Stella talked about her, Nick hadn't given her too much thought. But after he laid eyes on her two weeks ago, she'd taken up considerable space in his late-night fantasies. All those supple curves and those big blue eyes.

Today, it had only taken his short meeting with Syd to squelch those fantasies. She was as difficult as he remembered.

He pulled into his narrow driveway and flicked on the heat as soon as he got inside. Another day had passed with his forgetting to call the chimney sweep company his family used. The reason he'd bought the house was for the fireplace, which according to the inspection hadn't been cleaned in at least three years. On a night like this, a drink in front of a toasty fire would've been a nice end to a long and frustrating day.

Instead, he nuked some leftover lasagna. After dinner, he got the inventory list Syd had asked for from his truck, snapped a picture, and texted it to her. The woman was a giant pain in his rear end. It wasn't his fault that Stella hadn't discussed the kitchen project with Syd. Nor was it his fault that he was sticking to his and Stella's agreement. What did Syd expect? That he would break his promise to a dying woman? If he didn't know better, he'd think the real issue was that Syd was still holding a grudge from sixteen years ago.

The next day, Nick ventured out of his office to take in the parade. Thirty-two years and he hadn't missed one. According to his mother, he'd watched his first parade from a baby carriage. Now his nieces and nephews, at least the ones old enough to walk, marched in the ragtag processional dressed as ghosts and goblins and superheroes. It was cute as hell.

He spied Hannah Allan in the sea of crazy dressed as Little Bo Peep and gave her a wave. Her family owned the Corner Café, an institution in Moonbright. They'd gone to school together and Hannah now helped out at the café.

"Hey, what do you know? It lives." Nick's brother Sal smacked him on the back. "I thought you'd chained yourself to the desk."

Nick gave Sal a one-finger salute. "Where's Rory and the kids?"

Sal pointed across the street where his wife, dressed as Daenerys Targaryen, and Nick's niece and nephew—both dragons, of course—waited to be given the signal to join the parade.

"Where's your costume?" Nick asked.

"You're looking at it." Sal spread his arms wide. "It's called overworked contractor."

Nick snorted. "You and me both."

"How'd it go at the Byrne place yesterday? How's Syd doing?"

"As well as can be expected, I guess." Maybe he should've given Sydney another week of bereavement before tearing up the carriage house. "Stella never told her about the new kitchen and it caught Syd off guard. I don't think she's too thrilled about it." That had to be the understatement of the year.

"Shit. What about all the materials we bought? Wasn't it like fifty grand in appliances, fixtures, and cabinetry?"

More, but who was counting? "Something like that. We'll work it out," he said with as much optimism as he could muster.

"Is it true she's one of those celebrity chef types with a cookbook coming out?"

The cookbook was news to Nick. But according to Stella, Syd had been featured in a few gourmet magazines. "All I know is that she owns a bread bakery in San Francisco." And from what he could tell, she was anxious to get back to it.

"With that new kitchen, why doesn't she just expand her business to Moonbright?"

Nick looked at Sal as if he had a screw loose. "Right, Moonbright. Because expanding in a town the size of a hazelnut in the ninth least populous state in the nation would certainly be the natural progression of things."

"Give me a break—it was just an idea." Sal threw his arms up. "I'd better get back to Rory and the kids. I'm supposed to walk with them." Sal started to leave, pivoted, then put Nick in a headlock and whispered, "Jen's back for the parade. Just wanted to give you fair warning."

Though Nick wasn't surprised that his ex was in town, his first reaction was to search the crowd so he could take cover. He didn't want to run into her, which would inevitably mean rehashing the same old bullshit they always did. They'd made the right decision by breaking up. But when a couple had more than a decade's worth of history between them, things were never cut-and-dried.

He strolled, hugging the inside of the sidewalk, watching the parade over the heads of the throngs of bystanders. All the storefronts had been decked out in fall colors and Halloween décor for the event. Moonbright boasted having the largest pumpkin patch in Maine. Between that and the parade, people came from as far away as New York to take in the quaint flavor of the small town.

Nick zipped his jacket. Although there was no snow in the forecast, a brisk breeze had kicked up, chilling the clear afternoon air. After the parade was over, the shops would open to trick-or-treaters and patrons alike. His family usually got a table at the Corner Café. But this year his folks were out of town, escaping the cold. They'd finally taken that trip to Turks and Caicos that Nick's father had been promising his mother for ages. So, the rest of the Rossi family was free to roam.

A flash of red caught Nick's eye on the other side of the street. There she was, standing in front of the bakeshop, staring at the case of goodies inside, instead of the parade. He should've kept on walking, but like a dumbass he crossed the road, dodging cowboys, skeletons, and a few naughty nurses to keep from getting trampled.

"Hey," he said. "Nice to see you."

Sydney turned to face him, pulling her red coat tighter. "Is it?" Her lips turned up at the corners as if to say she knew he was full of crap. "I think the last time I was here for the parade was my senior year in high school. Gram always begged me to come, but this time of year it's difficult for a professional baker to get away."

"I imagine it would be. You're probably swamped all the way to Christmas, right?"

She nodded. "Gram loved this parade and this little town so much. Looking back on it, I wish I'd come more often. . . . Well, it's too late now."

"Knowing Stella, she understood."

She didn't respond, but there was a wealth of sadness in her silence.

"Did you get that inventory list I texted you?" On a scale

of professionalism, accosting a client at a Halloween parade to talk shop ranked a negative ten. But Sydney Byrne wasn't his client.

"I did." Her smile was tight. "If I didn't know better, I'd think my grandmother was planning to open a bakery."

Sal's words rang in Nick's head. "You think she meant it for you?"

Syd shook her head. "I'm fully entrenched in San Francisco and am about to open a second location in the city. She knew that. Our biggest dream was that she'd be there at my grand opening and book release party."

"I'm sorry she didn't make it."

"Me too. I've asked around a little, and so far no one besides you knew anything about Gram's plans." She squinted up at him accusingly.

The marching band launched into an off-key version of "Monster Mash." He pointed to his ears and shook his head. She laughed, and the way her face lit up just about knocked the wind out of him. For a few seconds they just stood there, holding each other's gaze.

Then he motioned that they should move farther down the street, away from the noise. She followed as he ducked into a narrow alley between two buildings that muffled the sounds of the parade.

"Better?"

She nodded. "I was just saying that besides you, no one had a clue about this kitchen of Gram's."

He'd heard her the first time. "Syd, why would I make it up?"

"I'm not saying you made it up."

"Then what exactly are you saying?" He waited.

"I'm just really confused. Gram and I talked every day. Not once did she mention this project."

"Maybe she wanted to surprise you."

"Oh, I'm surprised all right."

Hurt seemed more like it to Nick. How could he blame her? It did seem rather unlikely that Stella would've kept her plans from her only granddaughter. But, hell, it was just a freaking kitchen, not the end of the world.

"It won't take me long to finish it," he said. "And who knows, maybe the new owners will start a catering business."

She awarded his comment with a good amount of side-eye.

"I'll do a good job; you can depend on it." He hadn't said it to goad her but could see that his promise was having that effect by the way her face screwed up.

"Clearly, my grandmother trusted you more than she did me. So you at least have that going for you."

"A little melodramatic, don't you think?"

She rolled her eyes. "You ought to get out a little, Rossi. The days of men telling women they're being dramatic went out with girdles."

There was no winning with her. "All I was trying to say is that my family's company has a lot of history with your gram's Victorian." The house on Maple had been a regular patient of Nick's father. Window replacements, new flooring in the laundry room when it had flooded a few years ago, a screened-in porch for summer, and a myriad other fixes and additions.

"I know. I'm not questioning your qualifications as a contractor."

Nor should she. He took pride in the work he did and considered himself a craftsman. "Everyone in town loves that house. It's one of the crown jewels of Moonbright. I wouldn't do any work that would change that," including carrying out her earlier request to plunk the new appliances and cabinetry into the Victorian's period kitchen.

In a resigned voice, she asked, "How long is not long?"

"Five weeks. Four if I push it. But I've got a lot of clients who are pressuring me to get their jobs done by Thanksgiving. They're *good* clients." He emphasized the word "good" to drive his point home, because so far she'd been a giant headache.

She huffed out a breath. "Message received."

He took her arm. "Come on; let's watch the parade. Then I'll buy you a cup of coffee and a whoopie pie over at the Corner Café."

They found a spot on the sidewalk with a good view and watched until the grand finale—a giant pumpkin-faced helium balloon that brought up the rear. The crowd slowly dispersed and Nick and Sydney strolled to the café. It wasn't until they got a table in the corner that he noticed the gawking, inquisitive faces.

Like any small-town inhabitants, the residents of Moonbright liked their gossip. And Nick suspected that by tomorrow folks all the way to Bangor would be laying bets on whether he and Syd were an item. To his relief, she didn't seem to notice the speculative stares coming their way.

A server took their orders. Syd shrugged out of her red coat and draped it over the back of her chair. Nick once again noted how the scrawny high school girl he remembered had filled out in all the right places. Today, she wore her dark brown hair down, the ends curling above her shoulders. Despite her casual clothing—a turtleneck, jeans, and a pair of short boots with furry tops—she carried an air of big-city sophistication that unexpectedly turned him on.

Born and bred in Moonbright, he'd always considered himself a girl-next-door kind of guy. Probably why he and Jen had had so many problems.

"I always adored this place," Syd said, glancing around the room at the wood-paneled walls, the green vinyl counter stools, and the banquette seating, then up at the pressed-tin ceiling. The restaurant was a throwback to a simpler time.

"Nan sure can cook. But I'm guessing you go in for all that gourmet stuff."

She shook her head. "Comfort food will always be my first love."

"They have that out west?" He rubbed his chin. "Unless you consider kale comfort food."

She laughed again. "Maybe not whoopie pies, but San Francisco has its share of comfort food. And I don't mean kale."

He'd only been to California once and had never understood what all the fuss was about. Jen, on the other hand, got stars in her eyes at the mere mention of the Golden State. Perhaps that's why he'd gone out of his way to dislike it.

"So you're opening a second bakery, huh?"

"I'm hoping to, yeah. I just have to raise the cash."

"You mean like investors?" It was nosy of him to ask, but as a businessman he was interested.

"Only silent ones if any at all."

"Why's that?"

"I've learned that I don't play well with others."

"Big shocker there." He cocked a brow. "What happened?"

"I didn't have any money when I founded Bread and Cie. And I was too inexperienced to understand that by taking on financial backers, I was relinquishing control. It was a tough lesson but one I won't make again."

"It must be a pretty big business." For some reason, he'd visualized it as a mom-and-pop bakery not dissimilar to Moonbright's Bellaluna's Bakeshop.

"We provide bread, rolls, biscuits, croissants, muffins, and scones to a good many Bay Area restaurants, cafés, and gourmet grocery stores."

"Wow. When Stella described it as successful, I had no idea what kind of scale she was talking about. So is that the model for the second bakery?"

"Nope. The second bakery is a totally different concept.

Strictly business to consumer. But first, I have to find the right location. Somewhere with a lot of foot traffic that I can still afford. San Francisco is an expensive town to do business in."

He nodded, knowing firsthand the expense of running a company. His father had started as a one-man band with Nick and his brothers helping out on weekends and during summer vacations. But Nick had big plans for Rossi Construction, and the math to make it happen would take a truckload of Benjamins.

The server came with their coffees and dessert. Syd took a bite of her whoopie pie, closed her eyes, and let out a hum of appreciation.

As he watched her, Nick's groin tightened. Jeez, he needed to get a damn grip. Start dating again. But not in Moonbright, where there were prying eyes everywhere. And not with Sydney Byrne, who preferred the bright lights and the big city. Been there, done that, had the returned engagement ring to prove it.

"Boy, have I missed these." She wiped a crumb from the corner of her mouth, drawing his attention to her lips. Plump and pink.

Yeah, he really needed to start dating. All work and no play wasn't helping his libido.

"Nan could make a killing in California with these." She took another bite, this time using the tip of her tongue to lick away a dab of stray filling.

He wondered if she knew what she was doing to him.

"What's wrong? Aren't you going to eat yours?"

He quickly looked down at his plate and shoved half the pastry into his mouth, hoping it would feed his craving.

# Chapter 3

Syd woke up in the middle of the night, unable to sleep. It had been like that since all the upheaval in her life. Gram's death and Syd's breakup with Gage had caused a lot of tossing and turning.

Instead of trying to fight it, she wrapped herself in Gram's old woolen shawl and crept down to the kitchen for a cup of something warm.

The wind was still howling and an errant tree branch scraped against the window, making her jump. It was a little scary being alone in the large Victorian with its creaks and unfamiliar noises. And it was Halloween of all nights. Too late for any last-minute shenanigans from the neighborhood kids, which made the sounds even more ominous.

She lit a fire under the kettle. Gram would've suggested a warm cup of milk. But Syd worried that it would curdle in her stomach. Other than the whoopie pie she'd had earlier with Nick, she hadn't eaten anything solid all day. She unwrapped the rest of the ciabatta bread she'd made the previous day, cut two fat slabs, and popped them in her grandmother's old Dualit toaster. The refrigerator was filled with leftover casseroles the neighbors had brought over in the days following Gram's funeral. Tucked in the back, she found the Irish butter her grandmother swore by and a jar of homemade jam.

The kettle whistled and Syd made herself a cup of herbal tea, sipping it while she stood over the counter, waiting for her bread to brown.

Suddenly she wasn't alone.

The reflection of a man in the chrome of the toaster stared back, startling her. She jerked, her pulse racing, and quickly looked over her shoulder, expecting to see a ghost. Or, worse, an intruder. But no one was there.

Syd looked at the Dualit again, and the distorted image danced before her. It was hard to make out, but it was a man all right. He had a strong jawline and high cheekbones.

*And pretty soon I'll be seeing Jesus in my toast.*

Syd dismissed it as a trick of the light from the overhead fixture. Or was it that silly Moonbright legend? The thought made her laugh. According to the superstitious townswomen, including Gram, if you looked in the mirror at midnight on Halloween you'd see your future spouse. Syd glanced up at the clock on the wall. It was eleven fifty-two. *Take that, you old myth.* And a toaster wasn't a mirror. But more important, she wasn't in the market for a husband. Or even a boyfriend for that matter.

"You hear that, big guy?" She chucked the warped image on what she thought was his chin and a zing of heat from the Dualit went through her like an oven blast. She dropped her hand to the counter and a business card fluttered to the floor.

Nick had left the card the other day. On the semigloss stock was the Rossi Construction logo and a picture of Nick. It wasn't the greatest photo—truth be told, it looked more like a mug shot. But it was Nick just the same.

When she put the card back on the counter the image in the toaster reappeared. "Aha, not the legend. Just a simple reflection of a picture. Sorry, Gram."

She buttered her toast and ate at the kitchen table, listening to the fierce wind blow outside.

Monday morning, Syd surveyed the leftover Halloween candy. Most of the good stuff was gone, which was a blessing even though a Snickers with a cup of coffee would've revved her engine right about now. Even one of those mini Paydays. But the little scavengers had wiped her out.

She settled for a healthy plate of eggs and polished off the rest of her ciabatta toast while baking a pumpkin bread. If she had time today, she'd work on perfecting a new recipe for maple scones she'd been mulling. First, though, she had an appointment with Moonbright's premiere Realtor. Dot James was a Mainer through and through, who'd made a killing selling New England real estate.

She drove a 1979 International Harvester Scout that looked as if it had survived a nuclear holocaust, and her wardrobe resembled an L. L. Bean catalog, circa 1951. Her signature was a dun-colored man's wool fedora. People either loved or hated her. But if you had a house to sell, Dot was your agent.

She'd agreed to come to the house and give Syd a quick lesson on what and what not to do when selling a house in Moonbright. Dot had been Nick's idea, and he was coming too.

As soon as Syd finished breakfast, she hit the shower and took a little extra time with her makeup. For Dot, she told herself. She hadn't seen the woman in years and wanted to make a good impression. "Who are you trying to fool?" she asked herself in the mirror.

Her phone rang and she raced into the bedroom, nearly tripping over her towel. One look at caller ID and she let it go to voicemail. This was the fourth or fifth time Gage had tried to call her. Whatever it was, it could wait. She had no desire to talk to her ex. In fact, she had hoped never to talk to him again.

She had just changed for the fourth time when the doorbell rang. Show time. Syd dashed down the stairs to find Dot pulling weeds in the front yard.

"Gram's gardener is coming next week," she said, embarrassed that she hadn't seen to the garden since the funeral. But it was getting cold and soon the landscape would be covered in a blanket of snow.

Dot straightened, putting one hand at the small of her back and using the other to shield her eyes from the glare of the morning sun. "Well, look at you. The spitting image of Stella. Last time I saw you, you were an ugly thing. Gaumy as a toddler."

Syd wasn't sure whether she'd been complimented or insulted. "Thanks for coming," *I think*. "Nick should be here any minute."

"Let's get started without him. I've got to be in Bangah in two hours." She climbed the porch stairs and assessed the front door. "Paint this red. Buyers think it's a lucky color."

While Syd scrawled "red door" in her notebook, Nick's pickup slid up the driveway. He parked next to Dot's Scout and hopped out. Syd had never been much for men in plaid woolen shirts, but call her converted. The flannel stretched across his broad chest, and a crisp white T-shirt peeked out of his collar. His hair was damp as if he'd just jumped out of the shower, and his face was clean-shaven.

"Mornin'."

"Mornin'," Dot called back.

"Dot thinks I should paint the door red."

He nodded and joined them on the porch.

"The rest of this looks fine," Dot said, assessing the railing posts. "Maybe freshen up the trim with a coat of paint."

She let herself inside the house. And for the next thirty minutes they tailed her from room to room as she called off a long
list of repairs and renovations that would make the house more
appealing to buyers.

"We'll want to stage it," she said. "Put Stella's stuff down cel-
lah. Put all your focus on the bathrooms and kitchen, though.
That's where the return is."

Dot crossed the kitchen to the mudroom and stared out the
window at the refuse pile next to the carriage house. "What's
that mess?"

Syd caught Nick's eye and shot him a look, then turned to
Dot. "Before my grandmother died, she hired Nick to put in
a commercial kitchen. How well do you think that'll go over
with prospective buyers?" She couldn't hide the sarcasm in her
voice.

Dot let herself out and headed to the carriage house, where
she examined the outbuilding, a mini replica of the Victorian.
"I wouldn't put it on the market until it's done. The month before Thanksgiving is dead anyway."

Syd followed her. "But . . . a commercial kitchen . . . won't
that be weird?"

Dot shrugged. "If the new owners don't like it, they can pull
it out." She climbed over the construction debris in her duck
boots. "Add a bathroom in here."

*Great.* Just what Syd needed, more construction. "Is it really
worth the headache?"

"That and then some," Dot said with authority. "Moonbright's wicked popular. All those Portlandahs looking to get
out of the rat race. A nice family will scoop this right up." She
went back outside and stared up at the big house. "But to maxi-
mize the price you need to put the work in. Update it without
stripping out the charm."

Nick, who had tagged along, gave Syd an *I told you so* nudge.
*Five weeks of Nick Rossi. Ugh.*

Dot finished her assessment of the house and its selling potential and drove off in her ancient Scout for Bangor—or Bangah—leaving a cloud of exhaust behind her.

"You want a cup of coffee before you start?" Syd asked Nick. She'd brewed a fresh pot and it would be small of her not to offer.

"I could use one, yeah."

They went inside the kitchen, where she served him a piping-hot cup at Gram's little kitchen table along with a large slice of the pumpkin bread she'd made that morning.

"Mmm, good," he said around a full mouth. "You make this?"

"Yep."

"Best pumpkin bread I've ever had." He took another bite, washing it down with a sip of coffee.

She liked watching a man with a healthy appetite eat. The fact was she liked watching Nick eat. The way he chowed down her pumpkin loaf with unabashed gusto was hot. But given the way he'd once burned her, it wasn't wise to like anything about the man, she reminded herself.

Syd leaned against the counter. "Based on Dot's recommendations I suppose we should add a bathroom to the commercial kitchen." She rolled her eyes at the absurdity of it. "And what about the other stuff on her list?" As long as Nick was here for the carriage house conversion, she might as well have him do the rest of the work.

"I'll have to do some juggling and check with my brothers about their crews. We've got a lot of jobs going and are a little shorthanded on workers. But if all the stars align, yeah, I can do that too." He eyed the rest of the pumpkin bread like a dog would a juicy bone.

She served him another large slice and topped off his coffee. "I'll need a bid and a contract, of course." Every dime she had was going into her new bakery. Still, being a good shepherd of

Gram's pride and joy before passing the house on to the next family was important to her.

"You're getting a little ahead of yourself. Let's make sure I have the resources to even do it. In the meantime, let's walk through the carriage house and see about this bathroom."

He finished the last crumb of bread and drained the rest of his coffee, surprising her by taking his dishes to the sink, rinsing them, and putting them in the dishwasher. Gage never dreamed of getting off his ass to do something someone else would do for him.

She grabbed a jacket off a hook in the mudroom, and they walked together to the carriage house, where Nick proceeded to inspect the plumbing of the old farm sink where Gram used to wash her paintbrushes.

"I'm thinking we use this corner here." He pointed to the back of the room. "The sink for the kitchen will stay where this one is. But if I don't have to take the new plumbing too far, it'll save you money and me time."

"Sounds good."

"You want a shower too?" He started pacing off the area, seemingly calculating how much square footage he'd need.

"I don't know. I guess I should've asked Dot. What do you think?"

"It should be easy enough as long as we don't do anything fancy like tile or frameless glass doors. I'm thinking one of those fiberglass deals, a curtain rod, and call it a day."

"Okay." She nudged her head at the sink. "Can we repurpose that?" The cast-iron sink would forever remind her of her grandmother. Syd thought Stella would have wanted it to stay with the house.

"I don't see why not. It's all doable."

"Exactly what I like to hear." For all his other faults, he was the most amenable contractor she'd ever worked with. The construction company that had done her build-out at Bread &

Cie had given her every excuse in the world why they couldn't accomplish what seemed to her fairly simple tasks.

*The building's too old. . . . That'll cost you an arm and a leg. . . . Lady, are you out of your mind?*

But with Nick everything was possible.

Nick grabbed a sandwich at the Corner Café and was headed to the office to look at the schedule and work up a bid for Syd. The woman was wound tighter than a spool of thread. Most of the time, he gave his clients a simple time and materials bid and they sealed the deal with a handshake. But Syd had made it clear she wanted something in writing, which meant more paperwork for him.

He turned the corner on Juniper Street, where more than a decade ago his old man had bought a small building to house Rossi Construction. Nick had converted one of the back rooms into office space and a conference room. It was nothing fancy. But it was more professional than meeting prospective clients at his house.

He'd had a sign made, hoping it gave the company a little more presence in town. While the old-timers knew Nick and his brothers were here, Moonbright was seeing an influx of newcomers or, as Mainers liked to say, folks "from away."

He pulled into the alley, parked, and ducked under the partially opened roll-up door. Sal was sitting in the office with his feet on Nick's desk, eating a bowl of chowder.

"Where'd you get that?" Nick prodded his chin at Sal's soup. It smelled good.

"Rory made it to warm the kids up after trick-or-treating. I'd share with you, but I'm a stingy bastard."

Nick swiped Sal's feet off the desk and pulled up a chair. "I got an Italian at the café."

"You getting the Byrne place knocked out?"

"Yeah. Syd wants to hire us to spruce up the Victorian too."

Sal let out a low whistle. "The woman can't make up her mind, can she?"

"I think she's resigned to the kitchen now. Dot came over and gave her a laundry list of minor renovations that should be done before she puts the house on the market."

"We've got 'em stacked up." Sal sighed.

"Yep. But we're there anyway, seems foolish to turn the business away."

Sal hitched his shoulders. "I don't know. Between the Thompsons' new garage and the Michauds' second-story addition, we're stretched thin. That's not to mention the kitchens and bathrooms we've promised to our other clients before the holidays."

"I know," Nick said, still trying to figure out why he was letting Syd's job take priority over clients who were at the front of the line. Ah, he knew damned well why. Pretty face gets the space, which was bullshit and unevolved on his part.

"What, you got a thing for Sydney Byrne?" For a giant lug, Sal was smarter than he looked. "I remember a time when you wouldn't give her a second look. Though there were those rumors." He waggled his brows. "Wasn't she madly in love with you?"

"No, she wasn't. And that was like a hundred years ago, so grow up."

"Testy, aren't you?

"It's for Stella," Nick said. "She loved that old house. The least I can do is bring it back to its former glory."

"Ayuh, but why can't it wait until January?"

"Because we're already there. It doesn't make sense to do the kitchen, leave, and come back again. If it makes you feel better, I'll do most of the work myself and leave the crew to our other obligations."

"That's mighty generous of you, big brother." Sal went back to his chowder.

Nick unwrapped his sandwich and took a big bite. Despite the pumpkin bread and coffee he'd had at Syd's, he was starved.

"You see Jen?" Sal asked. "I saw her this morning at Bella-luna's. She was trying to get in touch with you."

That was news to Nick. He hadn't gotten a call or text from her. The truth was he was hoping to avoid her visit altogether. "She say how long she was staying?" After the breakup, she'd taken a job in Manhattan and moved in with two of her friends in a fancy high-rise with a doorman.

"Nope." Sal pushed his bowl away. "Just that she wanted to say hi." He poked Nick in the arm. "You two will be back together by New Year's Eve."

No, they wouldn't, despite what his family and the rest of Moonbright thought. No one puts off a wedding for ten years unless they don't really want to get married. Unfortunately, it had taken a decade for Jen and him to figure that out. A lot of lost time.

"How's the Thompsons' garage coming?" Anything to change the subject.

"Good." Sal nodded. "We're rushing to button it up before the first storm hits."

Sal washed out his bowl at the makeshift kitchenette. Tino, their baby brother, strolled in, holding a lunch box.

"A family reunion, huh?" he joked. Rarely were they all in the same place at the same time, unless it was Sunday supper at their parents'.

"As much as I'd love to catch up with you, Tino, I've got a garage to build." Sal gave Tino a noogie and headed out.

"What about you?" Tino asked Nick.

Nick held up what was left of his sandwich. "I got five more minutes; then I have to get back to the job site."

"Stella's kitchen, right? Marty saw you and Sydney Byrne at the Corner Café after the parade. Said you looked real cozy. Didn't you two have a thing in high school?"

*Here we go again.* "Nope. She was my math tutor. That's it."

"Not what I heard, but whatever. According to Marty, she's smokin' hot."

"Isn't Marty married?" The guy had been Tino's best friend since the fourth grade. Last Nick had heard, Marty had tied the knot with a waitress from Hampden.

"Divorced." Tino stuck a frozen lasagna in the microwave.

Well, that hadn't lasted long.

Nick tossed the wrapper from his sandwich in the trash and ducked into the head to wash his hands. He didn't have all day to shoot the shit with his brother. Like their father always said, "daylight was burning."

Nick grabbed his jacket from the back of his chair and shrugged into it. The temperature was getting colder. The previous night he'd had to double up on blankets.

"You're on your own," he called to his brother as he crouched under the roll-up door. "Stay out of trouble."

He'd just climbed into his truck when his phone chimed with a text. All he needed was another fire to put out. These days he spent more time hunting down materials that had gone MIA or making emergency trips to the lumber store than he did actually building anything. Sometimes it sucked being the boss.

He fished his phone out of his jacket pocket, glanced at the message, and grimaced. *Jen.* She wanted to meet for drinks, which he had no interest in doing. Nick sat in the cab of his truck, contemplating his options. None of them good. If he said he couldn't meet with her, she'd find a way to corral him at his house and they'd be there all night, most likely fighting. At least in a public place he could have one drink, claim exhaustion, and leave. It was the safest bet.

He quickly tapped out a message that he'd meet her at seven at the usual place and hit the send key. *Shit.* Nick banged his head against the steering wheel a couple times, then got on the road back to Maple Street. He hoped, if he kept his head down and focused on work, he could avoid a certain brunette.

No such luck. Syd was in the driveway, getting out of her rental car, wrestling with an armful of grocery bags.

He exited his truck and blew out a breath. "You need help with those?"

"There's two more in the trunk if you wouldn't mind."

He grabbed them and followed her through the mudroom into the kitchen, trying to avert his eyes from the sway of her ass. "You planning on doing some cooking?" The bags were heavy and appeared to be filled with baking supplies.

She began unpacking flour and yeast from the sacks. "I'm testing a few recipes."

He considered volunteering to be her taster, but that sort of defeated the purpose of keeping his distance.

"When do the new appliances come?" she asked. "I'd love to get my hands on that commercial convection oven. It's similar to the one I have at Bread and Cie."

"Appliances are usually saved for the tail end of the job."

"Any chance of installing them early," she asked, but the inflection in her voice told Nick it was more of a demand than a question.

"Nope."

"Why not?" She stopped putting away her ingredients and stood with her arms crossed.

"Because it's not the way I roll."

"What the hell does that mean?"

"That it's a construction site and I don't want to risk damaging a twelve-thousand-dollar oven while putting up drywall and cabinets."

"I'll take the risk," she said.

He leaned against the wall, trying to hide his annoyance. "Fine. But if anything happens to the ovens, I'm not eating the cost."

"Just be careful then."

As if he weren't always careful. The woman was busting on his last nerve. "Tell me you're not planning to bake in the middle of a construction zone."

"I could do it early in the morning before you arrive. Or in the evenings, after you leave."

He didn't bother to tell her all the reasons that was a terrible idea. Instead, he shook his head and returned to work. He needed to swing a hammer at something. Something hard.

# Chapter 4

By the end of the day, Nick had worked up a good sweat and needed a shower. He packed up his tools, cleaned up the carriage house the best he could, and went home to wash off the sawdust.

At seven, he took the first available barstool at the Thirsty Raven, steering clear of a private booth.

Salty, who'd been tending bar since Nick's parents were old enough to drink, brought him a Sea Dog beer. Nick ordered a burger, fully loaded.

Jen was late as usual. Nick killed time by snacking on a bowl of complimentary beer nuts and reading the names that had been carved into the wooden bar. A TV in the corner blared *Monday Night Football*. The Patriots were having a sucky season so far.

No one had bothered taking down the orange and black jack-o'-lantern lights that had been strung up along the backbar mirror. If Nick had to wager a guess, they'd stay up until December, when someone would remember to swap them out for the bar's plastic menorah and artificial Christmas tree.

Nick was halfway through his burger when Jennifer saun-
tered through the door, her shiny blond hair glimmering in the
glow of the Thirsty Raven's ambient lighting. She looked good.
Too New York sleek in a lightweight camel-colored coat for his
taste but good just the same.

She gave him a little wave from across the bar and wended
her way around the tables. One look at his dinner plate and she
frowned. "You didn't wait?"

"I was starved and you're thirty minutes late. You want a
burger?" Nick flagged Salty, so Jen could put in her order.

She looked around the crowded bar. "Why didn't you get a
booth?"

"This was the only thing available when I got here," he lied,
and tapped the stool next to him. "Hop up. It won't kill you to
sit at the bar."

She took off her coat, hung it on a hook on the wall next to
the restrooms, and joined him. "What, no hug?"

He stood up and awkwardly embraced her. "Good to see
you, Jen."

"You too, Nick." She smoothed down her dress and sat on
the stool next to him. "I've missed you."

He didn't know what to say to that, so he let the silence
speak for itself. "How's the job and Manhattan?"

"Good. I just closed a five-million-dollar deal, a town house
on the Upper West Side."

"Yeah? Good for you." He was proud of her. Five years ago
she'd gotten her real estate license, and now she was killing it
selling high-end properties to New York's elite.

"I'm having a good year." She took a sip of the cosmopolitan
Salty had placed on the bar in front of her. No one in Moonbright drank pink cocktails except for Jen. "If I had a dime for
every client who was looking for a good contractor . . . Nick, I
wish you'd reconsider."

If he had a dime for every time they'd had this conversation.

"I'm not moving to New York, Jen. I'm perfectly content in Moonbright, running my dad's business."

She reached out and traced the top of his hand with her finger. He meant to move his hand away, but the door opened, letting in a gust of wind, and Sydney. Her brown hair was up, with loose tendrils framing her pale face and accentuating her blue eyes. The sight of her made his breath catch and for a moment he just stared.

When he turned back to Jennifer, she was watching him, a look of panic in her eyes.

"I'd heard she was back for her grandmother's funeral."

Nick nodded. He didn't want to talk to Jen about Sydney. He wanted to go home, sit by his non-working fireplace with a stiff drink, and finish watching the Patriots game.

"She's pretty now. But then, you always thought she was pretty, didn't you?"

Jennifer's burger came and he hoped it would end any more discussion about Sydney Byrne. It had been sixteen freaking years ago. The fact that they were still talking about it showed how little their relationship had evolved.

"What are you doing for Thanksgiving?" she asked as she cut her burger in half and then in quarters.

As long as he'd known Jen, she'd been cutting her food into bite-size pieces. Tonight, for some reason, it bugged the shit out of him. Why couldn't she just eat her burger the way everyone else did?

"I haven't given it much thought." Before their breakup, they'd spent the holiday with either the Rossi clan or Jen's family.

"I was thinking that maybe you and I could go away. Try to . . . put us back together."

He stared at her, not knowing what to say. "Jen, why are you doing this?" He glanced to his side to make sure no one was listening and dropped his voice for good measure. "Nothing is going to change. I'm not moving to Manhattan. I don't want to remodel the homes of Wall Street tycoons. We've been over this a thousand times."

"I thought with time apart, you'd miss me enough to reconsider."

How did he tell her that time apart had only confirmed what they already knew? They wanted different things from life. And for the first time in years, he felt free to be himself and embrace the things that mattered most to him: his family, Moonbright, and the small business his father had grown from the ground up. The sad reality of their breakup was that it was a relief.

"Don't say anything." Jen's bottom lip quivered. "Just think about it, okay?"

There was nothing to think about, but he didn't want to hurt Jen any more than he already had, so he held his tongue.

"I'll be right back." She hopped down from the stool, swiped her eyes with the back of her hand, and crossed the floor to the restroom, trying to hold her head high.

He knew how much that had cost her and felt like an asshole. But he couldn't go backward. It wouldn't be fair to either of them.

He swiveled on his stool to find Syd watching him and bobbed his head in greeting. She quickly turned back to the two people sitting at her table. Nick had never seen them before and assumed they weren't from around here. The man had worn a cowboy hat when he first came in. It now hung on a hook near their table. The woman was an attractive blonde, maybe a few years older than he and Syd.

Ordinarily, he'd go over and introduce himself. But under the circumstances it would just exacerbate the situation with Jen. Besides, the three of them seemed pretty caught up in their conversation.

Jen returned to the bar, wearing her *everything is fine* face.

They spent the rest of the evening making small talk, pretending to the world—and perhaps themselves—that they were just old friends, having a drink.

There was that damn buzz saw again. Syd rolled over, took one look at the clock on the nightstand, and gritted her teeth. It was seven in the goddamn morning. The neighbors were going to kill her. Or better yet, they'd kill Nick.

She swung her legs off the side of the bed and made a split-second decision to brew a pot of coffee before jumping in the shower. Emily and Clay were coming for breakfast. And she wanted to pull out all the stops.

She shrugged into her bathrobe and jogged downstairs to the kitchen. Through the window, she saw Nick on the roof. In another life the man must've been a tightrope walker. She tapped on the window, motioning that he should be careful. But either he hadn't heard or he was ignoring her.

She got the coffee machine going and ran back upstairs to bathe and dress. If she rushed, she could have her new and improved maple scones out of the oven just in time for breakfast. She was working on the spinach frittata when Nick knocked on the back door.

"Can I borrow a cup of coffee?" He held up his insulated driving mug. "I bypassed the Corner Café on my way to work this morning. Big mistake."

"Sure. Come in."

He knocked his boots on the mat and met her in the kitchen. "Smells good in here. What are you making?"

"Frittata and scones. I'll make you a plate when everything is out of the oven." Well, weren't they being cordial this morning?

"Thanks." He cocked his hip against the counter and suddenly the room felt smaller. "Who were your friends last night?"

"Emily and Clay McCreedy. Emily's working with me on my cookbook. They're visiting from Northern California."

"San Francisco?"

"No, a small town called Nugget about four hours away. Her husband owns a large cattle ranch there."

"Huh, that explains the cowboy hat. Not a lot of those in Moonbright." He grinned and Syd wished he hadn't. That smile had once melted her teenage heart. Unfortunately, even after all these years, it still delivered quite a wallop.

"Jen looked good," she forced herself to say, and filled his cup with coffee. "You two look very happy."

He let out a humorless laugh. "We're not together anymore."

"You're not?" She jerked back in surprise. "I'm sorry. I thought I'd heard somewhere that you were engaged. And last night . . . well, I just assumed."

He hitched his shoulders in a halfhearted shrug. "Jen was just in town for the parade. She lives in New York now."

"Oh. I hadn't heard. I am truly sorry, Nick." And she was. Her breakup with Gage had crushed her. She wouldn't wish that on anyone.

"Thank you." He tightened the lid on his cup. "It was a mutual decision. We both wanted different things."

Was it? Syd wasn't so sure. Nick had been in love with Jennifer Gerard since he was sixteen years old. In high school, the girl had had him wrapped around her little finger. She'd probably run off to New York to bask in the bright lights. Be the star she'd always been destined to be.

Syd's kitchen timer went off, and she removed the scones from the oven.

He leaned over her to sniff, brushing against her back. His body heat spread through her like a furnace and she froze.

"They look good. How long until they're ready to eat?"

"A few minutes to cool," she managed without stuttering.

They stood like that for several moments. When he finally moved away, she felt bereft of his warmth.

"My friends are coming over for breakfast," she said just to fill the silence that ensued.

"The ones from last night?"

"Emily and I are working out a few details of my book before they head off for Portland. They're anxious to see the fall colors." Emily, who'd been dogged by tragedy until Clay had come into her life, was mixing a little business with pleasure. It was the first time the couple had been able to break away from the ranch without their children for a romantic week together. Syd was thrilled they'd chosen New England.

"Where are they staying?"

"Rose Cottage."

"Nice."

They both seemed to be using inane small talk to stall for time. Either Nick didn't want to go back to work or he was desperate for one of her scones. She was still reeling from the revelation that he and Jen were no longer together. Syd told herself that it was just interesting in the same way as finding out from Facebook that one of your old high school classmates has gone to prison for tax evasion.

Nick and Jen had been together forever. And when Gram had mentioned their engagement a couple years ago, it had struck Syd as odd that they hadn't already married and produced a brood of babies. At some point, maybe she'd work up the nerve to ask him about it.

"I'd better get back to the job," he said, but seemed in no hurry to leave.

"How's my bid coming along?"

He shook his head. "You don't mess around, do you?"

"Nope. The sooner I get everything taken care of here, the sooner I can return to my business." She had good people running Bread & Cie in her absence, but she was too much of a control freak to leave it in their hands for a prolonged period of time. And then there was Gage. Who knew what he would do behind her back?

"I'll work on it, Syd. But let me remind you *again*"—he bit out the word "again"— "that you're not my only client."

"Gotcha." She tried hard to keep the sarcasm out of her voice and searched for a metal spatula. Scooping one of the scones off the cooking sheet, she plopped it on a plate. "Here you go. I'll bring you a piece of frittata when it's done." She flashed him a fake smile.

He balanced the plate and coffee cup in both hands. When she tried to get the door for him, he opened it with his elbow just to be ornery.

Ten minutes later, the buzz saw was back and louder than ever. She turned on music to block out the noise and set the table with Gram's Royal Albert Rose Confetti china and frilly linen napkins. It was too late in the season for flowers from the backyard, but Syd made a centerpiece out of a bouquet of chrysanthemums she'd gotten at the market. Very festive.

Emily and Clay arrived just as Syd was pulling her frittata out of the oven.

"What a wonderful house," Emily said as Syd ushered them into the foyer.

"Thanks. How was Rose Cottage?"

"So charming and comfortable that it's the first time we've slept late since . . . I don't even know."

"What's going on in that building at the end of the driveway?" Clay pointed his chin in the direction of the carriage house.

*A nightmare on Maple Street.* "It's a long story and a bit of a mystery. But it seems that my grandmother commissioned the installation of a commercial kitchen in the carriage house before she died."

"Really?" Emily said, intrigued. "Was she planning to go into the catering business?"

"Not that I'm aware of. She'd already been diagnosed with cancer—a weird time to get a new business off the ground. Besides, she was eighty-two."

"What do you think she wanted it for?" Emily asked.

"Beats the heck out of me."

"Do you think it was for you?"

"I can't imagine. Before she died, we'd talked about my selling the house and using the money for my new business in San Francisco. It doesn't make sense."

"Was she . . . uh . . . ?"

"Losing her marbles?" Syd finished for Clay. "Nope, she was sharp as a tack."

"How odd," Emily said. "I suppose whoever buys it will get to enjoy a second kitchen." Emily had a gorgeous second kitchen in a converted barn. But she was a professional chef, cookbook author, and food stylist.

"I hope you brought your appetite." *Enough about Gram's crazy kitchen.*

Syd gave them a quick tour of the house before leading them to the dining room. They gathered around the table, which almost sagged beneath the morning's feast.

As promised, Syd quickly made up a plate for Nick. "I'll be right back. I promised the contractor a piece."

"Tell him to join us," Clay called to her. "There's enough food here to feed all of Maine."

Syd took the plate out to the carriage house, where Nick was crouched down, working on an electrical box.

"Hey, you want to eat this here or join us inside?"

In his rush to get up, he hit his head on the windowsill and groaned. "You mind not sneaking up on me?"

"Sorry." It wasn't as if she'd tiptoed into the room.

He stood up and eyed the plate in her hands. "I'll come in and say a quick hello."

It surprised Syd. Emily and Clay were strangers to Nick. Then again, people in Maine had nice manners.

He took the plate from her and they returned to the dining room, where Syd introduced everyone. Nick could be extraordinarily charming when he wasn't wielding an obnoxious buzz saw at seven in the morning. He engaged in a lively conversation about being a fourth-generation Mainer while scarfing down his frittata and a couple more scones—the man could eat—and eventually excused himself.

When Clay left to use the washroom, Emily whispered, "Oh my, where did you find him?" and fanned herself.

"I've known him since high school. His father used to be Gram's go-to contractor. Nick's now running the family company."

"Anything there?" Emily hitched an inquisitive brow.

"No . . . no . . . of course not." Sixteen years ago, she'd been foolish enough to think there was. She'd never let that happen again.

"Is he single?"

"I have no idea," Syd lied. "And as soon as I settle my grandmother's estate, I'll be leaving for San Francisco."

"It wouldn't hurt to have a little fling on your way out. Get back in the saddle so to speak." Emily knew all about Gage and what he'd done. He'd cut a wide swath through the food community in Northern California, even before he'd cheated on Syd. She only wished she'd known that before she'd gotten involved with him.

Clay returned to the table. "I thought I'd check out Nick's progress while you two discuss the cookbook." He stacked up their breakfast plates and took them to the kitchen on his way out.

"That one is a keeper." Why couldn't Syd find a man like Clay?

"Don't I know it." Emily got that gooey expression of a woman in love.

Years ago, Emily's little girl, Hope, had been abducted from her in broad daylight. The entire story had been splashed across the news. Understandably, Emily had gone into a deep funk, hiding away in her home for years. She finally sold the house and moved to the tiny town of Nugget, where she'd met Clay, who brought her back to the living. A few years ago, she'd found her daughter. It was a long story, but Syd always thought of it as a Christmas miracle.

"The book," Emily said. "Let's get to work, shall we?"

# Chapter 5

Nick heard Syd's California friends drive away. They'd spent the better part of the afternoon in the Victorian. The guy . . . Clay . . . had helped Nick install a new storm window. Nice having a second set of hands.

It had been a long day and Nick was ready to pack it up. He'd started to sweep a pile of sawdust when Syd came out to inspect his progress.

"The new window looks good." She wandered around the room, looking at all the changes. "Where are the ovens going?"

He was pretty sure that was a veiled reminder that she wanted them installed yesterday. "Over here. That proofer thing over there." He pointed to the location.

"A proofer is a warming chamber to help dough rise. It's a staple for a professional bread baker."

Nick cocked his head to one side. "You sure your grandmother wasn't building you a bakery?"

"Gram was more logical than that. Moonbright isn't exactly a thriving metropolis, and I need to make a living."

He didn't bother trying to persuade her otherwise. What

was the point? "The ovens are coming at the end of the week. If you still insist that I install them, I could have them in by the weekend."

"Excellent. I was thinking about talking to Nan over at the Corner Café to see if she'd like to carry some of my bread. I'd love to test some of my new recipes out on the townsfolk and get feedback on what's working and what isn't."

"I can save you the trouble and act as your official taster." He reached up and hung his hands from the top of the door-jamb, taking her in from head to toe. Sydney Byrne could sure fill out a pair of jeans and a sweater.

"Get my ovens in and I'll see what I can do."

"Do you drive your bakery employees like this too?"

She thought about it for a few seconds. "Probably. But no complaints so far."

He shoveled up his neat sawdust pile and dumped it in the trash. "Any chance you want to grab dinner?" He didn't know what had possessed him to ask and tried to convince himself it was to discuss the rest of the work she wanted him to do.

"Uh . . . I guess. What did you have in mind?"

"We could hit a restaurant in Bangor." Too many prying eyes and loose lips in town. "Or I've got a couple of steaks sitting in the fridge at home. I could fire up the grill and throw some potatoes in the oven. It's up to you."

He could see her deliberating and wondered if his suggestion to go to his place was a bit presumptuous. But, hell, they'd known each other since high school. It wasn't like he was trying to put the moves on her. For all he knew, she had a significant other in California.

He started to say forget it, they'd go to Bangor. But she said, "Your place sounds good. That way I can make an early night of it. I have this annoying alarm clock that goes off at seven in the morning. It sounds a lot like an electric saw."

He laughed, then made a point of saying, "You want the job done in five weeks?"

"You know I do."

"Then quit complaining. Give me a head start to get in a quick shower." He reached for the pencil behind his ear and scribbled his address on the back of an envelope he found in his truck, then raced home.

God only knew what shape his house was in. He couldn't remember the last time he'd cleaned it. He'd gotten the Roomba in the breakup and used the app on his phone to start her up. At least the house would be vacuumed. He'd clean the bathroom while he showered and wipe down the kitchen afterward.

By the time Sydney showed up at his door, he'd shaved, changed into a clean pair of jeans and a Henley, and tidied up the front room enough to make it presentable.

"Here you go." She handed him two foil-wrapped packages. "The leftover scones and yeast rolls. I just need to pop them in the oven. Lead the way."

He waved his hand across the entryway threshold, inviting her into his tiny foyer.

When they got to the living room, she glanced around. "Cozy. How long have you lived here?"

"A little more than a year. I bought it after Jen and I sold our place on Sycamore."

"Sycamore, huh? Fancy."

The colonial had been more than they could afford, but Jen had convinced him it was a good investment. As it turned out, she was right. In only five years, they'd turned a tidy profit. Enough money to get her to Manhattan and hold her over until her first commission.

He, too, glanced around the room, trying to see it through Syd's eyes. Though the wood floors were original, they were scuffed and scarred from many years of wear and tear. The fireplace surround had gotten a makeover in the eighties with fake stone that reminded him of *The Flintstones*. And the walls were a dirty beige. "I figured I could fix it up in my spare time. Maybe flip it. The problem is I don't have any spare time."

"I can relate to that. I bought my condo six years ago with all kinds of plans to renovate. Hasn't happened yet. And I can still roll a marble down the hallway."

"Foundation problems, huh?"

"I don't even want to know. But it's likely because it was built in the early 1900s."

"You live alone?" It was a weird non sequitur and none of his business. But he was curious.

"I do now." She left it at that and he didn't press.

But it sounded as if Sydney Byrne was single, not that it mattered or that he cared.

"Come into the kitchen," he said. "It's the only room worse than the living room."

She trailed behind him, stopping every few minutes to look at his family pictures on the wall. "How are your brothers?"

"Good. We're all partners in Rossi Construction and they're both married. Sal's got two kids and Tino's got a baby and one on the way."

"Wow. That's great."

"Yeah," he said. "I never would've pegged either one of those lugheads for fathers. But I guess it's a Rossi tradition."

"Your family must've been sad when you and Jennifer didn't work out."

"I'm pretty sure my folks saw it coming. We must've had the longest engagement in the history of the world. First, I wanted to build the business. Then, Jen wanted to wait until she got her real estate license. It was one excuse after another. I think it was a pretty big red flag; don't you?"

"Only you can know that. Is that what she's doing, selling real estate?"

"Yeah. She's good at it, super successful. Million-dollar places in Manhattan."

"Whoa, that's great."

There was a long, awkward silence, both cognizant of what was going unsaid.

"Don't hate her, Syd. She was just a kid back then. She grew up to be a good person."

Syd nodded, poker-faced. "I'm sure she did. It was high school, Nick. I'm over it."

He felt stupid for even bringing it up. Of course she was over it. Sydney was a beautiful, successful adult with a thriving business. The truth was she and Jennifer were a lot alike. Both had left Moonbright in their rearview mirrors, seeking fame and fortune. Neither had been satisfied with the simplicity of small-town life. Not like him.

"This is it," he said as they entered the kitchen.

"Nice wallpaper." She ran her hand over the kitschy yellowed pattern of teapots that covered the walls.

"The plan was to strip that. As you can see, I never got to it."

Syd stepped back to view the room in its entirety. "It's a big space. There's even room for a center island."

"Yep and a total gut job. Someday."

"You'll get it done." She turned the oven dial to Bake. "Do you have a cookie sheet?"

He searched through the cupboard, but the best he could come up with was a roasting pan. "Will this work?"

"Sure." She unwrapped her yeast rolls and spaced them a couple of inches apart on the pan.

"I'm just waiting for the grill to get hot before throwing on the steaks. I probably should get the potatoes in first." He wasn't much of a cook. Most of the time, he ate out or reheated one of the dishes his mother stuffed in his freezer.

"I'll help you." She took over. And in no time had the potatoes and her rolls in the oven.

"You want a glass of wine?" He was a beer guy, but he kept a couple of bottles of Chardonnay in the fridge for his sisters-in-law.

"I'd love one."

He got down two goblets and poured them each a glass. "I don't know if it's any good."

"I'm not that picky."

"Let's take them into the living room." It was too chilly to drink their wine outside.

He cleared his paperwork off the coffee table to make room for their glasses. They both sat on the couch, close enough that his leg brushed hers as he reached for his wine. She had changed from her earlier jeans into a red knit dress that hugged her curves. Every time the hem of the dress rode up on her thighs, he lost his train of thought.

"Your friends seemed like good people," he said. "Tell me about this cookbook you're putting together."

"It's been in the works for a while. Emily is helping me scale down my bread recipes for a home cook, because everything I do is on an industrial scale. We're including the history and tradition of each recipe and how it came to be part of my repertoire. I have a wonderful photographer doing all the pictures. It's scheduled to be in bookstores before next Christmas."

"Not this Christmas?"

"Nope. Once it goes to the publisher it takes about a year to go through production."

He had no idea how these things worked. "Pretty exciting. Is this your first book?"

"Uh-huh. I've been included in other books but have never had one of my own until now."

"So are you one of those celebrity chefs?" He used to give Jen crap for watching all those food and home and garden shows. Half the people on them were now household names.

The musical sound of Syd's laugh made his groin tighten.

"I'm well known in food circles but nothing close to a celebrity."

He suspected she was downplaying her importance. She had to be pretty well known to have a book deal; otherwise no one would buy it.

"Enough about me. What about you? What are your plans for Rossi Construction?"

Nothing as lofty as hers, that was for sure. "To build on my father's reputation, do quality work, make decent money, and live a good life. Nothing too complicated."

"That sounds perfect."

"You think so?" He was skeptical. For people like her and Jen, ambition was everything. His basic ideals were hokey in comparison.

"They're words I live by."

*Yeah, right.* He nodded just to go along. "I should probably put those steaks on."

"I'll help you."

"No need. It'll only take me a couple of minutes. No sense in your standing out in the cold."

"It's not so bad." She stood up. "Everyone thinks California is a perpetual summer day. You ever been to San Francisco?"

The side of his mouth hitched up as he remembered his one visit and how he'd had to buy a sweatshirt from a street vendor because he hadn't expected July to be so cold.

She helped him season the steaks and followed him to the small patio off the kitchen where he kept a gas grill. There was a breeze, and a couple of times Syd had to hold her dress down to keep it from flying up. He couldn't help but wonder what kind of panties she had on. Her bra was red and lacy. He knew because he'd caught a peek of it as she was bending over the oven to check on her rolls.

Here he was, a grown man acting like a high school kid, fascinated with a woman's damn underwear. Yet when they sat down to eat, he could think of little else, making it difficult to focus on the meal and their dinner conversation.

This had been a bad idea. Sydney Byrne was strictly off-limits because A) he didn't sleep with clients, B) they barely got along, and C) there was too much bad history between them.

Still, his thoughts continued to wander to the bedroom and how he'd like to take off that red dress of hers.

After dinner, she unwrapped the rest of the morning's scones and put them on one of the platters he didn't know he owned. "If I'd had more time, I would've made a real dessert."

"These work for me." He could've eaten them all day long. They were the best scones he'd ever tasted.

He made a pot of decaf and they ate dessert in the living room. Again, he wished he'd had the chimney cleaned. A fire would've capped off a perfect evening.

"I should get going soon," she said after a second cup of decaf, but lingered.

They wound up doing the dishes together, which probably made him a bad host for not insisting that he handle KP duty on his own. But he didn't want her to leave.

"I guess I'll see you bright and early tomorrow," she said.

"I'll try to lay off the power tools until eight. After that no guarantees."

"No worries, I'll be up by then." She folded the dish towel and went to the living room to get her purse.

"I'll walk you out," he said.

"Last I looked, Moonbright was still crime-free."

That wasn't exactly true. They had the occasional burglary,

and last year Jonesy Taylor's ten-speed got stolen. In the days after Halloween, it wasn't uncommon to see an uptick in vandalism. Small things, like spray-painted mailboxes and toilet-papered trees.

He accompanied her to her car, where they continued to linger.

"Thanks for having me. The steak was delicious."

"Thanks for coming. It was nice to have company."

"Even if it was me?" She slid him a teasing smile.

He waggled his hand from side to side. "Yeah, even if it was you. At least tonight, you weren't your usual pain-in-the-ass self." He winked.

She snapped back something smart-alecky, but he was too focused on her lips to pay attention. And that's when he couldn't help himself.

He leaned in and covered her mouth with his. Nick went slow at first to make sure she was on board. When she went up on tiptoes and twined her arms around his neck, he took the kiss deeper, reveling in the hot pull of her mouth.

She clung to him and he could feel her nipples pebble against the soft fabric of her dress. It was all he could do not to take her on the hood of her car. Instead, he cupped the back of her head, tasting the inside of her mouth with his tongue. She whimpered and ground into his arousal, which pressed so hard against his fly he thought the buttons would burst.

Somewhere in the distance, a door slammed and the purr of a car engine rent the night air. *Shit.* He had to shut this down before they reached the point of no return, his mind said. But his body was having trouble hearing the words.

He summoned every drop of willpower and pulled away. "Ah, jeez." He scrubbed his hand through his hair. "That shouldn't have happened. I don't know what I was thinking."

Her lips, bruised and puffy, quivered. "Really? We're doing

this again?" Her blue eyes sparked with anger. "I can't freaking believe it." She got in her car, closed the door with a thud, and squealed off in a huff.

He watched her taillights disappear as he called himself twenty kinds of stupid. It was their junior year of high school all over again.

# Chapter 6

Syd made sure to avoid Nick the next day by being gone before he arrived that morning. She went to the Corner Café for breakfast and asked for a table in the back of the dining room. Hannah Allan, her server, was happy to oblige.

Sydney wasn't in the mood to socialize. No, she was in the mood to stew. What was that saying? "Fool me once, shame on you. Fool me twice, shame on me."

She was so busy feeding on her mad that she didn't notice Hannah waiting to take her order until Hannah cleared her throat.

"Sorry. I'm somewhere else this morning." Like an empty classroom in Moonbright High. "I'll have a cup of coffee and whatever the special is." Syd wasn't even hungry.

Hannah returned with the coffee and left Syd to reminisce about all the reasons she'd once despised Nick Rossi.

In her heart, she knew it was silly. She'd been a sensitive sixteen-year-old, grieving the loss of her parents, feeling uprooted and lost. And there was Nick, the best-looking boy she'd ever laid eyes on, who'd come to her for tutoring. He was failing Algebra II and she was killing it. One more bad grade and Nick risked being benched from the varsity baseball team.

For the next four months, she routinely met with him in one of the vacant math classrooms after school. She'd lived for those afternoons like a starving person for a morsel of bread. He'd been so appreciative of her help that he'd begun paying attention to her even while school was in session, waving to her from across the crowded quad or inviting her to join the cool kids' table at lunch in the cafeteria. She was almost starting to feel like she belonged.

And then one day he kissed her.

He had just aced his algebra final and had met her at their usual tutoring spot. Caught up in the moment, he'd swept her off her feet and planted his lips on hers. And before they knew it, they were engaged in a full-blown kiss.

And like any good teen drama, that's when Jennifer walked in and caught them in the act. Her revenge was swift. Jen told anyone who would listen that Syd had misconstrued a friendly gesture and, in her desperation to be liked by the most popular boy in school, had thrown herself at Nick.

Going from being ignored by the other kids to being a social pariah wasn't even the worst part of the fallout. It was that Nick had never manned up. Not once did he correct Jen's story of what had happened that afternoon.

Over the years, Syd questioned whether she had indeed imagined Nick's attraction. As much as she hated to admit it, the whole episode had left a long-standing mark. The repercussions of that stupid kiss even made her second-guess Gage's cheating. Had she been delusional about his feelings for her in the first place?

And then last night . . . She didn't want to think about it.

Her breakfast came, an egg pie (otherwise known as quiche). The restaurant was famous for its mouthwatering pies. There was even a wooden sign on the wall that proclaimed: *Your Fa-*

*vorite Food Comes in a Pie—Lobster, Chicken, or Fruit.* Or in the case of today's special, mushroom and leeks.

It looked delicious. Syd only wished she had an appetite to eat it. She picked at it for a while, letting the buttery goodness melt on her tongue. Nan, one of the owners, came out from the kitchen and gave Syd a wave, then wandered over. Sydney wasn't in the mood to chitchat, but if anyone knew what Gram's plans had been for her commercial kitchen, it would be Nan. She and Stella went way back together.

"Well, hello, stranger." Nan pulled Syd out of her chair and enveloped her in her thin arms. It felt good to be held by one of Gram's oldest friends. "I won't keep you from your breakfast, but I wanted to check in and see how you're doing."

"I'm okay," Syd said, though it was a little less than the truth. Just seeing Nan made her nostalgic for her grandmother.

"I hear Nick Rossi's been over to do work on Stella's place. Between you and me, that handsome young man is even better than his father, who was the best carpenter this town ever saw."

"I wanted to ask you about that. Do you have time to sit for a few minutes?"

"For you, of course I do." Nan took the chair on the other side of the table.

Syd couldn't help but notice her gnarled hands. Arthritis, one of the hazards of being a baker. All that dough kneading and rolling wreaked havoc on the joints.

Syd told Nan about the kitchen and how Gram had commissioned the work even after she'd been diagnosed with cancer. "Do you have any idea why or what her plans were?"

"Not a clue, dear. If she had told anyone, it would've been you," Nan said.

Just hearing the words salved Syd's aching heart. It hurt knowing that Gram had done this without discussing it first with Syd.

"Do you think it was in the hope that you would stay?" Nan

asked. "I know how proud she was of the business you built in San Francisco, but maybe she wanted you to come home."

Gram had been Syd's home, not Moonbright. But to tell that to Nan, who adored the small town, would be an insult.

"I don't know, Nan. It seems like a lot of money to spend on a hope and a prayer that I'd stay. I have a lot invested in Bread and Cie. I couldn't just up and leave California. Gram knew that."

"It does seem like a long shot. But I can't imagine what other reason she might've had. In all the years we knew each other, she never spoke to me about starting a food business." Nan waved her hand at the café. "And I would've been the person she'd come to. You keep digging, dear, and let me know what you find out."

"I will," Syd said, trying to keep the disappointment out of her voice. She had so hoped that Nan could solve the mystery.

"In the meantime, I'm hoping you can help me with a problem." Nan looked down at her hands and sighed. "I've started thinking about outsourcing the café's bread, rolls, and biscuits, and just the other day it occurred to me that you might be just the person. Sadly, these old hands are no longer up to the challenge."

Syd sandwiched Nan's hand between hers and gave it a gentle squeeze. "It's the curse of a bread maker. But I can definitely help. And you'd be doing me a favor too. Gram might've told you that I'm opening a second shop in San Francisco. To differentiate it from the first one, I want to start a new line of baked goods and would love to get feedback from you and your customers on what's working and what isn't."

"Oh my, you're the answer to my prayers, dear girl."

By the time Sydney left, she and Nan had a deal. At least it would give Syd something to focus on while she spent the next few weeks in Moonbright, settling Gram's estate. She might have to fly to San Francisco a couple of times for various meetings and to keep her eye on the business. But she was now filled with purpose. And she hoped all the baking she planned to do would help her keep her mind off Nick. Because lord knew, he'd already taken up too much space in her head.

When she got home his truck was parked in its usual spot in the driveway. Syd made sure to park her rental car on the street. If she was covert enough, she wouldn't have to see him on the way into the house.

She got all the way to the door when he tapped her on the shoulder and made her jump. "For hell's sake, were you just lying in wait?"

"No, but I saw you drive up and thought we should clear the air about what happened last night."

"It's not necessary."

"Actually, it is." He put his hands on his hips where his tool belt usually sat. Good, maybe he was quitting. She could find someone else to make the repairs Dot had suggested.

"Did it ever occur to you that you're not the only one on a schedule? If you want to talk, take a number and get in line." With that, she let herself inside the house and gave the screen door an extra shove, so it slammed in his face.

She was halfway to the kitchen when her cell phone rang. Boy, Nick was persistent. And fast. He must've had her on speed dial. He'd waited sixteen years for the first apology, which he still hadn't made. He could wait another sixteen for the second one. Or maybe he wanted to blame her for last night's kiss. Accuse her of *throwing* herself at him.

Well, this time around, Syd was a grown-ass woman and there was no mistaking what had happened. She may have gone along with the kiss (enthusiastically, she might add) up until the second Nick had pulled away. But he'd initiated it, not her. And the worst part was that it was a really great kiss. Like up there with one of the best kisses she'd ever had. Even better than Gage's kisses, and her ex had had plenty of practice.

She let the call go to voicemail, waited ten seconds, then immediately played the message. It wasn't Nick.

"Hi, I'm calling about the Victorian on Maple and the bakery position," said a woman whose voice Syd didn't recognize. "I have five years of experience at Bread and Butter in Boston. But I'm looking to relocate to Maine. My parents live in Brewer." She left a phone number but no name.

Last Syd looked, there was no job position. If not for the fact that the woman had referenced "the Victorian on Maple," Syd would've thought it was a mistake, a wrong number. But the coincidence was uncanny. Too uncanny. She called the number back and got voicemail. Syd left a brief message and hung up. Either someone was playing a trick on her or this had something to do with Gram's commercial kitchen.

Syd stared up at the ceiling. "Gram, are you messing with me? First it was the reflection of Nick in the toaster and now this. What are you up to, oh grandmother of mine?"

No answer from the heavens came forth. But perhaps the so-called job applicant could help her unravel what the hell was going on.

At the end of the day, Nick decided to take another stab at an apology. Syd couldn't ignore him forever. From the carriage house he could see her through the kitchen window. She was either fixing dinner or baking.

He tapped on the back door.

"Go away," she yelled.

He told himself it was exigent circumstances and let himself in. "Will you give it a rest and just talk to me."

"There's nothing to say." She pulled a tin of muffins out of the oven.

They smelled so good that he was momentarily at a loss for words. He was also pretty sure that if he asked for one, she'd hit him over the head with the pan.

"I'm sorry, Syd. That shouldn't have happened last night. It was totally unprofessional. You're a client for hell's sake."

"I'm not your client." She put the muffins down and put her hands on her hips. "My late grandmother is, remember?"

Those were his own words coming back to mock him.

"Okay, well, in that case I'm not sorry." He flashed a wicked grin, hoping he could charm her into accepting his apology. But from the scowl on her face, it didn't appear to be working.

"Look, let's just forget about it, okay? It was a kiss in the heat of the moment. Nothing more. So can we drop it?"

"Yeah, sure." He held up his hands in the universal sign of surrender.

"Are the ovens still slated for the end of the week?" She was all business now. For some reason, that turned him on even more than last night's red dress, and he suddenly wanted to kiss her again. The first one, as good as it was, had only whetted his appetite.

He moved closer to her as if he were being pulled by gravity. "Yep, even though I'm advising that we wait."

Her response was to ignore him. So much for his recommendation.

"Like I said, it's an expensive piece of equipment to plunk in the middle of a construction zone. But suit yourself."

"I always do." She gave him a withering look but didn't back away. They were so close he could smell the sweetness of her breath. "I'm going to be baking for the Corner Café, so I need those ovens up and running. Pronto."

"I think it was you who only minutes ago said you're not my client." He jutted his chin at her in defiance.

That sort of took the wind out of her bullshit sails because she couldn't have it both ways. Either he worked for her late grandmother or he worked for her.

"If you would be so kind as to have the ovens up and running by this weekend as you promised you would, I would be extremely grateful." She spoke in a saccharine voice that would've given anyone a mouthful of cavities.

"I'll see what I can do."

She thanked him with a tight smile.

"You planning to keep this up for the next four weeks?" He wagged his hand between them. "I had hoped we could bury the hatchet." Clearly, she was equating last night to what had happened in high school and was still angry from all those years ago. "Why don't we clear the air once and for all?"

"Why don't we?" She waved her hand through the air. "Clear away."

"I told Jen the truth that day. That it was me, not you, who initiated the kiss. We fought about it for days."

"Yet you didn't tell everyone else. You just let our entire junior class believe that I threw myself at you. You let me be a laughingstock to protect your mean girlfriend."

"I told anyone who would listen."

"Right."

"What did you want me to do, Sydney, take out an ad in the *Moonbright Sun*. It was idle gossip. The only one who cared was Jennifer."

"And me!"

He pinched the bridge of his nose. "I'm sorry, Syd. I wish I'd been better equipped at sixteen to fix it. I was an immature, stupid kid, who thought honesty was enough. I told the truth. But people chose to believe Jen. I hurt her and she lashed out. Unfortunately, you were the one punished. I should've done better."

"Yes, you should've."

He scrubbed his hand down his face, wishing he had been more resolute in his defense of Syd. Looking back on it, he'd been so consumed with guilt where Jen was concerned that he'd let her run roughshod over the situation. He'd been too inexperienced to realize that wanting to kiss another girl might've been a warning sign that his and Jen's relationship wasn't as solid as he'd thought.

"If I could go back in time, I'd change it. But to set the record straight, last night had nothing to do with high school, Syd." He'd wanted her in the way a man wants a woman. Not the way a curious boy experiments with a girl. "It was wrong for professional reasons. But I'd be lying if I said I didn't want to do it again." The corner of his mouth tipped up.

His words seemed to stun her into silence. But lack of verbal response didn't stop her cheeks from turning bright red. Seemingly stymied about how to respond, she lifted one of the muffins out of the baking tin and handed it to him. It was still warm.

He took a chair at the breakfast table and ate while watching her plate the rest of the muffins.

She handed him a napkin. "Do you want something to drink? I can make coffee."

"Nah, I'm good." He held up his partially eaten muffin. "This is probably dinner."

She deliberated for a few seconds—Nick suspected she was trying to decide whether to forgive him—then took pity on him. "I can make you something. Leftover soup or I could quickly throw together some pasta."

"Soup would be great." He was just happy she was talking to him again.

She got a container from the fridge, a pot from the rack over the stove, and began heating the soup. Her phone rang. Syd checked the screen and turned it off.

"You don't need to get that?"

"It's my ex."

"You don't take his calls?"

"Not if I can help it. But he's also my business partner and the principal investor in Bread and Cie."

That had to suck. "Yeah, I try not to mix business with pleasure for that reason," he said, hoping to make it clear why he'd pulled away after their kiss the night before. Though there were plenty of other good reasons. Namely that she was just passing through and casual hookups left him cold these days.

But he was relieved that their conversation had veered past her hostility toward him and once again appeared to be on normal footing. Whatever that was.

"That's why I don't plan to have a partner the next time around."

"What happened between you two if you don't mind my asking?"

"Well, first Tatiana happened. Then Sue, along with Kelly. There may have also been a Rita along the way. But who's counting?"

"Ouch."

"Now he's engaged to my former assistant. Poor girl." Syd rolled her eyes.

"How long were you two together?"

"Since the inception of Bread and Cie, so about five years. We ended things last summer when I found him in bed with Kelly . . . my former assistant. As you can imagine, things went terribly downhill from there." She laughed, leading him to believe that she was over the guy.

"You seem to be taking it well."

"Oh, I didn't. Not at first. But you know what they say. Time heals all wounds. And he is an excellent businessman. I'll give him that."

Nick thought it was pretty generous of her, given that the guy sounded like a giant douchebag. "He doesn't have a problem with your opening another bakery? I would've thought there'd be a no-compete clause in your partnership contract." He and his brothers were as tight as any close-knit family. But their father had insisted on the clause to ensure that one of them didn't go off on his own because of a hotheaded familial squabble.

"As the wronged half of a couple, I was allowed some concessions." Her mouth slid up. "Besides, I would never compete against myself. The new place is much smaller in scope than Bread and Cie. It'll really be just a neighborhood bakery that specializes in bread. Most of the recipes will be markedly different from what we make at Bread and Cie. That's why I'm in a rush to start baking with professional equipment to test some of my new stuff out. This old oven isn't going to cut it." She took the pot off the burner and ladled them each a bowl of soup.

He nodded. "I'll make it happen."

"So, I aired all my dirty laundry. Now it's your turn. What really happened with you and Jen?"

He stretched his legs under the table. "We want different things is all. She wants the penthouse in Manhattan, a summer place in the Hamptons, and to hobnob with people who spend more money on their suits than I do on a truck. But it wasn't just the money. Moonbright, Maine, was never going to be enough for her." If anyone understood that, it would be Syd. She'd sped out of Moonbright at light speed after high school graduation and never looked back.

"No room for compromise?" Syd brought their bowls to the table.

"The only place I ever wanted to live was Moonbright. I like working with my brothers and carrying on the business my father built from the ground up. I've never been interested in joining Jen's business, remodeling the homes she sells."

"Was that what she wanted?" Syd tilted her head.

"Yeah. It makes sense and I probably would make a shitload of money. But it's not me. It's not where I want to be."

Syd didn't say anything for a long time, making him wonder

what she was thinking. That he lacked ambition? That he was too simple? Too unsophisticated?

"What?" he finally said.

"You really want to know?"

He nodded, even though he recognized that a woman like her wouldn't understand.

"It's only my humble opinion and perhaps I've read too many romance novels, but it seems to me that if two people are destined to be together, they meet each other halfway."

He'd spent a lot of time contemplating that idea. Was it that he and Jen had wanted two different things or was it that they didn't want each other enough to meet in the middle? He wasn't even sure he could love anyone more than he loved his life in Moonbright.

"Then again, maybe I'm being naïve," Syd said with a toss of her head. "Everyone knows that relationships are hard, especially for the long haul. So, it makes sense that if a couple doesn't share the same values from the start, there's probably a good chance they're doomed. Realistically, I don't think I could leave the life I've built for someone else. And if I did, it would have to be a life I wanted too."

"Yep." She'd summed up his entire philosophy on love in a nutshell.

# Chapter 7

The weather in Moonbright had gone from crisp and cool to downright blustery. Surely a storm was on the horizon. But Syd had lived in California so long that she'd lost her inherent skill to predict New England weather patterns. Nevertheless, she didn't need a calendar to tell her Thanksgiving was just weeks away. The leaves were a gorgeous burnt red and orange and everyone in town seemed to be anticipating the holiday.

It would be her first Thanksgiving without Gram. Even though it was a hectic time for a baker, either Syd had flown to Maine for a quick visit or Gram had come to San Francisco. Last year, Stella had even come with Syd to Bread & Cie and helped with the last-minute holiday rush.

Eight months later, Gram had received her diagnosis. Syd would always be thankful for the time they'd had together. This year, it would be just her. She planned to make the best of the holiday by baking up a storm for the Corner Café, where her bread would start debuting as soon as Nick finished installing the ovens.

"How much longer?" she asked while watching over his

shoulder as he slid the individual racks inside all that glorious stainless steel. Who knew Stella had such good taste in commercial baking equipment? The sight of the four-stroke heating coil made Syd's heart go pitter-patter. It was almost as good as the sight of Nick's muscles bunching as he swung a hammer.

"If you'd quit hovering, it would go a lot quicker." He put the last rack in and started attaching the doors.

"When you're done, could we cordon off the area from the rest of the construction site with plastic sheeting?"

He gritted his teeth. "How do you plan to get to the ovens then?"

"Oh, good question."

He rolled his eyes. "I'll make you a plastic door with some Velcro. But I still think it's a bad idea." He punctuated his opinion by making a show of staring at the tools and sawdust that littered the floor.

"I'll give it a good cleaning with the shop vac."

"You're going to have to do it every day," he said, then mumbled, "It'll get old fast."

"I'm not breaking my promise to Nan. And the kitchen oven in the house is woefully inadequate for baking nine to ten dozen loaves a day."

"Don't come crying to me if the health department catches wind of what you're doing and shuts you down."

"Way to be a buzzkill. Call me when it's done. I want to take a selfie of me with this bad boy." She slapped the steel and headed to the house to make a few calls and check in on her crew at Bread & Cie.

She left a message for Gage, thanking her lucky stars he hadn't answered. He'd sent her a couple of urgent texts to call him. But his idea of urgent was running out of shampoo, so she wasn't particularly worried. Syd got a daily status report from her head baker, who assured her that the bakery was running like a well-oiled machine.

After a twenty-four-minute conversation with her business manager, Syd moved on to emails. Emily and Clay were home in Nugget after their tour of New England, and Emily was ready to pick up where she and Syd had left off on the cookbook. Syd responded to the other messages that needed her immediate attention but left the rest for later.

She was too busy hoping Nick would take his lunch break in the house soon. It had become an unspoken routine for him to wander in about noon and for her to fix him something to eat. On most nights, they also shared supper. Syd had begun to watch the clock, counting the minutes to their cozy meals. Much to her wonder—and chagrin—she was getting attached.

Soon she would meet with her grandmother's estate lawyer and arrange to list the property come spring. Her work here would be done. Time to go home to San Francisco, where her business and condo waited. It wasn't wise to grow too close to Nick. Yet she couldn't seem to stop herself from spending as much time with him as possible.

She tried to tell herself that she was merely bereaved and lonely and he was good company. But deep down inside she knew there was a chemistry between them that she hadn't felt with a man in a long time. Perhaps ever. Not even with Gage, who had been fun and sexy but always a little distant. She'd never been able to talk to Gage the way she could with Nick.

As if on cue, he came through the door exactly at noon and washed his hands in the mudroom's laundry sink.

"I made beef stew," she called to him.

"Sounds good." He came into the kitchen and took her in from head to toe. He'd seen her only a couple of hours ago. Yet his hungry assessment made it seem as if it had been days or even weeks. The desire she saw in his eyes gave Syd goose bumps. She couldn't help thinking about their kiss and wondering why he hadn't tried again.

Syd, never shy about being the aggressor, had held back with

Nick. It was probably a great deal due to what had happened in high school.

"What've you been up to?" he asked.

"Catching up on work and phone calls."

"I imagine it's not easy running a business long-distance."

"Nope, especially this time of year. All our retailers are doubling their orders for the holidays. I have good people, though. They're clutch in a crunch."

He grinned at the sports reference, then wandered over to the stove, where he sniffed her pot of stew. "Smells good."

"It felt like a comfort food day." She got two bowls down and dished them up good-size helpings. "I made a sourdough bread too. Given my grandmother's oven, no guarantees on how good it is, though." Syd thought the kitchen stove needed to be recalibrated. Everything took twice as long to cook as it should.

Nick grabbed his usual spot at the table and she sat across from him. It had become their little domestic ritual.

"You want to have dinner at my place?" he asked. "I could grab a pizza on the way home."

"Okay. But I could make us something here."

He gazed around the kitchen. "I figured you could use a change of scenery and a break from cooking."

"No argument from me." She had been working on recipes all day and looked forward to getting out. And his place was rather cozy.

"Besides, the chimney guy is at my place right now. And if all goes well, we can test run the fireplace. Or we can set my house on fire. Either way, I wouldn't mind having a partner in crime."

"I'll pick up a pie at the Corner Café. I have to stop by there to talk to Nan about her order." She looked at him expectantly. "I'll be able to use the ovens first thing in the morning, right?"

He nodded his head. "Yeah. Good luck with navigating

the mess in there. But I'll get your plastic sheeting up before I punch out for the day."

"Thank you." She leaned across the table and flashed him her most appreciative smile. "I'll be out of your hair by the time you arrive tomorrow morning. Promise."

He gave her an acquiescent nod. While they finished their soup, she made a mental note of what she planned to wear to dinner, right down to her underwear.

Nick had a roaring fire going when Syd arrived at his place that evening.

"The house is still standing." She knocked on the mantle. "So I guess everything is working okay."

"Yep, just years of soot buildup. But it's all good now." He set a bottle of wine in the center of the coffee table next to trays of veggies, charcuterie, and cheese and crackers. "It's the best I could do for appetizers."

"Are you kidding? It looks great." Syd handed him the pumpkin pie she'd gotten from Nan on the way over, and he took it to the kitchen.

"I stuck the pizza in the oven to keep it warm," he called over his shoulder, and returned a few minutes later with a bottle opener. "I guess I should've let the Chianti breathe before you got here." He uncorked the bottle and poured them each a glass.

"I wouldn't know the difference." She took a healthy sip. "Mmm, it's delicious. See."

He laughed, then looked her up and down. The same hint of male appreciation he'd shown at lunch glinted in his eyes. "You look nice."

She'd worn a winter white fitted sweater dress with a plunging cowl neck and a pair of tall brown suede boots.

"Thanks. So do you." He'd changed out of his work clothes into fresh jeans and a flannel shirt that looked soft enough to curl up in, and his hair was wet. The faint scent of cologne settled around him. Whatever it was, it smelled woodsy and masculine. Syd wanted to eat him up.

He shrugged like he hadn't put any thought into his appearance. From the look of his carefully plated nibbles, Syd thought it more likely that he'd obsessed over the food.

"Did you do all this?" She waved her hand over the spread.

His expression turned sheepish and his shoulders gave a small hitch. "I called the deli at the market. Ginger did it for me."

Syd didn't know Ginger, but she'd done a lovely job. "Everything looks great."

"You're always cooking for me, so I wanted to do something nice for you."

Now when had Gage ever said that? Syd was pretty sure never.

She surveyed the table. "This is more than nice. It's a veritable feast."

"I figured you wouldn't die from store-bought food. As for my cooking, I make no promises."

"Your grilled steaks were fantastic."

"A barbecue I can manage." He winked. "But I've got to tell you it's intimidating cooking for a professional chef."

"I'm a baker, not a chef. But yeah, I get that a lot. Here's my dirty little secret: I'm not that picky. Feed me and I'm happy."

"Yeah?" He sat next to her and sipped his wine. "What else makes you happy?"

Him, sitting so close that she could feel the warmth of his breath on her neck. For a second it took her back to high school, when her palms would break out in a sweat at the mere rumble of his deep voice. But she was older now, more experienced. So why did he still have that effect on her? Even though they spent most of their time bickering, she was more than a little infatuated with him. Okay, maybe a lot infatuated.

"You ready for pizza?"

"Sure," she said, though they'd hardly touched any of his lovely appetizers. "You want help?"

"Nah. Nothing to do but take it out of the oven. Should we eat it here or at the table?"

"In front of the fire." There was something incredibly romantic about eating in front of a roaring fireplace.

"Okay . . . in here . . . then." But he didn't move and his eyes never left her lips.

She stared back, hypnotized. He leaned in and ever so gently brushed her lips with his. Hesitant at first, Syd kissed him back. It was all the encouragement he needed, because he cupped the back of her head and went deeper, his tongue exploring the inside of her mouth. He tasted delicious, like wine and heat. It was all she could do not to inhale him.

He moved over her until she was flat on the couch. She gripped his shoulders, pulling him down on top of her. His weight felt glorious pressing against her. Syd arched into his arousal, grinding against him. He moaned and she felt him grow harder.

Nick kissed her neck, and his hands roamed over her dress. She undid the top buttons of his flannel shirt. Impatient, he dragged the shirt over his head. A light dusting of hair covered his well-muscled chest. Swinging a hammer had paid off for him in more ways than one. Syd had never been with a man so ripped.

Unable to resist, she pressed her palm against his abs. They were as hard as granite. It made her a little self-conscious about never going to the gym.

He played with the hem of her dress, his work-rough hands skimming the inside of her thighs. "Can I take this off?"

She sucked in a breath and whispered, "Yes."

He rucked the dress up over her head and tossed it on the floor near his shirt, leaving her in nothing but a white lace bra and a thong. Nick lifted himself on both elbows and gazed down at her, taking his time to look. His eyes shined. "Damn," he said, a slow smile building. "I mean damn."

Her skin prickled with anticipation. She pulled him down again and tilted her head back, giving him full access.

"The couch is a little tight." His legs hung off the end. "Bedroom?"

"Uh-huh," she croaked, her throat suddenly dry. They were doing this. She and Nick Rossi, the boy of her high school fantasies.

He scooped her off the sofa and carried her as if she weighed nothing through the hallway to the master. She hadn't seen his bedroom on her last visit to his house and in the back of her mind was curious. But presently, the only thing she was focused on was getting Nick's pants off.

He laid her on his bed and came down with her. His kisses, hot and passionate, spurred her to desperation. In a frenzy, her hand moved to his belt buckle. When she struggled to get it undone, he impatiently pushed her hand away. In three seconds flat, he managed to unfasten his belt and shuck his jeans and underwear.

"Your turn." He slid her thong down her legs. The scrape of the lace against her skin made her whimper.

He unclasped her bra and fondled her breasts, weighing each one in his hand. "Ah, Syd. You're so freaking beautiful."

She threw her head back as his mouth laved attention on her breasts and his hands explored her body. Everything about him felt so good that she lost her mind.

"Nick . . . Nick, please."

Syd made it known exactly what she wanted. But instead of giving it to her, he continued to slowly torture her with exquisite foreplay. She arched up, silently begging him to fill her.

Finally, he reached into the nightstand, found a condom, and sheathed himself.

Within seconds he was moving inside her.

"Good?" he whispered in her ear.

"So good," was all she could manage. It was more like transcendent. But she could barely see straight, let alone speak in full sentences.

She touched him everywhere. His hair, his chest, his perfect backside. He kissed her again and again, never breaking stride, going faster, deeper, harder.

And just like a hair trigger, she shattered, calling out his name. Leaving her no time to gather up a second wind, he increased his pace, heightening her pleasure all over again. She met him stroke for stroke, and before she knew it she was climaxing a second time, something she never did.

Unable to hold on any longer, he threw his head back and reached his peak just as she was coming down. Afterward, they lay there together, tangled in each other's arms, breathing hard.

Nick rolled them to the side to take his weight off her and she burrowed her head against his chest. She could hear his heartbeat. The sweet sound of it along with the warmth of his body and the safety of his arms lulled her to sleep.

She didn't know how long she'd napped, but when she woke, Nick lay awake, gazing at her. He'd covered them both with a quilt from his bed.

"What time is it?"

"Only nine." He reached over and brushed a strand of hair out of her face.

Her messy bun had come loose and she was pretty sure she had crazy hair. But Nick was looking at her as if she were the most beautiful woman in the world. The heat in his eyes was heady. No one had ever looked at her that way before. It made her wonder if she was seeing things that weren't there, the way she had sixteen years ago.

"I should probably get going," she said because leaving now would be the safe thing to do.

She had to be up at the crack of dawn to start baking before the Corner Café opened for breakfast. But Nick made her want to believe, and his warm bed made her want to stay.

His phone rang, jolting them both.

"Shit." He fumbled around on the nightstand, took one look at the screen, and muttered an expletive. "Hang on a sec."

He took the phone into the other room, which signaled to Syd it wasn't about a leak or some other construction emergency. It was personal.

She strained to hear, grabbing snippets of the conversation, and quickly concluded that it was Jennifer. Of course it was. History repeating itself.

Syd gathered up her underwear just as she realized that her dress was still somewhere on the living room floor. She didn't want to walk through Nick's house in her thong and bra, so she borrowed a shirt from his closet. It smelled like laundry soap and shame. Shame that she'd yet again been reeled in like a hungry fish.

She crept into the living room to find Nick sitting on the couch. He motioned to the phone he held to his ear and gave an apologetic shrug, then mouthed, *Give me five minutes.* He waved his hand over the spread of mostly untouched food. They'd never gotten around to eating.

She swiped her dress off the floor and went back to his bedroom, where she fully dressed, then went in search of her purse. It was on the hallway console. She grabbed it and let herself out. Nick, so absorbed in his conversation with Jen, didn't even see her leave.

# Chapter 8

Syd pulled out her last sheet of breads from the new ovens when she heard Nick's truck turn into the driveway. He'd tried to call her several times after she'd left his house the previous night. She'd let every call go to voicemail.

In two weeks, she was going home, and as far as she was concerned, Nick Rossi was officially out of her system.

She'd started for the house with her tray when he met her in the driveway. "Why didn't you answer your phone last night?"

Syd didn't like his sharp tone. "You clearly have unfinished business with Jennifer, and I don't want to be in the middle of it."

"There is no unfinished business. It's finished. She and I are no longer together."

Syd shifted the tray to her other hand. "Really? Because it certainly didn't feel that way last night."

He took the tray from her and put it on the hood of his truck. "Look, she's been a part of my life since we were sixteen years old. She's having trouble adjusting."

"What does that even mean? Trouble adjusting." Syd held up

her hand as Nick started to talk. "You don't owe me an explanation. You don't owe me anything."

"Yes, I do." He tried to take her hand, but she wouldn't let him. "Syd, I like you. A lot. Last night wasn't just a . . . hookup. It was important to me. You're important to me." He scrubbed his hand through his dark hair. "Jeez, Syd, don't you see? I'm falling for you."

Syd took a minute to let that sink in. She was falling for him too. But it was an impossible situation. In two weeks, she would be gone, back to San Francisco. Everything she'd worked for was there. And everything Nick had worked for was in Moonbright.

"I can't do this, Nick." She picked up the tray and went inside the house, leaving him standing there alone.

She boxed up her breads and drove them to the Corner Café with a promise from Nan for a full report on which ones were the top sellers. On her way home she got a call. Gage again. There was only so long she could avoid her business partner. She tapped Bluetooth.

"Hi, Gage."

"What do you know? You finally answered your goddamn phone."

"In case you forgot, my grandmother died. I have a lot on my plate right now, Gage. And I know from Cecily that everything is fine at Bread and Cie. So what's so important that you couldn't wait?" *Or just have sent a damn email?* She knew full well why. He didn't want to give her time to respond to whatever it was he had to say. Syd had a sneaking suspicion that he was going to renege on his agreement to let her open a second bakery and was going for an ambush.

"Williams-Sonoma has been in touch." He paused for effect. When she didn't respond, he continued. "They want to include your biscuits in their mail-order food catalog."

"Okay." She waited for the *But*. When nothing was forth-coming, she said, "That's fantastic."

"I thought you'd like it. But"—there it was—"our agreement with Sugar Café is that they have exclusive dibs on the biscuits." Sugar Café was a California chain and represented a nice chunk of their business.

"I guess we have to pass with Williams-Sonoma then." As much as she'd like to do business with the kitchenware giant, a deal was a deal.

Gage let out a sigh. "I crunched the numbers and it would be more advantageous to work with Williams-Sonoma. The catalog has national reach."

"We can't just break our contract with Sugar Café."

"Don't you know contracts were made to be broken? Our lawyers can figure out a way."

How like Gage to take his commitments so lightly. It took everything she had not to make a snide remark. "I don't roll that way, Gage, and you know it. Tell Williams-Sonoma no. I have to go."

Before she could hang up, he asked, "How are you doing? Did you get my flowers?"

"I did. Thank you." It had been thoughtful of him to send them. He wasn't a total shit.

"Did the funeral go okay?"

"Uh-huh, it was a beautiful tribute to my grandmother. How's everything there?"

"Good. Our holiday numbers are up from last year, so I'm happy. I wish you'd reconsider on the Williams-Sonoma thing. It would be great exposure and business is business, Syd."

That's where they were different. To her, a good business-person kept her word. The way Nick had with Stella. "It's not always about the bottom line, Gage. Sometimes value comes in being honorable."

He let out a snort. "Whatever, Syd. You'll learn the hard way with your new enterprise that turning down good business is no way to run a railroad. But I don't want to argue over the phone about it. How soon until everything is wrapped up there?"

"I'm meeting with Gram's lawyer later this week and have a ticket home for the following week. I'll call you when I get back."

She hung up and parked in the driveway, leaving Nick enough room to get out in his truck. Syd sat in her car for a while, letting Nick's words roll over her: *Syd, don't you see? I'm falling for you.*

She'd fallen for him sixteen years ago. And despite the animosity she'd carried with her into adulthood, all it had taken was one kiss for her to fall all over again. Life sure knew how to throw a curveball.

There was a tap on her window, pulling her from her thoughts. She looked up and there was Nick.

She got out of the car, and without saying a word he took her in his arms.

"What've we done?" She rested her forehead against his chest.

He let out a wry laugh. "We've got a couple of weeks. What do you say we take it one day at a time and live in the moment?"

Why? It would only make the end worse. But she nodded because she wasn't ready to let him go.

They spent lunch in bed.

"At this rate I'll never get the carriage house done." Nick rolled to his side and propped himself up on one elbow. He traced a line down the valley between Syd's breasts.

She arched up and kissed him. "You hungry?"

"Yep. For seconds." He rolled her on top of him. "Let me look at you for a while."

She loved the way his eyes filled with heat. When the time

came, how would she be able to say good-bye? *I won't think about it now.* As Nick said, she'd live in the moment and enjoy every second of the time they had together.

Her phone rang. She was about to ignore it when she saw the Boston area code. "It's her," she blurted.

"Who?"

She climbed off Nick and grabbed her phone off the nightstand. "Hello."

"Hi. This is Fern Rogers. I called earlier about the baking position. I've been moving the last few days from Boston to Brewer and just now got your message."

Syd shrugged into her robe. "May I ask how you found out about the position?"

"Your ad on Glassdoor."

"Ah," Syd said. *Who knew that Gram had even known about Glassdoor?* "I'm afraid that the position is no longer open."

"Really? Darn, from the description, the job was perfect for me." Fern sounded so disappointed that Syd considered offering her a job in San Francisco at Bread & Cie.

"I'm a bit at a disadvantage," Syd said. "The person who placed the ad has since died. I'm her granddaughter and didn't know anything about her plans. What exactly did the ad say?" She turned to find Nick intently watching her.

"Oh, wow, I'm sorry about your grandmother. Uh, just that she was looking for an assistant baker to help open a tearoom."

"A tearoom?" Syd's eyes grew wide. The mystery continued to thicken.

"Uh-huh. In an old Victorian on a tree-lined street. There was a picture in the ad. It was lovely and got me really excited about the job."

Syd couldn't imagine what her grandmother had been thinking. There was already a bakeshop in Moonbright, and of course there was the Corner Café. She doubted a town this size could also support a tearoom.

"I apologize about the confusion," Syd said. "Best of luck with your job search."

"Thank you. And if you change your mind, you've got my number."

"What was that about a tearoom?" Nick asked when Syd got off the phone.

Syd shook her head, still puzzled. "Apparently Stella was planning to turn the house into a tearoom. She didn't tell you that?"

"Not a word." He looped his hand around Syd's waist and pulled her back into bed. "Not a bad idea, though."

"A tearoom? Really?" Syd pulled a face. "Just what Moonbright needs." From a business point of view, the idea was patently ridiculous.

"The town's growing, Syd. Yuppies moving in from Portland and Bangor. Kids who grew up here are coming back to raise their families. Moonbright's no longer the small town you remember. Hell, my brothers and I have more business than we can handle. And tourists no longer just flock here for Halloween. They pack the town in summer and are back for fall and winter. If you don't believe me, ask over at the Corner Café or at Bellaluna's Bakeshop."

Syd had noticed how crowded both establishments were but had chalked it up to the Halloween rush.

She blew out a breath. "What do you think Stella was up to?"

"I think it's pretty obvious." He kissed her deeply on the mouth. "She wanted you to stay and run her tearoom."

"That's nuts. She knew how important Bread and Cie is to me, that I was looking for a second location for a new bakery."

Nick gave her a pointed look.

"Nuh-huh, no way. My life is in San Francisco."

"I don't know what to tell you, then." He got out of bed and started to dress.

"Where are you going?"

"Back to work."

"Let me make you something to eat first." She collected her clothes from the floor and ducked into the bathroom.

Nick was waiting in the kitchen, looking at his watch, when she got downstairs. He pointed at the wall. "Your clock's eight minutes slow."

Syd stared at the minute hand, then checked the time on her phone. Sure enough, the clock was slow.

*Uh-uh, not that damned Halloween legend.*

A draft swept through the room and she checked to see if she'd left a window open. But everything was closed tight. She could've sworn she smelled a hint of Jean Naté, Stella's favorite scent.

*What are you up to, Grandmother dearest?*

Stop, she told herself, or she'd be accused of being as superstitious as the old women of Moonbright.

# Chapter 9

"Well, how did it go?" Nick asked as he installed a bank of shelving in the corner of the carriage house.

In the last few days, the project had come a long way. The large sink and small walk-in cooler were both up and running. The cabinetry was mounted and Nick had assembled the portable stainless-steel countertops and racks. It looked like a smaller version of Syd's setup at Bread & Cie.

Just a few things here and there and they could stick a fork in Gram's vision.

Well, almost.

"Gram's lawyer confirmed Stella's wish for a tearoom. Gram left the plans with him, including permits to turn the driveway into outdoor seating and to build a structure off the carriage house for a small dining room." Syd was still reeling from the news.

"Hmm, she never mentioned anything to me about another building, or an outdoor seating area. Just the kitchen."

Syd nodded. "She wanted it to be my decision and apparently hoped that going ahead with the kitchen would act as an enticement." Syd suspected that Stella had also hoped that the man building the kitchen would be yet another enticement. Gram had always been wily that way.

"What are you going to do?" Nick put down a shelf and wrapped his arms around her.

"There's nothing I can do. I can't run a business in Moonbright from San Francisco. And honestly, I could use the cash from the sale of the house to open my second bakery. But at the same time, I don't want to let Gram down." She closed her eyes, wishing Stella were here and they could have one of their heart-to-hearts.

"What did the lawyer say?"

"That Gram knew this would be a dilemma, and at the end of the day, she wanted me to do what was best for me. She just wanted to give me options, he said." Syd sighed.

She waited for Nick to add his two cents, maybe ask her to stay. But crickets, which in her mind spoke volumes. Syd didn't know what she expected of him. They'd only just reunited and although he'd said that he was falling for her . . . well, it didn't matter, because staying was out of the question.

Syd gazed around the room. "The place looks great. You know of anyone who wants to open a tearoom in a gorgeous Victorian in Maine with a killer commercial kitchen?"

"Can't say I do." He kissed her, making her pulse quicken the way he always did. Oh, how she would miss this man and his kisses. "On another note, how would you like to go on a real date tonight?"

"A real date?" She laughed. As far as she was concerned, they'd been "dating" like crazy.

"Yeah. Call me old-fashioned, but something besides my house or yours. Something like dinner and a movie."

"Sounds wonderful."

"I'm just waiting for the final inspections from the planning and health departments. Then I'll knock off, run home for a shower, and pick you up around six."

"Okay. How should I dress for this real date?"

"Any way you want. But just remember, less is more."

Nick was setting himself up for a world of hurt. Syd already had one foot out the door. In a week, poof, she'd be gone. Hadn't he learned from Jennifer? *No, because I'm a dumbass.*

He shaved, rubbed his hair dry with a towel, and slapped on some aftershave. He'd managed to snag the last reservation at Bucatini's in Bangor. It was the best Italian restaurant in the area. The chef made a risotto that was out of this world, even better than his mother's, though he'd never tell her that. Not if he wanted to live to see thirty-three.

Nick glanced at his watch. He was running late. The inspectors had left his job for last. They'd signed off on the work, but the planning department guy still needed to check off the bathroom, which Nick estimated would be done by the end of the week. Then he'd start on remodeling the Victorian. Syd had already picked out new bathroom fixtures and paint colors. The work was straightforward and would be done in plenty of time for Syd to put the house on the market in the spring.

Usually, Nick preferred working in a vacant house: no homeowners looking over his shoulder. But he was going to miss Syd's lunches. He waited for them like he did for his next breath. Even back in high school, he'd watched the clock to meet up with her for tutoring. She'd been so easy to talk to . . . so comfortable and at the same time alluring. Maybe because she hadn't originally grown up in Moonbright, which for him made her an exotic bird.

He'd had a shot at her back then and blown it. And now . . . well, you couldn't fit a square peg in a round hole. Syd would never be happy running a tearoom in a small town. From the sound of it, she had San Francisco at her feet. Why settle for anything less?

He grabbed a jacket on his way out and zipped through side streets to get to Maple. When he pulled up, Syd was waiting for him and climbed into his truck before he could get out and open the door for her.

"You look beautiful." He leaned over to kiss her.

"How can you tell? I'm bundled up like the Stay Puft Marshmallow Man."

"I can still see your face." He played with her scarf. "It's a really great face, by the way."

"Yours too." She sniffed his neck. "And you smell fantastic. Where we going?"

"My favorite Italian place. I hope you're hungry."

"Starved."

He reached over and took her hand, and they rode like that the entire way to Bangor. They filled the cab of his truck with conversation about each other's day. Nick couldn't remember enjoying another person's company as much as he did Syd's. She was the personification of beauty and brains—and a great listener to boot.

When they arrived at the restaurant, he ushered her inside. They were seated next to a stone hearth with a blazing fire. The waitress had just taken their drink orders when Syd's phone played the *William Tell Overture.*

"Shoot, I forgot to turn the ringer off." She fumbled in her purse until she found her phone. As she was trying to turn it off, a second call came in. "Sorry, sorry."

"Everything okay?"

"I don't know." She glanced at her phone screen. "It was Gage and now my head baker. I think I'd better get it." She got up from the table and walked to the restroom.

Nick checked his watch. It wasn't even five yet in California. He glanced around the restaurant, where every table was full.

Candlelight flickered, giving the dining room a romantic glow. A trio of musicians were setting up in the corner. He'd forgotten that the restaurant had live music. Hopefully, he and Syd would stick around after dinner, have a drink or two, and enjoy the entertainment.

But when Syd returned to the table she was ashen.

Nick immediately got to his feet. "What's wrong?"

"There's been a fire at Bread and Cie. I have to go home and book a flight to San Francisco."

"Ah, crap, Syd." *What a hell of a thing to happen.* "I'll get you home in record time, then drive you to the airport." He flagged their server down to let her know they wouldn't be staying.

"You know what? Skip Moonbright. Can you take me straight to the airport?"

"You got it."

Syd worked the phone while Nick headed to Bangor International. From her clipped long-distance conversations, Nick gathered that the blaze had been caused by faulty wiring and there was extensive damage.

He rested his hand on her leg. "You have good insurance, right?"

"Yes, but this is our busiest season. Losing the revenue could kill us."

As he listened to her discussion with the ex, it sounded to Nick like the bakery was in bad shape. "I'm sorry, Syd. I wish I had something better to say, something more reassuring."

She let out a deep breath. "Your moral support is enough. Gram was always that for me and without her—" She broke off.

"If there's anything I can do, I'm here for you."

"Thank you. It means a lot."

"Which airline are you booked on?" he asked as he navigated the entrance to the airport.

"American Airlines."

Nick doubted she'd get a flight right away. "I'll come in with you." The last thing he wanted to do was leave her stranded at the airport.

"You don't have to."

"I want to." He squeezed her knee. "At least if you have to kill time, I can get you something to eat."

"Ah, I'm sorry I ruined our date." She dropped her head on his shoulder.

"Promise me a rain check." But he had a bad feeling that this was it. Once she got to San Francisco, she wouldn't be returning.

"Absolutely," she said, but he detected a sadness in her voice.

His gut told him Syd was thinking the same thing as he. This was it, the end.

# Chapter 10

Syd's bakery looked like a burned-out refugee camp.

"It's even worse than you described," she told Gage as they walked through the building, examining the damage. The walls had charred marks on the drywall and you could see where the flames had licked the ceiling.

If it hadn't been for the sprinkler system, it would've been much worse, the firefighters said. Syd had trouble imagining the situation any graver than this. Ash and retardant covered the floor, the equipment was beyond repair, and the space stank like burnt toast if the toast had been on steroids.

It would take months to fix the damage. "What're we going to do?" Syd rubbed her temples. She was going on zero sleep, fueled only by coffee.

Gage shrugged. "We can't afford not to fill our holiday orders. November to January accounts for roughly a third of our revenue stream. I'm hoping we can find a temporary kitchen."

*Good luck.* As far as Syd knew, there was nothing large enough available on such short notice to meet their production schedule. But if anyone could find it, Gage could.

"What about insurance? How soon can we expect them to pay our claim?" They'd need money as fast as possible to replace their equipment.

"I talked to our agent, and as soon as we can come together on a dollar amount for damages, they'll cut us a check."

At least that was something.

"I guess we should get on the phone and start calling everyone we know about a new space."

Gage nodded. "In the meantime, I'll get some folks in here to see what we can salvage."

Syd doubted there was anything. Replacing all their cookware would be a job in and of itself. "I'll call our rep at Bay Restaurant Supply and see if he can hook us up as quickly as possible."

"Yep." Gage rubbed his hand down his face and glanced around the kitchen at the carnage. "You know a good contractor?"

Too bad Nick lived on the other side of the country. Her chest squeezed just thinking about him. It had been only eight hours since she'd left him at the airport and yet it had felt so final.

"I'll make some calls," she said. Maybe Emily would be a good resource. At least for finding a temporary commercial kitchen large enough to accommodate their operation.

And like that, she remembered the Corner Café. She was supposed to drop off a new order of yeast rolls, cheesy biscuits, and cinnamon bread this morning. In her haste to get to San Francisco, she'd forgotten to call Nan.

She stepped outside, moved away from her burned-down building, and inhaled clean air. At the bottom of her purse she found her phone, which was down to the last of its battery life. She quickly dialed and got Nan on the second ring.

"I am so sorry," she started to say, but Nan stopped her.

"Nick told us what happened, dear. Is everyone okay?"

Her evening crew had been able to get out of the building, unharmed. If anything had happened to one of her employees . . . well, the thought made Syd count her blessings. "Everyone is fine, thank goodness. But the bakery is a wreck and, in my frenzy to get here, I forgot about the order I promised you."

"Don't be ridiculous. We've survived this long without your delicious breads, though they're a giant hit, Syd. I wish you would reconsider staying. I don't know who will miss you more, me or my customers."

"That is so sweet of you, Nan." Gage had come outside and was motioning to Syd. He had news. "Uh, I have to go, Nan."

"Oh, hon, when you have time, drop us a line and let us know how you're doing."

"I will. Thank you for being so understanding." She hung up and made her way across the sidewalk to where Gage was standing. "What's up?"

"I may have a lead on a commissary kitchen we can rent."

Syd's mouth fell open. "How did you make that happen so fast?"

"It's not a done deal by any stretch, but Kelly called someone she knows and just texted me that she's driving over there to check the place out."

It took all of Syd's willpower not to pull a face at the mention of her former assistant's name. The worst part about Gage and Kelly's affair was that Syd had lost the best assistant she'd ever had.

"Fantastic. Let me know what she finds out. I've got to go home and grab a shower, Gage." Besides smelling like smoke, she'd been in the same clothes since her dinner date with Nick. "After that I'll start making calls about equipment and everything else we'll need. Who's been in touch with our accounts? Even if we're lucky enough to get this kitchen, I don't see us making our orders this week."

Gage ran his hand through his thinning hair. "I'll get my

staff to let everyone know. By now the fire has been all over the news, so it shouldn't come as any surprise. But, Syd, we've got to get up and running as soon as possible; otherwise we won't make payroll."

Syd sighed. The margins were so tight in the baking business that even a flush company could go down with one small catastrophe. "I know."

She took a Lyft home, her head throbbing. There hadn't been any time to grab food at the airport, and all she'd had was a bag of airline pretzels. Though the idea of eating made her stomach queasy. Sleep was what she wanted. But there was too much work to be done.

She was unlocking her front door when she got a text from Gage that the kitchen was a no go. Too small. They were back at square one as far as finding a place.

She'd been home less than three hours and she was already physically and emotionally drained.

After her shower, she called Emily, who'd already heard about the fire through the local food grapevine.

"I'm so very sorry, Syd. How can I help?"

"We need a large commercial baking kitchen. You have any ideas?"

"Not off the top of my head. But let me do some calling around. How long do you think it'll take to rehab the bakery?"

"I don't know. I need a good contractor."

"Let me make some calls."

As soon as Syd hung up with Emily, she called everyone she could think of. Though they all tried to be helpful, Syd was no closer to solving her problems.

Gage sent another text, his fourth one in an hour. "Any luck? None on my end. Kelly has a friend who's in construction and she's calling him now. Please tell me you've got good news."

She dialed his number. "Nothing so far. Emily McCreedy is reaching out to some of her friends, but I doubt she'll have any better luck than I did. This commercial kitchen we're looking for is a unicorn, Gage. We'd be better off paying a crew to work around the clock to repair our kitchen."

"I don't know what kind of cleanup is involved with fire damage or what the health department will require. We may be looking at months here to mitigate the odor, the ash . . . biohazards. This isn't my area of expertise, Syd."

"Is there someone we can talk to about it . . . an expediter or someone from the city?"

"Let me ask around. But even if we can get a cleanup crew to do it to the satisfaction of the health department, we've got open walls . . . an open roof. The place is in a goddamn shambles."

"What about Kelly's construction friend?"

"It's a possibility. We're working on it. You keep searching for a kitchen, because right now that looks like our best option."

Yeah, if it actually existed.

By nine that night, she couldn't push herself to make another call. She could barely keep her eyes open. Two hours earlier she'd made herself a sandwich, and it was still sitting on the counter, untouched. The day had been daunting, and she'd never felt more alone. Even with all the support from her friends and colleagues, she was terribly on her own.

She'd tried to call Nick but kept getting voicemail. She could really use some of his moral support about now.

The next morning, she met Gage at Bread & Cie. Kelly had come through with a contractor, and they planned to walk the site with him to get an idea of how long a rehab would take. The bakery looked even worse than it had the day before. Syd figured she'd still been in shock when she'd first arrived. Today, though, she was able to see the complete destruction.

"I need a few minutes," she told Gage and the contractor, and ducked into the alley, where she pressed her face against the neighboring building and cried until her tears ran dry. Everything she'd built was gone. And Gram, Syd's life guide, was no longer here to soothe her. If only . . .

"It looks pretty bad."

Syd didn't dare to look up. The voice sounded so much like Nick's that she was afraid to turn around and be disappointed when she found someone else standing there.

"Ah, honey, come here."

She slowly raised her head, and there was Nick with his arms wide open. It only took her a second to walk into them. "I don't understand . . . what are you doing here . . . how did you find me?"

He lifted her chin with his finger and stared into her eyes. "I buttoned up the carriage house, caught a plane, and Googled Bread and Cie. Figured you'd be here."

"I can't believe you came all this way." She buried her face in his chest so he wouldn't see how choked up she was. Suddenly she didn't feel so all alone. "I tried to call you. . . . You must've been on the plane. When did you get in?"

"Early this morning. I had a layover in DC."

"Oh, Nick, you must be exhausted. You didn't have to come, but I'm so glad you're here."

"Looks like you can use me." He bobbed his head at her charred bakery. "I wish I could've brought my tools."

"I'm just happy to have a shoulder." His were certainly wide enough to bear the weight. "I don't know how we'll get back on our feet. This is a huge hit."

"We'll make it happen. It always looks worse than it is. Have you called a fire damage restoration company to do the cleanup? As soon as that's done we can start rebuilding."

*We.* He'd said it twice—she'd counted. Never had her heart felt so full.

"What about all your work in Moonbright?"

"Sal and Tino have got me covered. Let's do this."

*  *  *

With little sleep, they spent the next week clearing enough of the damage to get the health department's blessing to start baking again. Nick worked tirelessly alongside Rafael, Kelly's contractor friend, installing flooring and drywall. They still had a mess to contend with, but engineers had deemed the building structurally sound. It turned out that the fire damage was mostly cosmetic. Still a ton of work, but a lot less costly and time-consuming than having to build from the ground up.

Every day, Syd fell deeper and deeper for Nick, who'd been her lifeline. Their nights, what little they had of them, were spent in bed, wrapped in each other's arms. She'd never experienced the kind of intimacy she had with Nick. But in her heart, she knew they were only putting off the inevitable. Soon he'd have to return to Moonbright and she would have to put her life back together in San Francisco.

Yet the thought of ending whatever this was made it nearly impossible to let go. She reminded herself that he'd never asked for a future together. *Jeez, Syd, don't you see? I'm falling for you* had been the extent of his voicing his feelings for her.

Still, he was here, working like a dog to help her salvage her business. That had to mean something, right?

But when he got on a plane back to Bangor two days later without discussing where they stood, she convinced herself that they were friends who could never become anything more. Now she just had to convince herself that it was for the best.

# Chapter 11

One look at Syd's big-city life and Nick had known he was doomed. Her condo reminded him of a commercial for expensive vodka. Views of the San Francisco Bay, the Golden Gate Bridge, and city lights made Moonbright seem like Timbuktu.

Then there was her bakery. The kitchen was ten thousand square feet, far larger than Stella's quaint carriage house. The little building wouldn't hold a tenth of Syd's employees.

And while her ex was a dick for cheating on her, Nick couldn't help comparing himself. The dude showed up to the bakery every day dressed in designer suits. The only suit Nick owned was the one he'd worn to Tino's wedding a couple of years ago. He doubted it still fit him anymore.

The week had sure opened his eyes to how differently he and Sydney lived. The crushing part was their week together had also cemented just how strong his feelings were for her. If he thought he'd fallen for her before the trip to San Francisco, he was now completely underwater. Sydney Byrne did it for him, hook, line, and sinker.

It wasn't easy letting her go but what choice did he have? He couldn't give her what she wanted, and she deserved someone who could.

*One day at a time*, he told himself. He'd get over her one day at a time.

But as Thanksgiving approached, he was no closer to getting over her than he had been a couple of weeks ago. He'd tried going cold turkey. Yet he found himself reaching for the phone at least three times a day to call her, using work on her grandmother's house as an excuse: *Do you want the shelves over the toilet or next to the sink? Did you get those paint chips I sent you?*

"Hey, what's your problem?" Sal asked.

"Huh? Sorry, what did you say?"

Sal threw his arms up in defeat. "Apparently that beer you've been staring into for the last ten minutes is more interesting than Marjorie Miller's change orders."

They'd met at the Thirsty Raven for happy hour and to discuss the Millers' project, which had gone over budget.

"You have to sit down with Marjorie and Dick and give them an accounting before they get the final bill and flip out," Nick said. "People don't realize that altering the plan in the eleventh hour of a project comes with a price tag."

Sal shook his head. "Why do I get stuck delivering the bad news?"

"Because you're the dipshit who allowed Marjorie to make all the changes in the first place."

"Fine." Sal rolled his eyes. "What's eating you, anyway? You haven't been the same since you got home from San Francisco."

Nick didn't think there was any sense in lying. His brothers knew him better than anyone. "I've got a lot on my mind."

"Like a certain baker you've been infatuated with since high school?" Sal waggled his brows. "What's going on between you and Sydney Byrne?"

"She lives across the country, Sal. So nothing is going on."
Nick went back to staring into his beer.

Syd fastened her seat belt while a too-cheery flight atten-
dant announced that the crew would soon be serving turkey
scrambles, cranberry jelly, and toast. For the third or fourth
time that morning, Syd questioned her sanity.

Showing up at Nick's doorstep unannounced on a holiday
had seemed like a brilliant idea after a couple of glasses of wine,
when she'd paid three times the going rate for a round-trip
ticket to Maine. This morning . . . well, not so much.

He hadn't invited her. Yet here she was on an eight-hour
flight with a stopover in Philly. On the upside, she didn't have
anywhere else to go. Her Thanksgiving orders were filled and
she'd be back in time for Monday's deliveries.

Worse came to worst, she'd have Thanksgiving dinner alone
in Gram's Victorian. She needed to check the remodel anyway.
At least that's what she told herself.

She slept through most of the flight, awakening just as
the plane prepared for landing in Bangor. Traveling light, she
grabbed her carry-on from the overhead and managed to de-
plane in record time. She wasn't looking forward to driving in
the dark, though the forecast called for mild weather. No snow
or ice.

At the car rental kiosk, she got an all-wheel-drive vehicle
just in case. In Maine, the weather could change on a dime.

An hour later, she sat parked in front of Nick's house, holding her breath. Of all the hairbrained schemes this one was
right up there with Gram's commercial kitchen. But she was
here now. Cold and hungry.

*Just do it.*

She forced herself out of the car and gave herself a pep talk
as she made her way across Nick's front yard. The fact that the

lawn desperately needed mowing made her smile. She rang the bell when she got to the door, but no one answered. More than likely he was at his parents'.

So much for her surprise. Then again, what had she expected? Of course he'd be with his family on Thanksgiving. She sucked in a steadying breath and slowly dialed his number on her phone.

"Syd?" He answered on the first ring, making her heart race. "Where are you?"

"Funny you should ask. I'm sitting in front of your house."

"Shit."

Okay, not the reaction she'd hoped for.

"I'm standing in front of yours," he said. "I guess that's why no one is answering your intercom."

Apparently great minds thought alike. They were each trying to surprise the other. She didn't know whether to be thrilled or disappointed.

"Stay where you are," he said.

"In front of your house?"

"In Moonbright. I'll catch the quickest flight home." He'd be lucky to make it here by tomorrow. "And, Syd . . ."

"Yes?"

"I love you."

The next morning, Syd walked through the carriage house. It was amazing how very different it looked from the last time she'd seen it. Just a few finishing touches had turned the granny flat into a dazzling commercial kitchen. Not nearly as large as Bread & Cie but big enough to accommodate a tearoom and then some.

"Don't you love it, Gram?" Stella had been the architect after all.

It made Syd wonder what other intentions Gram had had by throwing her and Nick together. She'd been well aware of Syd's crush in high school and had soothed her broken heart after the kiss fallout. And here they were, déjà vu.

*I love you.*

Nick had hung up before she could say the words back to him. She loved him. Perhaps she always had.

"Hello."

Syd spun around. "You're here." She hadn't expected him to arrive so early.

But there he was, in the flesh, standing in the doorway of the carriage house, looking exhausted, a little frazzled, and so good it made Syd's heart sing.

"I didn't hear your truck drive up."

"I parked on the street." He crooked his finger at her. "Come 'ere."

She rushed into his embrace. Before she could tell him how happy she was to see him, he caught her mouth with his and kissed her until she thought her knees would buckle.

"I love you, Nick," she said against his lips. "I've been a mess ever since you left."

"Me too. But I'm good now." He pulled her in for another kiss.

"I can't believe you flew all the way to San Francisco and then back again. I'm sorry you missed Thanksgiving with your family."

"I'm sorry you had Thanksgiving alone." He held her as if his life depended on it and pressed his forehead against hers. "How the hell are we going to do this, Syd?"

She let out a breath. "I don't know, but we'll figure out something. Love will find a way."

As they stood in the carriage house, holding each other, Syd felt Stella's spirit smiling down on them. *I told you so*, Syd could hear her say.

And that's when she knew for sure that love would indeed find a way.

# Epilogue

## One year later

## The *Moonbright Sun*

Sydney Ann Byrne, the granddaughter of the late Robert and Stella Byrne and daughter of the late Richard and Alexa Byrne, was wed to Nicolas James Rossi, the son of Dora and Nick Rossi Sr., Oct. 31.

The ceremony was held after the Halloween parade at Moonbright's Church of the Immaculate Conception with a reception that followed at Stella's Tearoom. More than a hundred guests attended the lavish affair catered by the Corner Café. The bread, of course, was provided by Fern Rogers, the head baker at Stella's Tearoom.

After a year of traveling back and forth between California and Maine, the bride is making Moonbright her permanent home. The groom, who has racked up more frequent-flier miles than he cares to count, couldn't be happier.

Byrne (now Rossi) said she is relinquishing her day-to-day duties at her San Francisco company, Bread & Cie, to an associate but will continue to own a share of the business. Her plan, she said, is to run Stella's Tearoom full-time, bake her delectable cheese *palmiers* for Williams-Sonoma, and write cookbooks.

Her new husband said he couldn't be happier with the plan. In the meantime, Rossi Construction has applied for permits to add on to the couple's Maple Street Victorian. Extra space in case of small visitors in the next few years, Rossi said.

The new Mrs. Rossi declined to say whether it was the Moonbright legend that brought her and her groom together. However, the *Sun* finds it extraordinarily coincidental that they chose Halloween as their wedding day.

Despite the coincidence, their secret is safe with us.

# Romance on Tap

## MARINA ADAIR

*To my friend, Alex,*
*who believed in me from*
*the beginning and fought for*
*me until the end*

*Friendship is born at that moment when one person says to*
*another: "What! You too? I thought I was the only one."*
*—C. S. Lewis*

*Thank you for being my one.*

# Prologue

It was official. Mila Cramer was going to die. A travesty, since she'd barely lived.

Oh sure, she had a passport with a few stamps, dual citizenship, and had won first place in the county fair art contest. But she'd never snuck out of the house, was still afraid of the dark . . . and even worse?

She had never been kissed. Sixteen and never kissed was bad enough. But eighteen? And now it looked like she never would be. Either the dark or the embarrassment would kill her.

"This is why you don't go to parties," she mumbled, wiping her sweaty palms on her jeans.

The only reason she was at Abigail Anderson's Halloween party was because Abigail had passed her a note in Physics, from Mila's secret crush, asking if she was going to the after-game party.

Okay, she'd also gone because last week, on Halloween, her two besties convinced her to cast a love spell. And, just as town lore predicted, when the clock struck midnight her soul mate's identity was revealed in the reflection of her compact mirror:

Moonbright High's quarterback, homecoming king, and the only student ever to be voted Prettiest Eyes three years running. Ford James, who—according to the whispers in the girls' locker room—was a kissing legend.

Her friends had pinups of their favorite boy band or movie posters with the Hemsworth brothers hanging in their rooms. Not Mila. She spent her days after school sitting on the bleachers, watching Ford from afar. Sketchbook in hand, she'd carefully detail his square jaw, electric blue eyes, and those oh so kissable lips. Sketch after sketch filled her journals, the insides of her binders, even the back wall in the attic behind a stack of boxes holding her dad's old tax returns.

She was bewitched from the moment Ford chose her first for his kickball team in sixth grade—she'd never been picked first. Not that he knew she even existed. An embarrassing fact, since they'd grown up together, their houses kitty-corner to each other.

But last week, at the Halloween dance, he'd smiled at her. Or at least in her direction. She couldn't be positive, but one of her friends swore that his smile was intended for Mila.

"He's totally checking you out," Kira had whispered. "It's the Princess Buttercup costume. Guys appreciate a girl who reads."

"Guys appreciate boobs. That padded bra takes you from mosquito bites to a respectable A cup," clarified the girl who put the B cup in their BFF posse. And since Dakota knew the most about boobs and guys, Mila believed her. Which was why she'd worn the push-up bra to the party. "And have you seen how many times he's cracked his head during a game? He probably watched the movie."

Either way, he'd asked her to the party and, when she'd arrived, Abigail had told her he'd meet her in the downstairs closet. Everyone knew what happened in Abigail's downstairs closet.

*Seven Minutes in Heaven.*

Had it been any another guy, Mila never would have willingly walked into that closet. Confined, dark places reminded her of the time her cousin locked her in the basement during her grandfather's wake. And just like back then, the tiny closet made her chest feel tight and her skin feel too small for her body. Not to mention the sweaty hands and armpits.

Not how she'd envisioned her first kiss going. But she was three minutes into her seven, and Ford James was a no-show.

She could hear Abigail and her friends on the other side of the door whispering about her. Feel the darkness closing in. Even straining her eyes, she couldn't see her hand in front of her face.

"Please, please, please don't let him stand me up," she whispered to the universe. "Just one kiss with Ford, and I promise never to ask for another thing as long as I live." Because according to town legend, that was all she needed.

After the spell was cast, a single kiss would seal the soul mates' love forever. It had worked for her parents and her grandparents. In fact, the Cramers had a long history of epic love stories, dating back to her great-great-grandparents, who'd met at the first annual Moonbright Halloween parade.

Out of the billons of people in the world, every Cramer had managed to find their person. And Mila Cramer was about to kiss hers. Because, as if the universe had heard her plea, the door slowly opened.

"Mila?" she heard someone whisper. A too-husky-to-be-anyone-but-a-guy whisper.

Relief flooded her. Partly because she hadn't been stood up in front of the entire cool crowd, but mostly because a beam of light flooded into the closet, eating away at the scary shadows.

She nodded and then realized he couldn't see her. "Um, it's me. I thought you were going to be a no-show."

"I'd never let that happen." He sounded so sincere that her heart melted into a puddle of goo.

He stepped inside and closed the door behind him, plunging them back into darkness. Her heart rammed against her ribs so fast, she was afraid she'd pass out. The tightening in her chest didn't help.

"Do you think we could open the door a crack?" she choked out past the lump in her throat.

"That's not how this game is played," he said, and she was pretty sure he was flirting. Then his hand bumped her arm, before clumsily sliding down to link his fingers with hers—and she knew.

Ford James *was* flirting with her, Mila Cramer, theater geek and art club president.

*Huh*, being in the dark wasn't so scary after all. Not when Ford was holding her hand. In a closet. Where they were about to play Seven Minutes in Heaven.

"I don't have much experience with this game," she admitted.

"Me either."

She felt the air stir around her, sensed his body shift closer. Uncertainty and inexperience twisted into a complicated knot in her stomach. Taking a deep breath, she mentally recited the tips her favorite magazine had listed in its "How to Get an A+ in French (Kissing)" article, which she'd memorized for this exact situation.

1. WITTY BANTER, PHYSICAL CONTACT LIKE HOLDING HANDS, AND MAINTAINING LINGERING EYE CONTACT ARE ALL WAYS TO BUILD THE CHEMISTRY.

Check. Check. And it was too dark to tell.

2. TO AVOID A STICKY SITUATION, BLOT YOUR LIP GLOSS.

She wasn't wearing any, but she'd started sweating again.

3. TAKE A DEEP BREATH AND RELAX YOUR BODY.

She exhaled. A little too loudly, because he froze. "You okay?"

Was she? She was nervous and probably going to throw up.

"Yes." *Crap.* Tip number four: DON'T SOUND TOO EAGER. "Sure. I mean, if you are."

"Doing better by the second." He brought her arms up and slid them around his neck.

He was so tall, compared to her travel-sized stature, she had to roll up on her toes just to hold on.

"Is this okay?" he asked.

It was better than okay. It was sheer heaven. In his arms she felt beautiful . . . seen. Out of all the girls at the party, Ford had chosen her. She'd captured a lot of different sides of him over the years, but she'd never witnessed this side. Patient, gentle, shy even.

She could feel his gaze on her, sense his slight hesitation. As if giving her the time she needed to feel comfortable. Her mind flashed back to the article.

4. TAKE SOME OF THE PRESSURE OFF HIM AND MAKE THE FIRST MOVE.

*First move. You totally have this.*

"Did you say something?" he asked.

She so did not have this. But instead of giving in to her fear, she channeled Bold Mila in the silky top with the push-up bra and made the first move. Only he had the same plan and, instead of making contact, her lips crashed into his chin.

"Oh my God." Horror flooded her. "I am so incredibly sorry. And clumsy."

"It's okay."

"No. It's not." She closed her eyes in embarrassment. "Am I totally blowing this?"

"You're not blowing it," he assured her, but he didn't move. He just remained still, his hands resting loosely on her hips. She realized he was waiting for her to initiate the next move. Perhaps he wanted to give her time to compose herself or he didn't want to risk losing an eye on attempt number two.

"Are you sure? Because it feels like I'm blowing it." And she was about to cry. She felt tears sting the back of her throat, and no matter how hard she blinked she couldn't stop them. She'd never imagined she'd be thankful for the dark.

"Inconceivable, Buttercup," he whispered, and she wanted to cry for a whole other reason. "I could go into all the reasons why, if that would make you feel better, but we only have three minutes left. And I can think of better ways to spend them."

"Me too."

He chuckled, then slid his hands to rest on her lower back, gently tugging her toward him until she was snug against his body. His head dipped, his cheek pressing against hers, and she broke out in goose bumps—and not the scared kind. They stayed like that for a moment before he slowly shifted, his mouth coming closer and closer, his lips only a breath away.

*True love* only a breath away.

"Earlier when I said I didn't have a lot of experience," she began, kicking herself for talking to fill the silence. Quiet always made her uncomfortable. It was a leftover from her first few years at the orphanage, when silence was a rarity. "It's more like I don't have any."

In front of her, she felt him go still. "This is your first kiss?" he asked.

"Is that a problem?"

He swore low, beneath his breath. His hands loosened, not all the way, but enough that she knew he was reconsidering this whole thing. Refusing to miss this chance, she made her second move. And this one hit him square on the mouth.

He hesitated and, for a heart-pounding moment, she thought he'd changed his mind. Then he groaned, tightening his arms around her so firmly, he practically lifted her off her feet. Ford wasn't just a kissing legend; he was a kissing wizard, delivering the best first kiss in first-kiss history.

After a few moments, he pulled back, just enough so that when he spoke she could feel his mouth move against hers. "What came next?"

Her eyes flew open. "What?"

"Lip gloss. Take a deep breath. Make the first move."

"I said that out loud?"

He chuckled. "Not all of it. But enough to make me curious."

This moment had all the makings of a rom-com. A girl in distress, a dashing knight who comes to her rescue, misunderstandings, humorous antics, the awkward first kiss. Which should immediately be followed by *the kiss*.

The heart-pounding, life-altering, fireworks display kind of kiss. Mila had waited eighteen years for fireworks. One silly misstep was just a part of their story; what came next was up to her.

She boldly tightened her arms. "What do you want to know?"

"What comes next on your list? Because after that kiss, I've got to know."

"My favorite part," she said coyly. " 'Practice makes perfect.' "

He smiled against her lips. "As you wish."

And just as she'd dreamed, when his tongue touched hers

the darkness faded and the nervousness dissipated, and she could hear the air crackle around them. It was as if she'd been transported to a magical place. If she hadn't believed in the legend before, she believed it now.

Mila Cramer had found her person.

# Chapter 1

*Seven years later . . .*

Everyone in Moonbright, Maine, knew that finding true love was as easy as saying, "Mirror, mirror on Halloween, will my future spouse be seen?" Everyone, that was, except Mila Cramer.

As far as she was concerned, enchantment spells were about as realistic as hopes of winning the lottery. Now curses? That was something she could vouch for.

"We're talking about your possible soul mate," Kira said as if this were the start of a Disney movie.

"Soul mate?" Mila snorted.

It wasn't that she didn't believe in true love. She just didn't believe it could ever happen for her. Once upon a time, Mila had thought she'd found her person, only he'd found someone else.

Lots of someone elses.

"Yes, soul mate," Kira said, her gold bangle bracelets jingling together as she tightened the corset of her fortune-teller costume. "Look around—everyone in this room is hoping to find their one true love."

"Suckers," Dakota said, and Mila couldn't agree more.

Tonight was the annual Till Death Do Us Part-y at the Thirsty Raven, a hole-in-the-wall tavern off Haystack Lane, where local singles, dressed in spooky garb, gathered to ring in All Hallows' Eve.

It was nearly the witching hour and the bar was packed, a sea of zombies and ghouls taking up every booth and stool. In a town that was home to Maine's largest pumpkin patch, Halloween was the biggest celebration of the year. Cobweb-covered lanterns swayed overhead, pitchers of Oktoberfest beer lined the bar, and a pumpkin the size of a tractor tire hung from the ceiling, like the New Year's ball counting down to the big drop at midnight.

Dakota was the recently promoted bar manager, and Kira's event planning company had been hired to organize the party, which was how Mila found herself at the counter, wedged between a balding Clark Kent and Pennywise, while dressed like Princess Buttercup. Kira swore it had been the last costume left in Mila's size at Charade, Moonbright's premiere costume shop, but Mila knew better.

Kira was trying to play cupid and re-create that wonderfully awful night back in high school.

"I think it's romantic," Kira said, clutching her chest.

"I think the idea of finding one person for the rest of your life is novel." Dakota slid two Poison Appletinis and a basket of fries across the bar. The fries were salty and hot. The cocktail tart and delicious. "A guy who wants to stay the night but doesn't expect breakfast in the morning is more my speed."

Dakota was no-strings. Kira had a subscription to six wedding magazines. Mila wasn't sure what her speed was anymore.

She could recite every Nora Ephron movie by heart, cried at Prince William and Kate's wedding, and her mind often drifted to how nice it would be to have a constant someone-special in her life. But she didn't daydream about "the ring" or have her dress picked out. And she certainly couldn't imagine inviting anyone to sleep over.

Not in her current situation.

Which was why she'd created a plan: itemized, detailed, multi-tiered, color coded, flagged and tagged—a strategy to get her life back on track.

- ☐ GET YOUR SHIT TOGETHER.
- ☐ APPLY FOR A BIG-GIRL JOB.
- ☐ GET A LIFE. ONE THAT DOESN'T INCLUDE SLEEPING IN YOUR CHILDHOOD BEDROOM.

More specifically, a life that belonged to her. It sounded so simple when put that way. However, there were a lot of steps involved, which felt like the equivalent of rolling a five-hundred-pound pumpkin up a steep mountain, but in the end it would be worth it.

Adulting was hard. And ever since her dad's second stroke last year, she did it every day, all day.

Mila never once regretted her decision to give up her downtown loft and great job as a set designer for a small theater company in New York to move home and care for her parents. They had adopted her later in life, but that never stopped them from showering Mila with unconditional love and support. Her dad had coached her soccer team and taken her to mommy-and-me ballet. Her mom bought Mila her first art set and introduced her to painting.

Her parents were amazing, even taking her to Heritage Camp when Mila started having questions about her Vietnamese heritage. Camp was where Mila met other kids just like her, Asian born and American raised by white parents. Ronald and Joyce went above and beyond to make sure Mila felt understood, accepted, and from-the-heart cherished.

Now it was her turn. Because, while most of her friends' parents were in their forties, Ronald and Joyce were in their seventies. Too sharp and active to go into assisted living, but too old to take care of a two-story house on an acre lot, which they weren't quite ready to let go of.

They'd asked for one more Christmas in the house and Mila would do anything in her power to make that happen. Even if it meant moving back to her small hometown.

But with the holiday season officially here, Mila's heart began to ache. Some of her best memories were tied to that house. The thought of someone else living there, painting over the height charts penciled on the kitchen doorjamb, tearing down walls, updating, renovating—all the things that came with the invention of DIY television. It made her sick.

What would happen to the original 1930 enamel-blue cast-iron stove her grandmother had received as a wedding present? Mila understood that sometimes to move forward, one had to let go. Didn't mean she had to like it.

As an adoptee, Mila took comfort in predictability. As an artist, repetition drove her batty. Which brought her to the next step. The biggest, scariest step. And that made her nervous. *Very* nervous.

*Ford James.*

Even after all these years, his name made her heart flutter. *Stupid heart.*

She glanced around the bar, noticing that Step Three was thankfully absent. After sustaining a permanent kink in her neck from craning to watch the front door, she'd decided to bribe the bouncer, Butch Burns, with one of Nan's famous pumpkin pies from the Corner Café if he signaled her when Ford showed.

If he showed.

He would. This was his kind of event—right down to the

former football team playing darts and the sheer number of sexy, single, scantily-clad females.

*This is a bad idea*, Mila thought, and grabbed her purse to leave. "It's getting late. My sweats and a bowl full of Halloween candy are calling my name."

"Oh no you don't. It's almost midnight and this is your do-over. Your last chance to change your destiny. Take life by the horns," Kira said.

"Did that once," Mila said. "And seven years later, I'm still living in my childhood bedroom and drawing on walls."

Okay, so she'd moved up from walls to windows. In fact, she'd created the Halloween-inspired mural on the windows that spanned the tavern's front. It had taken her a solid week to complete, landed her two new customers, and she was proud of the end result. But she wasn't exactly living the dream.

Mila was still paying off student loans from one of the top art schools in the country, yet she painted storefronts for a living. When she'd opened her mural-for-hire company, First Impressions, it was a short-term solution to a challenging problem. A Band-Aid really, to hold her over until she felt comfortable getting back to her dream of being a set designer.

Not that she didn't enjoy creating seasonal storefront art for the shops and restaurants downtown, but her life wasn't where she'd imagined it would be at twenty-five. It was as if, at some point, she'd mistakenly turned right instead of left and ended up back where she'd started.

"Aw," Kira sighed. "It's your golden anniversary. Seven years after your Seven Minutes in Heaven."

"I think that only works for birthdays," Mila pointed out. "And what do you want me to do? Next time I see him, drag him into the nearest closet for a replay?"

"Guys dig chicks who make a bold first move," the boldest musketeer said. Dakota was fearless, badass, and made bold look sexy. Her cocky, take-charge attitude was equal parts impressive and intimidating.

Mila didn't even know what badass and bold looked like on her, let alone know how to pull it off without appearing desperate. She wouldn't go so far as to say she had zero plays in the pickup game, but putting herself out there had never been easy. Especially when it came to someone who acted as if that kiss had never happened.

"Being bold didn't really work out for me last time." Not in the long run anyway.

"That's because you were a non-believer when you said the words. You tempted fate." Kira whispered the last part, as if "the curse" was contagious and would somehow infect her if spoken aloud.

"Or you did it wrong," Dakota said.

"Why is it always the woman's fault?" Because Mila *had* been a believer. Past tense.

She'd bought the town legend, hook, line and sinker. Listened to her family's stories about destiny and true love. Now she was older, wiser, and ignored her romantic side, even when it was the hard thing to do. Because her sensible side had never let her down.

"Well, there were two of you in that closet, and Ford James doesn't seem to have a string of bad kisses on his record," Kira said. "In fact, according to Instagram, he holds the title for best kisser in town. It's said his lips are like pillows. The expensive kind."

Didn't Mila know it. Sometimes, late at night, her body still tingled from those seven lip-cocked minutes in heaven. Too bad they'd been followed by nearly a decade of hellishly bad kisses.

Every relationship since had been plagued by one bad kisser after another. The tonsil licker, the teeth bumper, the face grabber, even the cobra. Kissing had ruined every relationship she'd ever had—including with her most recent ex.

She'd dated Leo, been in love with Leo, then sadly ended it with Leo when it became apparent that he was always going to be a consent seeker.

Mila was all for clarifying boundaries, even thought it romantic. At first. But asking for consent to kiss her while she was in the throes of an orgasm was the last straw. She'd settled in her career, but she wasn't going to settle in love.

Leo consented to an amicable breakup; Mila moved out and came up with her multi-tiered plan to break the curse. Kiss Ford again, then move on.

That had been two years and a bazillion missed opportunities ago. Either Ford was dating someone or Mila would lose her courage.

*Ridiculous.* Surely, she'd embellished the power of that teenage kiss.

"I've seen better," she lied.

"I'm with M, on this," Dakota said. "I don't think Ford's all that. Now his twin? Yummy. I've always had a thing for bad boys. Tall, dark, dangerous, rough around the edges, and a troublemaker. Hudson fits the bill."

"I didn't say I preferred his twin!"

*Hell no!* Hudson James was the exact opposite of what Mila was looking for. He always made her nervous, the kind of nervous that had her stomach drop and her palms sweat whenever he was around. And since her dad used to hire him to do odd jobs, he was around a lot while she was growing up. Mowing the lawn, trimming the trees, helping decorate the house during the holidays.

And with Joyce Cramer, decorating was a world-class event. *She* should have been a set designer for Hollywood. Her creations were legendary, keeping the power company in business and drawing spectators from three counties over.

"I'm not into alphas," Mila said. She'd dated enough to know that the fantasy was much nicer than the reality.

Kira sighed. "He's a war hero."

Great, he was probably even more dangerous and brooding now. "I'm into softer, sweeter guys."

"Guys like Ford?"

Guys like her dad, who were gentle natured, emotionally mature, and had a steady nine-to-five. Guys who read more than *Hot Rod* magazine, preferred a lighthearted comedy to an action flick, and possessed a wardrobe that extended beyond faded rock T-shirts and leather jackets.

A guy whose kiss was magical enough to break the curse.

When a dreamy sigh slipped out, Dakota lifted a brow. "I thought you were over Ford. Moved on."

"I have. He's a means to an end. Nothing more."

"Then why do you wake up at five AM so you can get your coffee at the exact time he gets to work every day?"

"The Corner Café has the best coffee in town." That didn't mean she didn't admire his butt every time he walked into the courthouse. "And I'm most creative in the morning."

"*Bullshit*," Dakota coughed. "You're a night owl who's broken three alarm clocks in the past year alone. Admit it—you're still mooning over a guy you haven't said more than 'boo' to in the past decade."

"We've talked." It was a year ago and she literally said, "Good work. Keep it up."

He'd smiled awkwardly, as if he still wasn't sure how they knew each other.

"And I was just pointing out the right kind of man for me." Who was not, *not*, some guy who'd kissed her one minute, then went bobbing for Abigail Anderson's apples the next. "Plus, he's dating the file clerk at City Hall."

"The redhead?" Kira shook her head. "They broke up. He's s-i-n-g-l-e."

"He is?" *Dammit*, she must have sounded too eager, because her friends exchanged a look. "Not that it matters. Means to an end," she repeated. "And he's dated nearly every single woman in town, which is in direct violation of article F on my list."

"She's talking about her Mr. Perfect list again." Dakota rolled her eyes.

"Not Perfect, Right." Mila didn't believe in the concept of perfect, but when it came to finding a partner she wanted to do it right. Hence, the list. She flipped to the correct page and read aloud, " 'Decisiveness. A trait that separates a man from a boy. A boy flounders, directionless. A man knows what he wants and goes after it.' "

Dakota laughed. "That man does not exist."

"Maybe. Maybe not. But it's important to put out to the universe what you want and then visualize it."

Kira threw her hands in the air. "That's exactly what the legend says."

The legend relied on romantic concepts like destiny and fate. Mila's plan was all about preparation and execution. Actionable milestones.

Painting outside the lines was great when it came to art, but in real life she wanted the safe bet, so she'd come up with a Mr. Right list. A detailed guide that outlined the traits and qualities of her perfect fit. It was solid, logical, something quantifiable and tangible.

An approach that wouldn't shatter her heart.

It listed seven traits that were crucial in a partner. Which brought her to the next step in her plan:

☐ KISS FORD AND **BREAK** THE CURSE.

As soon as she got this kiss over with, the curse would be lifted and maybe, *just maybe*, she could get on with her life.

"We're twenty-five. Aren't we too old to believe in fairy tales and legends?"

"What? Curses don't count?" Dakota asked. It was a question Mila refused to answer, so she took a big sip of her Poison Appletini. Dakota laughed. "That's what I thought."

"We're never too old for fairy tales, but we are *all* too old to still be single. Plus, I have a good feeling about it this time." Kira tapped the middle of her forehead. "Third eye."

"Just because you're dressed like a fortune-teller doesn't mean you have the Sight," Dakota pointed out.

"I come from a long line of fortune-tellers. Plus, my aunt Rose has the Sight and said if I could just focus, I'd have it too." Kira put her hand on Mila's arm, closed her eyes, and began humming.

"Just say the stupid spell so she'll shut up."

"Fine," Mila said. "Not that I put any stock in it." However, there was still a part of her, the naïve, shy teenager, who wanted to believe that love could really be as easy as chanting a few lines.

It had worked for her parents—forty-nine years of marriage. And all those rom-com movies couldn't be wrong. Nora Ephron wouldn't lie about something as important as love.

With a defeated sigh, Mila looked at the mirror behind the bar and admired her mural one last time. In just a few days it would be erased—just like her dignity.

"If you're going to do it, you might want to do it fast," Kira said. "You only have a minute or so before midnight and then you'll miss your window and have to wait another whole year."

Mila wasn't about to put her life on hold any longer. So when the pumpkin started its descent and the crowd began the countdown, Mila squeezed her eyes shut, so tight little white orbs appeared. In a low voice that only she could hear, she said, "Mirror, mirror on Halloween, will my future spouse be seen?"

And just like seven years ago, she felt a warm glow fill her chest. She held on to the feeling for a moment, relished what it was like to still believe in such things, then opened her eyes right as the countdown hit one.

She stared into the mirror. Waiting. Searching. For what, she wasn't sure. But suddenly it felt as if her life was about to change. As if the planets were aligning and Fate herself had come down to give Mila a big high five.

Only the longer she stared, the harder it was to see anything. The cheers and clapping around her faded, the warm glow grew stronger, and, for a moment, she had to admit that she wanted to be a believer again. But as the seconds passed and the glow faded, she realized that, once again, she'd been a fool.

"Told you. No truth to it. Just stupid folklore."

"What about before, when you saw Ford's face in your compact?" Kira asked, a flicker of romantic hopefulness in her eyes.

"I was a kid, with a huge crush, who saw what I wanted to see," she said, surprised at the disappointment knotting her belly. "Now, can I go home and put on my sweats? If I wait too long, my dad will polish off all the good stuff and I'll be left with Whoppers and raisins."

"Oh my God," Kira whispered, smacking Mila on the arm. "Butch Burns is signaling you."

"He is not. He's probably—" Mila turned and—*oh, holy Saints, each and every ghoulish one!* In the reflection of her Poison Appletini glass a flicker of a figure appeared.

Mila squinted, leaned closer, and—her heart fluttered to a stop. Because right there, as clear as a bottle of vodka, was a chiseled jaw, crooked smile, and pair of piercing blue eyes staring back at her through a black mask.

"Guys," she whispered, afraid if she spoke too loud, the apparition would disappear. "Look at this."

Only before they turned the mirage vanished, leaving nothing but the green-apple garnish.

"No, Mila. You need to look at this," Kira said. "Your Westley just walked in, and he's headed this way."

# Chapter 2

Mila's heart kicked hard, and she began sweating in uncomfortable places. Westley wasn't just headed their way. He was headed *her* way.

The black Dread Pirate Roberts mask concealed his expression, but Mila would recognize those piercing blues anywhere. And that grin, *whoa, baby*, she didn't remember it being quite so mesmerizing. Or him being quite so big.

Everywhere, she thought, giving him a once-over—three times.

Even though his costume covered him from head to toe, the shirt hugged his broad shoulders and chest to perfection and the leather belt cinched in his waist, hinting at the washboard abs beneath. Don't even get her started on how well he filled out those pants.

*Breathe. Remember to breathe.*

His long legs ate up the space between them faster than she could formulate her opening line. Or any line for that matter.

"Buttercup," he said, and she had to take a moment. That too-husky-to-be-anyone-but-a-James voice always left her

tongue-tied. Staring up at six feet and four inches of pure testosterone and unadulterated male made it worse.

"Buttercup?" he said again, and she realized she was staring
at his lips. *Busted.*

"Can I help you?" she asked and, *wow*, she hadn't meant to
sound so irritated. After all, he was the reason she'd come. But
there was an edge to him tonight that rubbed her wrong. Or
maybe it rubbed her all too right—and wasn't that problematic?

"Depends on what you're offering," he said, not looking irritated in the least. "I imagine it's something good, since Butch
said you've been waiting for me all night."

She craned her neck to peer over Ford's shoulder and saw
the bouncer, waving his hands as if to get her attention. "He's
here," Butch hollered over the crowd, then pointed at Ford before giving a double thumbs-up.

Mila thumbs-upped back, but the gesture lacked Butch's
enthusiasm. Ford's grin, on the other hand, was equal parts
amusement and smugness.

Mila hopped off the barstool, a mistake, since it was hard to
appear tough and in charge when forced to look all the way up
at someone. Especially when that someone made her feel like an
awkward teenager again. One grin and her heart raced, her lips
tingled, and her chest gave this annoying little flutter.

Treacherous chest. It had missed the "means to an end"
memo. She wasn't looking for tingles or flutters or happily ever
afters. At least not courtesy of him.

"You." She glared and poked his pec—her finger bounced
back. "Me. Coat closet. Now."

"As you wish," he said, his lips quirking.

Without another word, he calmly started across the tavern,
leaving her to follow, his cape billowing behind him. He moved
like a matador, confident, graceful—deadly.

She had to sprint to catch up, barely passing him by as they
reached the closet. She wasn't about to kowtow, to him or any

man. But especially him, not after he'd barely acknowledged her for all these years.

To change her destiny, she needed to be bold, badass, a real take-charge-and-mean-it kind of woman.

Shoulders back, she grabbed for the door handle before he could and yanked it open. He chuckled behind her, which she ignored, as badasses do, and she ushered him inside.

If she'd thought he was big before, he seemed larger than life now. He had to dip his head to make it under the door-frame. Once inside, his body seemed to expand to take up all the space. Mila had to suck in just to avoid pressing up against him when she closed the door.

"Closet is bigger than our last encounter. Then again, so are you," he said—to her chest.

*Let him look*, she thought. He wasn't the only one who'd filled out since high school. While Mila could never be called busty, in the right bra her cleavage could hold its own against any redheaded file clerk's, from Town Hall to Tucson.

"You have me here," he started. "Question is, what are you going to do with me?"

His tone implied he was open to suggestions. All kinds of flirty, sexy suggestions that her nipples were one hundred per-cent in favor of. She crossed her arms. Not fast enough, because he slid her a sexy grin that was equal parts amusement and male appreciation.

"Before we start, I'd like to clarify things, so there's no con-fusion."

He rested a shoulder casually against the door, effectively blocking her exit. "Clarify away."

"There will be a kiss."

"Don't I have a say?"

She thought about that. "No. And it will be a single kiss."

"Just one?"

"That's usually the definition."

He gave a low whistle. "You'd better bring your A game."

"There will be no games, A or otherwise. Just a simple smooch, then I'll leave the closet, where you will count to five before leaving. I will go right. You will go left."

"That doesn't work for me," he said, and she held her breath, waiting for the humiliation to set in.

Instead, it was a hot rush of irritation. She couldn't exactly force him to kiss her. Could she? "Fine, you can go right, but that closes the discussion portion of our evening. So to recap: Kiss. I leave. Go left. You count. You leave. Go right. Understood?"

"We talking tongue or no tongue?" he asked, stumping her. She'd hadn't thought that far. The way he was looking at her lips made it impossible to think at all. "Because I want to make sure you respect me for my mind first."

"Doesn't matter, since after this we're going our own separate ways."

He considered this. "Yeah, that doesn't work for me."

"I don't care what works for you. It's always been about you. Tonight is about me."

He shrugged. "I can live with that."

Mila opened her mouth to argue, then closed it. "You can?"

"Sure." He shrugged. "I've always been a ladies-first kind of guy. Plus, I get to be right."

"*Go* right, and you're missing the point."

"Then explain it to me," he said quietly.

She met his gaze, but instead of teasing, she found a tenderness that reminded her of the boy from her childhood. Not the one who'd passed by her at school the next day as if she were nothing more than the quiet girl from across the street, but the sweet boy from the closet who'd made her dream of forever.

"The point is you ruined me!" she said, surprised that he still had the power to hurt her.

"That's a pretty bold statement for someone you haven't

spoken more than a dozen words to over the past seven years," he said, as if he were the offended party. "Care to explain?"

The time for pointing fingers had come and gone. All that was left between them was to break the curse.

"That kiss, the one in Abigail's closet—" She felt the need to clarify, in case he had her mixed up with one of his many closet conquests.

"I remember the kiss in question."

"It was . . . well, it was . . ."

"Epic? Amazing? Mind-blowing?"

"We can go with good," she said—*liar, liar, pants on fire.*

"Good?" He sounded outraged. "It was a hell of a lot better than good."

"Okay, it was better than good."

He seemed comforted by her reassessment. "Then what's the problem?"

"That every kiss after you has sucked. Every single kiss. You." She poked his pec. "Cursed." Poke, poke. "Me." This time he caught her hand and held it against his chest. She tried to pull away, but he wasn't having it.

"Cursed?" He laughed. "I knew I was good, but seven years good? Can I get that endorsement in writing?"

"Don't let it go to your head. I'm sure it was just some kind of first-kiss deal, which will be proven when we kiss again."

"I wouldn't be so sure about that. What was that last tip? Oh yeah, practice makes perfect." He leaned down and whispered, his breath tickling her ear, "You should try me now. I've had a lot of practice."

She'd like to say it was bats she felt fluttering around her belly, but it was magical, whimsical butterflies.

"You say that like the whole town doesn't know." This time she did snatch her hand back. "All I want is one kiss. Then you can go practice on someone else and I can get on with my life."

"I don't know, Buttercup. It sounds like the last kiss lasted seven years. Just imagine how long this kiss will haunt you."

"Not concerned because nowhere on my list does it say 'haunting kisses.'"

His lips twitched. "Let me guess, Top Five Tips for Landing Your Dreamboat?"

"*Psh*. Nothing that ridiculous. It's just a list of traits I'm looking for in my partner."

"Partner? It sounds so clinical."

"Not clinical," she said primly. "Sensible, practical, compatible."

"We've already proven compatibility's not an issue," he said, and before she could tell him to dream on he pressed her up against the wall and planted one on her.

No hesitation, no room for question. It was a move so bold and decisive it made her head spin. Practice had indeed made perfect, because the once kissing legend had risen to the level of kissing god.

There was nothing sensible or practical about it. Their compatibility defied logic.

She gripped his face, reveling in the rough stubble of his jaw against her soft palms as she kissed him back, over and over again. One turned into . . . way too many to count and, *oh boy*, she was in trouble. All these years, she had assumed she'd oversold its power—his power—but if anything, the kiss was even more magical than she remembered.

More magical didn't sound like a safe bet. It sounded messy, dangerous, and like a direct violation of every step in her multi-tiered plan. How was she supposed to go on with her life after this kiss, when the second their lips touched it felt as if her life had finally begun?

Unnerved, she pulled back. "Wow."

"Yeah, wow," he whispered.

Neither could look away. "Ford, how is it possible that it was even better?"

One minute he was right there with her, in the heat of the moment, going on the same insane journey with her, and the next he was gone. Blank. Removed. It was as if someone had entered him in the ice bucket challenge and forgotten to tell him.

His hands dropped from her hips so quickly, she stumbled back and bumped into the coatrack, sending hangers and purses clattering to the ground.

He wiped his lips, as if wanting to wipe away any trace of her, then reached for the door. "Wrong twin, Buttercup. Again."

# Chapter 3

Hudson James was used to life moving at a steady 500 rotations per second. He'd traveled the world, first in the Marines and then as a chopper pilot-for-hire in some of the most remote and dangerous places on the planet—always in control and in charge. Those well-honed traits had saved his life more than once.

Seven minutes in a closet with a blast from his past had him rattled. He didn't do rattled. Which was why he'd come to his grandpa's hangar on his day off. To remind himself what was at stake.

His grandfather's legacy. A legacy on the verge of bankruptcy.

Good thing Huey had taught his grandsons the value of discipline and hard work. They'd survived their childhood together, the two of them against the world; they could survive running Huey's business. For that to happen, they first had to bring Huey's AirTaxi into the current century. And Hudson believed he knew exactly how they were going to accomplish that.

Reimagine. Rebrand. Revive.

Focus locked and loaded, he headed up to the loft that looked over the rest of the hangar, his tactical boots reverberating off the steel steps.

Ford peeked out from the upper-level office and smiled in surprise. "What are you doing here?"

"We've got a meeting at two."

"We? Since when do you sit in on business meetings? You hate business meetings."

Hudson had to laugh. Since Ford could befriend a rabid grizzly, they'd decided he would hold down the business side of things, while Hudson would stick to anything above sea level. Hudson would rather be neck-deep in enemy territory than sit around with a bunch of suits.

However, today's suit was going to be a doozie.

"I'm making an exception."

"Why? You hate anything that forces you to be indoors." Ford leaned forward, resting his elbows on Huey's old, battle-scarred desk. "What are you up to?"

*No good, that's what.*

"Maybe you don't know me as well as you thought. Maybe I'm turning over a new leaf."

Ford lifted a brow. "I knew you in utero, when I kicked your ass and got out first."

"Last time you've beaten me at anything." Hudson sat down on the old leather couch in the corner, which still smelled like cherry tobacco, motor oil, and simpler times.

"Seriously, why are you here?"

Hudson leaned back, stretching out his legs and casually crossing them at the ankles. "Grandpa wanted us to work this business together." It was part of the truth. "In order to do that, we have to be in the same room together. There's a dictionary on the shelf behind you; look it up."

His twin, doing the other-half thing he always did, called out, "Bullshit."

Before Hudson could reply, their suit walked in and, *Devil be dammed,* what a suit it was. Red, fitted, above the knee, and crafted for the single purpose of making a man stand up and take notice.

And notice he did. From the open toes of her do-me pumps, all the way up to her silky black hair, twisted into some kind of complicated knot at the back of her head. Then there was every glorious inch in between.

Ford jabbed an *I'm on to you* finger Hudson's way.

Great, just what he needed, his nosy twin all in his business. And how could a pint-sized princess pack a punch to his chest, with or without her lips on his?

"Gramps is going to whup you from the grave for that lie," Ford whispered, but Hudson wasn't listening. He was too busy watching Mila strut across the hangar floor, her heels clacking on the concrete, her hips swaying with confidence. Then she looked up, their gazes locked, and she came to a stop. A full and complete *I'm going to steam your nuts over a boiling cauldron* stop.

"What are you doing here?" she accused.

Hudson stood and walked to the metal railing, resting his forearms on the top. It put him in a dominant position, not to mention a glimpse-down-her-blouse position. Had he been a glimpse-down-her-blouse kind of guy, which he was not. Instead, he met her gaze.

"Why let Ford have all the fun?"

Ford snickered and then he, too, stood. "Are we here to talk about business or do you two need a closet?"

Hands digging into her hips, foot tapping the floor with irritation, she pressed her lips into a straight, pissed-off line. "You told him?"

He lifted a casual shoulder and she shot him a look that probably would have had her ex-boyfriends cowering and stumbling over themselves with an apology. Time she learned that Hudson didn't cower and he sure as hell wasn't a boy.

"Well, Buttercup, I figure since you called me Ford, twice, he had the right to know," he said dryly, wondering why he was acting so hurt.

"Twice, huh?" Ford grinned. They both ignored him.

"When I answered the ad, I had no idea you were even back in town." As if that made everything okay.

"Friday night proved that."

She considered this for a long moment before turning her attention to Ford. "I understand if you want to go with someone else."

Even from twenty feet up, he could see her confidence waffling. But it was the defeat in those big brown eyes, the resignation etched in her every muscle, that ate away at him.

This was supposed to be an interview and, instead of acting professional, he was acting like an idiot. The way she avoided his gaze was a forcible reminder that while his ego might have been bruised, the situation wasn't entirely her fault.

He'd never clarified all those years ago that he wasn't Ford, and, to be honest, he knew when she approached him at the tavern she thought he was his brother. This was all on Hudson.

"No," Hudson said. "Let's table this for now. I remember what a great artist you were in school, and from what I've seen around town, you've only gotten better."

She rolled her eyes. "I paint goblins and sales announcements on windows."

"It's so much more than that. I saw the mural you did at the Thirsty Raven. It was incredible, Mila," he said, confident that was what she needed to hear. That he believed in her, saw the talent she brought to the table. "And you're right; most people would have painted a goblin and some pumpkins. You went further, creating a story with this eerie forest landscape and a terrified woman running from a beast emerging from billowing fog."

"Landscape? Emerging? Billowing?" Ford snapped his fingers, then held out his hand. "Man card. Hand it over."

"All I'm trying to say is it was amazing," Hudson defended. "What she did was original and impressive, something out of the box that still honored tradition." He looked at Ford. "Three things we're looking for in the person who's going to rebrand our business."

Her eyes met his and, *pow*, there it was. A thousand-watt, adorably shy smile aimed his way. Had he known that all it took was a reminder that someone was in her corner, he would have said it the second she'd walked into the hangar. Because, *hot damn*, she was a sight to behold. Smiling Mila scrambled his brain.

"You noticed the beast?" she asked.

"Why do you sound so surprised? Just because I don't have some fancy degree on the wall like this asshole"—he jabbed a thumb at Ford—"doesn't mean I can't appreciate culture."

"I didn't mean that. It's just . . ." She shrugged. "No one else noticed him. I purposely made him a shadow in the fog, a little wink from the artist."

"A breathtaking wink," he said, rolling his eyes at himself. "It was Hồ Tinh, right?"

"Hồ Tinh?" Ford whispered under his breath, and Hudson shot him a hard look.

"He's a nine-tailed fox who lures villagers back to his cave and eats them. Could take you any day of the week," Hudson informed his twin, whose attention bounced between them as if he were at a Wimbledon match.

"How did you know you that?" Mila asked.

Because eleven-year-old Hudson had made it his adolescent mission to learn every detail about the beautiful girl across the street. "It was your Halloween costume one year, and when I asked you why your fox had nine tails, you explained how your dad would read you the story every Halloween night."

"I don't remember telling you that," she admitted.

"Well, clearly he does," Ford said. "Now are we going to talk about business? Or stand around listening to Hudson school us in folklore?"

"Business," Mila and Hudson said in unison, and she paused as if processing the moment, her expression wide with realization and another emotion he couldn't decipher. He was certain she was going to say something important, something that would give him the opening he needed, when Ford, always used to being the center of attention, clapped his hands.

Mila blinked and, *bam*, the moment was over.

"Now that we got that squared away, come into the office and let's hear your pitch." Ford waved her up, then led the way, taking a seat behind the desk. Mila chose the seat farthest away from Hudson. "I've already talked to a couple of other bigger firms from Augusta, but I'm interested to hear what direction you would take this."

She smoothed her hands down her skirt. "I actually wanted to get a better picture of what you . . . I mean, the two of you are looking for. I know how much this business meant to Huey, and I'm so sorry for your loss."

For the first time since entering the office, she looked Hudson's way, and the genuine sympathy she offered cut straight through his chest.

"Thank you," Hudson said, wishing like hell he'd been there when his grandpa passed. Instead, he'd been on the other side of the world, flying rich assholes from one oil refinery to the next. By the time he got home, he'd missed the funeral and saying good-bye to the man who'd raised him.

He hoped to God he wasn't too late to keep the small, family-run charter company airborne.

"I wanted to find a way to merge the old with the new," she continued. "Honor Huey's legacy while personalizing the company's image to the two of you."

Ford sent Hudson an impressed look. Fitting, since she'd just impressed the hell out of Hudson.

He was in trouble. Deep trouble. He'd already had a second taste and, after seeing her today, he wanted a third. No, he needed a third. Then he'd be a dead man walking.

"Are there any colors or images that inspire you both—" She stopped in midsentence and turned back to Hudson. "Wait. I'm sorry. There's something I need to clarify before we continue. Did you know I thought you were Ford when you kissed me the other night?"

*Hell yes*, he knew.

Hudson may have only had seven minutes in a dark closet with that full, lush mouth on his, but it was as if every one of those 420 seconds was imprinted on his mind—and a few other places. Not to mention the thousands of fantasies she'd starred in.

He'd been dreaming about a replay since that night. Clearly, from the way she'd reacted, she had too.

"Before you get all worked up, I think you're forgetting one important detail. You kissed me back."

Ford let out a low whistle. "That better have been a good kiss, because you were representing me."

She shrugged. "It was okay."

Hudson chuckled. "Someday I'm going to make you take that back."

She bit her lower lip, a sign that she was thinking about that kiss. Yeah, he'd blown her mind. She might not want to admit that now, but he'd intrigued her. And that intrigued him. Not that he hadn't already been intrigued. That Buttercup costume had shown just how much she'd grown up.

"Doesn't take away the fact that you tricked me. Or that I'm mad at you."

"Noted." He grinned. "Next time I'll remember to give you the treat first."

Even as he said it, he knew he was more off-kilter than ever. Hudson was used to ignoring his own needs, pushing aside his wants to take care of others. Huey had raised him to always do the right thing, which was rarely the easy thing.

With Mila, he didn't want to do the right thing. He wanted her, no matter the cost.

To either of them.

# Chapter 4

In hindsight, Mila should have known when she received the email from Huey's AirTaxi that it had been Hudson's doing. There was no signature at the bottom, just a generic reply to the ad she'd taken out in the local paper.

If they hired her, it would be her biggest deal to date. That kind of addition to her portfolio could make all the difference. Not to mention the money. All she needed was a handful of high-caliber clients and she'd be set. Fewer hours and higher rates would afford her the freedom to get her parents situated—and the time to work on her art.

Today, though, she was a window artist, hired to create a holiday-themed piece for the Corner Café, home to the best whoopie pies in the Northeast. The café was also Mila's favorite eatery in town.

Three generations strong, the Corner Café was an institution in Moonbright. Founded in 1946 and now run by Nan Allan, it was a place for families to come together and make memories over better-than-home-cooked meals and fresh-from-the-oven pies. Nan had a magic touch when it came to baking pies, whether meat, fish, or fruit.

Which brought to mind someone else who had a magic touch. A very sexy, very male someone else, who had turned Mila's world upside down and sideways, distracting her from what was important.

"You didn't blow the interview," said Annie, one of her oldest friends from Heritage Camp, her amused expression crystal clear though the phone's screen.

"You weren't there," Mila said, using a fine brush to paint a snowflake in the upper corner of the window while holding the phone in the other hand. "But Hudson was, and he's the problem."

"Wait, you got nervous and tongue-tied over Hudson? I'm confused."

"Join the club."

After tossing and turning all weekend, Mila knew she needed advice. Annie, the only friend in her life who'd found true love, was the obvious choice. When Mila caught herself painting a *U* instead of an *A* in the HAPPY HOLIDAY mural on the café's window, she immediately dialed Annie.

"For years, all you talked about was Ford James. Nine summers, I had to listen to you moon over your soul mate." Annie shifted the phone so that her face took up the entire screen. "You even doodled 'Mila James' all over the cabin walls the last year at Heritage Camp."

"And we all had to scrub if off with toothbrushes. Florence was so mad she didn't talk to me the entire summer," Mila said, referring to one of their camp buddies.

They both laughed and Mila was brought back to those summers in Colorado, when she felt free to be herself. Like her, all the girls in her cabin were born in Vietnam and raised by white parents—sharing a common experience of having one foot in each world.

They called themselves the East Coast Inbetweeners, and the bond formed in their youth connected them for life. One week every summer they still got together. While all the women had a place in Mila's heart, Annie was special. When Mila had received the wedding invite last spring, she couldn't have been happier for Annie and her new husband, Emmitt.

"But it was always Ford. You never even mentioned Hudson, except to say he was nothing but trouble," Annie said.

"I know," she said, wondering why she hadn't been able to take her eyes off the nothing-but-trouble twin at the interview. "But he kept baiting me."

*Sexy bastard.*

"Then go and bait him back."

"I tried." Mila lowered her brush, ignoring the new paint smudge it left on her overalls. "He's better at it than me."

"Impossible. The woman who was named Miss Fisherman five years in a row wouldn't back down because some guy had better bait," Annie said. "You're the camp champion fisherman."

With a sigh, Mila leaned against the brick wall of the café. "Only I'm no longer sure what I'm fishing for. I can't believe I interrupted a business meeting to talk about a kiss."

So much for being the champion fisherman. She'd caught the wrong fish and, instead of throwing him back for being too bigheaded, she'd kissed him.

"I gave up a job in Rome, Italy, to stay in Rome, Rhode Island, for a great kisser," Annie said.

"This isn't Emmitt. This is Hudson, a guy who pretended to be someone else to get some action."

Annie sighed. "I think it's romantic."

Mila pressed her AirPods against her ears to make sure she'd heard that correctly. "Romantic? I think it's rude." Mila thunked her head against the wall. "You know how badly I needed that job."

"You're going to get the job—I know it. How is Claudia working out?" Annie asked, referring to the in-home caretaker she had found for Mila's parents. Claudia was local, reliable, and had a huge heart.

"She's heaven-sent. I can't thank you enough," Mila said. "My mom loves her, and Claudia can put up with my dad."

"So, she's a keeper?"

"Definitely, but she's also expensive. If I don't land this contract, then I can only afford to keep her on for the hours I'm at work, which means preparing the house to go on the market while dealing with my dad's health needs. Not to mention, saving a nest egg for when I move to Los Angeles and get my own place."

That was if she got the job. Last month, Mila had applied for a position as assistant to the set designer at an up-and-coming movie studio in Los Angeles. If she landed it, she'd be working under some amazing artists.

"You're going to get the contract. And you're going to make it to Los Angeles."

"How do you know?"

Annie laughed. "About the job? You're too talented to be overlooked."

Mila snorted. "Hollywood, the biggest collection of talent on the planet. To be overlooked means you first have to be seen." Something Mila had spent a lifetime trying to master, without much luck. "Which is why I applied for the art director position at Moonbright Community Theater."

Annie paused. "Do you want to stay in Moonbright and be their art director?"

"It's a solid backup plan." Backup plans had saved her butt more than once and taught her to never put too much stock into something as finicky as chance. "Not to mention a bump in title."

"A backup plan is like telling the universe you're ready to fail, and, you, Mila Cramer, are not a failure. You know what your problem is?"

"No, but it sounds as though you do."

"Your problem isn't about backup plans or being seen. It's about going after what you want and then knowing what to do with the attention once you have it," Annie said gently. "Look at your meeting with the James twins. You laid it out there, told them how amazing you are, then sealed it with a kiss."

"God, that kiss." Mila covered her face, leaving a smudge of paint on her cheek. "I'd never admit to Kira or Dakota that there might be something to the Moonbright legend BS, but it *was* magical." It also had her questioning everything she held as true. Ford hadn't blown her off and pretended they'd never kissed. They never *had* kissed.

It had been Hudson all along, and he'd never said a word.

"Throws you for a loop when you find the right guy," Annie said.

"He's not right for me." She set the brush on her tarp, a few white drops dotting her paint-stained Converse, and pulled out her list. She held it up to the screen. "This is my Mr. Right."

"That's a piece of paper."

"It's a list of qualifications, Annie. Keep up. Number one." She pointed to the item in question. " 'Must rock a suit and tie.' "

Annie crinkled her nose as if she'd just gotten a whiff of dog poo. "If you want your man to be prettier than you, then I guess."

"Number two. 'Mild mannered, even tempered, and honest no matter what.' " She addressed the screen. "Which Hudson is not."

"I didn't know we were talking about Hudson," Annie teased.

"We're not. Number three. 'Understands the importance of throw pillows.'"

Annie laughed. "Are you looking for a man or an interior designer?"

"Number four," Mila went on. "'Must be considerate: of a person's time, situation, and emotions.' Number five. 'Is manly enough to watch rom-coms.'"

"The only reason a man watches a rom-com is to get laid. If he tells you differently, he's lying and therefore breaking qualification number two."

Mila lowered the list. "Not all men."

"Emmitt," Annie hollered in the direction of her kitchen. "If I said we were watching the new Reese Witherspoon movie, what would you think?"

"That I'm getting lucky tonight," Emmitt said in the distance. "In fact, I'm turning it on now. How about pizza with olives?"

Mila went back to her list. "'Will take charge in the bedroom.'"

"Any guy can get behind that." It was Emmitt.

Mila's face burned from embarrassment. "Did you put me on speaker?"

"Yes, you needed a man's perspective. What's next?"

"You take me off speaker," she demanded.

There was some rustling; then Annie was back. "Continue."

"Number seven. 'Must be an amazing kisser.'"

"So, we're back to talking about Hudson?"

"No. Too bad for Hudson, he only checked off one thing on the list." Okay, so two, but she wanted the whole package. And how ridiculous was it that she was just a little bit disappointed.

"Depends on what kind of list," came a husky voice from behind her.

Mila's heart lodged itself in her throat as she glanced at the reflection in the window. And, *Lord help her*, standing between the HAPPY and HOLIDAY were both brothers, side by side, with matching grins.

Never one to hide from her mistakes, Mila plastered on a smile and slowly turned to face the men in question, wondering how much they had heard—and feeling confused at how her attention automatically landed on Hudson.

Troubling, since Ford was the guy she'd wanted forever. In his suit and tie and charming smile, he checked all her boxes. Then there was Hudson, in cargo pants, a gray Henley that showed off his lean muscles, and a blue ball cap that matched his eyes—which were locked on hers.

He didn't look away. Neither did she. Not that Mila could when heaps of unwanted and unwelcome feelings flooded her. It was like a moth to a flame, one of those want-what's-bad-for-you situations where she felt the danger—and a whole lot of chemistry—crackle in the air. Likely from that voodoo shit Kira had sprinkled on her.

How could she have ever mixed these two men up? She certainly wouldn't make that mistake again.

Hudson's lips curled up into a challenging grin; then his gaze dropped—to her mouth. She swallowed and his grin got larger. Smugger.

Hands trembling, *from the crisp morning air,* she told herself, she stuffed the list in her front pocket. She wasn't going to feel bad for passing on a guy who didn't even tick off half the qualities needed to be right for her.

She deserved Mr. Right, just like she deserved this job. Sadly, both of them might be slipping through her fingers all because of Mr. Wrong.

"Annie, I gotta go," she said, and disconnected before her friend could say another word.

*Stay professional. Stay on task. Don't put a kiss before your job.*

She'd put her parents before her own wants, but they were

family. Now she had a chance at living her own dream life, but she needed this job to make it happen. And she wasn't going to let Mr. Wrong take that away from her.

No matter how earth-shattering his kiss.

"You're early," she said, looking down at her paint-stained overalls and grungy high-tops. She grimaced. Not quite the pantsuit she'd borrowed from Kira, which was hanging in her car.

"Early bird catches the worm," Hudson said. "Or the end of an interesting conversation."

"A private conversation," she said primly, then turned her attention to Ford. "Thank you for giving me the extra time. I have some things I wanted to show you. I just need to clean up and change; then I can meet you inside."

"Let me help," Hudson said, bending down to collect her brushes and paint cans.

"I got it." She grabbed the handle of her wooden paint box, but he didn't loosen his grip.

"Seriously, I got this. We were the early ones—it's the least I can do."

"Okay, but helping still doesn't get you off the hook for eavesdropping."

"Didn't expect it would," he said.

She had to admit, three were faster than one. They made quick work of her materials and loaded everything in her trunk. She considered changing but, in the end, decided her art would speak for itself.

"Thanks, I have a table waiting for us inside." She'd bribed Nan with a free wreath stencil on the glass pie display in return for reserving the corner booth during the lunch rush.

"After you," Ford said, and sent Hudson a look, which Mila couldn't translate. But it had Hudson glaring back.

They were ushered to the table by the youngest of the Allan

women. Hannah Allan had grown up two streets over from Mila and had been her favorite babysitter, the one who taught her how to play jacks, French-braid hair, and always let Mila stay up past bedtime. Hannah bordered on shy and had a habit of mixing up orders at the café, but she was as sweet as the pecan pies she served.

"Today's special is a Gruyère and Swiss Monte Cristo, served on brioche, fresh from Sydney's oven," Hannah said, referring to Sydney Byrne, a baker from San Francisco who'd recently come back to Moonbright to settle her grandmother's estate. "It comes with a side of fries or, uh—" Hannah pulled the notepad from her apron and quickly reread her notes. "Actually, scratch that. Today's special is lobster pot pie, with coleslaw or a green salad."

"Is there still some of Sydney's cheddar and artichoke bread to go?" Mila asked, knowing it was her mother's favorite. All of Sydney's artisan breads were delectable.

"I'll check for you," Hannah asked. "Do you need a minute?"

All three ordered the special with a slice of apple pie a la mode; then Mila pulled out the designs she'd spent all weekend working on and slid them across the table.

Hudson took the glossy binder and opened to the first page, his gaze never leaving hers. Mila hadn't imagined how nervous she'd be, waiting to hear their opinion.

*Gah!* Who was she fooling? She was waiting to hear Hudson's opinion. While there were two partners at Huey's AirTaxi she needed to impress, for some reason all she cared about was the bad boy's take on her designs.

After a long, nerve-wracking moment during which Mila peeled off strips of the paper place mat and wadded them into little crumpled balls, Hudson nodded. Just once, but Mila could feel his energy. Eager, excited, impressed.

"Wow," he said. "You nailed it. You're amazing."

There went those flutters again, taking flight from her toes to the tips of her hair. He didn't say *it* was amazing. He said *she* was amazing. And dammit if that voodoo shit didn't start to tingle and glow.

"Spot-on. I didn't know this was what I wanted, but now that I see it, it's perfect." Ford placed a hand on her shoulder. And even though he was touching her, she felt not one single flutter.

"Thank you." Uncertain how to handle the praise, she directed her attention to her purse and pulled out a notebook. "I have some color samples I think you will both like. Why don't you take a look."

"I'd rather look at this." Hudson held up her Mr. Right list.

"Give that back." She reached across the table, but Hudson held it out of reach. The smug jerk was so tall, he could still read it.

" 'Must rock a suit and tie'?" Hudson looked down at himself, then over at Ford. "Sounds like you're up, Bro. " 'Mild mannered, even tempered.' " He casually skimmed the list. " 'Must know his way around the kitchen.' " Hudson lifted a brow. "Just because a guy doesn't know his way around a kitchen doesn't mean he doesn't know his way *a-round*."

She rolled her eyes, then snatched the list back and scribbled down another trait. "Number eight. 'Any last name other than James.' "

Ford laughed. Hudson did not. And wasn't that interesting.

She shoved the list into her purse. "I came here to talk about the job."

"The job is yours, if you want it," Hudson said.

"I want to be up-front. I've applied for a set designer job in L.A., and if I get it I'd start after the first of the year."

"That's fine with us." Ford turned to Hudson. "Right?"

Hudson's response was to sit back, arms folded, and silently stare at her.

After a moment, she looked back at Ford. "Then it's a deal."

"Even though you're mad at me?" Hudson teased.

"I might be mad, but I'm not stupid."

# Chapter 5

There was a damn good reason Hudson had made his home base a good thousand miles from his past.

Okay, there were a lot of reasons, but none of those mattered anymore. His homecoming was all about fulfilling the promise he'd made his grandpa before leaving for boot camp. But as he walked into the hangar under the faded tin sign advertising Huey's AirTaxi, an unwanted and familiar feeling settled in his gut.

Anger.

Had he come home sooner, he would have seen the problems the company was facing, witnessed how hard Huey had struggled to save it, and, maybe, he could have said good-bye to one of the few people who saw more in Hudson than his mistakes.

The only good thing about the delay was that he'd missed seeing his SOB of a father, who'd headed back to Florida the second he realized he'd been removed from Huey's will.

Even though Hudson had kicked some serious ass alongside Uncle Sam's toughest and brightest, his dad made it clear that Hudson was still the family screw-up. So he'd come back to Moonbright prepared to take the brunt of the blows over Huey's decision to leave everything to his grandsons.

Hell, he'd come prepared for anything—except the Ghost from Halloween Past sneaking up and weaving her magic around him.

He knew kissing Mila would blow up in his face. Just as he'd known it was wrong not to correct her from the start. But when she'd glared up at him, those dark brown eyes sparkling with enough fury to have sent another soldier's balls retreating, he'd been amused. Turned on, even.

For the first time since hearing about Huey, he'd found himself smiling.

Mila had shocked the hell out of him when she yanked him into the closet. Shocked him more when she'd shrink-wrapped herself around him as if she couldn't get close enough. And that kiss—*holy hell*. He'd never bought into the mumbo jumbo of the Moonbright legend, but it was as if he was under her spell.

Only, just like back in high school, her kiss was meant for Ford. Not the troublemaking twin. However, Mila was no longer the naïve girl next-door, and there was no need to pretend to be Ford in order to save her from a cruel trick. So, he had zero problem letting her know exactly which brother had rocked her world.

Most women would have apologized for the mistake, then thanked him for being a knight in freaking armor. Not Buttercup. She'd come at him shoulders back, chin tilted high, five-foot-nothing of stubborn, pissy woman, holding him personally responsible for the bamboozle of a lip-lock and accusing him of cursing her with seven years of bad kisses.

As ridiculous as that was, now she was flaunting this Mr. Right list and, unlike his brother, Hudson was lucky if he ticked off even a single box.

*Right back at ya, babe*, he thought, walking up the ladder to access the engine compartment. He wasn't sure the last time

Huey had checked the hydraulic fluids or reset the avionics, so he intended to give the Bell 206 JetRanger a thorough inspection before he took her for a spin. She might have a good decade and a half on her, but the way Huey kept her polished, she looked brand-new—on the outside. The internals needed some love—and fast. Their reimagine-rebrand-revive inaugural flight was in less than a week.

Even splitting time between his law practice and the hangar, Ford managed to book six new, big-city commuters into their existing clientele. It was easy money and good money. The kind of regular clients they needed to dig the company out of the red.

"Why are you messing around, playing this game?" Ford asked, handing him a wrench.

Hudson loosened the fastener to the engine compartment and lifted the cowling. "She made it clear she wants you. You saw that list. I'm not on it, but guess what, Bro? You're the one who inspired it. Been there, done that, not going to compete with you again. Boxing a shadow is a no-win situation."

Hudson had spent his formative years being compared to his twin, whose charisma and flashy achievements cast a shadow wider than the coastline of Maine. Most of the time Hudson laughed it off. Or pretended to. When required, he could fake anything: calm during combat, cool headed when landing in a hot zone, and confident when uncertainty was eating him alive.

Why the hell couldn't he fake indifference with Mila?

Even thinking about that list put him back in the mind-set of being the kid who wasn't good enough—a place he hated going. So he locked her and that kiss in his "Do not break seal" compartment and moved on. But Ford, nosier than a group of pageant moms, couldn't keep himself from tampering with the fucking seal.

"I know what you're thinking, and you need to set aside the past," Ford said. "In the here and now, it was you she kissed.

She may have had the name wrong, but it was you. Both times. It was so good that after all these years, she came back for seconds."

Hudson would be down for thirds, but they were looking for different things. Mila was the exact kind of woman he'd spent his entire adult life avoiding—sweet, sensible, and with a big HEA stamped into her DNA.

"Even though she's lived in New York, deep down she's still that small-town girl trying to spread her wings and go after what she wants. She doesn't need another person trying to anchor her here," he said, swapping the wrench for a screwdriver. "I wouldn't do that to her."

"Kind of like how you just up and joined the Marines without telling me, so I could have the big college experience? Guess what, dumbass? It was fun, but it wasn't with you."

"Considering what a mess I was back then, that's probably a good thing."

"You put my wants ahead of yours and that's bullshit. We're a team. Or at least we were until you got it in your head that you had to leave in order for me to excel." Ford wadded a greased-up rag and threw it, tagging Hudson in the head. "Like you were somehow protecting me, even though I'm eleven minutes older. Newsflash, I can excel just fine on my own."

"We're not going there."

"Of course, we're not," Ford mumbled. "What are you going to do about Mila?"

That was the question of the hour. Hudson had left the Thirsty Raven telling himself he was done. Once bitten, twice shy and all that. Only, he couldn't stop thinking about her. Caught himself staring out his bedroom window in hopes of catching a glimpse of the girl across the street, the way he'd done when they were kids.

His crush on Mila had been immediate. First day of middle school, one look and he was spun. Not a bad way to start a move to a new town. Only while he was looking her way, she was looking Ford's.

"Nothing," he finally said. "It wouldn't work. She probably still doodles in her diary, and I'm jaded as hell. She's got a list. I'm not anywhere on it."

"Put yourself on it," Ford said. "Since when do you let a piece of paper and a few words stop you from getting what you want?"

He pulled his head out of the compartment and met Ford's gaze. "When there's a job in L.A. waiting in the wings."

"Jobs fall through all the time. Even if she does get it, that could be months away. I'm not saying get down on a knee, but don't let this chance go to waste."

"I don't know."

"Look, I've been steering clear of her all these years because of bro code, but—"

"Don't even think about it."

Ford smiled. "That's what I thought. She's going to get that worldly experience you think she needs. Why not with you?"

Ford had a point. Once Mila set her mind to something, nothing would stop her. Not even a three-month expiration date. If it wasn't him, then it might be some other prick, who would take advantage of her loyal and selfless nature, and then Hudson would have to kill him.

He might not be her Mr. Right, but neither was the guy on that list. A man's worth couldn't be measured by the number of checkmarks in fucking boxes.

He was going to prove it.

Mila was about as comfortable in confined, dark places as she was with confrontation. Which was why she waited for Ford outside the courthouse rather than meeting him at the hangar—where Hudson would be preparing for his afternoon flight.

She needed to clarify the events of Halloween night that had led to her mistaking Hudson for Ford. She might be easy to fool, but she wasn't the kind of person to kiss one brother and then kiss the other. Even if that wasn't what had happened. The way she saw it, Hudson had tricked them both. The only way to avoid the awkwardness, and keep things professional, was to get it all out in the open.

Mila burrowed deeper into her coat as a crisp November wind whistled through the large white columns of the court-house, the cold stinging her nose. The weatherman had called for gentle breezes and mild temperatures. He'd lied. Which was how Mila ended up downtown in the red-leather fashion-before-function jacket Kira had forced her to buy. It was during one of Kira's famous "expand your horizon" lectures, when buying the coat was easier than re-explaining that Mila pre-ferred to keep her eyes on the road ahead, not in the clouds.

"Never again," she mumbled, her breath turning to vapor. She stamped her feet to keep them warm. She was but a button away from becoming a snowman.

"Hey," Ford said, clearly surprised to see her there. "Did we have a meeting?"

*Wow.* This was the first time Ford had ever spoken to her in public and acknowledged her as more than a passerby.

"No." She shivered, and he ushered her inside City Hall. "I wanted to talk to you about the other night when I, uh, took Hudson in the closet."

He raised a brow. "Took or shoved?"

She covered her face and groaned. "That's beside the point. What I'm trying to say is that I wasn't kissing him—"

"You mean me?"

"Yes, I intended to kiss you, but not because I still have a crush on you."

"But you still intended to kiss *me*?" He looked a little too pleased with himself.

"Keep up, Ford. I was kissing you to get rid of the curse I got when we played Seven Minutes in Heaven. Or when Hudson and I . . . You know what I mean."

"Do I? Because, trust me, if I'd played Seven Minutes in Heaven with you, Hudson would have kicked my ass."

"Why would he kick your ass?" For some reason, Ford's answer seemed like the most important thing in her world, right then.

"Because he had a thing for you. He's always had a thing for you. From the time we moved in with Huey and he first saw you in the yard. Then you sealed it when you danced with him to 'Earth Angel.'"

She gasped. "That was in sixth grade and I stepped on his toes the entire time."

"And you apologized every time. That was his favorite part." Ford shrugged. "That's what he wrote in his diary anyway."

"You read his diary?" She was offended on Hudson's behalf.

"Your first question should have been why a dude keeps a diary. And yes, I read it. You'd be happy to know that you were in several entries."

"Like what?"

Ford ran a hand through his hair and looked over his shoulder as if he were being followed by a covert government agency. "Hud is going to kill me for telling you this, and if he asks, I will deny everything. But I guess Abigail and some of her friends heard about your crush on me."

She snorted. "The whole town heard about my crush on you."

"I didn't," he said honestly. "I never gave you a second look because I knew how gaga Hud was. But Abigail thought it would be funny to send you into the closet and lock you in there. I guess they were going to egg you when you came out."

Once upon a time, she and Abigail had been friends, played Barbies, had sleepovers. Then Abigail had grown boobs, which launched her to an entirely different social stratum, leaving Mila behind. She never understood how someone who had been such a close friend could suddenly turn so mean.

"She knew I was terrified of the dark."

Ford shrugged. "Hud figured it was something like that, so he did his hair like me, adopted my attitude, which I had plenty back then, and went to the party to make sure you weren't waiting alone."

"He hated parties. And he went there just to save me?" Here she'd thought Hudson only ticked off a couple of her boxes.

"And he let everyone think it was me," he said.

Mila groaned, because something else dawned on her. "He was trying to tell me who he really was and, when he found out it was my first kiss, he tried to stop it."

"No regrets, Mila," came a soft and husky voice from behind.

A warm glow oozed through her at the sound of her name sliding from his lips. Heart beating hard, she turned to find Hudson in his fly-boy uniform, looking hot and hard and edgy in the sexiest way possible.

"I thought you had a flight planned this afternoon."

"I do." He reached out and took her hand. "With you."

# Chapter 6

"Where are we going?" Mila shouted into the mouthpiece.

It was a legitimate question, since they were three thousand feet up, with nothing but the choppy waters of the Atlantic below. In the near distance she could see a row of small islands, lush and green, with fiery autumn trees peppered throughout. On the closest island stood a modest cedar-shingle house with a large dock that jutted out into the ocean. A lighthouse was perched on a nearby bluff, shining a golden glimmer over the rocky shoreline at its base.

"It's a surprise."

Excitement bubbled. "I love surprises." Especially when she was on the receiving end.

Maybe it was the altitude or maybe it was the pilot, but everything she thought she knew suddenly looked different. It was as if she'd been gifted a new perspective. From the ground, it was hard to see past the way things were, but up here she got a glimpse of what could be.

They flew until the sea kissed the sky and the spun-cotton clouds reflected the beginnings of a crimson glow on the autumn-painted horizon. As they circled back, the lighthouse came into view and she noticed a clearing in the trees bordering the steep cliffs.

"Are we landing there?"

"You aren't very good at surprises, are you?" Even over the headset, the low gravel of his voice had her heart thumping against her ribs. Then his eyes met hers, warm with bemusement and, as usual, giving away nothing about the reason behind this unexpected outing or why he was so determined to keep their destination a secret.

Then again, Mila had a secret of her own. One that involved her feelings and how they were slowly shifting.

"I'm just not used to being on this side of one," she answered honestly. This was an entirely new experience. As the caretaker of the family, she wasn't accustomed to actually being cared for. It not only felt novel; it felt good. No, more than good—it felt romantic.

"We'll have to work on that."

There were a lot of things Mila was interested in working on with Hudson. As they rounded the island once again and Hudson took the helicopter lower, Mila knew she was going to get that chance.

The sound of the propellers cutting through the air rumbled in her chest. The whirring blades stirred the leaves below and forced the meadow weeds and surrounding trees to bend at their will. The landing was so smooth, Mila barely felt the touchdown.

When the engine stopped, Hudson opened the door and walked around the back of the helicopter. Mila tracked his every move—she couldn't help it.

He was tall and leanly muscled with broad shoulders and a solid chest that was built for cuddling. Naked cuddling. After a full, long night of no-promises sex.

He opened her door. "Let me help. It's a big step down."

"Is that a jab at my size?" she said with no heat.

"No, it's an excuse to get my hands on you." As promised, his big, manly hands spanned her waist and he lifted her from the seat and let her slide, *oh so slowly*, down his body until she was safely on the ground. Only he didn't let go right away, holding her snug against him, so all their good parts lined up. "And I think your size is pretty fucking perfect."

*Man*, was she ever in trouble. Tingles sizzled, starting in her belly and moving to all the essential parts so quickly she could scarcely breathe. Stupid tingles, they were at the center of this mess. This problematic, complicated, and incredibly sexy mess that, as far as she could conclude, would only be solved one way.

"Buttercup," he whispered. "You keep looking at me like that and we're both going to be in trouble."

"I've never gotten in trouble," she said, sliding her hands up his chest. "I'm beginning to think I've been missing out."

Hudson groaned and rested his forehead on hers. "If we go there now, I won't be able to show you the best part."

"Funny, I was thinking by going there, we'd get to the best part faster."

"When we go there, it will be slow, and long, and will take all night and into the next day." The last part he whispered, his lips hovering over hers until she was certain he'd kiss her.

*Careful, he's better at this than you.* "I've always been a night person."

"I've always been a you person," he said, and a giddy zing ran down her spine.

"Take this." He shrugged out of his jacket. "It can get cold out here."

Mila began to tell him she was more turned on than cold when he slid his warm, soft, incredible-smelling jacket over her shoulders.

"There are gloves in the pocket." He pulled the edges of the jacket together and zipped her up.

She took in his long-sleeved but lightweight shirt. Gray, filled to perfection, and nowhere near thick enough to combat the frigid ocean wind. "What about you?"

"I always come prepared." He reached into the helicopter and pulled out another jacket along with a light gray scarf, which he wrapped around her.

"Lucky me."

"I was thinking the same thing." On the same breath, he lifted her hand to his mouth and blew on it, warming it before tucking it in his pocket.

That was how they walked the property, holding hands inside his cozy pocket, while she wore his jacket, as if they were in school and she was his girl. It was cute really, an innocent show of affection that had her heart rolling over in her chest.

He led her through a field, colored with blue and purple wildflowers gently swaying in the ocean breeze. Most of the island remained untouched, like a state park with hundreds of pine trees lining the meadow and reaching all the way to the cliff's edge.

"It's beautiful here."

"It's one of my favorite places," he said, and she had to agree. The farther they explored, the lighter she felt. The serene landscape brought her a sense of peace her life rarely afforded.

"Could you imagine living here?" she asked, taking in the sound of the waves and the crisp sea air. Imagining all her worries drifting out with the tide.

"Actually, I used to spend my summers here," he said, stepping up onto one of the rocks that lined the bluff leading up to the lighthouse. He lifted her hand, steadying her as they went.

"Vacationing?"

He chuckled. "No, more like doing manual labor. Ford would do his football thing and I'd come here."

"So, you weren't at some military camp for delinquents?"

"I thought the rumors were that I was prison?" he joked, but his tone sounded as if he struggled to find the humor.

Mila looked up to study the man who, little by little, was chiseling away every misconception she'd clung to. He was making cracks in the walls she so skillfully hid behind. If she wasn't careful, he'd slide right past them and into her heart.

"I think you just let people say what they wanted because it added to your bad-boy image," she said.

"Had I had known you were into bad boys, I would have started the rumors myself."

"Who said I was into bad boys?"

"Besides that cute blush warming your cheeks?" He waited for her to look at him, and when she did he winked.

He was on to her. No sense in hiding it anymore. "I've decided to expand my horizons."

He sent her a sidelong glance that was hard to read. He was quiet for a long moment; then he gently squeezed her hand. "Is that what L.A. is? A way to start fresh, try on new hats?"

"Maybe. I don't know." They reached the top of the hill and stopped to take in the ocean view. "Have you ever wanted something so badly you pushed and pushed to make it happen, only to have things out of your control push back?"

"More times than I'd like to admit."

"I treasure the time I've spent with my parents. Most people never get the opportunity to know their parents as friends and peers. Some of those memories are my favorites."

"Most people wouldn't do what you've done for their parents."

She smiled up at him. "Most people don't have my parents."

"No, they don't," he said, a quiet reverence in his voice.

She knew how much time Hudson had spent with her dad, following him around with tool belt hanging from his bony hips, swinging a too-big hammer. Looking back, she realized he'd been so deprived of positive male attention, he would take whatever he could get. Mila's dad understood that—so did her mom—which was why, whenever Hudson came around, there was always work to be done and an extra serving or two of leftovers in the fridge.

"Which makes me a jerk for saying this." She closed her eyes. "But sometimes it feels like life gave me three strikes before I even stepped into the batter's box."

"You deserve to live your own life, Mila. And sometimes when it's placed on hold for so long, it feels selfish to want something that you completely deserve."

"Yes. That's exactly it. No one else understands that."

"I do." He gave her hand another gentle squeeze. This time she squeezed back and they both laughed.

"Was that why you joined the Marines the day after graduation? To find your own path?"

Below them, the waves crashed against the jagged cliffs and mixed with the other sounds of nature.

"No," he finally said. "I joined the Marines to make sure Ford cashed in that free ride to University of Michigan. I knew if I stayed here, he'd blow an amazing opportunity to become something more than our father over some stupid loyalty pact we made when we were kids. So, I signed up and shipped out, and Ford went on to become a first-rate lawyer."

Chest aching, Mila released his hand to slide hers around his waist, then rested her cheek over his heart, trying to show him he didn't always have to go it alone. And somewhere between his arms coming around her and feeling his lips press against the top of her head, Mila wondered how she'd ever misjudged him.

She didn't know how long they stood there, on the cliff with the waves crashing below, holding on to each other and acknowledging the other's loss. But when they finally stepped back, she felt as though something fundamental had shifted between them.

"It's going to be dark soon and I want to show you the view from the top," he said.

Shading her eyes with her hand, she looked all the way up to the flashing beacon. "How many steps are we talking?"

"About two hundred, but it's worth it. I promise."

"Okay." She took his hand again and started toward the lighthouse. "On the way, you can tell me how you landed a job working here."

He laughed. "You make it sound like one of those fancy summer camps. My great-uncle was a fisherman and bought this property back in the sixties. Forty acres, a dilapidated cottage, and no dock to moor a boat. But to him it was paradise. He'd anchor his fishing boat about a quarter mile out, and we'd have to row in on a dinghy."

Ford pointed to a second smaller dock in the distance with a wooden dinghy moored to the side.

"I'm surprised it still floats."

He grinned down at her. "You should have seen my great-uncle's."

As they approached the lighthouse, a cottage came into view. No bigger than the size of her apartment in Manhattan, it was cedar shingled, with white trim, a bright blue door, and a small chef's garden enclosed by a picket fence. And windows galore. The place had more windows than walls, most likely because the wow factor came in the form of stunning, panoramic views of the Atlantic and other private islands.

"Did you stay there?"

He chuckled. "Nope, the cottage was for adults only. I slept in the boathouse." He pointed to an architectural masterpiece at the end of a long lawn that looked like it would list with Sotheby's. It was three times the size of the cottage, and its ceilings were two stories high, with floor-to-roof windows and a deck that made her parents' yard look shabby. "I recognize that look, and before you go saying something you'll regret, know that I helped renovate the boathouse into the main living quarters the summer between freshman and sophomore year.

Before that, it was me, a sleeping bag, and a stolen *Playboy* to keep me warm at night."

"Ford didn't come?"

He shook his head. "My time here always conflicted with football. There was camp, practice, preseason, playing season, off-season training. It never ended. When it came to football, my dad was worse than my first drill sergeant. We could be puking our guts out and he'd have us running bleachers in the middle of July."

"That's awful," she said, realizing that this was the first time he'd ever mentioned his father. "I didn't know you played football."

They reached the lighthouse and stopped at the door. "Until I was eleven. Then I got tired of playing my dad's game. I quit and he lost his shit." Hudson pulled a key from his pocket and opened the padlock. "I was never really into it like Ford, but after I handed in my jersey, my old man acted as if he only had one son. It didn't take long before I moved in with Huey, and Ford followed. My dad and I pretty much lost touch after that."

"I'm sorry you're not close." She was so close to her own dad, it made her heart ache for Hudson.

"I used to be sorry too, but then my grandpa took us in, and life with him was so much better." He shrugged as if it were no big deal, even though it was a huge, gut-wrenching deal.

Mila didn't know what to say. Her heart was breaking for everything Hudson had endured. She'd been abandoned by her birth parents, so she understood the issues that came with being unwanted. But she'd had Ronald and Joyce Cramer, two of the most loving and caring parents in the world, who had endured three flights, sleeping at the Tokyo airport, and traveled over seven thousand miles to find Mila. Her mom said she heard her child cry out from across the world and had to find her and bring her home.

Hudson had been abandoned by his parents too, just in a

different way. She knew he didn't want pity or empty plati-
tudes. He was too honest for that and he deserved more from
her. So when he pushed the lighthouse door open, she stepped
in front of him.

He raised a questioning brow. "Chickening out?"

"I hate that he made you feel like you didn't matter. Nobody
should ever be treated that way. Especially someone as sweet
and wonderful as you."

He tugged at the collar of his shirt. " 'Sweet' and 'wonderful.' Two adjectives that would definitely have Ford revoking
my man card."

He was making light of things, something she was coming to realize he did when faced with kindness. "You're a good
man, Hudson. Your dad's a jerk and a bully for not acknowledging that."

His face softened and he reached out to cup her cheek, his
thumb tracing her jaw. "I don't know about all that, but when
I'm with you, I feel like I can be a good man."

His admission was as surprising as it was endearing. She
wondered how she'd never noticed this tender, vulnerable side
of Hudson before. Then again, she guessed she had, only she'd
given credit to the wrong brother.

"Thank you." She went up on her toes and pressed a gentle
kiss to his cheek. "Everything about today has been incredibly
special. *You* made today incredibly special."

To her surprise, he blushed. The tough-as-steel army of one
was thrown by a compliment. They'd work on that, she decided.

"Are we going up?" he asked, pointing to the endless spiral-
ing steps that hugged the wall like the red on a barbershop pole.

"Damn straight."

Laughing, he took her hand and led her to the top, where the
view was worth every one of those two hundred steps. Fishing boats dotted the waters and pelicans flew overhead, diving
down to catch their dinner.

Silently, he and Mila stood side by side, gazing out at the ocean, as the sun slowly sank into the horizon. Much prettier than focusing on the road ahead, she decided.

"Did you learn your love of flying from your grandpa?" she asked, breaking the comfortable silence.

"I learned everything from him. When I think of the man who raised me, it's Huey." He turned to look at her. "How old were you when you were adopted?"

"Six."

He looked a little staggered at that. "Was it hard being dropped into a foreign country at that age, not even knowing the language?"

"Not any harder than you being dropped into enemy territory, not knowing what was waiting for you."

"At least I had my training and my unit."

"And I had mine. From day one, my parents went out of their way to make me a part of their family. Which is why I don't mind caring for them now. My dad was nearly fifty when they adopted me, so I always knew there would come a time that they'd need me."

He went back to staring at the waves crashing against the shoreline. "How do they feel about the possibility of your moving to Los Angeles?"

"That's actually why I needed the job with Huey's AirTaxi. The money will help pay for an in-home caretaker when I leave for L.A. They won't need full-time care, just someone to come by and check on them a few times a week." She looked over at him. "Isn't it pathetic—I'm a foreign national who's never left the Northeast."

"I'd go with 'honorable'"—he moved behind her—"'selfless'"—his hands rested on the railing, caging her in—"'incredible.'" He whispered the last part in her ear.

She looked at him over her shoulder. "Funny, those were the same three things I was thinking when Ford told me what really happened at Abigail's party. How you came to my rescue."

"I hate that you were left alone in the dark, but it did check off one of my teenage dreams."

"What was that?" she whispered.

"Kissing the girl who starred in every single one of my teenage fantasies."

"Every single one, huh?"

"Well, Kate Beckinsale may have had a few walk-on roles." She turned in his arms. "I have a confession."

"Tell me in minute detail. Can you use that sexy voice you used in the closet?"

She cupped his cheek. "I'm glad it was you."

He leaned down, his mouth hovering over hers, so close she could practically hear, *Houston, we have contact*, in the background. Her lips parted in anticipation, and—

"Wait," she heard herself say. "Before we take this to the next level, I need to tell you something."

He chuckled. "I wouldn't expect anything else."

"I made it through the second round of interviews." She cringed, waiting for his response.

Instead of sadness or even a hint of disappointment over the possibility that she could be moving three thousand miles away, he said, "Congratulations, that's amazing," then pulled her into his arms.

It wasn't a sexy embrace either, more like one step shy of getting a "way to go" tap on the shoulder for winning a free slice of cake in the annual Harvest Cake Walk.

Mila wasn't sure what she expected, but his wholehearted support stung a little. Which was ridiculous. She wanted a guy with enough emotional intelligence to understand what a great opportunity this was for her, to encourage and support her unconditionally. He was giving her all of that and more, yet her stomach was a big, complicated knot of emotions.

As if sensing her uncertainty, he tipped his head down to meet her gaze. "This is a good thing, right?"

"Yeah, it is," she said. "It's an amazing opportunity with lots of potential for growth. New York would be closer and more convenient, but you go where the job takes you. This job is taking me . . ." She almost said *away*, because that's what it was starting to feel like. "It's taking me to sunny L.A. How could I pass that up?"

"You can't, unless you're having second thoughts," he said gently.

"I'm not."

"It's okay if you do."

"Well, I don't," she lied, her eyes stinging with emotion. "It's just, how am I going to leave my family, my friends?" *How am I going to leave you?* "The thought of never being able to come back to my house or hang my Christmas stocking over the fireplace makes me sick. I'd still come home for the holidays, but I won't be coming to *my* home. Christmas will be celebrated in a condo or town house at the new retirement community across town."

"Change is hard, sometimes it's scary, but it's a hell of a lot easier to live with than regret. Don't let fear come between you and a great opportunity."

"So then I didn't need to let you know about L.A. before anything happened? In case you wanted to . . ."

"Change my mind?"

"Yeah."

"Buttercup," he said, his thumb tracing her lower lip. "As far as I'm concerned, it's already happening and there's no going back. At least not from where I stand, so I think we should take advantage of the time we have left."

Staring into those deep blue eyes, Mila felt seen, understood, safe, as if he'd catch her when she fell. If she wasn't careful, that was exactly what she was going to do. It would be a fast, hard landing that would break her, which was why transparency was so important.

If everyone knew where they stood, no one would get hurt. He might not be her Mr. Right, but he was a front-runner for Mr. Right Now. At least, that's what she was told herself as she pulled the list from her back pocket and plucked a pen from his fly-boy getup.

"I need to do one more thing," she said, and made a big deal of finding "Must be an amazing kisser." Only before she could put a check in the box, something at the bottom of the list caught her attention. The new item was certainly important in a partner, but the penmanship was too scribbly to be hers. She glanced up at him. "Did you write this?"

"Your list was a bit shortsighted, so I may have added a thing or two." He didn't sound the least bit apologetic. "Think of it as me, helping you find your Mr. Right."

"How thoughtful of you." She read from the list aloud. " 'A guy who knows how to get things done.' " She looked up at him through her lashes. "Did you mean like change my tires or . . . ?"

"We can do that too." He laughed. "A topic to discuss further anytime you want. Just not right now."

"Actually, right now I want to check something off."

"Name it."

"I'm working on becoming more of a show than tell person." With that, she brought his mouth to hers. One touch was all it took for fireworks to explode. His arms tightened around her, pulling her against him as her hands slid into his hair.

When he pulled back, they were both breathing heavily.

Mila picked the pen up off the ground, where it had fallen in the midst of lips locking and hands grabbing, and finally put a check in the "Must be an amazing kisser" box. Instead of handing him back his pen, she decided to add one more thing.

She handed him the list, which he read, then gave a low, sexy chuckle.

" 'Is interested in joining the mile-high club.' I've got just the chopper for that," he said as he kissed her again.

Hudson had sunk to a new low.

What had started out innocently enough with a quick glance out the bathroom window had turned him into a peeping tom when he spotted Mila, in a pair of ass-hugging leggings, bending over—all the way over—to grab a hammer from the toolbox.

How had he never noticed that his childhood bathroom window had a direct view of the Cramer house? And would you look at that—if he craned his neck a little, he could see over the fence to their front porch, where Mila was hanging holiday decorations.

He should have closed the blinds five minutes ago, but when it came to Mila there were a lot of should'ves and would'ves he chose to ignore. Which was why, after a long day of cleaning the helo from top to bottom, he chose to stand barefoot and dripping water on the tile floor, instead of heading downstairs for ice-cold beer and his already-made dinner.

She kept digging and he kept watching as she dove waist deep into a box of décor, ass in the air, and dug around for a good . . . hell, he didn't know how long. Didn't care. All he knew was that she had the most delectable derriere—so marvelous it was in the running for the eighth wonder of the world.

By the time she reappeared with wreath in hand, Hudson had his face pressed against the glass, the window was fogged, and the only thing he was hungry for didn't come in a to-go bag.

She hung the wreath on the front door and started draping garland over the door and around the railings of the yellow and white New England–style cottage. The lampposts challenged her five-foot-nothing reach, forcing her to roll onto her tippy-toes. Her light blue sweater rode up her body, high enough to expose a tiny strip of torso—tan, silky—two inches above and below the navel.

With the last post finished, she disappeared into the garage, only to return dragging an extendable ladder. Her second trip produced a life-sized, light-up Santa, followed by a trip for every one of his reindeer. On her final return, she came out with strands of twinkling lights draped across her chest like a band of ammo, a pink tool belt hanging around her waist, and a few dozen ornaments dangling from each pocket. Then there was the way she shimmed her hips to what he imagined must be Christmas tunes.

She was the collision of Santa Baby with G.I. Jane, making her the sexiest Santa's Helper he'd ever seen. An image that gave him a lot to be thankful for this holiday season.

As a teen hoping for a glimpse of Mila, Hudson took every odd job he could at the Cramer house, from cleaning out the duck coop to unloading groceries. He'd even once volunteered to model Mrs. Cramer's mermaid costume while she altered the shimmery skirt and coconut shells.

After their mile-high date the other day, Hudson didn't need coconut shells. Just as he didn't need to be stealing peeks of Mila from his bathroom window. Sure, it had been too soon to join the club on their return flight, but she'd given him a good-night kiss that was still with him come morning. Then she'd given him her phone number. *Which* he'd already had. But getting digits from a business card was a hell of a lot different from hearing it whispered by a pair of just-been-kissed lips.

So then why was he standing there in nothing but a wet towel and hard-on, watching her dance in the yard, instead of heading over?

Knowing it was smarter to make dinner than answer that question, he went for the blinds at the same moment Mila did a little booty shake, glanced across the street and up—then froze, her mouth a perfect circle of surprise.

"Shit." He considered ducking down, but it was too late.

Squinting, she raised a hand to block the sun and—even from across the street, two doors down, and through a slightly foggy window—he could see the humor in her eyes.

She recovered a hell of a lot faster than he, gifting him with a smile that stopped his heart.

Hudson hadn't seen her smile like that, bright and carefree, since he'd arrived home. Probably a good thing, since it made him want things he shouldn't. Things that came with expiration dates and countdown clocks attached.

Her fingers gave a cute little *I see you* wiggle. He wiggled back, not caring if he looked like an idiot because then she signaled for him to wait—as if he were in a rush to lose that view—and dug into her tool belt, pulling out her cell.

He watched her fidget with the screen, then hold up her phone and point. A moment later, his cell vibrated across the counter. With a grin, he picked it up and read the message:

**TEXTING WHILE NAKED IS A GOOD LOOK ON YOU.**

*Would you look at that*, Mila was initiating flirt zone. A good sign that their good-bye kiss had been as good for her as for him. His fingers eagerly typed a response:

**HOW DO YOU KNOW I'M NAKED?**

**ONE CAN WISH.**

**WHAT ELSE ARE YOU WISHING FOR?**

Three little dots appeared at the bottom of his screen, blinking so long he was afraid she'd changed her mind. He was about to type CHICKEN, followed by three chicken emojis, when a text came through:

> TO SEE YOUR MOVES. ONLY FAIR, SINCE YOU SAW MINE.

> MY BEST MOVES REQUIRE A PARTNER.

> DOES THIS PARTNER ONLY GET TO WATCH? OR IS PARTICIPATION REQUIRED?

*Hot damn.* Hudson hadn't been this excited about writing a girl since he'd made Mila a valentine card in the sixth grade.

> YOU APPLYING?

> YOU TAKING APPLICATIONS?

> FOR YOU BUTTERCUP, ALWAYS.

> REFERENCES MIGHT BE AWKWARD.

> NO NEED. I WATCHED HOW YOU HANDLED THOSE BALLS. I WAS IMPRESSED.

Her brow furrowed in confusion. Then she looked down, spotted the ornaments hanging from her tool belt, and laughed. She was still grinning when his phone lit up.

NOT SO BAD YOURSELF.

WHAT ARE YOU DOING FOR DINNER?

He hit send and watched the screen. His growing anticipation over her reply was almost embarrassing.

DEPENDS.

ON?

WHAT YOU'RE DOING.

Hudson got dressed, packed up his dinner and a few beers to go, and made it across the street in record time. When he arrived, his excitement turned to concern because she was two stories up, precariously perched, with one foot on the ladder and the other on the giant oak, stringing up holiday lights.

"Jesus, what are you doing?" he asked, gripping the bottom of the ladder to steady it.

"Hanging Christmas lights," she said as if the idea of gravity fell under the category of fake news. "What are you doing here?"

"Dinner."

She paused, sniffing the air, then closed her eyes. "That smells amazing." She met his gaze. "You cooked for me?"

"I can neither confirm nor deny the origin of this outstanding dinner. But don't worry, what I lack in cooking skills I more than make up for in other ways." He waggled a brow and she laughed.

"When you said dinner, I figured sometime after five."

He looked at his watch. "It's nearly six."

"Really? I must have lost track of time," she said, reaching over even farther.

"I see that. Can you come down? I'd hate to ruin this meat-loaf sandwich by watching you go splat."

She looked down at the to-go bag and blew a hair out of her face as if unaware she was an inch from disaster. "You brought me one of Nan's meatloaf sandwiches? Thinly cut goodness, topped with gravy, and nestled inside one of Sydney's fresh baguettes?"

"Actually, I brought one to share with a slice of pumpkin pie for dessert."

"Who gets the bigger half?"

"Depends on if you fall off the roof and die. Then it's all mine."

"You play dirty."

"You play dangerously."

"I'm not going to die. I've done this every year since I was a kid."

"You say it like that should make me feel better. And for the record, I cleaned those gutters from sixth grade through senior year, so I know just how high it is, and how hard this balancing act is."

"Then you should also know how pretty they look," she said, still not coming down the ladder. If anything, she dug in deeper. "Move out of the way or you're going to end up covered in leaves from the gutter, and that looks like a clean shirt."

"You know, Sawyer Finn does this for a living. Why don't you hire him?" Not that Hudson wanted the local landscaper sniffing around Mila's place. Even if the guy was married.

"Do you know how much he charges? A lot. And you're still in my way."

"Not as much as the doctor's bill if you fall."

"No kidding, all I've got is catastrophe coverage, and you should see the deductible. Now seriously, scoot. I don't want that sandwich anywhere near what's about to rain down."

He didn't move and neither did she, except to flash him a grin that said she was up to no good. Seconds later, a huge pile of leaves and debris landed on his head and went down the back of his shirt.

Hudson had to laugh. No one ever pushed his buttons. Most people gave him a wide berth. Not Mila. She was fearless in a way that was as frustrating as it was impressive. She'd always been impressive, but watching how she cared for her aging parents, the sacrifices she made for her family, had him wondering what it felt like to be on the receiving end of that kind of devotion.

That kind of love.

"I'm going to make you take that back too," he warned, climbing up the ladder behind her.

"Big words," she said in mock fear.

"I'm a big guy." He didn't stop until reaching the rung just below her, his body caging her in and showing her just how big he was.

She looked at him over her shoulder, and he realized he could look into those beautiful brown eyes forever. "Is this where you show me your moves?"

"One of them." He captured her lips in a kiss that ended with her moaning. "The rest will be added to my list, since none of them can be fully appreciated while balancing on a ladder."

"You have a list?"

"Started it after our first meeting," he said, sliding his hands over hers to take the string of lights, loving how she shivered at the simple contact. "It's getting pretty big."

She leaned back against him. "Your list or . . ."

"Both," he whispered in her ear, then gave her ass a playful swat. "Now climb on up so we can get these hung and move on to dinner."

"And the list."

"Definitely the list."

# Chapter 7

When the last of the holly was strung and the last of the twinkly lights hung from eave to eave and all seven reindeer were perched on the roof, Hudson sat down on the porch and patted the step next to him. He wanted to make this moment stretch a little longer because he knew, the second she walked through that front door, she would morph into selfless, nurturing Mila.

She deserved a break, even if it was just sharing a sandwich and watching the sunset.

"Hurry up or you'll miss the best part," he said.

"One second, I just want to make sure my mom put the casserole in the oven."

"One second and you'll miss it." When she didn't look as if she were about to sit, he snagged her phone from her tool belt and texted Joyce. "There. Done."

Stubborn as ever, Mila waited until her mom texted back before giving in. With a grin, he stood, then took her hand and gently tugged her toward the street.

"Where are we going?" she asked.

"To have a dinner that isn't chaperoned by your parents," he said.

She looked over her shoulder, laughing when she spotted the two inquisitive faces watching from the front window.

"They'll just ask what happened when I get home."

"But I won't have to listen to what you tell them," he said, once again struck by the deep connection her family shared.

Hudson had witnessed tight-knit families before, but never one like the Cramers. Maybe it was because of all the time he'd spent there as a kid, but Hudson promised himself that if he ever did settle down, it would only be when he found that same kind of fierce, unconditional love Ronald and Joyce shared.

Any man lucky enough to be in Mila's life had big shoes to fill, and Hudson had never really been all that lucky.

Their lives were going in different directions and their upbringings couldn't have been more opposite. Where Mila was loved and accepted for exactly who she was at every moment of her life, Hudson was ridiculed and beaten down, eventually seeking shelter on his grandpa's doorstep. Ironically, Hudson was home to stay, while Mila was hoping to make her home across the country.

"Is this another surprise?" she asked.

He stopped a few feet from his front porch and faced her. She might not have had a say all those years ago, but he'd give her a say now. "Do you want it to be?"

She shook her head. "No. When I walk through that door, it's going to be because I want what *you're* offering."

"I was thinking dinner under the sunset, drinks under the moonlight, and then *dessert* under the covers."

With a smile that was a thousand percent trouble, she took both his hands, lacing their fingers. "I was thinking kissing under the sunset, *dessert* under the moonlight, and leftovers under the covers."

"What about the pie?" He knew how much she loved pie.

"A girl can't give away all her secrets."

Especially the epically stupid, best-left-in-the-box, life-will-never-be-the-same-if-you-spill secret Mila had been doing her best to ignore.

Admitting it now, even to herself, would be way too dangerous. Which was why, under no circumstances, would anyone ever know that she was falling in love with Hudson James.

Not only was he the wrong but somehow perfectly right brother, but this was the worst time in her life to be having these kinds of feelings. She was leaving. He was staying. End of story.

It boiled down to two options: walk away with her heart intact or accept the risks and fulfill a decade old fantasy. Either choice came with upsides and pitfalls, just as they'd both—

Oh, who was she kidding? Her heart was already so far involved, it had a PROPERTY OF HUDSON bumper sticker adhered to it. Heartbreak was guaranteed at this point, so she might as well reap some of the benefits.

She moved to the step above him, teasing him with a kiss. "We'd better hurry. The sun's almost set, and we don't want to miss it."

"It will be so amazing, there's no way you'll miss it." He cupped her hips and maneuvered her up another step, then the next, until she was standing on the porch stoop, her back against the door, Hudson against her front.

"Again, some mighty big words."

"I look forward to proving to you just how big"—palms flat against the door, he leaned all the way in to her—"my *word* is."

Oh, it was clear how *big* it was. Just as it was clear that deep down, beneath the confidence and swagger, was the shadow of a boy who felt the need to prove his worth to the world—and the man who still carried those scars.

"Hudson, you don't have to prove anything to me," she whispered with a gentle kiss.

He didn't move, just remained stock-still. Those deep blue eyes, always calm and assessing, looked a bit wild and uncertain. His throat worked as he swallowed hard, telegraphing how foreign that kind of acceptance was in his life. How terrified he was of disappointing her.

"Mila." Her name sounded like a plea. "I'll never be a suit and tie guy."

"A suit and tie would never work a mile up." Beneath her hand, she felt his heartbeat quicken. "I'm more interested in numbers six and seven."

" 'Must be an amazing kisser,' " he recited.

"And 'take charge in the bedroom.' " Her fingers trailed down to tangle in the hem of his shirt. "I've been looking forward to an up-close, hands-on demonstration with your *word* ever since the closet." She took the to-go bag with her free hand.

"Buttercup, I've been looking forward to hearing you say that for more than ten years."

"You mean, seven," she corrected.

"I know what I mean," he said, and then took her mouth as if it belonged to him.

His lips were amazing, full and skilled, but unlike the purposeful and patient Hudson of the closet, he was all testosterone and raw need, as if kissing her were his God-given right.

Being kissed by Hudson was a religious experience, one that made her want to convert. In his arms she felt reborn, as if being kissed for the first time.

It was epic. Amazing. Mind-blowing. Everything he'd promised and more. Love might not be as simple as reciting a spell, but kissing Hudson James was absolutely, positively, undeniably the most magical moment of her life.

Mila understood firsthand why Hudson was such a successful pilot. *His mission statement must be Defy Gravity*, she thought, because he drove her higher and higher until she was floating. The ground disappeared from under her, her limbs went weak, and the altitude made it impossible to catch her breath.

His hands hadn't left the door, but their bodies were engaged in a silent get-to-know-you that had Mila rolling so high on her toes that her sixth-grade ballerina teacher would have been impressed.

Mila let the moment wash over her, the intensity, the unleashed need, the feel of him beneath her hand. But it was the way he held her, as if he'd finally found his co-pilot for life, that had her heart silencing her brain.

The longer the kiss, the hotter she became until she was certain she'd burst into flames from the sexual chemistry. He was mesmerizing, habit-forming, drawing her further into his vortex one kiss at a time. Then there was his thigh, his big, strong thigh sliding between hers, creating a delicious friction that had her groaning.

"Sunset."

"Sunset," he agreed, but he didn't stop kissing her, which worked for her, since his thigh shifted higher, pressing harder, until she was so wrapped up in everything that was Hudson, she forgot her name, that they were on his front porch in clear view of the entire block, and that the only thing keeping her upright was the door. Which suddenly and unexpectedly opened with a click.

Not prepared, she stumbled backward, readying herself for a fall, but Hudson slid his hands down to palm her ass.

"Up," he commanded, but she was already climbing him like a tree. With her legs locked around his waist, the to-go bag crashing to the floor, he moved her through the house, onto the back porch, and had her lying beneath him on the patio table without their lips ever separating.

Then he was on the move again, his mouth on her neck, the

hollows of her throat, and lower—so much lower, unbuttoning her sweater as he went. Slowly, button by button, driving her out of her mind, until he finally reached the last one, gently parting the fabric.

"Damn," he said, staring at her as if she were the most beautiful thing he'd ever seen.

"Damn," he repeated, then lowered his head and pulled her into his mouth, nibbling and licking and getting her so hot, the crisp November air didn't stand a chance.

He continued his journey south, divesting her of her clothes as he went. Her sweater, her bra, her leggings, which caught on her shoes until he yanked them off in a single move that sent nuclear-powered tingles exploding though her body.

She reached for his belt at the precise moment his hands gripped her hips, lifting them off the table for optimal positioning. Which he took full advantage of, pressing an openmouthed kiss to her inner thigh, first the right, then the left and back to the right, before kissing her straight up the middle.

He gently tugged her panties to the side and, watching her watch him, delivered a kiss that was almost as hot as the big ball of fire raging between them.

"God, don't stop," she moaned, and, man of big words, he did not. Using his tongue, his teeth, teasing and tempting, he set a delicious pace that had her pressing against him. Harder and faster, he launched an all-out attack until breathing became nonexistent.

He got her body so primed it was humming and, in an embarrassing amount of time, he had her careening toward the finish line.

The finish line was good. The finish line was great. She hadn't crossed that line in a really, really, *really* long time. It almost pained her to stop, but Mila was a team player and determined that, when those champagne bottles exploded, they'd fly high together.

"Come here." She fisted her hand in his shirt, yanking him forward and his shirt up and over his head. She made quick work of his belt and jeans, then slid her hands down the front to his—*my word, indeed.*

"Mi," he breathed, so she did it again, only this time beneath his BVDs. Pushing his jeans around his ankles with one hand, she kept up a steady pace with the other.

"Slow down," he groaned, but she noticed he didn't make a move to stop her, instead pushing harder into her palm. "One more stroke, and it's game over, Buttercup. I've waited too long to have it end in three seconds."

She gave a little squeeze. "Big words go both ways."

Okay, more than a little squeeze, but he didn't seem to mind. His eyes darkened. His expression was dazed.

"Is anyone home?" Not that it would stop her now, but she was looking for an uninterrupted, dusk-to-dawn meet-and-greet.

"No. We've got the whole place to ourselves."

He leaned in to kiss her, and before she could stop herself she asked, "For how long?"

"However long it takes," he said, sculpting her hips and yanking her forward until she was teetering on the edge, literally and metaphorically. "Now, unless you have any more questions."

She grabbed his face. "Lucky for you, I'm done with words."

Thank God, Hudson was fluent in silent communication, because all it took was a single look from Mila to snap the waist on her teal thong, then—*holy shit*—lift her hips in silent invitation.

Hudson RSVPed to that show-and-tell in no time flat, easing his thumbs under the waistband and slowly tugging the thong down her legs. The lower he went, the harder he got, until she gave a little shimmy that had it sliding. All. The. Way. Off.

Hudson couldn't look away, because she leaned back on her hands, giving him a no-lace-required view that officially blew his mind. Then, back to that non-communication, she fisted her hands in his hair and locked her ankles around his back, holding him there, as if he didn't already know what she wanted.

He knew all right, and he was going to give it to her.

Then her lips crashed down on his, and while she was kissing him he grabbed a condom, was covered, and—miracle of all miracles—slid home in a single, earth-shattering stroke.

She groaned. He dropped his head to her shoulder. Just absorbing the feeling of finally, *finally*, being inside her. Being with her like this. She was silent and he wondered if, like him, she was taken by how right everything felt.

He wasn't sure how long they held each other like that, but suddenly the sky had grown dark, moonlight glowed over her silky skin, and she shifted—ever so slightly. Not enough to be considered a first move, but enough to know she was giving the green light.

Wanting to check off every box on her list, Hudson took control. Gentle at first, building from a slow burn to surface-of-the-sun. They moved together, faster and more frantic, their momentum catching fire. Desperate for leverage, he leaned her back against the table, and they quickly became a sweaty tangle of arms and legs.

Touching, sliding, exploring.

He knew when it happened, when she forgot about tallies and checkmarks and gave herself over to the possibilities.

Gave herself over to him.

Her hands slid up and down his spine, her eyes shining up as she started to tighten around him. The air burned his lungs, so he gave up on breathing. His chest felt too big for his skin, his knees began to buckle, and he wanted to run away and come home all at the same time.

Her legs pulled him down until there wasn't even a breath between them. She buried her face into the curve of his shoulder, holding him as though he was one of the good ones.

For the first time in his life, he was determined to be that guy—to erase every hesitation she'd had about them.

"I'm almost there," she moaned, clenching and drawing him all the way in, which drove him right over the edge.

The pressure built, hotter and higher, and he fought to keep himself in check, but her thighs tightened around his waist until he thought he'd pass out and then, *hallelujah*, she began to shake. She pushed up as he came down, sinking so deep he knew he never wanted to leave.

Then the sexiest thing he'd ever heard broke from her lips: "Hudson."

A-OK with him, since he was mumbling her name as everything narrowed, came into focus, and they both fell at the same time in a shared kind of raw tenderness that had so many feels going through his chest, it made speaking impossible.

Not that there were any words to describe what had just happened.

A long time later, after they'd shared dessert and he'd given her a double helping of *dessert,* Hudson lay on his back, with Mila snuggled against his side, fast asleep.

He watched the stars above with a big, goofy grin on his face. They hadn't made it to the bed. They were still on the back porch and Mila had stolen most of the blanket, but he wasn't complaining.

Tonight had been, hands down, the best night of his life. For the first time since enlisting, he had clarity. The soul-deep, without a doubt, conviction that he was in the right place. And Mila was the right woman. Only he didn't know where her head was at.

He knew where her body stood, but her heart was a whole other matter. And that made him nervous.

"I can almost hear you thinking," she said, her sleep-roughened voice making him ready for another helping. "What's up?"

He looked down and lifted a brow. She laughed. "I mean besides the obvious."

"I was thinking about how good this feels, you in my arms."

"Mmm." She snuggled deeper and his heart rolled over.

"And that I want more of this," he continued. "More of you." He felt her grow still and he closed his eyes with a grimace. This was why he shouldn't ever talk when sex drunk. It rarely turned out well. "Never mind. Forget I said anything."

"No, it's not that. I want more of you too." Her arms tightened around him. "But I heard back from the job this morning."

"The one in L.A.?" His chest pinched painfully.

"Actually. I heard back from two jobs."

"Two?"

"Turns out that the Moonbright Community Theater is looking for an art director. It doesn't pay as much as an assistant set designer, go figure, but it's a bigger title. I'd run the entire art department."

And she'd stay right here in Moonbright, with him.

"What about L.A.?" he asked, working really hard to smile. She looked up at him, her eyes sparkling with hope. "They want to do another interview with me on Thursday. There are still a ton of people left to interview, but that I made it this far is pretty cool."

"It's amazing." He leaned down and kissed her. "You're amazing."

"Tonight was amazing." She slid her thigh over his and straddled him, the moonlight casting a glow over her naked body.

"It's getting better by the moment."

He brought her down for a languid kiss before he said something that would influence her decision. "Art director" might be a bigger title, but their small town didn't hold a candle to the experience she'd get in Hollywood.

He knew how hard she worked, making everyone else's life fuller and better. It was about time she was able to make her own dreams come true. If anyone deserved some happiness, it was Mila.

Watching her tonight, working to get her parents' house ready for the holidays after putting in a full day painting windows, was an emotional game changer. It made him realize that this was about more than proving that her Mr. Right list was complete BS. This was about becoming the kind of man who deserved to be Mila's Mr. Right.

He'd finally found the woman he wanted for the long haul, only there was a big TBD in her flight plan.

# Chapter 8

Mila was glowing.

It had started Friday morning when Hudson fed her breakfast in bed and lasted straight through the weekend. It stuck with her during Monday and Tuesday's mural painting at the Bellaluna's Bakeshop, Wednesday's pitch to become Rose Cottage's official window artist, and this morning's house tour at the new retirement development—her dad liked the simplicity of the condo and her mom said over her dead body would she be denied a garden.

It had even withstood the winter storm that had blown in.

This was more than a sex glow. Of that she had no doubt. It was an inside-out, axis-tilting kind of glow that made her a believer—in the legend, in soul mates, and in true love.

And therein lay the problem. Mila was, head over heels, totally and completely, forever and ever amen, in love with a man who was so perfectly wrong, he couldn't be more right for her. Which was why, after her two interviews that afternoon, the first with the community theater and the second with the production company, she'd called an emergency meeting at the Corner Café.

All life-changing decisions were best made in the company of good friends and a slice of Nan's pie. Today's special was cran-apple cobbler served warm, with a generous helping of cinnamon ice cream. A favorite, but Mila couldn't seem to find her appetite.

"Okay, spill," Dakota said.

"Who said I had anything to spill?" Mila asked, because now that she was there, she didn't want to talk about the interviews.

Dakota laughed. "The constipated look you always get when you're overthinking plus the fact that you haven't touched your pie."

"I had another interview with the company in L.A. today. The entire executive team was there. It's down to me and three other candidates. They said, either way, I'd hear back by the end of the week."

"This is great news," Kira said.

"It is?" Mila hadn't meant for it to come out more query than statement, but it was hard when she'd been questioning her next move all week. Painting windows had never been more than a means to an end until her parents were settled and something better came along.

Then again, *means to an end* hadn't exactly worked out as planned for her lately.

"It is if you want it to be," Dakota said. "Do you still want it to be?"

Mila snorted. "Of course I do. I mean, it's my dream job. I'd be stupid to pass it up for a small-town community theater."

"Not necessarily." Kira covered Mila's hand with her own. "The beauty of dreams is that sometimes they change and we have the choice to change direction with them or stay the course."

Mila thought back to her time on Hudson's island and how one impulsive decision had led to a day of excitement and rightness. Standing there in Hudson's arms, being open and vulnerable with each other, had changed her. She wasn't sure if the things that had made her happy before would make her happy now.

And she couldn't forget the generous job offer here in town, which would provide a new challenge for her. It wouldn't give her the chance to network or make the kind of connections she could in L.A. and the growth potential was minimal, but it would allow her to stay in Moonbright.

Maybe even buy her parents' house. They were moving on to a new chapter of their lives, and so was she. Why couldn't she start hers with the man she loved in the house she adored?

It had served three generations of Cramers. Why change a tradition that, so far, had resulted in love and happiness?

"What does Hudson think?" Kira asked.

"He said he wanted more. With me." She shrugged. "But his life is here."

"So?" Dakota said. "The question is, where do you want to live your life?"

Her heart went *boom boom boom* at the possibilities, at the clarity that came when she chose to take her eyes off the road ahead and focus, instead, on what could be. She'd always dreamed of using her imagination to create alternative realities. How was that any different from creating her own reality, right here, in Moonbright?

"I don't know," she said, but knew it was a lie. "I don't want to get ahead of myself. There are still three other candidates. Why get all worked up over something that likely won't happen? Even if it did, the job starts relatively soon and my parents' house is nowhere near ready to go on the market."

Not to mention her heart wasn't ready to walk away from Hudson.

"You keep telling yourself that," Dakota said. "But eventually an offer will come in and, when it does, you'll have a heavy decision to make. You shouldn't pass on a job because of your parents or because of a guy. If you pass, it should be because staying here is the right choice for you."

A comforting peace filled her heart. She'd spent most of her life making decisions based on other people's needs. Her family, her friends, she'd even stayed with exes well past their expiration date because she'd been afraid of disappointing them. Maybe Dakota was right, Maybe it was time she started asking herself what would make *her* happy.

Hudson made her the once-in-a-lifetime kind of happy that no job could ever match. Moonbright might be her home, but he was her future.

"I have to go."

If someone had told Mila that she'd ever consider passing on a job for a man, she would have laughed in their face. But there she was, walking into the hangar, more excited about the prospect of a future with Hudson than the possibility of a job in L.A. He was worth staying for. And yes, while she wanted a life of her own, she didn't want to live life alone.

"Hey, Ford," she said, practically bouncing as she walked. "Is Hud around?"

Ford smiled. "*Hud* is buffing his precious baby."

"Thanks." Mila walked to the chopper to find her man, looking mighty fine in his fly-boy gear, his biceps bulging as he wiped down the front of the chopper. "Hey, you," she said.

He turned and, with a smile that made her body break out in the goosies, walked over to her, right up into her space, and, without hesitation, cupped her cheeks, giving her a long, delicious, drugging kiss.

"Hey." He kissed her again. This one shorter, but not any less potent. "How did your interviews go?"

"Good." This time she kissed him. "I should hear back soon from both. But enough about that. I missed you," she said, even though it had only been three hours since she'd left his bed—

for the third morning in a row. But a lot had transpired in that time.

"I missed this." He went in for another kiss just as her phone pinged. They both froze.

"It could be the community theater."

"Or not," he said. "You should check to be sure."

"I can do it later." She went up on her toes, and her lips had just brushed his when her phone pinged again with a reminder that echoed off the cement floor and around her stomach. "I should just . . ."

He took a step back and shoved his hands into his pockets. "You should."

Mila pulled her phone from her purse and opened her inbox. And there, in bold text, was an email from the president of the company in L.A. She tapped the screen and, *oh my God*, it wasn't about another interview. They'd offered her the job—and for more money than she'd expected.

"So?" he asked. She looked up at him and a smile snuck out. "You got it."

"I got it! Well, they want to fly me out for an in-person interview, but if that goes well, then the job is mine," she said, and for a second, just a second, she hesitated. Ignored the certainty that she wasn't going to take the job and let the pure euphoria of beating out some stiff competition rush through her.

She'd done it. She'd landed her dream job, all on her own.

"They'll love you." Hudson's gaze turned serious, and something flickered in it that gave her hope he felt the same way she did. "I—"

"You, what?" she asked, her chest thumping hard.

Instead of saying the three words she wanted so badly to hear, he said, "I'm really proud of you. What are they offering?"

"Ah." She swallowed. "Instead of an assistant to a set designer, I'd be an actual set designer. And they offered me twice as much as the community theater position."

"You're worth all that and more." His eyes remained locked on hers. "I never had any doubt."

"I did," she whispered. "But I'm glad someone had confidence."

"I have every confidence in the world," he said, and she realized he wasn't smiling. In fact, he appeared resigned, distant even. The emotions she'd seen a moment ago were extinguished, and along with them that small bead of hope.

"I should email them back."

"Wait, before you . . ." He stepped toward her, then stopped and shook his head. "You're right. You need to email them and accept the offer."

"No, wait, what were you going to say before?" she asked, anticipation causing her heart to beat so fast, she was afraid she'd pass out.

"Just that I'll help your parents get their house ready and look after them until it sells, so you can get settled."

"You'll look after my parents?" she asked, confused.

She was ready to stay. Thought that after the past week he'd ask her to stay, maybe even move in with her. Was he being standoffish because he'd had time to think, reconsider what her staying would mean, realize that the things he'd said had been in the moment and their time together hadn't changed him the way it had her?

And how embarrassing was that? It was like high school all over again. She knew if she hesitated, he'd ask her to stay but not for the right reasons. Her backbone snapped straight, and the weight of the world went back to where it had been her entire life—only this time it felt heavier, as if she would crumble the second she walked out of the hangar.

She forced a smile. "You're right. I should take the job."

"Of course you should. This is everything you've ever wanted. You've worked hard for this. You deserve to finally start your life."

"In Los Angeles?"

"Where else?" he said as if there were no other option than starting a new life, three thousand miles away—from him.

Her heart sank to her toes and her stomach hollowed out, making her want to throw up. Here she'd been thinking about the possibility of buying her parents' house, moving in with Hudson, and he'd been, well, she didn't know. But they clearly weren't looking for the same things.

"There were two options on the table, but I guess I chose the wrong one."

"Mila," he said, but she didn't look at him, couldn't for fear she'd lose it.

She was tired of waiting for the right time, the right opportunity, the right man—only to realize she'd once again gotten it wrong. For once she wanted someone to see her magic, to choose her. To tell her she was their person.

But the longer she waited, the more certain she became that he wasn't going to say any of those things, so she turned and headed for the door.

"I'd better go," she said, not looking back, knowing if she did, she'd cry. "I have tickets to book, plans to make. Oh, and I have to tell my parents the news."

Outside, it had started raining hard, matching the pressure building in her chest. So she clutched her hands over her heart, to make sure it stayed in one piece until she made it to her car.

She reached for the handle as the first sob rolled through her chest and broke free. Followed closely by another, and by the time the third one wracked her body she was soaking wet, leaning against her car, the rain crashing down around her.

# Chapter 9

Hudson sat at the bar, sipping a beer and feeling as if his heart had been tossed through a propeller.

"What are you doing?" Ford asked, taking way too much joy in Hudson's current situation.

"What does it look like I'm doing?" He picked up the glass and drained it.

"You know she's leaving today."

A whole month early. Hudson rubbed his hand over his chest, trying to ease the raw ache that had been gnawing at him. It didn't help. Nothing he seemed to do helped. It just got worse—deeper, hollower.

"She texted me good-bye yesterday."

"Did you text her back?" Ford asked, and Hudson remained quiet. "Man, you're an idiot."

Maybe, but he'd come to terms with his decision. It had been a week since Mila had walked through that hangar door and out of his life. He knew if he'd asked her to stay, she would have put her life on hold to retrofit it around someone else's needs. He cared for her too much to let that happen.

So, he'd let her go. And he sure as shit didn't want to rehash it all. "Love you too. Now, get the hell out of my face."

Instead of walking away, Ford took the stool next to him and signaled for another round.

"That's the opposite of what I asked you to do." Not that Dakota would bring Hudson anything. She'd been sending him the buzz-off-and-die glare since he'd walked in. He didn't blame her. He knew he'd hurt Mila, had seen it in her eyes, but he'd made the right call. In a few months, when her life was full of opportunity, she'd see that.

"You're not the boss of me," Ford said. "Thank Christ, because ninety-nine-point-nine percent of the time you get it wrong."

"Maybe." He shrugged. "But this is one of those point-one times."

"Let me guess, you breaking her heart is your way of protecting her." Ford clapped him on the back. "Then congratulations, Bro, job well done."

"What would you have had me do?" he asked in a tone that would have a smart man running. "Make her choose between me, a guy she's been with for less than a month, and the job?"

His twin was never the smart one. In fact, he was as stupid as they came, because he leaned forward, bringing his smug mug within punching distance. "You should have given her the choice. Not made it for her. You didn't just screw this up. You took her choice away."

He stared at the inch of foam left in the bottom of his glass. "What if she didn't choose me?"

Ford sat back and crossed his arms. "She's not Dad."

"I know that."

"Do you?"

Hudson wasn't sure anymore. He thought he knew a lot, but, apparently, he knew jack shit when it came to women.

"You should have more faith in yourself. And if that's too hard, then at least have faith in Mila."

He looked over at his brother. "And if she still leaves?"

"You really think that's what would have happened? I have no idea how you've ever gotten laid." Ford smiled. Hudson didn't. Because, looking back, he realized she wouldn't have left. He'd essentially chased her away and he knew exactly how that felt.

"You know what your problem is, right?" Ford asked.

Hudson shot Ford a hard look. "I guess you're about to tell me."

"You love her."

He shoved Ford nearly off the chair. "You take that back."

"Can't. Not when it's the truth." Ford snatched Hudson's phone and hit Mila's speed dial, then held it out.

Hudson looked at the phone as if it were radioactive. "What the hell are you doing?"

"I'm going to do you a favor and call her, then ask her not to get on that plane." Ford paused. "Maybe you should ask her. And be sure to say please."

He hated it when Ford was right. But Hudson wasn't just in love. He was in so deep he couldn't see a future without Mila. He should have given her the choice. He owed her that. She deserved that. And God help him, if she chose L.A. it would hurt more than the bullet that had pierced his shoulder in South Africa, but he'd live with whatever she chose.

"What are you going to do?" Ford asked.

Hudson took his phone. "Tell her I love her, then ask her not to get on that plane." He hit dial and heard it ring—in stereo.

He turned around and there she was, standing at the tavern door, dressed in a pretty yellow sweater and matching scarf. With her phone to her ear, she walked across the floor toward him. "I didn't get on the plane."

"I can see that," he said into the mouth piece, standing and walking toward her.

"I couldn't. Not without telling you what I was going to say in the hangar."

"What were you going to say?" he asked, and then she was right there, in front of him, those big brown eyes, red from crying, staring up at him.

"That I want to stay." She was still talking into the phone. "In Moonbright. Not for a job and not for a guy. But for my guy."

He liked the sound of that, but he needed to be sure of what she was saying. He took the phone from her and pocketed it along with his own. "What about your dream?"

She stepped so close he could smell the rain on her skin. "You're my dream. You're who I've been waiting for and I finally found you—why would I leave?"

"God, Mila, I don't even know where to begin," he whispered, resting his hands on her hips. "I'm a disaster in the kitchen, no one would ever call me even tempered, and I don't even own a tie. The only thing throw pillows are good for are naked pillow fights and I am so far from perfect I'm holding my breath, waiting for the day when you decide to call me on it."

"I burn eggs, have been known to honk at slow pedestrians, and I'm realizing ties are overrated. I'm up for a good pillow fight and you *are* perfect. For me." She slid her arms around his waist. "And I would always choose you, Hudson James, because I love you."

Ford smacked his arm. "You were supposed to say that first."

Hudson ignored him. "I love you so much, I didn't want to take anything from you. I just wanted what was best for you."

"You will always be what's best for me." She smacked his chest. "That was a dumb move you pulled, and I almost fell for it. Don't ever do something that stupid again." Then her eyes welled up and she smoothed her hand up and around his neck. "You love me, Hudson James?"

"Guilty as charged, Buttercup."

And then she kissed him and, in that moment when her lips met his, he knew not only that magic existed but, out of all the people in the universe, he'd found his person.

Enjoy these recipes from the Corner Café!

# Blueberry Butter Cake

(This recipe was handed down from a great-aunt who extensively traveled New England. She first sampled the cake during a summer visit with an old friend who owned a small restaurant. Desserts were a specialty. The owner graciously shared the recipe with my aunt. It became a family favorite over the years. —Kate Angell)

Yield: 12 servings

*Ingredients*

½ cup butter or margarine
¾ cup white sugar plus 1 tablespoon
¼ teaspoon salt
1 teaspoon vanilla extract
2 large egg yolks
2 large egg whites
1 ½ cups all-purpose flour plus one tablespoon
1 teaspoon baking powder
⅓ cup milk
1 ½ cups fresh blueberries

*Directions*

1. Preheat oven to 350° F (175° C). Grease and flour an 8-by-8-inch-square pan.

2. Cream butter or margarine and ½ cup of the sugar until fluffy. Add salt and vanilla. Separate eggs and reserve the whites. Add egg yolks to the sugar mixture; beat until creamy.

3. Combine 1 ½ cups flour and baking powder; add alternately with milk to egg yolk mixture.

4. Coat berries with 1 tablespoon flour and add to batter.

5. In a separate bowl, beat whites until soft peaks form. Add remaining ¼ cup of sugar, 1 tablespoon at a time, and beat until stiff peaks form. Fold egg whites into batter. Pour into prepared pan. Sprinkle top with final 1 tablespoon sugar.

6. Bake for 50 minutes, or until cake tests done.

# Classic Chocolate Whoopie

(This recipe is from *Whoopie Pies* by Sarah Billingsley and Amy Treadwell, whom I had the pleasure to interview when I worked as a food writer for the *San Francisco Chronicle* about how whoopie pies, once an East Coast treat, were sweeping the nation. —Stacy Finz)

Prep time: 20 minutes
Cook time: 20 minutes
Yield: 24 whoopie pies

*Ingredients*

*For the Cakes*

1 ⅔ cups all-purpose flour
⅔ cup unsweetened cocoa powder
1 ½ teaspoons baking soda
½ teaspoons salt
4 tablespoons unsalted butter, at room temperature
4 tablespoons vegetable shortening
1 cup (packed) dark brown sugar
1 large egg
1 teaspoon vanilla extract
1 cup milk

*For the Marshmallow Filling*

1 ½ cups Marshmallow Fluff (or other prepared marshmallow cream, which will do in a pinch)
1 ¼ cups vegetable shortening
1 cup confectioners' sugar
1 tablespoon vanilla extract

## Directions

### For the Cakes

1. Position a rack in the center of the oven and preheat the oven to 375° F (190° C). Line two baking sheets with parchment paper.

2. Sift together the flour, cocoa powder, baking soda, and salt onto a sheet of waxed paper. In the work bowl of a stand mixer fitted with the paddle attachment, beat together the butter, shortening, and brown sugar on low speed until just combined. Increase the speed to medium and beat until fluffy and smooth, about 3 minutes. Add the egg and vanilla and beat for another 2 minutes.

3. Add half of the flour mixture and half of the milk to the batter and beat on low until just incorporated. Scrape down the sides of the bowl. Add the remaining flour mixture and ½ cup milk and beat until completely combined.

1. Using a spoon, drop about 1 tablespoon of batter onto one of the prepared baking sheets and repeat, spacing them at least 2 inches apart. Bake one sheet at a time for about 10 minutes each, or until the pies spring back when pressed gently. Remove from the oven and let the cakes cool in the pan for about 5 minutes before transferring them to a rack to cool completely.

### For the Classic Marshmallow Filling

1. In the work bowl of a stand mixer fitted with the paddle attachment, beat together the Marshmallow Fluff and the vegetable shortening, starting on low and increasing to medium speed until the mixture is smooth and fluffy, about 3 minutes. Reduce the mixer speed to low, add the confectioners'

sugar and the vanilla, and beat until incorporated. Increase the mixer speed to medium and beat until fluffy, about 3 minutes more.

## To Assemble the Whoopie Pies

1. Spread the filling onto the flat side of one of the cakes, using a knife or spoon.

2. Top it with another cake flat side down. Repeat with the remaining cakes and filling.

3. Alternately you can use a pastry bag with a rounded tip to pipe the filling onto the cakes, which will give you a smaller, neater presentation.

# White Bread Rolls

(This is a family recipe that my mother and aunt used to make as a braided loaf. In the last few years, my sister altered the loaf into dinner rolls. She usually makes them during the holidays and they are the first thing on the table to go. —Stacy Finz)

*Ingredients*

2 packages of active dry yeast (¼ oz. each)
¾ cup warm water
2⅔ cup warm water
¼ cup sugar
1 tablespoon salt
3 tablespoons shortening (Crisco)
9–10 cups flour

*Directions*

1. Dissolve yeast in ¾ cup warm water. Stir in rest of water, sugar, salt, and shortening. Add 5 cups of flour and beat with an electric mixer until smooth. Add remaining 4–5 cups of flour until it feels a little sticky but not so sticky that you can't get a ball of dough to drop from your hands.

2. Turn dough onto a lightly floured board and knead for 10 minutes. Place the dough in a greased bowl, then turn the dough over so both sides are greased. Cover the bowl and let the dough rise for one hour. Punch the dough down and divide it in half, putting the second half in another greased bowl. Let both doughs rise to double in size, about another hour.

3. Take handfuls of dough (a little smaller than the palm of your hand), roll into a ball, and flatten on an ungreased baking sheet. Brush the tops lightly with melted butter or egg wash. Bake at 375° F (190° C) for 20 minutes or until golden brown.

# Grannie Stowell's Pumpkin Custard Pie

(Granny Stowell spent most of her childhood picking what needed picking from farm to farm all over the South. She never missed *Wheel of Fortune* and prided herself on having the best pie at every potluck. In the 1950s Granny opened Hot Biscuit, a locals-only diner that served homemade blue-plate specials, gravy-covered scratch biscuits, and three-layer-crust pies so deep they had to be baked in a lasagne pan. But her signature dessert was her pumpkin custard pie, a family-only treat that graced our table every holiday season. Even though Grannie Stowell is no longer with us, I make sure her pumpkin custard pie is the centerpiece of our holidays. —Marina Adair)

## Ingredients

16 oz. room-temperature cream cheese
½ cup granulated sugar
1 teaspoon vanilla extract
2 large eggs
1 (9-inch) graham cracker crust (store-bought or homemade)
½ cup pumpkin puree
½ teaspoon ground cinnamon
¼ teaspoon ground ginger
⅛ teaspoon ground cloves
⅛ teaspoon ground nutmeg

## Directions

1. Preheat oven to 325° F (175° C).

2. Combine cream cheese, sugar, and vanilla extract and beat until creamed. Add eggs one at a time, beating until smooth.

3. Spread 1 cup of the cheesecake batter into the bottom of the graham cracker crust. Set aside.

4. In a separate bowl, combine pumpkin puree, cinnamon, ginger, cloves, and nutmeg. Add the remaining cheese-cake batter and whisk gently until well combined. Pour the pumpkin batter over the cheesecake layer and smooth evenly over top with a spatula.

5. Bake 35 to 40 minutes until center is almost set. Allow to cool for an hour, then refrigerate for a minimum of 4 hours or overnight.

*If you enjoyed THE CAFÉ BETWEEN PUMPKIN AND PIE, you can visit Moonbright, Maine, again!*

*Love is the sweetest treat. . . .*

## THE COTTAGE ON PUMPKIN AND VINE

*USA Today* Bestselling Author
Kate Angell
Jennifer Dawson
Sharla Lovelace

"Delightful and spicy."—*RT Book Reviews*, 4 Stars

*Welcome to Moonbright, Maine . . . where the scents of donuts and cider waft through the crisp night air . . . with just a hint of magic.*

It's time for the annual Halloween costume party at the cottage on Pumpkin and Vine, the perfect place to celebrate the pleasures of the season. Guests return to the picturesque B & B year after year to snuggle up in its cozy rooms, explore the quiet, tree-lined streets, and enjoy all the spooky fun of the holiday. But local legend whispers that it's also a place where wishes have a strange way of coming true.

For three unsuspecting revelers, it's going to be an enchanted weekend of candy corn kisses and midnight black kittens, along with some *real* Halloween surprises—the kind that make your heart skip a beat—for many more celebrations to come. . . .

*The recipe for love always includes a dash of magic. . . .*

## THE BAKESHOP AT PUMPKIN AND SPICE

*USA Today* Bestselling Authors
Donna Kauffman
Kate Angell
Allyson Charles

"Brimming with costumes, cookies, love, and
a pinch of magic . . . an excellent time."
—*Library Journal*

Every autumn, Moonbright, Maine, is the picture of charm
with its piles of crisp leaves, flickering jack-o'-lanterns . . .
and a touch of the sweetest kind of enchantment.

Witches, goblins, the occasional ghost—they're all sure to be
spotted at the annual Halloween parade, where adults and
children alike dress in costume to celebrate Moonbright's
favorite holiday. And no place has more seasonal spirit than
Bellaluna's Bakeshop, a family business steeped in traditional
recipes, welcoming warmth—and, legend has it, truly
spellbinding, heart-melting treats. . . .

Between good-natured Halloween tricks, frothy
pumpkin lattes, and some very special baked goods,
for three Moonbright residents looking for love—
whether they know it or not—the spookiest thing
will be how magical romance can suddenly be. . . .

# Connect with 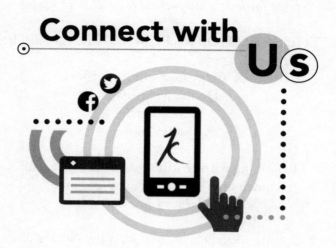 U(s)

Visit us online at
**KensingtonBooks.com**
to read more from your favorite authors, see books
by series, view reading group guides, and more.

**Join us on social media**
for sneak peeks, chances to win books and prize packs,
and to share your thoughts with other readers.

🅕 🐦

facebook.com/kensingtonpublishing
twitter.com/kensingtonbooks

## *Tell us what you think!*

To share your thoughts, submit a review,
or sign up for our eNewsletters, please visit:
**KensingtonBooks.com/TellUs.**